THE CURSE OF OPHELIA

NICOLE PLATANIA

First paperback edition February 2023

© Cover design: Franziska Stern - www.coverdungeon.com - Instagram: @coverdungeonrabbit

Edited by Kelley Frodel
Interior design by Lorna Reid
Map design by Abigail Hair

ISBN 979-8-9862704-0-1 (Paperback)
ISBN 979-8-9862704-1-8 (eBook)

www.nicoleplatania.com

PRAISE FOR *THE CURSE OF OPHELIA*

"Ophelia's inner fire will have readers lusting for more in this heart-wrenching and emotionally healing New Adult Fantasy book! A must read for all romantasy lovers, and the next big thing."

—L.B. Divine, author of *The Prince of Snow*

"A wonderfully immersive world filled with unbreakable friendships, strong women, curses, lost love and the heartbreaking search to find it. Nicole has outdone herself in this sweeping fantasy debut, and it's a book and a journey you won't want to miss!"

—K. Jamila, author of *Mine Would Be You* and *Golden Hour of You and Me*

"A much-needed addition to the NA fantasy romance world. TCoO takes you on an adventure full of first loves, found family, healing and self-discovery. Once you start you won't be able to put it down until you know what happens next."

—Carmen Meeker, @bookingitwithcarmen

"A sweeping fantasy that bends morality and blurs the lines between desire and necessity."

—Taylor Gingrich, @taylorgingichauthor

"A story of strength, love and bravery, TCoO is full of charming characters, tragic heartbreak and healing."

—Stephanie Skilling, @bookishly.steph

"Nicole's debut is filled to the brim with heart-wrenching stakes, incredibly strong women, and such immersive world building that you'll find yourself lost in the pages and never wanting to leave. Ophelia's journey is one that I'll come to time and time again to be reminded of what it means to face a challenge head on and always fight for what I believe in and for those I love. I cannot wait to see what comes next!"

—Chey Parkerson, @cheysreadinglist

To anyone who's ever fought against fate,
and everyone who's ever had their heart broken.

Author's Note

This book contains depictions of grief, alcohol dependency, blood/gore, death of a loved one, violence, torture, some sexual content.

If any of these may be harmful to you, please read carefully.

GALLANTIA
AMBRISK
CAPRECION
VALYN
LUMIN LAKE
SPIRIT VOLCANO
TUNDRA
MYSTIQUE TERRITORIES
WILD PLAINS
TURREN
STARSEARCHERS
DAMENAL
SOLSTINE RIVER
PALERMAN
CLIFFS OF BRONTAIN
XENOVIA
SEA WATCHER'S OUTPOST
SOULGUIDERS
BODYMELDERS
PTHOLE
THORENTII
MINDSHAPERS
SEA WATCHERS
GAVERAL
ENGROSSIAN TERRITORIES
BANIX

Pronunciation Guide

Characters and Creatures

Akalain Blastwood: *Ah-kuh-lane Blast-wood*
Alvaron: *Al-vuh-ron*
Annellius Alabath: *Uh-nell-ee-us Al-uh-bath*
Astania: *Uh-ston-ya*
Bacaran Alabath: *Bah-kuh-ron Al-uh-bath*
Calista: *Kuh-liss-tuh*
Cypherion Kastroff: *Sci-fear-ee-on Cast-Rahf*
Damien: *Day-mee-in*
Divina Delantin: *De-vee-nuh Dell-in-tin*
Elektra: *Ill-ectra*
Erini: *Ih-ree-nee*
Glawandin: *Gluh-wahn-din*
Gerrenth: *Gair-inth*
Hectatios: *Hehk-tay-shus*
Illia: *Ill-ee-uh*
Isobeth: *Is-uh-beth*
Jezebel Alabath: *Jez-uh-bell Al-uh-bath*
Kakias: *Kuh-kye-yus*
Lancaster: *Lan-kaster*

Lucidius Blastwood: *Loo-sid-ee-yus* Blast-wood
Lynxenon: *Leen-zih-non*
Malakai Augustus Blastwood: *Mal-uh-kye Uh-gus-tus Blast-wood*
Ophelia Tavania Alabath: *Oh-feel-eeya Tuh-vahn-yuh Al-uh-bath*
Santorina Cordelian: *San-tor-ee-nuh Kor-dee-lee-in*
Sapphire: *Sah-fire*
Tavania Alabath: *Tuh-vahn-yuh Al-uh-bath*
Thallia: *Thall-ee-uh*
Tolek Vincienzo: *Tole-ick Vin-chin-zoh*
Victious: *Vik-shuss*

PLACES

Ambrisk: *Am-brisk*
Banix: *Ban-ix*
Caprecion: *Kuh-pree-shun*
Damenal: *Dom-in-all*
Gallantia: *Guh-lawn-shuh*
Gaveral: *Gav-er-all*
Palerman: *Powl-er-min*
Pthole: *Tholl*
Thorentil: *Thor-in-till*
Turren: *Tur-in*
Valyn: *Val-in*
Vercuella: *Vair-kwella*
Xenovia: *Zin-oh-vee-yuh*

Appendix of Angels and Gods

Angels of the Gallantian Warriors

Bant, Prime Engrossian Warrior
Damien, Prime Mystique Warrior
Gaveny, Prime Seawatcher
Ptholenix, Prime Bodymelder
Thorn, Prime Mindshaper
Valyrie, Prime Starsearcher
Xenique, Prime Soulguider

Gods of Ambrisk's Pantheon

Aoiflyn, The Fae Goddess
Artale, The Goddess of Death
Gerrenth, The God of Nature
Lynxenon, The God of Mythical Beasts
Moirenna, The Goddess of Fate & Celestial Movements
Thallia, The Witch Goddess of Sorcia

-PART ONE-

ALECTO

Chapter One

The scrape of metal against metal rang out across the dusty enclosure that formed our family's training circuit. Three sharp clangs, followed by a thud as the double-edged blade of my short sword, Starfire, slipped past Jezebel's sword arm and came to rest gently against her wrist brace. Without the gold band, she would have lost her hand.

My sister was lucky I had pulled back at the last second, falling into our training habits rather than unleashing the rage that had festered inside of me for two years.

"Good one," Jezebel encouraged, tossing her cropped blonde hair out of her face and smiling mischievously. "Again," she spat the word at me, baiting my anger.

It wasn't irritation at my sister that fueled me. It was fury at the world. At the perfect life that slipped through my fingers two years ago as Malakai walked away from me for the last time. The image burned behind my eyelids as I gripped the leather hilt of Starfire and raised the two-foot blade in front of me: our hands outstretched, holding on until the very end.

That moment my fingers broke from Malakai's, a cold loneliness slid into his place, and everything in my life shifted.

My heart stuttered, and I blinked away the emotion.

Dawn's light glinted against Starfire's immaculate steel and the gold-and-topaz pommel. I'd polished her after yesterday's training, as I had every time I'd used her for the last decade. She'd seemed so heavy when I was gifted her for my tenth birthday.

She'll grow into it, my father had assured my mother.

I flipped the blade between my calloused hands. Grown I had.

Jezebel sheathed her sword and braced herself with a spear before me, our weapons unmatched, but our skill equal. Neither of us acknowledged the fact that training was futile. These sessions were our solace. A place where we bore the weapons we were born to carry and honed the skills that *should* have delivered us our birthright.

Had the war not devastated our people.

Had the Curse not been cast against our bloodlines.

Had the Undertaking not been forbidden for our future.

As I swung my blade in the direction of my sister's heart, I felt the power of the Mystique Warriors sing through my blood. That ancient magic tunneled through the land and into me. Into all seven warrior clans across Gallantia. It manifested as strength and connection; I felt it now, in the precision of my strike, the focus on my target, and the swiftness of my feet as I staggered away from Jezebel's spear.

It surrounded us, stemming through the willowy branches of each cypher—the trees growing throughout Gallantia since the Angels roamed the continent. The ash-white trunks and vibrant green leaves were pure conduits of power. As we fell deeper into spring, I could feel the magic blossoming in the small white buds dotting the space between the leaves.

I flexed my muscles, reveling in the gift of the Angels.

Jezebel lunged, a low growl escaping her lips as she thrusted the shaft of her spear in front of my sword. "You'll have to be quicker than that," she taunted, throwing my weight back against me. She twirled the spear fluidly above her head and brought the tip just below my rib cage.

Spears. I had never liked them.

"And you'll have to be less obvious," I retorted. My free arm struck out, catching her spear hand off guard and knocking her weapon to the ground.

She was quick. By the time I raised my sword again, she had unsheathed her own long sword from her hip to meet Starfire. Sparks shot up from where the blades collided.

The clashing of metal echoed again, and for a second, I thought this may be the day we were caught. Never mind the fact that our training circuit lay a half mile from our manor, on the outskirts of the Alabath estate. Since the war, many people had grown bored—and meddlesome.

With the suspension of the Undertaking, young warriors were forbidden to train. A bitter taste filled my mouth when I thought of the pointless order. I gritted my teeth against it and swung Starfire.

If war had not broken out, the Curse had not ravaged our people, and Malakai had not disappeared, I would have plunged through the ritual that ascended young trainees into adult Mystique Warriors two years ago on my eighteenth birthday. Jezebel would have been attempting her own Undertaking six months from now—assuming our parents allowed it. Often, second children were discouraged from the risky endeavor if the firstborn succeeded. It was a means of keeping the bloodlines alive and active while also ensuring the safety of their precious children.

But Jezebel never would have allowed that chance to be taken from her. Though, I supposed that no longer mattered.

The Undertaking. Another thing stolen from my life.

Despite the ban, Jezebel and I found ourselves in the training circuit every morning. We danced swift-footed across the dust bordered by the cypher trees and created our own challenge to the authority ruling our lives.

Those first few weeks, our parents had been suspicious when we showed up to breakfast with rosy cheeks and ravenous appetites. They had not said anything, though. Two years later, I suspected it was feigned ignorance. Our father was the Second to the Revered Mystique Warrior—our leader. He could not be found with knowledge of flouting the restriction.

I smiled to myself at the thought of anyone trying to stand between me and Starfire. I had been cheated out of my birthright, but I would not let them steal the power threaded through my blood.

Still, each morning that we donned our training leathers—covering our bodies from neck to foot in the slick, nearly impenetrable black material—and strapped on gold reinforcement bands, a shadow of worry hung around me. Not for myself, but for Jezebel. At seventeen, she still occupied the space in our culture when you were neither regarded as a child nor respected as a grown warrior. If we were to be found training, I could not say what repercussions she would suffer.

I closed my eyes for only a moment and channeled my hearing to catch any threats, but that slight adjustment was a distraction I couldn't afford. In one blink, Jezebel twirled around me, a perfect balance of delicacy and force, retrieved her spear, and swung the weapon behind my legs.

A cloud of dust surrounded me where I fell.

"Focus, Ophelia," she growled, extending a hand to help me up. Her tawny eyes burned with anger, stark against her bronze skin. They were the most notable difference between us, my eyes being a bright, inexplicable magenta. My parents thought it might have been a temporary discoloration when I was born, but it never faded.

Beyond that, our heart-shaped faces, full lips, and coloring were nearly identical, her features a bit slenderer than mine.

As she hauled me to my feet, it was clear she knew what had distracted me. That protective guard an older sister held over the younger.

And she hated it.

When the sun had fully risen, we opened the creaky wooden door of our family's weapons shed and disarmed. The structure had once been guarded against intruders with impenetrable wards on the lone door, but no one in Palerman bothered to lock their weapons up anymore. They had no use. Now the space only remained free of cobwebs and rodents due to my and Jezebel's weekly cleanings.

We polished our weapons in silence, peeled off our leathers, and discarded them into a soiled pile that was growing steadily. *Wash those soon*, I reminded myself. We'd have to sneak them to the manor.

A thin beam of light shone through the cracked door, brightening Jezebel's frame where she stood in only her undergarments. She held her hands before her, turning them over slowly. Her lips twisted to the side, eyes narrowing.

"What is it?" I asked, tossing one of the dresses we were forced to wear at her and pulling my own up my body. I tugged my long golden hair free of the backing, cursing when it tangled in the bindings.

I should not be wearing such restrictive clothing anymore. I should have spent each day in the leathers of the ascended Mystiques, having completed the Undertaking. The garb was customized by each warrior, with leather straps and bracings to the wearer's preference, providing flexibility and weapon storage. The sketch I'd designed years ago for mine was tucked away in my room for the day I needed it—a day that would never come now.

Jezebel freed my hair, still wearing nothing more than her lace undergarments. "It's odd, isn't it? The way the Curse just disappeared."

My stomach turned to ice as the spot on the inside of my elbow tingled. "Yes."

"I don't understand why it stopped when—"

"Get dressed," I ordered, storming out of the shed. Dust swirled around my skirt as I stalked the half mile back to our house and crawled through my open window. With my back pressed against the cool glass, I exhaled, forcing away the pain that twisted its way through my body and prodded at my already-shredded heart.

My father's study had always been my favorite place in our house.

Books overflowed the dark wood shelves, stretching from floor to ceiling. Volumes were piled in corners amid scrolls and maps, and two plush velvet armchairs sat beside a fire that never extinguished thanks to the mystlight flowing directly from the earth to power every building on the continent.

The scent of leather, parchment, and smoke accenting the air had wrapped itself around me in childhood, nurtured my curiosity, and transformed me into the wandering mind I embraced now.

My favorite piece of the room was the dark wooden desk positioned beneath the window. From this spot, mounted behind the surface of study and knowledge, I had felt powerful as a child. When I had looked out over the cypher-packed land and heard the calls of wild animals, I felt alive with possibilities. The study had symbolized comfort and warmth, wisdom and wonder.

Now, it was the place I came to brood and obsess over my losses. Where I searched for something—anything—that might help me restore the future I deserved.

A soft knock sounded at the door, and I knew I could tell him to go away, but I didn't. "Come in," I called without looking up from the volume I was reading, *The Six Gods of Ambrisk, Volume One: Thallia, the Witch Goddess of Sorcia.*

My father's blonde head poked around the door. I appreciated the way he yielded his space to me, knocking before entering when he knew I was lost in my world of research. "It's time for dinner," he said.

"I'll be there in a moment," I droned. Dinner didn't interest me. Nothing did but training for the future I'd lost and researching how to restore it. And rum—to numb the painful present.

"Two minutes."

My head snapped up at the cold tone in his voice. His jaw was set, his beard quivering as he exhaled. His tawny eyes—a perfect mirror of my sister's—narrowed, daring me to challenge him.

I didn't have the energy to fight my father tonight. I nodded, closing the book in my lap and rising to follow him as he turned from the room.

His footsteps were echoing down the hall when the rendition of the Mystique Mountain Range above the fireplace caught my eye. The source of Ambrisk's magic stared back at me. I felt as though I was there, standing atop a boulder at its base and soaking in the beauty of our cause.

Atop the peaks, warriors lived in the city of Damenal where they guarded this majestic mountain range and the secrets within. The purpose I had been born into. The birthright the fateful Undertaking would have confirmed.

The sky around the snowcapped mountains was peppered with stars, and hovering above the highest peak, one particular star outshone the others. I exhaled when my eyes landed on it, unable to tear them away as the sight of the North Star crawled beneath my skin and tore my heart to pieces. I didn't know it was possible for a broken heart to repeatedly sever, but mine found a way.

I inched closer to the painting, lifting a hand to graze the star. The paint was rough beneath my fingertips, but I lingered there, as if that touch might guide me in repairing the scraps of the life I once dreamed of.

The spot beneath my inner elbow tingled.

A reminder of another lifetime, two years ago, when the stars shone brighter.

A reminder to hope for the day that they may again.

Chapter Two

Two Years Earlier

GENTLY TWINING HIS FINGERS through mine, he lifted our hands to his lips. His breath was hot against my knuckles as he whispered, "We spoke the Words ages ago, Phel. It's time."

The Warrior's Words.

The declaration of commitment we had proclaimed privately to each other on my sixteenth birthday, before war broke out and the Curse had tilted our lives toward madness. We had been naive then, tangled in our blissful promise of the future, and as I stood among the ruined city of Palerman, I longed for that innocence again.

His eyes sparkled with the excitement of childhood, bringing me back to the many days we spent chasing each other through our city. His jet-black hair had reflected the sunlight above Palerman, like a beacon calling to me among those crowded streets. He would duck between shops or into narrow alleys in the center of the city where the buildings were stacked closely together—and I would always find him. The freckles across his nose had wrinkled when he teased me, and even now I remembered the fluttering that motion drew into my stomach.

Back when I didn't even know I loved him.

I brought my hand to his cheek, his jaw much more angular

than it had been in childhood, and leaned up to gently press my lips against his. He smelled of the jasmine and honeysuckle that marked the entrance to our secret clearing, where we had spent the winter afternoon rolling through the lush grasses.

I pulled a stray petal from his hair, smiling at the intimate memory that landed it there. The war may have destroyed so much, but I would still hold on to the good.

"You're right, Augustus." He had many names: Malakai Augustus Blastwood, Mali, Destined Warrior Child, Future Revered of the Mystique Warriors—but Augustus was mine.

"Tonight?" I asked. Bliss gripped my heart as I gazed back into his forest eyes. They deepened with my agreement.

He nodded, our lips brushing together. "We'll meet at the parlor."

His free hand grazed my jaw, calluses rough against my skin, and slid into my hair. My toes curled in my boots. I gasped at the energy that coursed through my body, at the heat pooling low in my stomach.

Augustus leaned closer, coiling the long blonde strands around his hand and pulling my head back slightly to claim my lips with his own. His movements were urgent yet gentle, as he always was each long night we spent tangled up in each other beneath the stars.

"I'll see you then," I whispered against his mouth, breaking apart before either of us could go too far in the public square of Palerman. There were always eyes on us, children of the two most powerful Mystique bloodlines. Augustus, the son of our current Revered, and me, firstborn daughter of Bacaran Alabath.

We were the most promising future of our people, a symbol of hope and strength among the death and pain.

The heart of the city was emptier since the war had ended last month, but restoration efforts had begun, meaning there were plenty of onlookers today. Though most of the fighting had been contained to the Wild Plains north of Palerman, enemy warriors swept through every large Mystique city. Pillaging what they could. Killing who they could.

It didn't help that in the denser part of Palerman, many families lived in old, apartment-style buildings above shops. It only made the target easier. Some days, I thought I could still see rust-colored stains on the worn stone streets.

It was easy to forget about that when it was just Augustus and me, his hands on my waist, the shadows masking us. White bricks and debris surrounded our feet, but when I looked at him, everything felt okay. We were rebuilding. The Curse was gone. Soon, we would complete the Undertaking, and all would be right.

"I love you," I whispered as I left him.

"Until the stars stop shining," he responded.

Mystique Warriors had three causes for tattoos. Each was etched by ink imbued with minerals of the Mystique Mountains, giving life to nearly unbreakable promises. The Bond was the first to be received, given after completing the Undertaking. A mountainous symbol printed into the skin at the back of the neck to mark success and everlasting commitment to our cause.

The Band came next, a design that declared rank to the world. Different forces received variations of entwined florals and vines. The highest bore a delicate band of budding peonies connected by a thin strand. This was the rendition Augustus and I would one day receive. As you traveled lower in the ranks, the flowers became less rare, the vines more brutish, but the tattoos equally as beautiful.

The Bind was the last a warrior was *supposed to* receive. The artwork was personal, decided between you and the partner you chose to speak the Words to. An irrevocable symbol of the commitment that was to be the final step in that agreement.

Though illegal, it was the Bind that Augustus and I received that night.

I settled into the rickety wooden chair in the parlor, my forearm clasped firmly in the artist's grasp, a light angled at my skin. I locked eyes with Augustus, pulling my bottom lip between my teeth as I smiled in anticipation. He grasped my free hand between his.

"Squeeze if it hurts," he whispered.

Marxian, the lone remaining tattoo artist in Palerman, dipped the needle into the ink. A low buzzing bounced off the boarded-up windows, the parlor not officially reopened since the end of the war.

I smiled at Augustus, leaning toward him for a kiss, but Marxian pressed my arm to the table. "No moving, Ophelia." His voice was stern, but there was a hint of a smile behind his black beard.

He was young by warrior standards—in his forties. His family had inked the promises of our clan for generations in both Damenal and Palerman. After the war, he settled back in our city, hoping to reopen the parlor in honor of his brother, who fell during battle. I had a feeling that he was willing to twist the rules for our tattoos due to that loss. We had all suffered so vastly; any opportunity for a little bit of shared joy was cherished.

"Right. I'm sorry." I grinned at the artist, and he shook his head.

"Ready?" Marxian asked.

"More than ever."

My heart jumped when he pressed the tip of the needle to the skin below the inner elbow of my left arm. Reflexively, I squeezed Augustus's hand, relaxing when he smiled at me in encouragement. It didn't hurt exactly—or, at least, I did not mind the slight pinching feeling as the fine needle bit into my flesh.

The sensation was odd as it printed a prickling promise into my skin. The ink merely lay on the surface, but this substance was more than that. It contained the essence of the Mystique Mountains, and it was that very magic that I felt entering my bloodstream, weaving itself through my bones and being.

I bit my lips, doing my best to remain still as that power poured into me and the pain deepened. The ink worked its way through me like pins driving into my bones. They stabbed into the marrow, and I nearly cried out, squeezing Augustus's hand. His gentle words were drowned out by the magic embedding itself in my life. But once the pins found their roots, they stilled, and a soothing warmth spread through my body. It wiped away any hint of discomfort, a radiance taking its place like an invisible string, now as much a part of me as my blood and bones.

It was the most intimate experience of my life, but it felt incomplete, waiting for its other half to join it.

It only took a few minutes to complete, the design simple but significant.

"This will heal it within hours," Marxian explained. He wiped a special ointment across my arm. "It will be a little sensitive."

"Thank you," I whispered.

I looked at the new artwork on my body and smiled. Something fluttered through me, twisting, searching for the other string to twine itself around.

It was Augustus's turn.

He unbuttoned his linen shirt and tossed it across the back of the chair. Marxian instructed him to lie on a low wooden table and fetched a fresh needle. The lights reflected off the tan skin of Augustus's pectorals where the twin Bind would be inked, locking us together from this day forward.

I pulled my chair over to the table, settling down and grasping Augustus's hand. His head rolled toward me, and there was something in his eyes I didn't recognize. A fleeting impression of wistfulness that had me wrinkling my brow in uncertainty. Without saying a word, he reached up and ran a thumb across my forehead to smooth away the worries.

"Let's do this," he said, turning back to Marxian.

Buzzing filled the room once again, and I watched our futures be tied together through ancient magic and thin lines of black ink. With each stroke of the needle against his skin, warmth spread through me. The dancing string within my own blood was mated with its match, the two spiraling together, a pair promised for eternity.

We crept through the city afterward, our partnership forever sealed between us. Shops and homes were closed up, mystlights in windows extinguished as Palermanians settled in for the night. We wandered down the cobblestone path between ivy-coated apartment buildings.

Overhead, bright orbs of light sprinkled a deep sheet of black streaked with violet. The stillness of the air wrapped itself around us in our state of bliss, and though it was much later than my father requested his seventeen-year-old daughter return home, I did not care.

Not that night.

I extended my arm between us to appreciate the beauty of the artwork in the moonlight. It was a small symbol, something understated to the outside world but a constant in our lives. A simple recreation of a star, with four large points and smaller ones blinking out between them, complete with tiny detailing that made the star appear to twinkle like those above us.

As I slowly rotated my arm, the ink absorbed the starlight from above and reflected it back to me, the tattoo shimmering silver. A celestial acknowledgment of the significance of this decision. A promise between Augustus and me to guide each other home, no matter the bleakness of the night.

"It's perfect," I whispered.

Augustus grazed his thumb over the tender symbol, still red around the edges. My gaze traveled up his chest to where he bore the twin, larger than mine and beneath his left collarbone, hovering slightly over his heart.

I met his eyes and imagined the smile on my face matched the one he flashed at me, every soft curve of our lips full of a love so powerful it threatened to break us.

"My North Star," Augustus whispered, bending to brush his lips over the freshly inked spot on my arm and sending shivers down my spine. "So that we may always come back to each other."

Chapter Three

Present Day

MY FINGERS CURLED AROUND the cool metal of my fork and knife as I dug into whatever roast bird my mother had prepared for us. I chewed each bite methodically, missing the plentiful meals we used to indulge in before the war. With so many lives lost, those remaining had to redirect their work. Trade suffered under the new organization. Mystique cities throughout the territory had to sustain themselves, rather than exchange goods as we used to. All efforts were now internal, leaving us without even the minor clans to deal with.

Before, any given meal was rare game and rich produce from the Wild Plains, foreign seasonings brought from the eastern lands of the Seawatchers Clan and presented to my father in exchange for dealings with the Mystique Warriors.

Sure, we still had more than most due to our last name. My father's bloodline and rank as the Revered Warrior's Second afforded us a more comfortable life than most after the war, but it was little in comparison to the old days.

Our home, once overflowing with an abundance of rich foods, luxury goods, and well-compensated staff, was now reduced to the bare necessities for survival. Expensive paintings that once adorned the walls had been sold, leaving the grand dining room an echo of what used to be.

Only one long table with a dull green tablecloth occupied the space below the mystlight chandelier. I sat at it now, looking out the floor-to-ceiling windows to my left that framed the soft pink sky of a setting sun. At least we still had beauty amid this dreary world.

The built-in bookshelves to my right were emptier each time I entered the room, the belongings sold piece by piece to provide for the Mystique Warriors and Palermanians. I did not understand why, two years later, artwork, statues, artifacts, and books were still required to be exchanged for food and clothing to keep others alive.

The dining room had two entrances: one into the foyer of our home, and one swinging door into the kitchen. Illia, our lone remaining housemaid, was the only one to enter through the latter now. What used to be a room fit for divine feasts had been stripped to its bones.

My mother kept the house running with the help of Illia and my sister, but the difference was stark. Our lives were dimmer, like a layer of decay had settled over our home, city, and people. Each day, it ate away at us more and more. The war had ended, the Curse was lifted, we worked to restore our land, but still Mystique Warriors suffered. They lost loved ones—a feeling I knew too well—and without them, it was hard to move forward.

My stomach twisted with guilt at the thought of those suffering. I set my utensils down, unsure I could continue to palate the dull food, though my sister ate as voraciously as she always had.

"I was wondering today, Father," Jezebel began, spearing a roasted carrot on her fork. The conversation had been a distant buzz in my mind, but the mischief coating her tone caught my attention. "We haven't discussed the progress of the Curse in some time." She popped the carrot into her mouth.

"That's not a question, dear," my father responded, cutting himself another generous slice of dry bird.

Jezebel's brows rose. "I have many questions." She tore a piece of bread.

"Don't get her started," I mumbled, my chin lowered and eyes glued to the muted blue fabric of my skirts as my fingers fiddled with the lace cuff at my elbow. I hated the color—too soft. I hated the lace—too dainty. I hated the way the binding ran up my back and framed my torso, the skirts wrapping around me—too restrictive.

My mother shot me a glare, but my comment went otherwise unacknowledged.

"Curiosity is a gift, Jezebel. What would you like to know?" my father encouraged.

I gaped at him, unable to believe he was indulging her when I had spent the past two years searching for answers and being told it was a hopeless cause. The light in Jezebel's eyes only infuriated me further.

"Where did it come from?" she asked innocently, though I knew she knew this already. Everyone knew it. What was she playing at?

"The Curse was placed on the Mystique Warriors during the war, my dear. The leader of the Engrossian Warriors, Queen Kakias, recruited a sorcia from the Northern Isles for this purpose." My father spoke with patience, but I could feel the wonder bustling beneath his skin. Clearly, he also suspected a deeper meaning behind Jezebel's questions.

I clenched my fingers in my lap, tearing my skirts slightly at the mention of the Engrossians, the guards of the pools of dark magic in the Engrossian valleys to the far southwest. As the only other major clan, their jealousy of our mountains was the root of all my misery. Their wicked queen's vendetta against us was the reason the Undertaking was suspended.

Of all the clans, the Engrossians were the only ones who referred to their leaders with the regency titles. It reflected their inability to accept shared power—a trial we felt the repercussions of in the war.

Our groups protected the two largest sources of magic on Gallantia—truthfully, in all of Ambrisk—but ours was stronger, winding through the land like a living being. While dark magic was manipulative, there were goals only our power could achieve.

Envy and suspicion had positioned us as enemies for centuries leading up to the war, when their queen sought to wrench the mountains from our grasp. Though a truce had been reached, I often felt as though we were waiting for the day she would strike again.

Jezebel nodded, pursing her lips in mock consideration of our father's words. This conversation was clearly progressing as she planned. "How did the Curse manifest itself?"

"Jezebel, what—" my mother began, but paused when my father held up a hand, intrigued by his younger daughter's game.

"It started with the darkening of the veins, the paling of the skin, and the redness of the pupils, until all sense was lost. It drove one mad, bloodthirsty, turning them into a threat to everyone around them—even those they cherished the most. If it had continued, it would have meant the extinction of our people."

"And how—"

"Was it passed?" He anticipated her next question. When Jezebel nodded, my father's lips pulled into a tight line, his face grim. "It targeted our people at our most imperative source. The place where our power lives. Our blood. If one was plagued, it was a guarantee that anyone who shared their blood would be, too, starting with the eldest. It was also contagious, should you come in contact with the blood of a Cursed victim."

All four of us examined our own veins, silently thinking the same, unanswered question. *How did we, one of the most powerful bloodlines in Mystique history, escape unscathed?*

The question hung in the air, a taut string of guilt stretching between my family.

After a moment, my father cleared his throat. "Was that all, Jezebel?"

I knew it wasn't. I knew my sister better than anyone, and I felt that she was building to strike. Jezebel viewed the world as a series of opportunities. Just as when we trained, her common tactic was distraction. She led her opponent down one path, sensed when her chance was strongest, and attacked where they were blind.

Who was her opponent now, though?

My sister brushed her cropped blonde hair behind one ear and straightened her shoulders. This was it, the moment she would hit her unnamed target. I glanced at my father. The crease between his brows deepened.

"What changed? What caused the treaty ending the war and lifting the Curse? Why has no one been struck in two years"—the tattoo on my arm heated—"since Malakai disappeared?"

Breath cascaded from my lungs at a dizzying speed. No one in my family dared speak Malakai's name around me, but my sister was a ruthless fighter, and for a reason still unclear to me, I realized I was her opponent.

The bindings on my dress felt too tight. I struggled to catch my breath. I couldn't think, couldn't understand. It was as if the blood in my veins stilled then heated, igniting every ounce of rage I had built up over the past two years.

I pushed back from the table. "You're cruel," I hissed, leaving before she could respond.

The gentle noises of our family's horses calmed me, though each inhale felt like it would burst my lungs. I timed my breaths to my mare's.

Brushing my hand down Sapphire's nose, I brought my head to rest against her cool coat and inhaled deeply. She was one of the few that didn't set me on edge these days. I always had a sense that during these past two years she understood me better than most people did.

As a warrior horse blessed by Lynxenon, the God of Mythical Beings, she would live over a century and be my support throughout that time. I didn't want to think about the years after, when my extended lifetime would allow me to live for centuries after her. Another thing I was destined to lose.

White moonlight reflected on her pristine, snow-like coat. I stared into her turquoise eyes and wound my hand into her deep blue mane—the feature that was her namesake. She exhaled gently against my cheek, as if to say she read my ricocheting thoughts and held all the same questions but was here for me.

"I don't know, girl," I whispered. "I don't know where he is, but I know he'll come back." My voice cracked over the end of my sentence as I remembered Malakai's words on the night we received the Bind, mere weeks before he left: *My North Star, so that we may always come back to each other.*

But why hadn't he?

Soft footsteps punctured the stillness, crunching over layers of hay, and I prayed it wasn't my sister. I wasn't ready to dissect her strategy.

Thankfully, it was my father's strong hand that snaked across my shoulders and tucked me into his side. I fought every instinct to push him away.

"That was callous," I said coldly when he finally released me. I picked up Sapphire's brush to busy myself and kept my eyes on the soft silver specks that glowed in her coat, smoothing them with each brushstroke.

"Your sister will apologize," he assured me, braiding Sapphire's mane with his nimble fingers as he had regularly since he brought her home to me. "But she is right. Though her methods may be harsh, she only hopes to push you toward acceptance. She loves you, and she does not wish to see you suffer, Ophelia."

I stilled at the sound of my full first name from my father instead of the nickname he usually opted for: *Sorrida*, a word in a tongue I didn't know, which he claimed roughly translated to *smile. For the smile your birth brought to my face*, he always said, though now it felt so misplaced.

"She is wrong. You are all wrong." The bite in my words was clear—I had no use for their doubt.

My father turned to me but kept braiding. "You are living in the past. We must move forward." This wasn't the first time he had given me this speech, but it had become more frequent as of late.

I couldn't bear to speak of Malakai at this moment, not with the flaring heat still surrounding my Bind. "The Undertaking," I whispered, choosing a safer subject. A pain that still ripped through my body when it was taken from me, but one my father understood as a warrior.

His voice was softer when he spoke. "What about it, dear?"

"It's all I ever wanted. All I ever saw for my future." I closed my eyes, seeing the life I would now never have, with Malakai as Revered and me as his Second.

"Now you will find a new vision."

"I was born to be a legendary Mystique Warrior. Without that chance, I have no purpose. I feel useless, aimless." *Broken*, I didn't add aloud. "That's why I do it. That's why I cannot give up hope that our people will be restored." My hands froze on the brush. I took a determined breath to collect myself. "That *all* of our people will be restored," I added. And he understood. Malakai.

He sighed, and I could tell by the dramatic rise and fall of his shoulders that his next words would be heavy. "*Sorrida*"—there it was—"our people were born of the Angels. The First Revered Mystique Warrior, Damien, ascended as an Angel himself, as did the prime leaders of the other six clans. No matter what fate has befallen us, we are still Damien's faithful servants and he our guide. We are still protected by the Spirits of past Mystique Warriors. We are still *us*, regardless of it all. Sometimes, change is okay."

"We didn't change. We were obliterated." I tossed the brush aside, my fingers growing twitchy, and moved to the wall where a number of tools were hung. I removed a length of rope and knotted it, untying and retying different styles as I waited for him to speak. The quick actions of my fingers and required focus steadied my breathing.

"It was a check on the balance of power. Just because we are no longer the premiere clan doesn't mean we are any less significant. You still have a role to play in the world." He spoke with such tenderness that I knew he believed the words, even if I didn't. The balance of power was what magic demanded, a justification for the order of the world. But I would never understand why something we defended would require our downfall.

"My purpose feels squandered now," I admitted, squaring my shoulders. "But I *will* make it right."

"Your faith is inspiring, Ophelia. It truly is. But there is a point when blind faith becomes reckless. That time has come and gone." I knew he meant it to be soothing, but it had the opposite effect.

"I must complete the Undertaking." I threw the rope aside and whirled on my father.

"You know that you cannot," he reminded me, keeping infuriatingly calm. "All Undertakings were suspended after—" I flinched, and he paused, reconsidering his approach. "Our people had grown too weak. We couldn't risk any more loss of life."

"But why?" I demanded. "It is senseless to cease the training of warriors when war is always a threat."

"The Revered made the decision, Ophelia." He crossed his arms, the motion sharp after over a century of training with swords and spears. When he spoke again, his tone left no room for argument. It was the voice of the Second, born of a different form of training. "You will *not* be completing the Undertaking now or in the future."

Though my father's eyes heated, I did not back down. He may no longer see a future for me as a warrior, but I could see nothing else.

"I was not made for *skirts*, Father. I was made for *swords*."

CHAPTER FOUR

THE COOL NIGHT AIR grazed my flushed cheeks, but it did nothing to calm my temperament.

The city was quiet at this hour, its inhabitants having retired to their homes at dusk after a day of restoration efforts beneath the Palermanian sun. Sometimes it seemed that the work would never end, like we would be trying to repair ourselves forever. We had seen progress in the past two years, but the trauma was a stain on our city.

Flashbacks of the battles that swarmed our home still crossed through my mind daily. Enemy warriors running through the cobblestone streets of Palerman, targeting it as the strongest Mystique settlement. We had been weakened by the Curse before they arrived, making the fight quick and brutal. Engrossian axes flew through the air, finding target after target. Their screeches as they cut us down still roused me from fitful sleep often, another reason I was headed to my destination tonight.

I had been kept out of the battles. *Too young*, my father had claimed, despite my advanced skill. I had watched from a hillside, though I had been told not to. Watched as an Engrossian blade skimmed the flesh of my father's neck, within a hair of his life, and I swore I would get revenge.

Now, as I passed the newly reopened apothecary, I thought about all the ways life had been damaged. Half of our shops were permanently shut down. Some, like the blacksmith's, were no longer necessary. Others, like the leatherworker's, with the shattered windows, had lost their owners to the war.

Some of the white brick buildings had been repaired, their brown wooden doors and glass windows replaced, signs repainted and strung up. The apothecary with salves straight from the Bodymelders, the herbal shop selling tinctures of the Starsearchers, a spice tradesman with blends imported directly from the Seawatchers—all three had been restored on this block alone, though wares from minor clans were nearly impossible to receive at present. It left us attempting to replicate them as best we could.

Still, much of our main street had been healed. Those who survived and did not own land in their family's name had relocated to the apartments above the shops in the center of town, centralizing life around the fountain that marked the heart of Palerman. With its towering figure of the First Mystique Warrior, Damien, in his Angel form. Wings stretched wide to encompass all who sought shelter, it became a source of comfort for many.

Despite the Curse and the war, the sun shone brightly over our land each day, heating the calming breezes we reveled in, kissing our skin until it glowed, and giving us back a little bit of the warmth our lives lacked.

"Ophelia!" An enthusiastic call bounced off the sealed doors and windows of our main street. I hoped the ivy draped across the buildings would muffle it. "Where dost thou journey to tonight?"

Tolek Vincienzo appeared at my shoulder and slowed his stride to match mine. I didn't turn to look at him, but if he had arrived, Cypherion Kastroff would be just behind him. Malakai's best friends had become shadows of mine in the past two years, anchored to my movements and monitoring my moods as Seawatchers did a storm-ridden tide.

"I'm not in the mood, Vincienzo," I growled, the sound out of place in the serene night.

Tolek shrugged, a light laugh escaping his lips. "You're never in the mood, Alabath. Since when does that stop me?"

A third set of footsteps fell in with ours as we crossed the deserted street. "Hello, Cyph," I called over my shoulder without turning.

Tolek tutted, "He gets a 'hello,' and I get 'I'm not in the mood'? Well, I guess that answers who the favorite is around here, Cyph. What do I owe you?"

I rounded on him, my anger at my family rising again. We stopped in the middle of the street, light from the apartments above spilling around our figures, dancing with the highlights in Tolek's dark brown hair. He'd dyed them himself using citrus juice and sunlight, and though I would never tell him, they were rather flattering against the amber specks in his chocolate-brown eyes. He raised his thick eyebrows playfully at me, those accents igniting.

"Ah! She's stopped," he said without looking at Cypherion, who danced like a shadow at the border of our square of light.

"And where were you headed, Ophelia?" Cyph's deep voice filled the street. The authority in his tone did not align with the tender heart hiding behind those deep-set blue eyes. Wavy auburn hair brushed his shoulders, shadowing a chiseled face that would look good brooding, but usually bore a gentle expression. His appearance was a lesson in contradictions.

I glowered up at the two of them. Tol stood a few inches shy of Cyph's height and was lean muscle where Cyph was more solid, but both were at least a head taller than me. When had they grown so large? Gone were the days of adolescence when I sprang up to tower over them both.

Many things had changed since those days.

"*I am* going to the tavern." I left no room for dispute, charging across the street and turning abruptly down a side alley. My skirts left a swirl of dust in my wake.

Tall, stacked buildings crowded the street, leaving little room to walk. More broken glass and discarded trash swarmed my ankles the farther I traveled from the heart of the city. I looked up at the empty residences around me—faceless skeletons with windows broken in, wooden shutters hanging on hinges, not a spark of life inside.

Everywhere I turned was a stark reminder of the fall.

Tolek and Cypherion followed me, footsteps light for men of their size. It was Cyph's smooth voice that broke the still air of the deserted alley. "Ophelia, you've been at the tavern every night for the past month. Would you not benefit from one night off?" In the moonlight, his pleading eyes against his tan skin were almost convincing. *Almost.*

"You're not my father," I answered.

"As if you would listen to him anyway." Tolek rubbed a hand across the dark stubble on his jaw, the shadow of which never quite disappeared.

"For fucking Damien's sake," Cyph mumbled, and I knew he wished Tol wouldn't fuel my anger.

I narrowed my eyes at Tolek. "You're right. I wouldn't, so why should I listen to you?"

I hadn't a clue why they always tried to keep me from drinking. It wasn't like they weren't by my side every night. It was a hypocritical attempt, if you asked me.

We approached the steep staircase that descended into the back entrance of the Cub's Tavern, the one Santorina left open for me each night. While I always drank in the barroom with other patrons, I tried to avoid prying eyes from the street and windows overlooking the front door. It was no one's business how I spent my evenings, but as an Alabath, I was accustomed to everyone caring. I pushed past the boxes and reeking trash bags that crowded the stairs, careful not to slip.

"You can't honestly—"

"Because we care about you, Ophelia," Cyph cut off whatever retort Tol was about to make. I wasn't sure whether I was relieved that he did or annoyed that I didn't get to respond. Going head-to-head with Tolek Vincienzo was one small outlet I was afforded for my anger.

Cyph continued, "As does your family. You spend every night in a tavern, and you're not partaking in the *casual* refreshment. Rina said you drained three bottles of her strongest supply last week."

I froze, searching for a denial, but only hazy memories surfaced. Hiccuping my way home under the moonlight, engaging in a round of illegal gambling with a small man of elvish descent, staring up at the spinning stars and wondering why my life had crumbled so. I couldn't even be mad that Santorina and the boys had been discussing my habits when he was right.

"Ophelia, you're a warrior." Cyph said it like a promise, though we'd been told we could not become ascended warriors anymore. "Your body is your greatest weapon, and you're poisoning it every night. What would..." He trailed off, his unspoken words lingering in the air. *What would Malakai think?*

"You can't imply that it's not a part of warrior culture to drink." It was a behavior seen as frequently as a training session in the pre-war days.

Cyph shook his head. "Not for the reasons you do."

The implication stung, but it only strengthened my resolve as memories of Malakai and the future I'd dreamed of flashed across my vision. I needed to blur them with something as strong, warm, and intoxicating as his presence. To forget the ghost lurking among us.

I raised my chin and looked into Cyph's beseeching stare, his jaw firmly set. I cursed his Spirit-damned rationale and how impossibly correct he always was—though I refused to admit it.

"You're right, I *am* a warrior. And I make. My. Own. Decisions." I punctuated each word with cold deliberation.

Holding his stare, I curled my fingers around the metal door handle and wrenched it open, throwing a beam of light onto our trio. As I stepped into the storeroom of the tavern, an ache echoed in my heart.

"We should know by now that with her fire, she wins every argument," Tol mused from the stairs, and I couldn't help the smirk that lifted my lips. He clapped Cyph on the back. "Nonetheless, that was a valiant attempt at persuasion, CK. After you." Tolek held the door open, and they followed me past shelves crowded with dark brown bottles.

When I reached the bar, I pulled my favorite stool out from under the countertop, the scrape of its wooden legs cutting through the dim chatter. The Cub's Tavern was nearly empty tonight, save for a handful of burly men gathered in a booth near the fire.

My friends and I had frequented this tavern for years, its presence serving as a haven for those under eighteen prior to the war. Post-war, it became a place for those who wanted a little solace and a strong distraction, regardless of age.

In the dimly lit room, I could practically see the past, our group packed along a table in the dining room. Now it was coated with stains and splinters, but then, friends would have surrounded us, drinks being drained and games gambled upon.

I remembered the cool stone wall beside the fireplace biting into the back of my neck as I leaned against it. Malakai's hands on either side of my head, broad shoulders shadowing me from view of the room as he brushed his lips against mine, almost innocently. A teaser of what was to come later. Now, crumbled stones stood in our place, a fire weakly fluttering in the grate.

Perhaps most painful of all, I remembered the barkeeps. The way Santorina's parents welcomed us with warmth and ale—never strong enough to cause our younger selves any harm, just a bit of fun. The bar had glowed with their presence, infecting everyone who passed through the door with a buzz of delight and wrapping the room in a familial embrace.

But Santorina's parents didn't survive the war, casualties of a Mystique and Engrossian dispute though they shared blood of neither clan.

As memories of two bloodied, lifeless bodies flashed through my mind, their daughter swam into focus behind the bar. "What can I get you tonight?" Her greeting was neither cold nor warm but layered with exhaustion.

"Hi, Rina," I greeted my close friend dully. "Indulge with me?"

"Ophelia, you know I cannot." The liner she'd swept across her eyelids emphasized the upward lift at the outer corners of her round eyes, but it couldn't take away from the dark circles beneath them. Years of pressure, of being tied to this bar since the night her parents died. "Besides, you have other friends to spare you the loneliness."

The stools on either side of me scraped back. I rolled my eyes as Tolek and Cypherion took their places.

"We'll have three of your finest ales, please," Tol chirped. I felt his eyes burning into the side of my face but didn't tear my stare from where my fingers chipped away at splinters on the bar.

"You know we only have one kind now," Rina reminded him, a sweet smile gracing her angular face as she reached beneath the bar.

"Ah, my favorite." Tol nodded in appreciation as she handed him the bottle.

When she placed mine in front of me, I said, "Actually, I'll have a glass of rum. A large glass."

My friends exchanged glances.

"Start with a small one," Rina offered, pouring a meager amount of the dark liquid into a chipped glass. I took it from her, holding it before the light of the fire. The flames turned the liquid into an alluring array of amber hues. The sweet, intoxicating aroma begged my body to consume it.

I brought it to my lips and tipped it back. The warmth slid down my throat and pooled in my stomach. It sent tingles through my limbs and eased the pressure that had built since dinner with my family.

I locked eyes with Rina. "Another small one, please." She did as I asked, and having made my point, I sipped this one slowly.

Her thin frame was tense, seeming close to buckling under the weight of her work, and I took a breath. When I spoke again, the harshness fell from my tone. "You're certain there's no one you can write to in Caprecion to help you run this place?" I asked after her home city for the hundredth time. "No family?"

Santorina didn't look at us when she answered. "You know that when my parents left they lost contact with our family. I don't even know if anyone heard about what happened." Her voice shook over the end of the sentence, eyes on her fingers where they picked apart threads on the rag she had been using to dry glasses. I squeezed my beverage between clammy hands. Santorina and I may be tough on each other, but her pain pierced my own heart.

Cypherion extended a comforting hand across the bar and patted Rina's shoulder. "What about your grandparents?"

"I don't remember them really," Rina told him. She had been a child when her parents left Caprecion permanently, and they had traveled often before that. She took a deep breath and threw her sleek black ponytail over her shoulder. The fire ignited her dark eyes when she lifted her chin. "I think I'm doing a fine job."

Tol raised a glass to Rina. "You most certainly are," he encouraged. He took a swig, then turned to me. "Will you be doing a summer exchange this season?"

"I don't see the point." Why would I spend weeks of the summer in a different territory, learning their trades and techniques, when I was not allowed to ascend?

For the five summers before the war, Malakai, Tolek, Cypherion, and I—along with other trainees our age—had visited each of the minor clans. We never made it to the Engrossians, and a part of me wondered if we had, if the war would have been avoided. I knew it was a ridiculous hope, though. Four adolescents could have done nothing to stall a war.

"It doesn't appear we'll be doing anything else." Tolek shrugged.

I tightened my grip around my glass and took a sip. The flavor was a bit off. I suspected Rina had been watering down my beverages for weeks now and sighed in frustration.

"They likely won't even let us train if we attend," I nearly growled.

"I'd quite like a bit of an escape." Tolek ran a hand through his hair until it stood on end. "Perhaps we should visit the Seawatchers this time—but the Western Outposts, not the Eastern Territory. I've heard the island beaches have sand so soft it resembles an Angel's wings."

Cypherion laughed into his ale. "Curses, Tolek, it is not a

vacation. It's a diplomatic effort for future generations. To build relations with other clans and better understand each other."

"And who's to say it can't be both?" Tolek dropped his voice, nudging my shoulder. "What do you say? With Cypherion constantly studying or polishing his unnecessarily large collection of weapons, I could use the company."

"You read just as much as I do," Cypherion argued.

"But I read *literature*—poetry and philosophy and stories of the heart. Not the history and strategy bores that you love so dearly, CK." Tolek flashed him a grin.

"Yes, you and your *heartfelt sonnets*. Care to tell us what you're constantly scribbling in your journals?" Cypherion raised one eyebrow as he lifted his bottle to his lips, and Tolek went silent.

"I won't be going," I hissed, and their argument ended.

"Well, your mood is certainly pleasant tonight," Rina muttered. Her eyes were downcast, but I read the annoyance in her expression. It added to the pain caused by my sister and melded with the fire from arguing with my father, threatening to overcome me.

I didn't want to tell my friends what had happened tonight. Opening up about my constant rage felt so personal, but I was drained, my fight dimming. "I argued with my family again." I took a deep breath, twirled my glass between my fingers, and voiced the words I had been afraid of speaking for so long. "I feel as though I am breaking."

Their silence was a painful reminder of why I didn't share my pain. Waiting for their responses in that empty space of vulnerability left me feeling exposed, each second like dragging a blade across an open wound.

"One needs to break fully in order to heal," Cyph finally said.

I looked into his deep eyes that were wise beyond his years and thought back to the day he met our group when we were twelve. The day we had become complete. His understanding eight years later solidified that.

Cypherion had battled his own demons since birth. With a

semi-absent but fully Mystique mother and a father who disappeared before he was born, Cyph had been forced to raise himself, giving him an understanding of the world the rest of us couldn't quite grasp. It was in moments such as these that I was reminded of that.

Jezebel and I were obstinate rule breakers, but we always had our mother and father guiding us. Tolek was as reckless as they came, but he was born of a strong warrior heritage, both parents present in his home his entire life. Cypherion—he was not as fortunate.

How many nights had we dragged him back to Malakai's house in the past eight years, just to ensure he could bathe and eat? Malakai's mother always had an empty room for him, should he need it. When he showed up in the night, his own home too cold or empty, she never looked at him with pity, but rather gratefulness that he turned to us.

He may have been embarrassed, refused our larger attempts at care, but we had always looked out for him. He may not know where he fit, but it was never a question to Malakai, Tolek, and me. Just like it was never a question of whether Rina belonged with us, despite the fact that she was entirely human and had not a drop of Mystique blood in her veins.

I turned Cypherion's words over in my head. *One needs to break fully in order to heal.* I knew he understood healing because each day he straddled the line of his heritage, his mother never revealing what bloodline his father was of. She didn't speak of him at all. Cypherion's head was full of questions of where he belonged in the world and how to feel whole—how to prove to *himself* that he belonged with us.

"Cyph is right," Rina said, pulling me back to the present. "But I don't think you'll be able to break fully until you accept what is true." Her words were quiet, and my blood ran cold at the implication.

Tolek's hands clenched atop the bar, his entire body recoiling at Santorina's words as if she had punched him. He closed his eyes and rolled his neck slowly, loosening the strain.

"I'm sorry," Rina muttered. "But we can no longer deny it to placate ourselves or encourage outlandish behavior." Her eyes were wide. Pleading.

"I know," Tolek whispered with a stiff nod. His gaze flicked to me, and his hand twitched, as if he wanted to grab mine but stopped himself. He looked back to Rina. "I know you're right, but it doesn't make it any easier to accept the fact that my oldest friend is gone. I understand why Ophelia refuses to—"

Rina whipped her rag against the counter, cutting through Tol's words. Every one of her frustrations broke through her tight composure. Exasperation with always having to be the one to speak what we couldn't—what I refused to believe.

"Truths aren't always pleasant, Tolek. It has been two years of this, and we *must* move forward." Her entire frame drooped. "Malakai is dead. He died during the last Undertaking."

Chapter Five

THE FIRE IN THE grate burned low as I worked late into the night, my eyes slowly drooping shut, begging for the reprieve my mind and body wouldn't allow.

This was the first night in weeks that I did not find myself deep in a bottle of rum at the Cub's Tavern. After Rina's words last night, the world had begun spinning. The atmosphere was too warm, everyone's voices making me claustrophobic. My skin felt like it was crawling to get off of my bones, and if I didn't get away into the cool air, I might claw it off.

I had no desire to return tonight.

Instead, I busied myself with research. To my left, piled high on my father's desk and casting an ominous shadow in the fading light of the fire, were books. Each spine divulged a different facet of the Undertaking. My nose had been buried in a volume that housed theories of the Spirit Volcano—*Undertakings Past: The Rituals, Rules, and Ruptures of the Mystique Warrior Tradition*—for the past two hours. The words were starting to bleed together before my eyes.

If only I could complete the Undertaking myself, maybe then I could tap into an unknown piece of knowledge that would unlock the key to what had happened to Malakai. My father, the Mystique Council, even Malakai's own parents had completed the Undertaking, yet none of them offered any assistance. Why they didn't understand my determination was a mystery to me, but when the Revered gave the order to forget the Undertaking, everyone obeyed.

The flames crackled, cutting into the silence of the study. My eyes snapped open. I could not rest yet. I planted my elbows firmly on the desk, cradling my chin in my hand, and continued to scan the page.

With sorceresses, warlords, and Angels haunting its depths, it is unknown precisely what Spirits will greet a fledgling warrior as they embark on their journey through the volcano.

That much I knew. Legends shared with us as young children explained the process of the Undertaking: one ventured into the Mystique Mountain Range against physical feats, climbed to the rim of the Spirit Volcano, and journeyed within. It was believed that the ancient land mass housed the souls of all Mystique Warriors past, as well as select other magical beings, and it was their choice to deem one worthy in the first step of the Undertaking—the mental challenges. Only those who had attempted the ritual and were approved by the Spirits knew what happened next. When a warrior entered the Spirit Fire—the final phase—they were tested emotionally, each journey unique.

I always believed that the Spirits of your Undertaking were tailored to each individual. Ancestors of your bloodline, predecessors of any gifts you wielded. Who were Malakai's? If I had been granted the chance, who would mine have been?

The Spirits may grow greedy should a blessed soul cross their path, choosing to claim it as their own, harboring it as a true life among the dead in their realm.

I bolted upright, sending the leather wingback chair shooting out behind me. My pulse quickening, I reread the line to confirm what I took it to mean. In all of my lessons, never had it been said that the Spirits could *claim* someone during the Undertaking.

A blessed soul…

Certainly, a blessed soul would be one who was worthy. But beyond worthy, blessed implied touched by the Angels themselves.

A child of the First Revered Warrior, the blood of the Angels running within their own.

Malakai...my mind flashed to his strength, power in both mind and body. His conviction as a future warrior. *Blessed.* Could Malakai have been deemed a blessed soul by the Spirits and now reside—alive and whole—within the Spirit Realm of the volcano?

My hands shook as I traced the black ink on the next page, all thoughts of sleep fleeing my mind.

Though this theory still resides in folklore, there has never been evidence of a blessed soul crossing the paths of the Spirits, deeming this tale as false. Most likely, this was a story created to encourage warriors to complete the perilous Undertaking with the hope that they may be revealed as an Angel descendant. Over the centuries, bloodlines have become so entwined that one would be hard-pressed to find a source of Angelblood pure enough to qualify as blessed.

My breathing stilled, the spark of hope I briefly felt extinguishing as I realized how ridiculous it was. Warriors had descended from Angels ten thousand years ago. Angelblood was nearly impossible to find nowadays.

"Fucking Spirits," I cursed, throwing the book from the desk and collapsing back into my chair in frustration. Heat roared through me. I wanted to tear this office apart, tear the world apart until I righted these wrongs. Reestablished our people's glory, completed the Undertaking, found Malakai.

"He is alive," I whispered the reminder to myself, massaging the spot below my inner elbow that burned brightly, answering me. "I will fix it all." Even to my own ears, my voice sounded disheartened.

The flames cast dancing shadows on the endless books lining the walls. Endless pages in which I had searched for answers. Endless dead ends I had met in the past two years.

How had my friends, my family, even Malakai's own family, given up so easily? I knew what they all thought. Rina's words from last night had echoed through my mind since she spoke them. Everyone believed that Malakai, Augustus, the son of the Revered, and *our future leader*, had somehow failed to complete the Undertaking and died in the process.

They were wrong.

If Malakai had truly died, I would feel it. He couldn't cease to exist without a piece of me dying as well, thanks to the imbued ink of the tattoo on my arm. Distantly, as if pulled through tar, I could feel the twin threads tangled together within my blood. But the link that should have formed between our souls was silent.

Despite the pressure on the Bind every time I thought of him, I had never felt further from the man I loved. The distance opened a trench of hopelessness in my soul, and the wider the cleft became, the harder it was to fight. I felt as though I was grasping at the air of memories without a solid reminder to tether me down.

I sank down further into my chair and ran my fingers through my hair, trying to imagine his touches, his kisses, but it all felt so distant. Watching the flames flicker with a heat I longed to feel, I realized that if intimacy was what I lacked, then I must go to the place where we were closest.

Brushing aside the curtain of jasmine and honeysuckle that shielded our clearing from the world was like stepping back in time. It was like years past, before the war, before the Curse, when Malakai's footsteps echoed my own.

Moonlight flooded our clearing tonight as it had then, reflecting in the crystalline water of the pond and catching the wildflowers, turning each petal into a drop of starlight. My gaze swept over the space, twenty feet across with knee-high, featherlike grasses. A dense grove of trees wrapped around the field, concealing it from unwanted eyes. The trees were in the throes of spring, with fresh leaves and budding flowers decorating their branches.

Despite the tragedies that befell my life, the clearing alone remained untouched, its beauty only tarnished by memories.

Limbs shaking, I staggered to the pond and fell to my knees, the grass under my skirts cushioning the blow. A shadow crept across my heart as I looked around our haven and endless hours played out before my eyes.

"Come on, Augustus," I called, grabbing his hands and slipping my slim fingers between his. It was the third night in a row that we had crawled out of our bedroom windows and met at the edge of our city, walking the mile to our clearing under the moonlight.

He laughed, and it was a breathtaking, husky sound that caused my heart to flutter like a caged bird. "I'm right behind you, always."

Wildflowers reflected in his glossy emerald irises, starlight outlined the freckles across his nose, and my heart swelled within my chest. I had never known such happiness as these stolen moments.

"And when you aren't, I will always find you," I promised.

I brushed the gentle curls of dark hair from his forehead and stood on my toes to press a soft kiss to his lips. They were full and willing against my own. The moment our mouths met, his lips parted to welcome me, and I was undone by the taste of him. My hand continued past his forehead to the spot where his curls rested against his neck. I tangled my fingers among the thick strands, grazing my nails down his skin and tugging gently. He groaned against my lips, something deep within me heating at the sound.

Firm, familiar hands slid up my arms and back down the sides of my dress, exploring my body, as he so often had, each time as exhilarating as the last. Every time we were together was different. New and exciting. I could never get enough of this. Him. Us.

His hands gripped the backs of my thighs and lifted me effortlessly despite the layers of my gown. When he settled me across his hips, I relaxed into him, tightening one hand around the cool skin of his neck and the other against his broad chest.

I explored every part of him, my mouth moving from his lips to his neck while I slowly undid the buttons on his shirt. Each fastener that slid through the thin linen intensified the moment. We weren't in a rush. We had all night in this clearing—our clearing.

Gracefully, Malakai lowered us to the ground, all the while staying tangled together. He moved one hand from my thigh to brush my hair behind my shoulder, and I rolled my head to give his mouth better access to my neck.

"I love you, Ophelia," he mumbled against my skin between kisses. The bindings of my dress loosened as he swiftly untied them. He pulled back, his eyes darkening with a shadow I didn't understand. "For every day my heart beats, I'm yours. My heart, my soul—it's all yours."

"I'm yours," I repeated.

His lips brushed mine. "I will love you until the stars stop shining."

His nimble fingers trailed up my exposed spine, coaxing me to arch into him. As I had many nights before, I completely gave myself over to him.

Afterward, we lay hidden among the billowing grasses, beneath our stars and moon. The shoulders of my gown had been pulled up, but still hung loosely around me. I rested my chin on Malakai's bare chest as I gazed up at him, fingers tracing his tattoo. From the jasmine tangled among his dark curls to the blissful smile on his lips, I loved every piece of him.

"Until the stars stop shining," I whispered.

I staggered up on trembling legs, breathing heavily over the hole widening in my heart. The intimacy of this space only intensified my loss. A phantom hand dragged nimble fingers up my spine in that familiar fashion, and I shivered, my eyes stinging.

Coming here had been a mistake.

If possible—standing here in our personal cocoon—I felt further from Malakai than ever. This space, the moonlight against white petals and glassy water, pushed me toward what I had fought for so long—breaking. My breaths came quick and shallow as I looked to the sky, one star brighter than the rest, winking at me.

I turned my back on the clearing and lifted the jasmine curtain, praying to the Spirits that the stars had not stopped shining on him.

The white petals were bathed with the barest hint of yellow as they moved, and I froze. Something within my body stuttered—like my blood had flowed backward for a moment, only to ricochet back in the right direction. Everything within me seized at the unnatural sensation, my hands clenching around the flowers and ripping them from where they hung.

The tightening within me hurt as deeply as the tearing of my heart, like something was tinkering with the very essence of my life.

But as quickly as the feeling washed through me, the pain was gone. I was left standing with a sheen of sweat across my brow and a pale, trembling hand gripping delicate strands of jasmine.

The world spun. I collapsed to my knees, vomiting into the feathered grass until my body had nothing left to give.

I wasn't sure how many minutes or hours passed as I remained curled over my knees, forehead pressed to the dirt with only the moon and stars to keep me company. My body alternated between dry heaves and waves of pain, quiet moments of night echoing in between. Through it all the only thing I could think of was how this moment confirmed the tarnishing of this clearing and everything it once stood for.

When my legs regained enough strength to support me, I rose slowly, bracing a palm against a cypher. Unsure if I could ever return to this place, I cast one last longing look over my shoulder.

And what I saw nearly knocked me to the ground again.

It was impossible. It hadn't been there before I was sick, yet it now slashed a golden line through the middle of the clearing.

I approached slowly, as if rushed footsteps would scare it away. A voice in the back of my mind laughed at me—it was not alive. It could not flee. It had appeared here somehow, though, meaning it must also have a means of escape. Objects did not simply spring into being.

My legs wobbled as I knelt beside the spear where it was cushioned by pillows of grass. The golden metal shone, an impeccable ray of sunlight amid the darkness of the night, but I knew it would have that effect anywhere. I could see it in my memory: a streak against the sky, lighting a path where it swung.

A trail of engravings traveled from end to end, etching a story along the length of the shaft. Flowers and vines tangled together, the thickest and roughest starting at the bottom with the most delicate wrapping toward the blade. They circled a jagged emblem holding tiny aquamarine stones in the shape of a mountain, symbolizing that this was a historic weapon forged to guard all Mystiques.

Hesitantly, I dragged my fingertips along the cool metal. It rolled toward me, and the gems gleamed in the moon's reflection. The largest stone in the center cast light on the smaller ones trailing it, like a crown on a weapon fit for a future Revered.

For Malakai.

Malakai's spear.

It shouldn't be here. He had taken it with him when he left for the Undertaking, and it would have gone with him into the Spirit Volcano. My breathing turned ragged; my head spun. I whirled to my feet, searching the clearing. Was he here? Had Malakai returned?

"Hello?" I called, my voice weak.

Only the pounding of my heart answered.

"Malakai?" Saying his name felt like dragging a hot iron through my throat. Like tearing a spirit from their living body. A part of me knew that there would be no answer, and I shook my head at my false hope. If Malakai had truly returned, he would not play such games. He would not hide from me. Nothing on Ambrisk could keep the two of us apart if there was any route around it.

I looked back to the weapon on the ground. Curiosity mingled with another emotion—fear. Some sense within me was frightened by its presence.

Regardless of the foreboding swirling in my gut, I stooped to pick it up. It warmed in my palm, the golden metal flaring like a burst of mystlight in the night. In time with the spark, something within me thrummed, the odd, reversed blood flow sensation returning. I bit down on my lip against the pain, but it settled in the hand that grasped the spear, like it was speaking to the weapon. I didn't understand how, but a kinship was forming. Perhaps already had.

Half of my mind wanted to abandon the spear here, arguing that I should not trust its suspicious appearance and sentient feel.

The other half wanted to bind this weapon to my body and never release it—one last reminder of Malakai.

He may not be here, but I had this piece of him. I could feel his spirit pulsing within the weapon that had been handed down to him at birth as the future Revered. The only weapon he ever wielded. His most cherished possession.

By right it was his, and I didn't know how I found it now, but I knew that leaving it behind would be like leaving him, and that was something I could never do. The Bind pulsed as if in agreement as I hugged the spear to my chest.

Something else pulsed along with it, a second heartbeat pounding through my body.

CHAPTER SIX

"IT'S ONLY THREE DAYS away, sweetheart, and you haven't given us any indication of how you'd like to celebrate." My mother's attempt at a calming tone had the opposite effect on me. I was too consumed by the discovery of Malakai's spear and the subtle pulsing sensation that had yet to leave my body to care about my upcoming birthday.

The occasion was nothing but a reminder of what I had lost, and after everything I felt last night, my losses weighed heavily on my heart. It didn't help that Jezebel and I had to skip our training this morning to assist our mother, so I had not even been able to show her the weapon—or use it myself. All I could think about as I roughly shucked another ear of corn was where the spear was now tucked away in our weapons shed.

"I'd rather not celebrate at all," I grumbled, plucking hairs from between kernels and discarding the scraps into the growing pile on the floor.

When we had extra food, my family prepared what we could to donate to the less fortunate of Palerman. This usually required the help of Jezebel, Illia, our grandmother when she was available, and me. Today, the five of us gathered in the kitchen, washing, chopping, and cooking vegetables that would be delivered to the group homes tonight.

"Twenty is an important year in your heritage, Ophelia," my

mother noted. Her dark hair swayed behind her as she bustled through the kitchen.

"Sixteen and eighteen are the significant birthdays," I corrected her, because I was a Mystique Warrior, and twenty was not a significant year to *us*.

The memory of my sixteenth birthday—the last before the war—gutted me. The day Malakai and I had spoken the Warrior's Words to one another in the confines of our clearing.

Ophelia Tavania Alabath, his promise echoed in my mind, memories of soft kisses brushing across each of my cheeks, *my partner in life, from this day forward. I offer my heart, my soul, and my hand, that all will be yours until the Spirits beckon us into darkness.*

I'd known he would say them eventually, and that I would repeat them in earnest, but I had not expected the Words on that day. In the solitude of our clearing. At the first moment possible on the day that I was deemed a woman.

I could not have chosen a better time.

My response echoed his own words in my memory. *Malakai Augustus Blastwood, my partner in life, from this day forward. I offer my heart, my soul, and my hand, that all will be yours until the Spirits beckon us into darkness.*

Every word, syllable, and letter that had crossed over my lips held weighted truth and a flame of promise that bound us together for eternity.

Neither of us knew that in two years' time, the promises would be stolen from us.

"You're more than just Mystique, and you know that." My mother's sharp tone called me back to the present. Her hands braced on her slender hips, fingers tightening like she was holding her patience together, but it was wearing thin. Good. This storm between us had been brewing for years.

I tossed the ear of corn I had been cleaning into the bucket beside me and took a sip of my tea. It was my favorite herbal blend, fruity with a bit of tart, and it calmed me enough that I relaxed back into my chair and chewed over my response.

Jezebel promptly picked up the corn I had discarded. "Ophelia, you barely even finished this one. Look at all the hairs remaining." My sister redirected the tension, proceeding to show me how to *properly* prepare an ear of corn. I barely noticed her fingers effortlessly sliding over the kernels, correcting my mistakes.

I ignored Jezebel, glaring at my mother as she filled a large pot with water from the tap. She moved with the grace of someone who had trained, but not with the fluidity of a warrior. My fingers curled around my teacup. How did she think it was acceptable to lecture me on my heritage when she had scorned her own?

"And you are of Mystique blood," I hissed. "But one would never know that."

Her spine stiffened where she bent over the sink, but she ignored my jab, hoisting the pot to the stove. Mystlight flared beneath it. Illia repeated the action, placing a second pot beside it. The water started to bubble almost immediately, softening the tense silence we'd fallen into.

The blow was low, but the anger building inside me did not quell. My mother had chosen not to partake in the Undertaking when she turned eighteen, claiming that she was only half a Mystique Warrior and therefore unsure if she would be worthy, never mind the fact that her parents had raised her in Palerman. It was not an unusual choice for one of her blood composition, but to have my mother—the woman who married into one of the most powerful Mystique bloodlines and birthed two rightful warriors—turn her back on that chance…I was ashamed.

I knew I shouldn't be. She and my father had fallen in love among the dizzying summer days of Palerman over a century ago. She had only been seventeen. He was twenty and already in line to serve the next Revered. They'd explained it was safest for their—our—future if she did not attempt the Undertaking, but I would do anything for that chance, and she had refused it.

I frowned at the Bind on the fourth finger of her left hand. She and my father had them inked where some might wear a ring if they chose to go through a proper marriage ceremony beyond the Words and the Bind.

She didn't deserve the tattoo without the commitment of the Undertaking. Without the Bond and the Band, it broke the rules as much as my own, but given my father's ascension, it was permitted.

"Do not throw around insults you don't understand, Ophelia," my mother finally said.

"Tavania..." my grandmother's tone around my mother's first name was chastising, and the latter did not reply.

Sitting beside me at our round worktable, my grandmother gripped my wrist between her darkened, weathered hands. "Twenty is the year *my* people begin their lives. It is the year you accept your role in society, whatever it may reveal itself to be." The emphasis of her words was not lost on me, and her subtle nod was a confirmation that she understood how I viewed my heritage. Understood and even—maybe—supported the choice. "The Soulguiders are powerful spiritual readers, leaders, and healers, guiding mystical beings to their final rest. At the age of twenty, our paths are made clear."

She knew that like my father's parents and her late husband, I identified as Mystique. The quarter of me that came from her—the blood of the Lower Soulguiders—was dwarfed in comparison to the ties I felt to the Mystique Warriors. That had nothing to do with the power we held as a major clan over the minor clan of the Soulguiders, or the low position in society of my grandmother's family. I understood the importance of each of the five minor clans.

The Soulguiders, Starsearchers, Seawatchers, Bodymelders, and Mindshapers were instrumental to the survival of magic on Ambrisk. They helped ensure the balance of power, but it was the Mystiques and Engrossians given the heavier tasks of guarding sources of magic, while the others guided it or read it, each in their own way. Together, all seven clans protected power for this world and every other that may exist. Each held a unique strength among us, and ours lay in the mountains.

So, no, my disinterest in my Soulguider heritage was no slight to my grandmother. The Mystique Warriors were the song of my blood.

Wisdom of centuries past swirled behind my grandmother's wide golden irises. She knew how I felt, but one night was what she asked of me. One night in celebration of her traditions, people, and symbols. My future.

Birthdays had been insignificant to me since my eighteenth passed without the Undertaking. They reminded me of where I should be compared to where I was now. For my grandmother, though—one of the only people who didn't force me to be someone I wasn't—I could stifle my pain. The second heartbeat in my blood, the one that surfaced with the spear, pounded as if in encouragement.

I inclined my head toward her, and her face softened, the lines in her forehead and mouth loosening. When I grabbed her hand and squeezed tightly, a wave of agreement passed between us.

"I will celebrate," I confirmed, though the excitement in my voice was false.

My grandmother's gold eyes glowed against her light brown skin as she leaned forward and placed a kiss on my cheek. Her two long braids brushed against our clasped hands as she whispered, "This year brings you promises of fortune, you will see."

The older my grandmother got, the more her predictions as a Soulguider went unmet, but this one sent a shiver down my spine.

My mother's expression brightened, and for a moment, she looked so like Jezebel. Though we'd both inherited my father's coloring, it was her heart-shaped face, full lips, and slight nose that we bore. Seeing that light in her eyes, guilt swished through my stomach.

I almost apologized, but my grandmother's hand tightened on mine. When I looked to her, her gaze swallowed me whole, drowning out the noise in the kitchen as it burrowed within me. She called on the magic that guided her and saw into my soul.

A peaceful glaze passed over her face. Though weathered with centuries of experience, she looked more alive than before. Younger, untouched by the hardships of her life.

She blinked and the fog cleared, releasing me from my trance.

"Have a cookie, dear." She passed me the plate stacked with my favorite lemon cookies. She'd baked them for me this morning. A satisfied sigh left me as I bit into one and shook away whatever had passed between us.

For the next hour, I tried to mimic the skilled manner with which my sister worked. As I struggled through tasks, her hands flew across a chopping block, sending perfect circles of produce into the boiling water before moving to scrub dishes. Jezebel didn't bat an eye as she worked beside my mother, their brains one.

"Jezzie, can you pass me the wooden spoon and the thyme?"

Jezebel had the spoon extended before my mother finished her request. "Rosemary will complement it better," she said, offering my mother a small jar.

The effortless manner in which they communicated the running of our household and their skills in the kitchen were all a mystery to me. I had no interest in chores, but still I gawked at my flawless sister, trying to find any similarity between the fighter I trained with and the woman before me.

She was both insightful and strong. Soft, yet fierce. Where I was made entirely of the rough edges and honed minds of Mystique Warriors, Jezebel Alabath truly was the daughter of two bloodlines.

Her dress, a weightless, pale pink fabric with two layers of skirts and a tightly drawn corset up the back, swished about her as she spun through the kitchen faster than my eyes could register. The pale-yellow sunlight streaking through the window picked up the subtle iridescence of the top layer of skirts and danced across her tanned skin. She kept her cropped hair behind her ears, and a golden chain hung around her neck, a crescent moon pendant and amethyst glittering in the light.

When I finished preparing the final ear of corn in my pile, I pushed back from the table. Scraps fell from where they had piled in the skirts of my olive-green dress. Something heavy weighted down my pocket.

"Jezebel?" I asked, my tone as light and innocent as possible.

"Care for a walk?" I wiggled my eyebrows tauntingly.

Jezzie turned toward my mother, questioning if she required any more help. When my mother shook her head no, Jezebel followed me from the kitchen.

"Only if we practice spearwork," she whispered.

As we exited through the front door, the thrum within my blood increased, until it reached a crescendo of excited beats in my ears.

"That's exactly as I hoped."

Twenty minutes later I was in the weapons shed, strapped into my leather training gear, the worn material molding to the curves of my body. It flexed and contracted where my muscles moved like a second skin. I stretched and practiced a few gentle kicks and punches to warm up, relishing the freedom of the leathers compared to the binding of my dress.

It was reckless to train in the middle of the day, but I thought of the spear and that thing pounding beneath my skin—and I didn't care.

Jezebel finished tightening metal guards around her wrists, neck, and ankles, the places deemed her weaknesses. The places I always struck. My own guards shone from around my neck and shoulders, but I had long ago abandoned the ankle and wrist braces. The longer you trained, the less guarded you became, until one day your instincts acted as your shields entirely. In proper battles, armor could be worn, but the goal of our exercises was to teach us to not rely on those protections, but on our own strength and speed.

I buckled Starfire's sheath to my waist, strapped daggers around my thigh, and looked to my sister. She raised her brows at me.

"I—" I fidgeted with my belt, unsure how to explain the spear. How to explain anything I experienced last night.

"You?" she asked. Sunlight streamed in through the open door, outlining her frame.

My pulse and the new essence within my blood hammered. Last night felt so intimate. The experience held so many unexplained truths, folded within layers of pain, that I was frightened to share the memory with my sister. But the heat of the spear still lingered against my flesh, and I knew I had to dissect it. I couldn't do that without a partner to fight against.

Jezebel had always been my confidant, even before Malakai left. Though she antagonized me to the Spirit Realm and back, the bond between sisters was unique and impenetrable.

I chose my words carefully, unfolding the hurt within me and baring it before her, explaining why I went to the clearing the night before, what I hoped to gain, what I did not find, and what seemed to have found me. Reliving the pain of the spear's appearance felt like something twisted its way through my bloodstream, but when I finished, relief unspooled in my chest. Perhaps sharing the weight of pain truly was a good thing.

Jezebel crossed the shed to wrap her arms around me. We were silent, but I relaxed into her embrace. When she pulled back, she appraised me with wide eyes. So many thoughts swirled in those tawny irises.

"Where is it?" was the first question she voiced.

One locked cabinet remained at the back of the shed. Before the war, it had been the place my father kept his most cherished weapons. Now, he rarely visited the room at all. I fished an iron key from the pocket of my discarded dress and took a breath, unsure why I was so nervous. It was only a spear.

With shallow breaths, I removed the weapon from where I had stashed it last night. The second it met my hand, the familiar heat surged along my arm. It was empowering and endangering all at once, in ways I neither expected nor felt able to handle—it fueled me but also seemed like it could kill me. I did not release it, though. The power surged into my body, stronger now than last night.

Jezebel came to stand beside me, eyes lingering on the place where my fingers wrapped around the weapon, but she did not touch it.

"This shouldn't be here," she whispered, tone reverent.

"I know," I agreed. It should be with Malakai.

"You're certain there was no one else in the clearing?"

I nodded. "Positive." I had checked the perimeter extensively before leaving, and with my heightened senses, I would have known if someone had entered the clearing to deposit the spear. Although, I had to admit that I was sick at the time. But anyone planning to leave this there would not have known that was going to happen. It was mere convenience.

"Describe it again," Jezebel said, still not looking at me.

I adjusted my grip on the spear, searching for the words to explain the sensation when I touched it. "It feels like there's something in me that's reaching out to it, and something within it struggling to get to me. Like threads through my veins—tugging. Like my blood was a river whose current was being warped."

"Could it be the Bind?" Her eyes narrowed at the weapon, and I could practically see her mind turning.

"Perhaps." I shrugged. "But I know what that pull feels like, and this feels different."

"But it's Malakai's spear by the hands of fate," she mused, one hand fiddling with the charm on her necklace. "Maybe he's somehow tied to it—like it's connected to his spirit, so it calls to the tethers within the Bind."

I stared at my sister, wondering when she became so profound. I often forgot she was not the young girl who followed us to training sessions each day in secret and watched from the trees. She spoke of the Bind and the forge it drew between two souls as if she had experienced it.

"You may be right," I said, unsure why the explanation disappointed me.

We stood in silence, the power in my hand swallowing us up. Outside the shed, birds called to each other, and breezes rustled the trees; I found it incredible how the rest of the world could seem so untouched by this new mystery in our lives.

Finally, Jezebel asked, "What do you want to do with it?"

I turned the spear over, testing its weight. "I want to use it."

"You?" She quirked a brow. "*You* want to use a spear?"

I nodded.

"I've been trying to get you to use spears for years."

"Not this one," I replied, strapping it to my back. It settled between my shoulder blades as if it was meant to be there, warmth spreading out from the metal and seeping into my skin.

Jezebel's answering smile was dazzling. "After you." She threw the door open, the wood creaking as we stepped out into the spring sun and began our training.

With the cool breezes dancing along my cheeks, I truly enjoyed the power of a spear for the first time.

I twirled the weapon above my head, my hands moving swiftly. When I was within striking distance of Jezebel, I slashed diagonally, aiming not for her but for her weapon. It flew to the dirt beneath her feet.

"Excellent," she cheered. Though I had beaten her, a smile crept across her flushed face. For the first time in years, mine truly matched it.

My chest rose and fell rapidly. Fighting with a spear was different than a sword, and my muscles were not quite used to the exertion. The burn was foreign but welcomed.

"Let's go again," I panted, taking large paces backward to put the appropriate distance between us.

My sister matched my steps, resetting her position. "In spearwork, unlike swordwork, you want to keep distance between you and your opponent," she reminded me. My instincts always sent me charging at an enemy, to close the distance between our weapons and get my blade upon them. I liked the directness of my short sword and the control it granted. This kind of fighting was different, though. A recalculation of my instincts.

"I know. Quick feet and quicker stabs," I finished the quote for her. It was one we had both heard, many years ago, the last time I had trained with a spear. Jezebel had been underage, not allowed to train at our level, but Malakai and I didn't much care for the rules.

Quick feet and quicker stabs, a deep voice echoed in my head. Malakai's voice. I breathed in the fresh air of our training ring, and for a moment I smelled the rush of worn leather, cedar, and honeysuckle that was Malakai.

I had practically trained from the moment I could walk. I knew how to hold a spear, how to strike, and how to crush an opponent beneath the piercing point of its blade, but I had never understood the grace it took to truly be one with the weapon. An energy poured out of the metal and into my hand, crawling up my arm like it was claiming me for its own. I was unsure whether it was because of the Bind, as my sister suggested, or for another reason, but as it embedded itself into my muscles and veins, I felt something shift within me.

With Malakai's spear, I channeled his power. That unnamed essence flowed from the weapon into my body, forging a connection, and the distance between us seemed to shrink.

Chapter Seven

JEZEBEL THOUGHT I WAS unaware of her following me to the tavern every night, but I always knew she was there. Be it through the faint shift of the silence, infiltrated by the most subtle of footsteps, or the scent of gardenia that clung to her skin, my keen senses didn't miss a beat.

Still, I had to admit as I prowled down the main road of Palerman, she was stealthy. I wasn't sure how many nights she followed me before I took notice of her presence. I couldn't be sure if she was doing it to watch out for me or to train herself, but I suspected the latter. My parents may have never intended for Jezebel to complete the Undertaking—even before its suspension—but she had had different plans.

Her featherlight footsteps echoed mine as I turned abruptly down the alley leading to the back entrance of the Cub's Tavern. I left the door ajar for her.

The familiar room brought me comfort. The fire in the grate cast ominous shadows across the barroom's dusty floorboards, but the darkness mirrored that within me, and I smiled at my friends as I crossed the room. My skin still buzzed with the energy of the spear, the training session having awakened something sleeping beneath my skin.

"Good evening, Ophelia," Tolek called from the bar, waving and flashing me a lopsided grin. I smiled back, nodding in greeting.

"You appear to be in better spirits tonight than when we last saw you."

Cypherion exchanged a weary glance with Santorina where she refilled drinks behind the bar. They constantly begged Tolek not to challenge or question my moods, but he never listened. Instead, he drew my fury onto himself whenever it peaked.

"You're in luck, Tol. For the time being, I am." I slid into the seat waiting for me between him and Cyph, and nodded at the other patrons along the wooden counter.

Rina placed a modest serving of my favorite rum before me, and as I raised it to my lips, I saw a golden-haired girl slide into a booth in the back corner. She truly was stealthy—and always vigilant.

Jezebel would blend easily with the young Mystiques scattered throughout the tavern tonight. Though I preferred the evenings spent with only my closest friends, I didn't comment. I knew Santorina would be grateful she had more customers. And Tolek didn't seem to mind the men and women throwing him seductive glances that were not entirely subtle. Even Cyph had been making hushed conversation with a beautiful girl with dark brown skin and black curls.

Angels, why did my friends have to be attractive? I would likely have one drink and leave them to their frivolity, having no interest in flirting myself.

"Let us drink to your happiness, then," Tol sang, raising his glass. A group of three girls beside him mimicked the motion. I recognized them from our year of school—there were the Bristol twins, one of whom was leaning across the bar, batting her lashes at Rina from beneath fringed bangs. I'd thought Santorina had been seeing a man whose name I couldn't remember, but perhaps that had ended. I could admit I'd been distracted as of late.

The third girl was a brunette whose name I also struggled to recall, though her soft features and expressive eyes were familiar.

She caught my gaze. "Hello, Ophelia," she greeted.

Dammit, I should know her name.

"Hylia here was just taking Cypherion's side in an argument

against me," Tolek explained, swinging his arm across the girl's shoulders and lifting his drink. *Hylia*, I repeated to myself as she whispered something to Tol that made him laugh.

I pursed my lips until he stopped. "Tolek, I am certain that if there is a bet being made, Cyph has considered the outcomes thoroughly."

"Are you taking his side, as well?" Tol's arm left Hylia's shoulder, palm pressing to his chest. He didn't appear to notice the slight drop of the girl's smile.

"She would be correct to," Cypherion noted.

"Nonsense!" Tol yelled.

Smiling to myself as they debated, I ran my hands along the deep maroon of my gown, the color making me feel powerful. Coupled with the easy conversation around me, for once it was hard to feel angry. I smoothed the gold patterns shimmering in the thin top layer of the skirt. It picked up the light in the tavern, reminding me of the shade the spear emitted when I first touched it. The thing beneath my skin shifted.

The boys and Hylia continued their banter, and I roared with laughter when I learned that the bet actually was that Tolek could not—or should not—attempt to shoot a moving target with a bow and arrow while standing atop his horse, Astania, as she galloped.

"Perhaps if the lovely Rina dares to refill my glass a few more times, I will give this challenge a valiant effort," Tol declared.

"You barely even know how to handle the weapon," Cyph argued. He had a point—archery was a Seawatchers' practice.

Tolek smirked. "Oh, I can handle a weapon."

"Damien's balls," Cyph muttered, rolling his eyes. "How was your day, Ophelia?" The firelight in the room darkened his auburn hair, casting shadows across his straight nose.

Do I dare share the truth? With the essence warm beneath my skin, I couldn't keep the revelation to myself. Nor did I want to, because for once, though I held so many questions, something felt right.

"I trained with Jezebel today." I sipped my drink, cleared my throat. "Using Malakai's spear."

"Malakai's spear?" Santorina whispered. It was the first time in months—years, maybe—that my friends heard me speak his name. Not the name I used for him, but his given name. To me, he was always Augustus, but it felt too personal to voice since his disappearance.

I nodded as Rina moved down the bar to deliver a glass of whiskey.

When she returned, Tolek turned his back on Hylia and the Bristols. My friends created a fortress around me as I dropped my voice to a whisper and explained in vague detail how I had found the spear, answering their questions without describing precisely how connected I felt to the weapon. I needn't cause suspicion until I knew what was going on.

My stare remained on the amber liquid swirling in my glass as they watched me, digesting all the information I had revealed and forming their own conclusions.

"How do you feel about that?" Cyph broke the silence first, though I knew his actual question was, *Have you accepted Malakai's fate?*

I took another sip to calm the nerves fluttering through my stomach. "It felt right. My body reacted to having that spear in my hands like nothing I've ever felt." I recalled the way I had struck with such ease, driving away my hatred of spearwork one slice at a time. The weapon was no Starfire. It was something…different. Unspeakable. The power that flowed through my veins, stemming from where I held the weapon and shooting throughout my body, was an unleashing of something long dormant.

I locked eyes with each of my friends in turn as I braced myself for their reaction to my next claim. "It's Malakai's by right, though. I will only keep it until I can return it to him."

The lighthearted spirit of the night dissolved in an instant. The collective breath had been knocked out of them, the progress they thought I'd made slipping through their fingers.

But what they called *progress*, I called *surrender*. I was not made to surrender.

"How will you return it to him?" Rina asked carefully, twisting her long black ponytail between her slender fingers. She was proceeding with caution after the last time we spoke, but her eyes narrowed at me.

Another sip of rum. "When he returns to me." The tethers of promise that lived within my Bind burned ferociously.

"Ophelia—" Cypherion began.

My glare silenced him. "I have told you this many times before. He *will* return to me," I said calmly but through gritted teeth, the ice seeping from my voice and into the air around us. All hint of joy I had gathered today went with it.

"It's been two years, Ophelia," Rina stated. There was a softness in her features that resembled pity.

I shook my head, throwing back the rest of my rum and shooting to my feet. "You may have all given up on him, but I will not."

My stool clattered to the ground as I stormed out of the Cub's Tavern, leaving every ounce of burning bliss simmering into ash in my place. The buzz of energy that had awakened within me shook, cascading through my blood as I stalked up the staircase and through the deserted alley.

I didn't know where I was going. Surely, I did not want to return home.

Once on the main street, I stopped walking and leaned against the window of an empty alehouse. The glass was cool against the back of my neck, calming the emotion that welled up in my chest and clawed into the back of my throat.

It was my own fault for expecting any other result from telling them of the spear. They all surrendered so easily. I didn't know why that fact caused me to implode when I had known it for two years now, but something felt different tonight. My emotions had been thrown about so wildly today—from my mother to the spear—and this was the final straw. Hearing them say once again that Malakai was *not returning* felt like a shard of ice slicing through my heart. Cold and sharp and damaging beyond repair.

Turning my face to the stars, I listened for the footsteps that I knew would follow me. One set, as there always was. The only one who dared confront me in these moments.

Citrus and a note of something spicier drifted around me as he stopped. He leaned against the glass beside me, shifting his gaze to the sky, as well. In this moment of silent camaraderie, I was relieved Tol had sought me out. Though I did not act like it, I needed his presence.

Tol was silent, waiting for me to speak or not speak. Giving me the strength of silence and the power to break it. He always knew what I needed, even when I did not.

"I miss him," I whispered after many long moments of silence. My eyes did not stray from the sky, but I couldn't bring myself to look for that one star that shone brighter than all the rest.

Tol deflated a bit at my words. "We all do, Ophelia." It was a simple sentence, but it cracked something in my icy heart.

"You don't always act like it." My voice was not harsh. I felt defeated.

"Just because I hide my pain doesn't mean I feel it any less than you do. Just because I have accepted his absence doesn't mean I am happy for it." A rare hint of sadness cracked his voice—the raw edge of mourning.

I turned my attention from the moon, an orb of bright light against the pitch black of the night, to Tol. That's what Tol was for me—a beacon of pure hope, guiding me through life's darkest moments.

The crack in my heart widened. I took a breath, holding Tol's eyes as I said, "I feel as if a piece of me will always be missing while he's gone. It's that lost piece that keeps me from believing what you all believe." I'd not dared divulge those words to anyone.

"You don't need to believe what we do, but I know that Malakai wouldn't want you traveling through life with this darkness in your heart." Tol's words were gentle, and as he spoke, his voice worked its way into that cracked space in my heart, forging it back together.

"How do you know that?" I faced him, leaning one shoulder against the window. With my pinkie, I drew a star in the dust coating the glass, watching how it caught the light.

Tolek faced me, eyes on the dirt now covering my finger. "You are brighter than this, Ophelia. Meant to be a shining star among us. But since he left, your light has dimmed."

My eyes stung, and the back of my throat tightened. I bit my lips to fight what was inevitable.

Tol stepped closer, lifting my chin so I was forced to look into his eyes. Swirls of sorrowful deep brown and hints of amber longing stared back at me from behind the hair drooping forward across his brow. It had been rumpled, likely from his own hand, and the highlights caught the moonlight.

"My heart broke the day Malakai left," he whispered. "But it has continued to break every day since, seeing what his absence has done to you."

Tears rolled down my cheeks. Tears I had fought for over two years, not allowing myself the weakness of crying for the man I loved or the life that had been taken from me.

Tolek tugged me to his chest, one hand coming up to cradle the back of my head as a sob worked its way up my throat. His citrus and spice scent enveloped me, and I breathed it in greedily, needing to calm the roaring in my ears. I fisted my hands against the thin black linen of his shirt, my tears staining him as he breathed a soothing whisper against my hair.

Under the cover of night, with Tol siphoning off my pain and shielding me from the world, I leaned into his embrace and surrendered.

Chapter Eight

My head felt like it was packed with damp leaves. The dull, lingering cloudiness was most definitely a residual effect of the time I spent crying into Tol's chest.

I rolled onto my back, squeezing my swollen eyes shut and stretching my hands above my head. Spirits, everything was stiff—likely a result of training my rusty spearwork. That pulse beneath my skin had not calmed overnight either. It centralized in a burning sensation in my right wrist, spreading throughout my forearm. Maybe I had not been quite as flawless with that weapon as I thought. Training this morning would be a challenge if I'd injured myself, but I didn't care.

Still, the pain did not feel like bone or muscle. It went deeper—starting at the surface and sinking into me.

Reluctantly, I sat up in my four-poster bed, rubbing circles against my temples. Once the pressure eased, I sighed and opened my eyes. Dull purple light peeked through my cream curtains, illuminating the dresses, books, and scrolls I had left on the floor in the past week.

There was no fire in the grate this morning, the air streaming through the open window pleasant enough on its own.

I scooted out of bed and reached to pull up the covers, but when I extended my arm, I saw it.

It was not a training sprain.

It was not a stiff muscle.

It was a delicate patch of green-and-gray webbing, starting in the veins of my wrist and working outward. The visible progress was subtle, isolating itself to the wrist for now, but it was digging deeper. It seeped into my body, my blood. Contaminating it. A slow crawl through my veins as it ripped apart what was most precious.

The Curse.

I stumbled against the bed, my legs no longer able to support my weight. Everything around me disappeared. The only sound was panicked blood rushing through my ears. A clammy sweat broke out on my forehead. My body seized and trembled in waves as it fought to understand the foreign agent that had somehow found its way into my skin.

"How?" I exhaled, the word barely distinguishable between my panting breaths.

The plague of our people was gone. It had disappeared two years ago when the end of the war was negotiated. The Engrossians had the sorcia who had cast the Curse remove it.

Maybe they fed us false information, I said to myself, horrified at the possibility of this disease lurking through our territory unexpectedly for the past two years.

But no. I quickly realized that couldn't be. Even if they had lied, not one case of the Curse had been reported in two years. Someone would have known if this disease was still infecting our people.

How is it now embedded on my skin?

My stomach clenched, but not from pain. It was uncertainty. Fear.

I struggled to breathe deeply. *How would an ascended Mystique Warrior approach this threat?* I asked myself.

The obvious answer was to fight. And the first step of any battle: strategize. My heart beat faster as I fought through the fog still clouding my head, attempting to organize the information I knew to be true. I stood from the bed and paced my messy bedroom, the cool floorboards a steady constant beneath my feet.

There were two facts of which I was sure.

The first: If I had been Cursed, then my family was wrong in our suspicion that our bloodline had escaped unscathed. That meant that either my father's or mother's lines were at risk. Since the Curse manifested in descending age order, one of them must have already been struck.

My chest constricted, but I didn't have time to panic because the second fact barreled into my mind: I was going to die.

Soon.

Within days I would begin hallucinating, and from there the progression would be quick. Unaware of my surroundings and starved for blood, I would pose a risk to both loved ones and strangers. The only solution, for the safety of those around me, was execution.

I waited for the swoop of terror through my gut, but it didn't come.

Sliding into the dark embrace of death for the safety of those I loved did not frighten me. Truthfully, I harbored little fear about my death. If I met my fate this way, so be it, but my family did not deserve this doom. It was the thought of the Curse spreading, infecting the innocent around me, and condemning them to an untimely death that had fear gripping my heart.

Bile rose in my throat as the stinging in my wrist deepened. I swallowed it and grabbed a pillow from the bed, pressing my face into it to stop myself from screaming out. Clamping my hand down over the gray webbing, I pulled my wrist to my chest to smother the pain.

It was a tree burrowing its roots, and I was the soil. The endless digging ebbed throughout my wrist, working to corrupt my blood with a gleeful pleasure.

The Curse was like a living thing, latching on to me.

Conceal it, I thought, steadying myself against the pain. That was what I must do. Hide this affliction from everyone I knew until I figured out how far it had stretched. As long as no one came in contact with my blood, those who had not yet been infected would remain safe.

I stormed to my armoire on shaking legs, and wrenched the doors open to reveal an overwhelming assortment of gowns. Trying to make sense of the gossamer, tool, chiffon, and silk of all colors that stared back at me was nearly impossible. Frantically, I ripped dresses from their hangers, cursing myself for insisting on as little material as possible when these were made. Never had I thought that I would be looking for something more modest.

A navy-blue sleeve caught my eye, and I shoved through the collection to grab it. Within seconds, I was struggling to do up my own corset. Dark skirts flowed around me, heavier than I preferred, but it had sleeves. Long and fitted, they extended past my wrists, a soft fabric falling to cover my hands almost completely.

I held my arms out and rotated them, taking care that the Curse was concealed with every movement. A burning twisted around my veins where the webbing lay, as if fighting the cover, but I swallowed my cry of pain.

Once I knew no one could possibly see it, I folded my hands before me and looked at my reflection. My swollen eyes were resuming their usual shape. I wiped a thin sheen of sweat from my forehead and looked otherwise normal. The Curse had not yet caused my skin to pale or my eyes to redden—though I supposed that wouldn't be too noticeable with their magenta shade, thank the Spirits.

My expression was grim, but that was typical of me nowadays. My heart felt heavier than it had in my lifetime as I imagined what was waiting in my household below. Who may be experiencing the steady pulse of pain that I now endured? Whose breaths may be ticking toward their last? My teeth ground together, heat flushing through my body. They all deserved better than this cruel twist of fate.

With a steadying breath, I shook my long hair behind my shoulders and let it fall to my waist as it pleased, still disarrayed from slumber. I turned from the mirror and left my room to decipher who among my family faced death.

Seconds after the door closed, I met Jezebel on the landing. She took in my heavy dress, her brow furrowing. "What are you—"

"No training today," I grumbled, pushing past her to descend the stairs, sneaking glances at both of her wrists as I went.

Bare.

Not an inch of gray webbing to be found. *Thank the Angels*, I thought, a weight lifting from my chest.

Jezebel trailed me down the stairs, clearly afraid to question me too loudly for fear that our parents would hear. Though they turned a blind eye to our training, open discussion of it would not pass their judgment. I felt her shadow following me, laden with unspoken questions.

At the bottom of the staircase, I looked to the stained glass set in the entrance of our home, a depiction of the First Revered Warrior in his Angel form. Would my spirit soon be joining his and the other warriors past? *Whatever happens, I will accept it*, I reminded myself. *For now, find the source.*

I paused in the foyer and considered my two options. Did I start right, to the kitchen where my mother was preparing breakfast, or left, to the study where my father spent his mornings?

I went left. My father's bloodline was stronger, a more useful target for the Curse.

Nerves wracked my body as I raised a hand to knock on the heavy wooden door. *Remain natural*, I coached myself. Jezebel's observant eyes tracked my every movement, making my jaw tick.

I sucked my bottom lip between my teeth and took a deep breath. Behind the door, I heard my father's low cough followed by the shuffling of papers. The sound of my fist against the door was hollow, little force behind it.

"Come in," he called.

I entered with as much bravado as I could muster, trying to mimic my usual confident step. The window behind the desk framed the Mystique land, the morning light reflecting off the white bark of cypher trees, draping branches and tall grasses dancing in a light breeze. My father did not appear to notice anything was wrong.

"Ah, girls. You're here early." He inclined his head, his golden hair unbound from its usual low bun and falling to his shoulders. He appeared healthy, a glow to his bronzed skin.

"Good morning, Father," I said, stepping into the office and toward the desk. I needed to get closer to be sure.

"What can I do for you?" he asked formally.

My head spun with the questions I needed answered but couldn't ask. "What are you reading?" I inquired.

He flashed the cover of the file that lay open on his desk. But I couldn't focus on the title because as he raised it to eye level, his shirtsleeves rolled up his arms. Unmarked wrists stared back at me. No Curse.

His words washed past me as I tumbled through a mix of relief and fear, not pausing to indulge either emotion. My father was safe, *thank the Spirits*, but that meant...Mother's bloodline.

My stomach turned to ice, but I nodded compliantly as my father stopped talking. "Sounds fascinating," I agreed in a voice much stronger than I felt.

"Well, it's more of an obligation to be up to date on the latest excavation developments in the mountains than it is of personal interest, but it comes with the job, I suppose." He shrugged but didn't ask after my feigned interest. My father learned long ago not to question my mind.

"I suppose it does." My fingers twisted within my sleeves, sweat pooling in my palms and along my spine. It was much too hot for this dress, but that was not the source of my distress.

"If you'd like to learn more, I can send a note to the Revered. Perhaps we can set up a tutoring program for the summer." He gestured to the inkwell on his desk that held the same liquid used to etch Mystique tattoos. Made of the mountains. A warrior must simply scribe a note with the dark ink and the parchment would transfer to the recipient instantly. It was to be used sparingly, and I did not wish to send any messages to the Revered in my current state.

Not that the man ever returned to Palerman anymore. He hadn't since his son disappeared. It was rumored that he had locked himself in the Revered's Palace in the city atop the mountains for shame of his son's failure.

"No, thank you, Father. I'll leave you to your work." I dismissed myself, closing the door quickly.

Jezebel looked at me with raised eyebrows. I scanned up and down her sunshine-yellow dress. With the short, capped sleeves at her shoulders, her arms were entirely exposed, and I couldn't help checking one more time to ensure she was safe.

But Jezebel was younger than me. Just because she hadn't shown the Curse yet didn't mean she wouldn't. The webbing pulsed as a reminder of what she'd face. I'd have to pay close attention to her behavior in the coming days. Before I—

"Breakfast?" I asked, turning toward the kitchen and nearly stumbling on my shaking legs.

We entered to the sound of meat sizzling on the stove, the smell not enticing my twisting stomach. At the table, my mother engaged my grandmother in a conversation about seam work while they drank freshly brewed herbal tea. It would have been a pleasant morning—had I not been marked to die.

My eyes landed on my grandmother, and for once I was grateful for her Soulguider heritage. It meant she was safe.

I took one deep breath in through my nose and released it out through my mouth before speaking. "Good morning," I interrupted their conversation.

"Good morning, girls," my mother responded. Her brow knitted. "Ophelia, why are you wearing such a heavy dress? It's not seasonal."

I shrugged. "The color suited me." A horrible lie. My obvious preference was one layer of skirts, sheer bodices, and short sleeves if I could not convince my mother that a strapless dress was suitable.

Jezebel nudged my rib cage as she walked to the stove to

prepare her plate for breakfast, and I had to fight the instinct to snatch my wrist away from her reach. "Ophelia is acting rather odd this morning."

I glared at her.

My mother turned a worried expression to me, but my grandmother stared resolutely at the teacup in her hands. "Are you feeling all right, sweetheart? Perhaps a cup of tea?" My mother reached for the teapot in the middle of the table, and my heart nearly stopped.

There was nothing on her wrists. No hint of the green-gray webbing that was burrowing further into my skin with every minute that I stood here.

I felt like the world was tilting, and I was going to fall off the end of it. This was not possible. The Curse targeted bloodlines, yet I was the only one of my blood who bore it.

"I'm going to have breakfast with Santorina." I excused myself, shooting a glare at Jezebel as I added, "Alone."

Once outside, I marched across our generous land and into the tree line. I fell against the sturdy trunk of a cypher, taking heaving breaths. Though I was baffled, relief brought tears to my eyes, loosening my tense muscles with each drop that rolled down my cheeks.

It was only I who faced death. I could accept that.

The green-gray lines had not spread up my arm yet, but I could feel them tainting my blood. There was a subtle, constant pain throughout my wrist, with short excruciating bursts as the Curse dug its roots deeper into me. Biting my lip to keep from screaming, I watched the dark epicenter pulse as quickly as my thoughts.

None of this was possible, yet the evidence was here.

The Curse had returned, and I was the lone victim.

Chapter Nine

FOR TWO DAYS I tracked the Curse, but my efforts were futile. No one I crossed paths with in Palerman showed visible signs of sharing my fate.

The agreeable weather meant that most residents wore sleeveless dresses or cuffed them, making it easy to glimpse the vulnerable wrists of Mystique descendants as I walked the dusty streets. I pushed my nose into shops, made friendlier conversation than I had in two years, and lingered around the First Warrior fountain, taking any advantage to earn a glimpse at one more wrist.

My own hands had remained within the long folds of my sleeves, and I fought the urge to clamp my hand over my wrist. As if leaving it exposed beneath the fabric would somehow make it visible.

Relief or disappointment—I couldn't be sure which emotion rose faster within my heart as I saw each bare wrist belonging to a familiar face. Comfort that no one else was to suffer my fate battled the selfish uncertainty of *why* the Curse had chosen me.

But when I remembered everything else that had been taken from me, it seemed a cruel but expected joke that the fates would bestow this end upon me.

So, it was with a silent satisfaction that I prepared myself for my twentieth—and what would be my last—birthday celebration. I was not afraid of the unknown bleakness of death. I welcomed the numbing reality, sure that it would alleviate the ache planted in my soul two years ago when my future was ripped away.

Darkness infringed on the night as I brushed my long, wavy locks, setting them back from my face with two studded combs. The diamonds glittered in the mystlight of my vanity, sending shimmers across the sun-kissed highlights in my hair. I had not worn these combs—or any jewels—in years. But as I drew closer to my fate, a fresh desire bloomed within me. Tonight, I would celebrate my life with splendor.

The dress I had selected hung on the door of my armoire, the long train trailing to the ground. It was made of a deep red silk, the precise shade of blood. *Ironic*, I laughed to myself, aware that no one else at the gathering would understand my morbid thoughts. They would see the silk and chiffon skirts trailing behind me, the tight bodice with shimmering gold embroidery laced up to accentuate my curves, and the plunging neckline and exposed shoulders that were captivating and elegant.

The crowning feature was the sleeves: They hugged the muscles in my arms tightly, gathering at the wrists, with a loop that slid over the middle finger of each hand. No part of my secret would be exposed.

Yes, it is the perfect dress to welcome the year of my death.

Wearing only my undergarments, I stepped into the skirts and painstakingly laced up the corset. It would have been quicker to call on Jezebel to assist me, but the week's events made me feel isolated, and I retreated into that solace now. More than that, I wanted to see this through on my own.

When I looked in the mirror, my jaw nearly dropped at my own reflection. For years I fought against the refinement I now embraced, opting for barely-there dresses when I could not don my leather training garb. The full skirts and tightened bodices had never felt like me. Now, surrounded by silk the color of my tainted blood, prepared to greet my encroaching death within a matter of days, I looked entirely myself.

A devious smile crept across my face, my magenta eyes flaring with excitement. Thanks to the cosmetics my sister had gifted me, they stood out more than usual. *You're to use all of these tonight, no exception*, she had said, shoving the box into my hands over breakfast. I knew better than to question her eye for everything glamorous.

Before leaving my room, I stole one last glance at my wrist. It had been two days, and the Curse had barely spread. Odd and inexplicable, as the Curse should have ravaged my blood by now. The pain was still a nearly unbearable reminder of its presence, but the webbing remained isolated to the veins on the inside of my wrist.

I chose not to question the progress. With one last vicious, satisfied grin, I tucked my sleeve over the affliction, and turned for the door. Tainted blood pounded through my veins, louder with each step down the darkened hallway. Dim chatter floated up to me as I stood on the top landing and gathered myself for that first step into the last frivolous night of my life.

Shock. That was what filled the air as I descended the staircase that curved toward the door of our grand room. From me, from my family, and from my friends.

My mother went above everyone's standards for this party, transforming our home with cascading golden drapery and glittering mystlight chandeliers. It was finery we had not seen since we fell into a state of mourning following the war. It appeared that for tonight my mother had returned to the old ways.

We had but a small number of guests—my closest friends, family, and warriors of honor who would expect to receive an invitation, such as the Mystique Council members. Long tables of bountiful food lined the far wall of the room, an array of my favorite dishes calling to me. Vested servers stood to one side, awaiting the signal to begin distributing hor d'oeurves and glasses of sparkling wine from polished trays. In the corner beside the door was a trio prepared to entertain us with fine music.

But no one paid any heed to the decor, food, or musicians. When I entered, I stole their attention. It was as if all air had been sucked from the room, and I was the source of everyone's breath. The scornful woman of just a few days past would have hated the attention, but tonight was different. Tonight, I wanted to live one last time.

Crossing the wooden floor, my heels echoed through the stunned silence, transporting me to another life. One where this night would have seemed entirely normal—understated even. I stood in the center of the room, soaking in the astonished expressions of my guests with wicked glee.

"Thank you all for coming," I called in a clear voice. The ringing tone belonged to the girl I used to be. The one I was saying goodbye to.

When I looked to my family and closest friends, I saw confusion crossing over their faces. My mother leaned in to my father to whisper what I was sure was a statement about my appearance, finally indulging the feminine side she often forced on me.

A silent chuckle went through me at the group's inability to grasp my pivoting mood—that is, all of them except two. My grandmother, who met my mischievous grin with a twin smirk of her own, and Tolek. He did not appear confused, but enchanted. His deep brown eyes widened as they met mine, and he rose onto the balls of his feet before clasping his hands behind his back and squaring his shoulders, as if fighting every instinct to meet me in the center of the room.

"Tonight, we celebrate twenty years of my life. They have been full in ways one could never expect in such a short time. Both in loss and in blessing." The Bind tingled. "Though not all whom I love are here tonight, let us revel in honor of what has certainly been a life unlike any other. I can say it has been twenty years that have felt like thrice that." I held out my hand to summon one of the servers, and the cool stem of a glass slid between my fingers. Around the room, his peers filled empty hands with glasses. I waited until all thirty guests held one, then raised mine before me. "To this year delivering whatever dark paths fate has gathered for me."

Brows furrowed at my ominous words, but a hesitant echo chorused around me as I drained my glass and passed it off to a waiter. I winked at my grandmother as she downed her wine, and a flicker of that silent understanding passed between us.

My mother and father said a quick hello, before departing to greet their esteemed guests, many of whom I could not be bothered with. As they left me, my father hugged me tightly, whispering against my hair, "I am proud of the woman you have become, *Sorrida*, but I am sorry for the events that shaped you."

The hole in my heart stuttered, a lump threatening to form in my throat, but I shoved the grief down for the evening. I nodded at my father and raised my chin. "Thank you" was all I could manage.

My grandmother stepped up before I could give in to the emotion flooding my system.

"May I?" She held a small gold charm in her hand. A pin, I realized, as she fastened it to the thin fabric of my dress above my left breast. "A family trinket for the important year you are entering. Allow it to guide you." She squeezed my shoulder, and it felt pointed.

The pin was small, a cluster of tiny rose-colored gems beside a clouded blue one. It was an odd combination, but rather beautiful. A gift I'd treasure forever.

"Thank you." I kissed her on the cheek.

"It's as radiant as the woman wearing it," Tolek said from behind me. He handed me a second glass of sparkling wine.

"You have excellent taste, young man." My grandmother had always loved Tolek. In his tailored black jacket and fine white silk shirt, it was obvious she was correct.

"I think so, too." He bowed slightly to her as she left, and I spied a faint blush against his tan skin. "Happy birthday, Ophelia." He leaned in to kiss my cheek.

"Thank you, Tolek." I grinned at him, my nose scrunching,

and performed an exaggerated curtsy. Tolek had a manner of bringing proper behaviors out of me, yet at the same time encouraging me to act with reckless abandon, embracing my wild heart. The unique balance of etiquette and foolhardiness forged his own gleam in the world.

He extended his glass to clink against mine, and I pivoted to stand on his right side, keeping my Cursed wrist as far as possible. I may have made peace with my fate, but I did not need others concerned with it. Nor did I need to risk contaminating anyone else should I spill a drop of blood.

"Which among your guests do you believe will be the first to fall to the impurities of the evening, Alabath?" Tolek asked, wiggling his eyebrows at me as we surveyed the room. His hair was coiffed upward, more tamed than usual, and the highlights caught the light as he tilted his head toward me. The persistent scruff on his chin had been trimmed, but the shadows lingered, emphasizing the definition of his jaw and cheekbones.

"Ah, Vincienzo. I believe that is most likely to be ourselves," I said, clinking my glass against his and taking a sip, batting my lashes over the rim as I did so.

Tolek's eyes darkened, but he shook his head and shrugged, speaking stiffly, "Sometimes the most fun is found at the bottom of a glass, though my money is on Alvaron." He tilted his head at the Master of Coin of the Mystique Council, who appeared to already be spilling hor d'oeurves down his shirtfront and laughing at himself with a glassy-eyed stare.

I laughed along with him, raking my eyes over the room for another target for our humor. It had been so long since we had had anything to celebrate. Though I felt energized at the thought, my cheer fueled by the secret on my wrist, my heart ached at the thought of who was missing.

How would this day have been spent if Malakai had not disappeared? I supposed it no longer mattered. If he were truly…I refused to think it, but if I were to die soon, perhaps we would be reunited. My heart fluttered wickedly at the idea.

"I have a gift for you," Tolek began, but when Cyph, Rina, and Jezebel joined us, he whispered, "I'll give it to you later."

I frowned at him, but he only laughed.

"Not to upset you, sister, but your speech was rather...dismal." Jezebel, resplendent in a gown of rose silk with a sheer décolletage and silver threading, crossed her arms.

"I thought it was fitting." Cyph shrugged. His navy-blue jacket brought out the dark accents in his eyes as they crinkled with his grin.

"Thank you, Cyph. And thank you again for the present." He had dropped off a matching set of exquisite daggers earlier, unsure how my guests would react to the gift given that I was no longer supposed to train. They were small, lethally sharp, and fit securely to each thigh. I should have known that our personal master of blades would have done as much.

Cypherion smiled at me, promising to show me how best to care for them.

"Useful," Rina said, an edge of disapproval in her voice, if only for concern of us getting caught.

She had let her hair down from its usual ponytail tonight. It fell in an intimidating curtain around her shoulders and the plum-colored gown that skimmed her figure down to the floor. She raised a brow. To anyone else, the expression in her round eyes might have been sultry, but I read the challenge there.

I lifted my chin. "You're jealous of my shiny new toys."

"I had to ensure you'd like my gift as much," Santorina said, tipping her glass toward mine.

"It's perfect," I told her of the perfume she had made specifically for me, laced with jasmine and citrus.

Around us, couples twirled across the floor without direction, not following a formal dance routine, but simply letting the music guide them. Operating on instinct fueled by the earth's rhythm in our veins. Cypherion led Santorina to join while Jezebel disappeared to the buffet table.

"May I have this dance?" Tol asked, extending one hand to me and tucking the other behind his back.

My heart fluttered as I flashed him my most charming smile and assumed my most dignified tone. "Why, certainly you—"

But the words were stolen by an exigent presence that entered the room.

All eyes flocked to him. He nodded to my father but did not stop to greet him. Somehow, his light-as-air footsteps drowned out the music, echoing hollowly against the wooden floor.

An inexplicable chill seeped through my body as I took in his dark gray coat, so long it traveled well past his knees. He must have just arrived from Damenal if he was wearing such a protective jacket. Underneath, he wore shades of black so deep my mind could not perceive how they were real. The air around him seemed to vibrate. Out of intimidation or force of power, I couldn't be sure.

Tolek met my numb gaze, turning to see who had caught my eye, and his lips parted, expression freezing. With a quiet exhale, he mumbled something that sounded like "*Holy hell Spirits.*"

Lucidius Blastwood, the Revered Mystique Warrior, leader of our people, and Malakai's father, stopped before us. There was something different about him—an aura I could not place.

His authority chilled me—every spot save for the tainted web on my wrist, but something cold and furious curled within me. Based on the way he tensed beside me, Tolek was experiencing the same rage, but his features remained calm.

"Ophelia," Lucidius greeted me, and his authority saturated that one word, seeping into the air around us. "Happy birthday." He extended his palm, and I placed my hand in his, the contact turning my fingers icy. He raised our hands in a silent salute before speaking words I was unprepared to hear. "I wish my son could be beside you on this of all nights. He is certainly missing out, wherever he may be." His eyes gleamed in an unsettling way. Not mourning or misery, but disappointment in his heir and a swirling depth I didn't recognize.

Though Malakai's strong jaw, dark hair, and green irises so looked like his father, they could not be more different.

I took a deep breath and pulled my hand back from his,

ensuring that my sleeve had not rolled up. I nodded gracefully at him, fluttering my dark eyelashes in an innocent impression. "Thank you, sir. You know I miss him dearly, but I do hope we will be reunited soon."

Lucidius's jaw tensed as he raised his hands before him, shrugging slightly. "As do we all. Though I fear that time has come and gone."

"That may be your fear." My patience was wearing thin, but I kept my voice light, pretending we weren't discussing the possibility of his own son's death and his hopelessness at his survival. "But I do not share it. Malakai is the strongest warrior among our generation."

A disturbing smile spread across his face, eyes darkening beneath hooded brows. "Ah, how I wish I could carry the hope of the young once again."

"I wish for your sake that you could, as well, sir." My words were becoming bitter. "He and I will see each other again, soon." The finality in my voice implied the end of the conversation.

"Mm-hmm," Lucidius hummed. He bowed to me slightly, clasping his hands behind his back before nodding in Tol's direction. "Vincienzo" was his only acknowledgment of his son's friend before he left us.

When he was out of earshot, Tol leaned closer to me and whispered, his breath hot against my neck, "I know that we're supposed to honor him, but that man makes my blood boil."

I turned my face toward Tol's so that our cheeks were an inch apart. Though still reeling from the encounter with Lucidius, I whispered, "I hear wine cools boiling blood nicely." I pulled back to flash him a mischievous smile.

Hours later, long after the clock had struck midnight and my birthday had officially passed, the grand room was emptying. My head spun from the bottles of sparkling wine Tolek and I had stolen from the kitchen, racing to see who could finish theirs first. The bubbles had coated the evening with an intoxicating, golden hue. For the first time in years, I felt gleeful, and I was certain it was not strictly due to the alcohol.

In another life, tonight would have been a dream. I would have worn my official Mystique Warrior leathers and held the evening in Damenal. I would have danced with Malakai, possibly Tolek and Cypherion, too, reveled with Rina and Jezebel, and fallen into my bed with my partner at the end of the night, questioning my luck in this life.

Instead, I was facing a cursed fate, but accepting that path had relieved my shoulders of the weight of life, and I was able to enjoy myself. I would find peace in another life, and potentially rejoin Malakai if he had truly fallen to the fate others believed. The thought sent my heart swelling.

The air buzzed with a heavy feeling of expectation. Though I didn't know what caused it, my stomach fluttered nervously, like it knew a secret I was not aware of. I bounced around the grand room on the balls of my feet, floating from that unnamed sensation, until the clock chimed three in the morning.

I kissed my family good night and stumbled into my darkened bedroom.

"Ouch," I muttered, clumsy fingers scratching my skin as I tore off my corset.

When the dress pooled around my knees, I stepped out of it, kicked off my heels, and crawled into bed in only my undergarments. The sheets felt cool against my body, especially the burning spot on my wrist. I was grateful to the alcohol for dulling that pain.

It could have been my drunken mind, but the air seemed different tonight. Delicate. Like the atmosphere was a precious realm of glass, waiting for someone to come along and gently send it shattering to the ground. A cool night breeze fluttered across my flushed cheeks, lulling the thoughts from my mind.

But I had barely reached the shallows of sleep when a blinding light flashed through my room. I scrambled to my feet atop my mattress in search of a weapon that wasn't there.

I squinted through the golden light that poured into every corner of the previously dark room, disoriented but prepared to fight. The rays resembled physical sunlight, but brighter. Inhuman and unnatural, yet the purest substance in existence. Through the burning beams I saw a figure that brought me to my knees.

An Angel.

Chapter Ten

LIGHT FLOODED MY VISION where I knelt on my bed. Every inch of bare skin it touched heated, my blood pumping faster in response to the ancient source of magic. Angellight—the substance of myth that no living warrior was blessed to see. Or so legends told. Born of the magic of the mountains, it was pure power only the seven Angels ascended to.

I remained in only my undergarments, my comforter pooling around my knees. In an attempt at respect for this honored being that found its way into my room, I grabbed a knit blanket from the foot of my bed and wrapped it around my shoulders. Though the window was open, a night breeze ruffling my curtains, the room was warm from the Angellight.

My head pounded from a combination of the wine, light, and shock. *How in the fucking Angels was this happening? And why?* All I could do was bow my head gracefully. My blonde waves blurred my field of vision, but I peeked up through my lashes, afraid to lose sight of my guest. One shouldn't make eye contact until summoned—it was defiant of me. But I could also argue that it was rude to appear in someone's bedroom in the middle of the night.

The Angel hovered inches off the ground. An embarrassing assortment of garments and books lay strewn across the dark wood floors. My armoire was flung open, my vanity cluttered with the combs, jewelry, and cosmetics I had used earlier that evening. Had

I known I would be visited by an Angel tonight, I may have tidied up.

No, I probably would not have.

The light pulsed with each breath the Angel took, and I found it odd that this being before me even needed to draw breath. Maybe it was an act to make me more comfortable. Despite all the questions running through my mind, I waited for him to signal that I could rise.

"Ophelia Tavania Alabath," he spoke in a voice that dripped with antiquity. It pushed against the walls, filling every inch of available space. It was a melody in my veins, vibrating along my bones and coaxing me into serenity.

At the sound of my name, I raised my head. Having adjusted to the intensity of the golden gleam, I took in his sculpted cheeks, broad frame, and golden curls. My breath caught in my throat. The eyes, a deep purple set against his bronze skin, were recognizable to any Mystique child. They were depicted in stained glass windows and ancient watercolors, adorning every dwelling of Mystique Warriors. Hung in the foyer of my own home. Marked the center of Palerman in fountain form.

This was Damien, the First Revered Warrior, the sire of the Mystique Warrior Clan. And he had appeared to me.

His presence swarmed my room, blurring out everything around us. I imagined the only thing that would compare to this pulsing power was that of a god, but as warriors we kept no gods. Other races of magical beings on Ambrisk, like the fae and sorcia, worshipped one founding god each, but the warriors kept seven Angels to ensure our balance of power was upheld. Some minor clans' magic was linked to the gods, and they even communed with them, but as our founders, the Angels were held above those ancient beings.

Trembling, I rose to my feet, pulling the blanket tighter around me. Had I chosen to meet the First Warrior, I would not have selected a time when I was still a bit drunk and wearing nothing but sheer undergarments. Though I was sure he was aware of my inebriation, Damien did not express any care.

"To what do I owe the honor?" I asked, unsure how one should greet a legendary Angel. These were not things taught in school.

"Chosen Child, the time of thy reckoning has reached us." Damien's voice wrapped itself around me, each syllable echoing through my bones.

"My reckoning?" I asked shakily. Why was he referring to me as *Chosen Child*?

Damien remained in his position, hovering at eye level just feet from my bed, and nodded, his curls falling across his forehead. He did not need to flutter his glorious, golden wings to stay afloat—his power suspended him. "At this, thy twentieth year, it is time that thou hear, a warrior born with blood of two is the blessed of me and you." The words rolled in melody from Damien's mouth, leaving little impression on me beyond confusion.

"What—"

"The task ahead will try thy spirit, but the Chosen is composed of strong merit."

Try my spirit? I squinted up at him, my brow furrowing. It was impossible to decipher anything he said over the pounding in my head.

He continued, not fazed by my confusion. "Thy deepest wish awaits thee, once thou claims thy destiny. Ophelia, time is running short, for thou art our last resort." The poem ended, but the words continued fluttering around me, a mix of rhyme and senseless song.

I blinked at Damien, but he said nothing more. "What does *that* mean?" I threw my arm out in exasperation, and the blanket slipped off my shoulder. The intricate webbing on the inside of my wrist caught the golden light.

The Angel's eyes flashed to the vulnerable spot, and it pulsed with pain as the Curse's roots burrowed deeper into my veins. As if the affliction could sense the presence before us and needed to claim me. Or hide. I could not be sure which.

Damien studied my wrist for a long, silent moment, and I waited for him to speak, but he did not utter another rhyme. His eyes returned to my face; the frustrating calmness still painted his chiseled features.

"Is this about the Curse?" I asked, my voice sharper than one should speak to any Angel, let alone the First Revered Warrior.

He opened his arms wide, as if to engulf the entire world. "It is about everything that will be nothing if you do not act."

I rolled my neck, hoping that working out the tension budding in my shoulders would help me to understand his cryptic message. My head continued to throb. *Everything that will be nothing.* "Am I going to die?" If I could get at least one answer, maybe I could begin solving the riddle.

"Not even the Soulguiders or Starsearchers could predict *your* death, Ophelia. The fate is too precarious." I really wished he would move in a less statuesque manner, but every sweep of his arm or bob of his head was rigid.

"But they are interpreters of everyone's fate. It has all been written." My grandmother had taught me as much of her people in the past twenty years, uttering prophecies her Soulguider genes bequeathed unto her. And the Starsearchers...they were even more notorious for translating one's death as written in the universe. Where the Soulguiders made predictions about your future guided by the Goddess of Death and led souls home after they departed, the Starsearchers read astrological fates at the hand of the Celestial Goddess.

If anything was to befall you, the Soulguiders or Starsearchers would know of it.

But Damien nodded his head gently, locking those vivid eyes on mine. They were almost the same shade, more purple than my magenta. "Your fate has not yet been decided, Chosen Child."

"Why do you call me that?" My tone was harsher than necessary, but I was never known for my patience. First Revered Warrior or not, Damien's presence was infuriating me. Not simply his being, but his elusive answers that only sparked more questions. His appearance was imposing, his power and avoidance unwelcome.

I opened my mouth to ask him—unkindly—to leave if he was not going to answer. Before I could speak, he said, "You will see."

I groaned at the Angel, but he only smirked at me, as if he understood my frustration and it amused him. At least that was a lively reaction. "If you succeed, you will right the wrongs you have staked your heart against."

My mouth went dry, my grip on the blanket almost slipping. "The wrongs?"

He closed his eyes and nodded reverently. After a beat of pulsing light, Damien muttered, "Goodbye, Ophelia," and his light shuddered. In a blink, the Angel had vanished.

"You cannot go!" I turned frantically around my room in search of him as the blurring effect of the Angellight faded and the chaotic mess of my life returned to clarity. "I don't know what to do. *Damien!*" I hissed, daring to use his first name.

"The truth lies within you, Chosen Child. It is yours to uncover." The voice echoed through my room, but Damien was gone. When the words faded, the night breeze drifted in through my open window, penetrating the heat the Angellight had brought.

Pulling my blanket up around my neck, I fell back to my knees. My brain swirled with a fog of questions, but at least Damien's appearance had dimmed the effects of the wine. Feeling slightly more sober, I took one deep breath. Then, I spoke out loud to myself. "First step—recall the rhymes he spoke."

I threw my blanket aside and picked up the first piece of parchment and ink I saw on the floor. Moving to the bench beside the window, I curled up to write by the light of the moon.

My reckoning, I scribbled, shivering. It sounded as though I was to be put on trial. Had I committed a crime that upset the Angels?

No, that could not be, for I remembered the words he spoke later. *I am their last resort.* If I existed as a chance at salvation, then the trial he spoke of could not be punishment for a crime. They needed me. Specifically, *me.* What did I have that others did not? I was a fierce warrior, though I wasn't fully ascended. But I was determined. Was the challenge a test of strength or will? Surely, that would be something I could conquer, if I set my mind to it. But what exactly would the trial present?

Though I wasn't sure what group Damien referred to when he said I was their last resort, I could only assume it was the Mystiques. He was our forefather, watching over us for eternity. I scribbled the possibility in my notebook, quickly followed by the few other lines I recalled from the Angel's mouth. Each was discouraging in their own right.

Your deepest wish awaits.

Try your spirit.

Everything that will be nothing.

You will right the wrongs.

The rest of his words were lost in a rush of rhymes and Angellight, but what was before me did not make sense. I was to undergo a test, and this trial would decide my fate. Not only my fate, but that of the ambiguous "them." I did not see how I could be anyone's last resort. Sure, my father's bloodline was honored in its own right, and I was a strong candidate to ascend, but I had not even completed the Undertaking. Without full status, what was I to do?

My stomach turned over in uncertainty as the list of unknowns grew, and I wrapped my arms around my bare torso in an effort to keep myself from being sick. I rocked back and forth in the moonlight, shuddering at the predictions the Angel had voiced. My eyes scanned the page in circles. *Chosen Child.*

Something deep in my bones purred the longer I stared at Damien's words. A part of me, be it soul or fate or pure intuition, acknowledged the Angel's premonition and hummed in acceptance. It was that small piece that told me it was true, despite my doubts.

After all, I had been promised to the future leader of our people and received the Bind with him. The magic of that promise ran through my skin, blood, and bones. We would have been a force among warriors, two powerful bloodlines merging.

And I was powerful on my own. Spirits, with Malakai gone, I may even be the strongest warrior of our age. Cypherion could likely beat me in a fight, but I had been trained at my father's hand as future Second, and I had observed the cunning instincts of female warriors before me, adopting them as my own.

So how could I truly deny the Angel's proclamation? The thrum of my Mystique Warrior blood coiled hungrily at the possibility.

I held my wrist out beneath the moonlight, running my thumb over the stinging spot where the Curse manifested itself. I barely wanted to admit the question brewing in my mind. Could this heal my affliction?

It was unlikely. The Curse had no known cure. If it was capable of being healed, we would not have lost so many warriors to its cruel fate.

Fate. My fate... *Your fate has not yet been decided.* Maybe I was not to die by the hand of this plague. Maybe I could do something, anything, to right the path my people were put on, restore our grand standing.

Right it...

The words I had last written in my notebook seemed to darken. Something connected in my brain like the end of a fuse being lit. My thoughts burned up the incinerating trail. "Right the wrongs..." I whispered.

My mind traveled at warp speed, begging to reach the result I was scared to admit. I had been wronged—cheated—in a number of different ways in the past two years. My future, my destiny, my love all ripped away. There were pieces of Damien's words that hinted at what I must do and what results those actions could derive, but I was almost afraid to voice them. My blood pumped faster in encouragement, that second pulse awakening.

Your deepest wishes...

The closer I got to the answer of Damien's quest, the louder my heart and the new pulse in my blood beat. The fuse that had lit was about to combust, the spark burning faster to its destination. I only needed to accept the task for it to explode. In its wake, I would travel the path burst open by the Angel.

There were two truths that I was certain were hidden beneath Damien's words. I did not know what results they would yield, but my blood sang in confirmation, encouraging me to trust the First Warrior—

I must complete the Undertaking.

The trial before me, the path meant to test my spirit, was not a punishment for crime. It was the Mystique Warrior's greatest journey. I had to claim this fate. I did not know if or how this was tied to the affliction burrowing into my wrist, but it was the future for which I always knew I was fated. And if the Curse was to kill me, I needed to act quickly—I had days at best.

The second truth, the greatest desire of my blackened heart—Malakai was alive.

I fell back against the windowsill, staring up into the heavens. At my understanding of Damien's message, the stars seemed to shine brighter. As I watched, one constellation—a long line of stars with a shorter one intersecting near the bottom—winked at me. It was the Sword—the constellation of the First Mystique Warrior. Tonight, it was brighter than the other six constellations of the clans.

And above that, pulsing to capture my attention, was the North Star. I watched it as it twisted and gleamed before my eyes, alive under my stare. Somewhere out there, *my* North Star was waiting to come back to me. I was sure of it.

I could almost feel Malakai's strong arms wrapping around my waist at the thought, a warm band of hope consuming me. I remembered the gentle brush of his lips over my tattoo each time we were together, like it was the most precious piece of either of us.

"I'm going to become a Mystique Warrior, and I am going to find you. If this Curse kills me, I will right the wrongs the universe has inflicted upon us first," I whispered my promise to the stars.

As if he heard me, a cool whisper of air tickled my neck, a simple exhale of a lover standing at your back.

I leaned against the window as a plan began to take shape in my mind.

Chapter Eleven

Malakai

Calloused hands shoved me through the stone archway, digging into my bare skin and slamming my body to the floor. I groaned internally as my shoulder caught my weight. Bone crunched painfully against cool rock, but I stayed silent. They must have weakened me somehow to be capable of forcing me to the ground so easily.

The fucking whiskey…

They had graciously pushed a bottle of something strong through the door of my cell late last night. One dizzying sip was all I took, but it was enough if laced with the right drug. I was usually more cautious than that, learning early on in captivity to be wary of beverages handed to me. I cursed myself for my sloppy behavior, but last night was the eve of—

No, I couldn't think of that now. I needed whatever strength they hadn't robbed in order to maintain a sliver of my Spirit-damned dignity.

A metal gate slammed shut, the frame rattling. Heavy boots stalked across the stone floor, circling me and moving to the front of the room. I sensed that there were two sets of them.

I relied only on my hearing, scent, and touch, the thick black blindfold stealing my sight. Still, I knew where we were. I didn't need to see the sheen glistening on the walls to know that it was there from our last session. Damp with the mixture of sweat and blood that clung to the air, floor, and walls. Stuck to my skin.

My sweat. My blood. But not my tears. No, I would not allow them that satisfaction.

I didn't need to see the heavy chains hanging from the center of the ceiling—or the matched sets on the walls—to know they were there, providing a variety of ways to bend, restrain, and destroy a captive. Whatever cruel means entered the guards' minds.

I was theirs to torment, for their entertainment, because they knew I wouldn't fight back. I couldn't. Not if the promises were to be upheld.

An iron scent penetrated the air, but that was usual. I had grown accustomed to the scent of my own blood over these two years of torture. They liked to extract it in a number of brutal, creative ways.

Afterward, they always left the mess on my torn skin as a reminder of their sport.

The chains rattled—the haunting clatter that tore me from sleep each night, gasping for breath. I showed none of that fear as I was dragged to my feet. They may own me, but I would not bare my soul.

One heavy cuff closed around each wrist and ankle, and the guard pulled the ends of the chains tight. My arms stretched outward, pointing toward the walls, and my blindfold fell to the floor. This was their favorite position in which to restrain me. The irony of my body resembling the tattoo inked on my chest was a cruel joke to them.

A reminder of the path that led me here, as if I would otherwise forget. Some days I wished I could.

I locked eyes with the man standing on the dais before me as the crack of a whip whistled through the air. The chamber filled with the snap of leather on skin, but I barely registered the pain. In the two years since my imprisonment, my body had grown numb to the feeling. The torture—though it had been hard to admit at first that that was what was happening to me. It became easier to accept over time, but there were some things I still chose to ignore.

I heard rather than felt the impact of the whip, a tearing sound that radiated through my body as my flesh ripped. It wasn't hard to break it—the wounds never had time to fully heal.

Everything around me was just noise. Nothing could hurt me anymore. *Nothing physical at least*, I thought as a hot trickle of blood trailed down my back.

"Again," the guard in charge instructed from his platform, his voice even and demanding, as if nothing he saw done to me fazed him or pleased him enough.

I raised my chin to meet his icy stare. With my arms spread wide as they were, chains binding me to the walls, I should have felt vulnerable. That was his hope. But I held his eyes as I heard the whip make contact again. The blood thickened, trailing under my shorts and down the back of my legs.

They never tortured me enough to kill me, though sometimes I wished they had. But it was impossible to kill me here; my body healed too quickly. They knew that I would wake each day with the fresh pink scars of mending injuries, the blood crusted onto my skin.

They knew that. The ones responsible for this.

"One more," the guard directed his fellow holding the whip.

"Only three today?" I spat the words, my voice croaking and hoarse from disuse. Those first weeks, I had screamed through the torture. Each blow, hot iron, and carving drew a cry from deep within me that shook the room. Since those weeks, my voice had barely been used beyond my meager taunts during these sessions.

I shook my matted black hair from my eyes as I threw my head back, authority I didn't truly have demanding that his gaze meet mine. I shouldn't goad the guard. He held the ears of my captors closely and acted with their orders. But if this was my fate, I would not be entirely submissive.

A cruel smile curled the guard's lips. The whip whistled through the air a third time. I didn't flinch—didn't blink—when it landed.

"Would you like more, Warrior Prince?" They liked to mock me with reminders of who I was destined to be, but the harsh words didn't sting. The one they called *Warrior Prince*—a false title, for Mystiques had no princes—no longer existed. Not as he had before.

I held his black gaze to mine, unrelenting. "Do your worst," I growled.

Today of all days, my body was filled with restless energy. I couldn't fight the baiting words that came to my lips, expelling a sliver of that wild heat growing inside of me. Anger at what I missed.

The man on the dais nodded at the inflictor, whose hands reached for the cold steel sword at his belt. It slid out of its sheath, shining against his leather armor. He flexed his hands around the hilt, muscles tensing, savoring the moment that my eyes locked on the blade before he struck.

Maybe this will be the final blow, I thought, hopeful at first. But as he raised the sword a pair of magenta eyes swam into my vision, and fear sank low in my stomach. The fear of never seeing those eyes before mine again. The fear of never running my hands along her warm, tanned skin or through her golden hair.

The memory of jasmine and honeysuckle made my knees go weak with terror, and I stumbled. The cuff chaining me to the wall—the only thing keeping me upright besides my own fortitude—dug into my skin, a new line of blood trailing down my arm.

My eyes followed the sword, but I thought of her, swearing to the Angels that if this was the end, she would be my last memory. The blade rose high before me. It was a streak of lightning against the night, slicing through the air with devilish intent and precision. In one powerful swipe, he cut through the skin and muscle stretched across the right side of my rib cage. It cut deep enough to leave a scar, but not so deep as to cause permanent damage. The guards were calculating where they struck, not wanting to anger their boss.

I panted as the metal slid against my skin.

I crumpled to the blade, but righted myself quickly, ignoring the growing puddle of blood obscuring the stone floor. It was sticky and warm beneath my bare feet, and I felt the loss radiating through my skull.

My captor smirked as if he had tasted something sweet. "You're lucky he only ordered three lashes today." His voice rang through the chamber as he jumped off his platform and landed before me. In my contorted state, he seemed bigger than me, but if I stood to my full height, I would have defeated him. A chance I'd never have.

He continued, voice cold and face just inches from mine, "If I had my way, you'd have been dead long ago, Warrior Prince." His eyes trailed over my body. When they flashed back to my face, an unsettling spark flared in their dark depths. He smiled hungrily. "Hold him down. I have one more *enhancement* I'd like to make."

There was a sharp click, and a blade shot into his hand. The inflictor sheathed his sword and rammed my shoulders against the wall, holding me still. The first guard prowled forward. "Your tattoo," he purred. "It's quite…sentimental, is it not?"

I squirmed beneath the inflictor's hands, the wound in my side throbbing and the slices in my back stinging against the wall. "Don't fucking touch it!" I growled, but that erratic energy was the reaction he wanted.

"Oh, no…I would never," he purred. "I'm simply making an improvement."

My eyes widened in horror as he raised the delicate blade. The tip pressed into the flesh on the right side of my chest below my collarbone, opposite the Bind.

"Get off of me," I panted, a soft bubble of red beading with the first prick. My vision was clouding from blood loss.

"Hold still, or we'll have to start over." His words were a cruel promise, and I knew from experience that he meant it. If I moved, he would allow the wound to heal and then begin again.

I wrenched my head upward and bit down on the scream that rose up my throat when the tip of the blade tore slowly through my flesh. He carved my chest for agonizing minutes, the hungry look never leaving his damned face. I did not cry out as the sharp point sliced along my muscle and skin, leaving his personal mark on me.

When he stepped back, he smiled. "Now you have been marked with our constellation, as well. Since you seem to have an affinity for stars."

I wanted to vomit at his feet. Their precious constellation, forever etched into my skin. The wounds would heal, but the scars would be a permanent reminder of who inflicted them. Marked me as a representation of their Angel-damned selves.

"Release his chains. Return him to his cell," he barked, taking a step back. His pale skin glowed in the moonlight from the one small window cut high into the stone. "We'll continue next time, Warrior Prince. Sleep well."

I glared at his retreating figure, swearing to the revenge I may never get to enact, until the gate closed behind him.

My chains slackened, and I fell to my knees in exhaustion. Defeat swarmed me as the inflictor returned my blindfold. My goading was met in this session, and though I brought it upon myself, I felt drained as we left the iron-scented room behind.

My cell was nearly identical to the bloodstained chamber, but instead of chains and a dais, there was a cot in one corner and a bucket in the other. The only entrance was a heavy iron door with a small window cut into it through which one of my four guards passed food daily. It remained locked at all hours; they didn't realize that I wouldn't try to escape. I couldn't. I heard them whispering about it sometimes. Speculating how I, the destined future of the Mystique Warriors, had come to this fate. How they had been so lucky to easily capture me and why I had not once attempted escape.

It seemed none of them were privy to the truth.

An ache started to creep along my muscles, beginning in my shoulders and spreading slowly down my back and arms. That fucking spot on my chest that I couldn't bear to look at was the most prominent. Light licks of fire crept into the flesh, muscle, and bone. The sting was subtle, my body healing as quickly as the sparks ignited. Ice tangled with the flames until it filled the space, sealing over what had been ripped apart.

I touched my hand to the spot on my ribs where the sword had sliced me. It stung when my fingers grazed the open flesh, but they came away clean. The blood had already clotted, leaving a shallow gouge in its place, exposing pink muscle. As I watched, the muscle became less tender. The blood on my skin dried and crusted, but it gave me little comfort.

Stumbling to the musky cot, I turned my head up toward the room's lone window. Three feet above me, its bars framed the rising moon and the sea of glimmering stars surrounding it. The iridescence broke the bleakness of the night. The moon appeared closer than usual, the sight planting a seed of something warm inside me—hope.

"Eight hundred and twenty-two," I whispered into the empty cell. I leaned my shoulder against the wall, my back still too raw to rest against the cold stone.

Eight hundred and twenty-two days since life as I knew it ended. Eight hundred and twenty-two days since I had kissed her goodbye.

I brushed my sweat-soaked bangs out of my eyes to view the moon better, imagining her skin bathed in its glow somewhere out in the world. Her eyes would reflect its light like a pearl placed in a sea of deep magenta flowers. I thought of the things we had done beneath the moon in our clearing. The way her body felt against mine all those nights ago, holding her to me. Protecting her. Protecting us. I could still feel her, like she was pressed against me now, our bodies rising and falling and releasing together.

My head sank against the wall, giving into the sleep my body craved as thoughts of her danced through my head. I hoped she was happy tonight, the radiant smile gracing her face, softening her exquisite features.

"Happy birthday, Ophelia," I breathed into the still air.

I'd like to think she felt it.

-PART TWO-

MEGAERA

Chapter Twelve

Ophelia

Two Years Earlier

The gate to the Blastwoods' sprawling property—the largest estate within Palerman—creaked slightly when I nudged it open. The silver gilding along its metal spikes glinted in the sunlight as it swung inward. The scent of freshly trimmed grass and sun-warmed gravel wrapped itself around me as I strolled up the pathway to the house, shaded by the willows.

I smiled at the memories of Augustus and myself tearing through the winding trails as children, ducking in and out of cyphers with screeches and laughter, using sticks as pretend weapons. The rule had always been that we were free to roam, so long as we stayed within the gates—which was easy considering how much land the Blastwoods owned.

As we'd grown older, the games had matured with us. It was within the willows of their property that we learned to trust each other both with our blades and our hearts.

The stone columns of their home loomed through gaps in the trees, but I turned left. Should I have knocked, the grand front door would have been opened immediately by a member of their staff, but I preferred my personal side entrance.

The gold handle was warm beneath my hand as I turned it. Though the shutters on the double doors were still closed, they were never locked to me. I entered into one of the house's smaller rooms, with dark wood floors and a simple set of couches and chaises arranged around a small glass table. Akalain Blastwood, Augustus's mother, sat upon one of the settees.

"Ah, Ophelia!" She jumped to her feet, her Mystique blood making her as silent and spry as a mountain cat. "I was hoping to catch you before you and Malakai took off for the day."

She gestured to the couch across from her, handing me a cup of tea, and I settled into the worn gray cushions, letting the familiar scent of the Blastwood home wrap itself around me in a cloud of cinnamon and vanilla.

"Good morning, Akalain." As a Mystique over the age of sixteen, I had the honor of referring to all ascended warriors by their first names.

"How are you?" she asked, handing me a cup of my favorite tea, a blend she made sure to always keep in the house.

I stirred in a spoonful of sugar and sipped it, the sweet herbs washing across my taste buds, and contemplated her question. With the war over and the treaty signed, there was much I *should* be grateful for. There was still so much wrong, though.

"I'm…recovering." I chose the word carefully.

"As are all of us." Akalain nodded, and I could tell there was more she wished to say.

I set my teacup on the table, running my palms down my skirts. "Is there something you wished to discuss?" Though I enjoyed the company, there was a gleam to her blue eyes that I couldn't ignore.

"As you know, Malakai's eighteenth birthday is approaching." That sparkle in her eye—it was pride. Utter delight at the prospect of her son reaching his destiny.

"I can hardly believe it." I curled my fingers into my skirts, the soft velvet absorbing my anticipation.

In a few short days, Augustus would be embarking on the journey to the mountains to complete the Undertaking. In three months, it would be my turn, and we would become the most powerful Mystique Warrior partners in history.

But the potential power didn't matter to either of us, nor did the fact that we were an Alabath and a Blastwood merging our lines. Even if we had not chosen to speak the Words to each other and received the Bind, we likely would have been pushed together. But we *had* chosen, and for us, the Undertaking was the obvious next step down our life's path. The fact that we were to take it together was what mattered.

"I'm overjoyed for the two of you. It's been over a century since I completed my own Undertaking, and it was a…*formative* journey." She fidgeted with the teacup, refilling it until it nearly overflowed.

Questions buzzed through me, but I bit my lips against them. By law, we were not allowed to discuss specifics, no matter how long ago she had completed the Undertaking.

Though a century was only a fraction of the life she would live. For warriors of all clans, the aging process decelerated once you reached adulthood, stretching a normal lifetime into many times that. Not immortal, as that would upset the balance of the universe, but decelerated to span centuries, potentially longer if the Spirits so blessed you. Judging by Akalain's smooth skin, I guessed she was near my father's age of one hundred and fifty-seven.

"I'm certain ours will be formative, as well," I said.

A tangle of fear and exhilaration danced across her expression, but she shook her head, red-brown hair tumbling around her shoulders.

"You two have an incredible future ahead of you." Akalain brought a hand to her throat and ran it along the delicate jeweled necklace she always wore. Sapphires dangled from the chain, winking at me in the morning light, and I knew she was thinking of the man who placed them there.

"Do you miss the Revered?" I asked, tracking the gentle tightening of her fingers around the largest sapphire. The one he added to the necklace after Augustus's birth.

"I miss him every day, but he is doing our family and his

bloodline the highest of honors by serving our people," she clipped, pain buried beneath the claim.

As Revered, Augustus's father was required to reside in Damenal, in the Revered's Palace at the highest peak. He rarely returned, but Akalain kept their home in Palerman. It had been her family's estate, passed down to her.

But when Augustus eventually stood in his father's place as Revered, we had no intention of being separated. Not only would I be his partner, but as my father's daughter, I was to be appointed Second. I would stand by his side, regardless of any children I may bear.

We had at least a century until we would have to consider that, though.

"Anyway, there was something I wanted to show you before I lose you to my son for the day." Akalain grinned, and I returned the smile.

She unfolded her legs and was across the room in one swift motion. The grace and agility of a fully grown warrior woman was transfixing, each movement fueled by magic itself as she removed a small wooden box from the credenza in the corner.

Born of an esteemed Mystique family, Akalain embodied what a woman was to me. She honored the legacy of her Deneski heritage, taking over the responsibility after her older brother died more than a decade ago.

She chose to wear her official leathers at all times, a statement I admired: She was a warrior at heart. Her unique garments consisted of a brown corset and fitted pants, boots lacing up to the knee. Gold and cerulean thread wove through the bodice, with matching accents stamped into the leather, detailing the story of her people by way of delicate symbols: mountains, flowers, swords, and spears. The images shone as she returned to the couch and placed the box on the glass table between us. Gold cuffs at her wrists sparkled as she folded her hands in her lap, a smile curving her lips.

"I had this made for my son, but it feels right that I share it with you first. For approval." She nodded at me to open the box.

The glossy surface was smooth and cool beneath my fingers. I held my breath as I flicked the latch, the lid sliding open to reveal a deep blue velvet lining with the gift nestled in its center. I gasped, stunned by the subtle beauty of it. My eyes snapped up to Akalain's, and I blinked at her, unable to speak.

"Go ahead," she encouraged.

Gently, careful not to damage the leather—though it was so sturdy I doubted even a sword could slice it—I lifted the strap from the box. The material was weightless in my hands, smooth and expertly crafted. Somehow, it already carried the familiar scent of worn leather and honeysuckle that I associated with the man I loved.

I ran my hands along the length of it, fingers passing over the fastening that would fix his spear to his back. This would be his warrior's sash. It would be strapped across his chest every day following the Undertaking, until the end of his days, carrying him into battle, locking the warrior and his greatest weapon as one.

But it was not only the gravity of the object in my hands that struck me, it was the detailing his mother had crafted on it.

Stars.

Not just any stars—*our North Star.* Imprinted repeatedly into the leather, identical to the Bind we had illegally tattooed on our bodies weeks prior.

My fingers trailed over the soft leather. This was no arbitrary design. It was a mother's way of confirming that regardless of where he was, I would be with him. Supporting him. Guarding him. A seal of approval from Akalain that burned its way through my heart, emotion welling in my eyes.

When I looked up, my fingers still tracing the stars on the sash, Akalain's eyes were shining, too. "It's beautiful," I whispered.

"I hoped you would think so."

"I could not have designed a more perfect sash for him." I took a deep breath to steady myself. "Thank you," I added.

Akalain winked at me. "It will be your turn soon," she promised, but then her face turned grave. "I have been worried about him—about Malakai."

"Worried?" I asked.

"He does not seem himself lately. He's off, his steps through the world faltering." She hid her emotions well, but the slight frown of her lips and crease between her brows was that of a concerned mother.

I thought back to the last few weeks with Augustus. He had been quieter, a bit aloof, but I had thought it was my mind playing tricks as I grew jealous of his upcoming Undertaking. The soul-tied connection through our Bind had been flaring with emotions I could not place, but I had assumed it was because the tattoo was so new, still learning us.

"Yes, I guess I have noticed some odd behavior. His spirit seems dampened." I gripped the leather sash tighter as I spoke, careful not to dig my nails into its pristine surface.

"I'd hoped it was all in my head." Akalain's shoulders drooped. "I suppose it could be nerves for the Undertaking."

"He has nothing to fear," I encouraged. "He's the strongest of us, born of two powerful warriors."

She smiled appreciatively, leaning forward to squeeze my hand. "I suppose it is natural. Will you try to reach the root of it, though? Instill your fortitude in him."

For her, for him, of course I would. I would do anything, and I told her as much.

I could have looked at the sash for hours, but a shuffle from above had me reluctantly packing it back into its shiny box. Akalain hid the gift and was returning to her settee when her son rounded the corner into the small sitting room.

When his eyes landed on me, his face broke into a grin, but something was wrong. The light did not fully reach his eyes—the forest green deeper than normal.

"Good morning," he greeted us both, but his eyes never left my face. "I didn't expect to find you two in here."

"We were having tea," his mother responded calmly, but worry flashed through her eyes at his subdued expression. "I'll leave you to your day," she excused herself.

"Thank you…for the tea." I smiled at Akalain as she exited, the secret of his sash humming between us.

She cast me a glance heavy with a mother's concern, and my throat tightened. I nodded slightly, confirming that I would always look out for him, and she blinked a brief thank you.

When she rounded the corner, I turned my attention to her son. "Hi, Augustus," I breathed. *Angels*, every time I saw him my breath was taken away. This man, this warrior…this strong, beautiful being was *mine.*

I extended my hand, and he was near me in a moment, strong arms lifting me off the couch. He crushed me to his chest, as if he could not get close enough, and my arms wound around his neck.

"Hi," he whispered, his breath fanning across my ear. "What were you and my mother discussing?"

"You," I laughed, breathing in the honeysuckle and leather scent of him that was my home.

He only exhaled in response, pressing a long kiss to my temple. His arms were tight around me, and I had to arch my back to look up at him.

"Is everything all right?" I asked, bringing a hand to his cheek.

He leaned into the touch as he whispered, "With you, everything is perfect." But I didn't miss the dimming of his eyes as he shut them, savoring the warmth of my hand against his cheek.

I had hoped Augustus's spirit would lift as we worked in the city, assisting with the clearing of debris around Palerman's largest music hall, but he was quiet. Even as I recounted my favorite shows we'd seen performed over the years, he barely grunted in response.

The rift in my heart spread with each minute that passed. Akalain and I had not been misreading his behavior. His eyes never reached their full warmth, even with each of his charming smiles, and his hair hung limply around his face and neck. Every inch of him seemed duller.

Around midday, he perched on the edge of the Angel fountain in the center of town, and I folded myself into his side. In silence, we shared bits of bread and soft cheese, passing fruit back and forth between bites.

We were surrounded by the bustle of shopkeepers, patrons, and children, everyone working to fix what was left of our town since the war had ended over a month prior. Our people—though many were worse for wear following the war—waved to us as they passed, and we politely greeted each. But I kept one eye on Augustus's sunken frame the entire time.

"Is something bothering you?" I finally asked, waving at a group of young warriors from across the square.

He raised a shoulder in response.

"Augustus," I whispered, grabbing his face and turning it to me. My eyes traced every inch of bronzed skin, seeking any explanation for the unease I felt within him, the one snaking into my Bind and throughout my whole body, as if in warning. "What is it? And do not claim there is nothing weighing on your mind."

"There truly is nothing. I'm only thinking about my journey in three days." His eyes did flare in the slightest as he spoke, but it wasn't his usual warmth. It felt forced, a vulnerability seeping into his gaze though he fought it.

"I can see in your eyes that you are not yourself, Augustus." Something tugged on the Bind, confirming the off-kilter step of the other half of my soul. I flicked my eyes to the spot where the tattoo hid beneath my sleeve. "I can feel it. Please, whatever your burden may be, whatever trial you are working to decipher, share it with me."

I could see his mind calculating, working through whatever harped on his conscience in that moment. He appeared torn, battling internally over…something.

He reached to where my palm cupped his cheek and removed it, grabbing both of my hands between his two calloused ones and pulling them to his chest. His green eyes locked on mine, and now I was the one being searched. "I love you, Phel. I love how deeply you wish to protect me and carry any weight on my soul." He pressed his lips to my forehead for a long moment, every ounce of adoration forced into that singular touch burning through me.

He pulled back, speaking so closely to my face that I felt his breath against my lips, "There is truly nothing I need to share at this moment. I promise you, if there is, I will tell you."

His words would haunt my dreams for the next two years.

Chapter Thirteen

Present Day

A ROARING WIND SHOOK the shuttered windows of Rina's apartment above the locked Cub's Tavern, but the gusts rocking the building were nothing compared to the storm raging inside of me. Between Damien's appearance last night and the Curse on my wrist, I had been unable to settle. Unable to do much but harp on the challenges laid before me and my approaching death.

"So, what's this about, then?" Tolek asked. He sprawled on a chair beside the fire, the flames casting shadows on its high back, shielding his curious face from view. Rina and Cyph fell onto opposite ends of the couch, the former tucking her knees to her chest and crossing her arms atop them.

At my request, Tol and Cyph had stayed behind to help Rina close up. After an hour of washing cloudy glasses and attempting to sweep away the permanent dust circles in the floor, we had retreated upstairs. My friends' eyes had stayed on my back for the duration of the night. They bore into me with questions as they made themselves comfortable in the sparse living room, echoes of Rina's parents surrounding us through the worn furniture and treasured keepsakes.

I chewed on my lip, wondering how to begin. Undertaking, Malakai, Curse. The trio echoed through my mind, reminding me of my goals and limitations until they were eating away at me. I needed to start. I needed to tell someone.

Santorina's fixed stare felt anticipative as she toyed with her sleeve and nodded, telling me to get on with it.

I turned toward the fire, staring into the glow that so resembled the Angellight that had spilled into my room last night. With a deep breath, I let that imaginary power settle into my skin and give me the courage I needed.

"I have something to share with you, and you'll likely find it outrageous, but I beg you to listen for the duration." I looked over my shoulder, my eyes meeting Cyph's first.

He nodded in agreement, but it was Tol who spoke from his shadows. "Ophelia, you know we often find the words from your mouth preposterous." I could hear the casual smile coating his words.

If only my heart felt as light in that moment.

And so, I told them. Of Damien's appearance in my bedroom in the hours following my birthday celebration. Of his riddled words and the dance of fate that was left in his absence. Of how I interpreted the two tasks he left before me. Of what I planned to do next.

My three closest friends stared at me when I finished speaking. There was no sound but my uneven breaths, the distant banging of a door shutting, and the beginnings of a light trickle of rain in the rusted gutters. I allowed them a moment to absorb everything I had admitted, then it was Rina whose gaze I sought first. Her judgment, always the harshest, carried the most painful truth—and was thus the one I would rather face head-on.

She grasped her knees tighter to her chest, and she looked so much younger than her twenty-one years. My mind flashed back to the girl I met thirteen years ago, a stranger among a world of warriors.

"You're going to attempt the Undertaking?" she asked. When I nodded, she added, "Are you mad?"

The task ahead will try thy spirit...Damien's words trickled through my body, leaving a warmth along my bones.

"It's the only way." I let a hint of desperation seep into my voice.

"No, Ophelia." She shot to her feet, looking down on me. "It is a *death wish*."

I threw my arms out at my sides. "And if I meet my death in this fate, then so be it. I will die a Mystique Warrior's death." Her cold stare met mine, and though Rina was not a warrior, I felt the power of one radiating from her.

"I won't sit by and watch you die." Her voice cracked over the last word. Suddenly, she looked three years younger, watching her parents brutally slain in a war that was not their own. The memory of her tear-streaked face cleaved a small piece of my heart, but not enough to dull the edge I had carried with me all day.

I took a calming breath, reminding myself that my friends were not aware of the impending scourge burrowing into my wrist and the fate I had already accepted. Of course they would fight my decision to risk my life, as they saw it. In the past day the Curse had only grown slightly, its green-gray trail darkening as it crept up my forearm. It was slower than expected, but it was still claiming me with each painful stretch of the web—and it was still a secret I must shoulder.

Wind battered the windows again, the old walls and stairway creaking in response. A chill trailed through the small room, wrapping itself around the four of us.

"I will not die in the Undertaking," I whispered, and it wasn't a lie. I did not believe *that* was how I would lose my life.

Rina's shoulders slouched in defeat, seeing the resolve in my stance and tight jaw. The fire crackled behind me, echoing my burning determination.

"But the Undertaking has been suspended," Cyph interjected from his spot on the couch. He was leaning forward, elbows braced against his knees, his tall frame entirely too big for the cushions. "How will you even attempt the ritual?"

"In secret," I answered simply. "You cannot stall the Spirits."

Though I hadn't been certain of the answer until it left my lips, something within me knew it was the truth.

Tolek's voice cut through the shadows. "You believe that if you arrive at the Spirit Volcano, you will be welcomed in." It wasn't a question; he sounded incredulous, yet impressed.

Not even the Revered could command the warrior Spirits that ruled the Undertaking. He could only stop *us* from entering. If I could make the journey undetected and slip through the defenses at the mountain range, I should be able to reach the Spirit Volcano. Angels bless me.

Tolek rose from his chair and came to my side. I felt his eyes on my face, but I did not meet them. "Rina's right," he declared. "This is madness."

I swung toward him, lips parting on a shout—he had been the one I was counting on for support. But he was smiling.

"I dare say we could use a bit more foolishness in our lives." He grinned at me with mischief dancing in his chocolate eyes, the fire emphasizing the strong cut of his jaw beneath his stubble, and I smiled back.

"This is not a time for jokes, Tolek," Rina argued, breaking our trance. "Do you understand what Ophelia is suggesting?"

"Yes, Santorina, she has painted the quest quite clearly. I did not find it hard to follow, did you? Are you feeling all right?" Leave it to Tolek to lighten the mood when I was confessing an unbelievable appearance of the First Revered in my bedroom and my decision to attempt a life-threatening, forbidden ritual.

Rina's answering glare could cut glass. "Why do you indulge her reckless ideas?" she muttered.

"I rather like Ophelia's mind."

"Mm-hmm, is that—"

Cypherion rose and moved to stand between Santorina and Tolek. "We have bigger problems than your bickering." He placed a hand on Rina's shoulder and guided her back as I did the same for Tol.

"Cyph is right. Lay your arguments aside." The authority in

my voice shocked even me. The two continued to glare at each other, Tol's nostrils flaring with heated exhales, but neither spoke.

"Ophelia, let's assume that you *do* successfully complete the Undertaking and become a full warrior," Cyph began.

"I *will* complete it."

He nodded, placating me. "Yes. What then? How does becoming an ascended warrior solve anything?"

Rina looked between us, mouthing *thank you* to Cypherion.

"I do not know exactly," I admitted. Before Rina could voice the victory that crossed her face, I continued, "But I am sure that it will open the path to whatever is right." I took a breath. "None of you faced Damien. The words he said to me…they hummed through my body. My blood knew that he spoke the truth." As did the energy I had gained from the spear. "That this is my duty as a warrior. I understand that this is a ridiculous claim I'm making, but it doesn't feel that way within me. I *must* do this." I would do it, with or without their support.

"You choose to follow this path on blind faith?" Rina still sounded dubious, but her eyes softened, and I appreciated her challenge. She always tempered my impulsive decisions.

"I do. But not blind faith. Faith in the Angels."

Rina's eyes heated, and I only felt slightly guilty for using the Angels—a faith system of the warriors—against her.

"*Believe in the Angels, be guided by the Spirits, and align with the stars,*" Tolek whispered the ancient quote of the warriors. Not only the Mystiques, but all seven clans, before mistrust had torn us apart. The words sent a bolt of hope through my body.

Cyph swallowed, his throat bobbing with the uncertainty in the air. "And what of Malakai?"

I had been waiting for them to broach the subject of the Angel's second message. *Your deepest wish awaits.*

"If he's not…We don't know where he may be. Where would you start?" Cypherion urged. Whether he was eager to strategize for my mission or attempting to dissuade me, I was still unsure.

"I'll ask the Spirits," I stated matter-of-factly. I had been raising the same question myself, but in that moment, when Cyph asked, the answer sprang to my lips, as if guided by another force.

No one could argue. The power of what I said hung in the air as rain pounded against the tin roof over our heads, each drop piercing the tension in the room. Flame cast shadows on the wood-paneled walls as I studied the rug beneath my feet. The red-and-brown pattern was faded from years of Rina pacing in front of the fire. Now, I assumed her position, rubbing the spot on my wrist where the Curse hid beneath my velvet sleeve. With its stagnant progress, it was safe to assume that I would have a few more days to conquer this journey than I originally thought, but I needed to move swiftly.

Two years ago, a victim would have been dead within the week. There was nothing I could do against fate, but I would fight with every ounce of power within me to prolong it. To complete this quest, restore the Mystiques as Damien implied, and find Malakai.

And if I was meant to die, I'd greet death with a wicked smile.

"I'll leave at dawn," I whispered under my breath, watching my feet pace in circles before the fire. "It will be best to stick to the forest and deserted plains. Perhaps along the Solistine River once I meet it." I pictured the layout of our territory. The snaking strip of water flowed from the mountains in the north, across our land, until it crossed into the Seawatchers' eastern shores and finally emptied into the Neptitian Sea. If I traveled west, I should meet the river within a few days, and I could follow its path north from there.

"Once I'm out of Palerman, it will be best to avoid other Mystique towns." Though I hated to admit it, I was recognizable among our people, and I didn't know who may try to stop me. Riding through the forests and groves of cypher trees and crossing empty fields would be a less risky path than stopping in cities for shelter.

I nodded as the path painted itself into my mind. "If I ride hard and take Sapphire, I can cut days off the journey. Perhaps arrive in ten. That may be enough time, I hope—"

"Why are you behaving as if you will be embarking on this

journey alone?" Tol narrowed his eyes, no hint of his usual whimsy visible. He stood with his hands behind his back, but his shoulders were tense, jaw clenched.

I straightened. "Because I am."

"Over my damned spirit," he roared.

"This was a task presented to *me* by the First Warrior." Though that was not the real reason I rejected him. My Cursed wrist twinged in warning.

"But not once in his speech did he say that you must be the only one to journey to the mountains, did he?" I blinked at Tol, but he was right, and he knew it. He stepped closer to me, looking directly into my eyes. Our chests were nearly touching as he spoke, his voice harsh and slow. "I am coming with you."

"I am a daughter of the Alabath bloodline. You do not command me, Tolek Vincienzo." I rose onto my toes to match his force, though he still towered over me. "I go alone."

"That you may be, but you are not our Second yet. You cannot wield authority that is not yet yours." In that moment, he could have been a fully ascended warrior, power spilling from his body and permeating the air around us.

Our gazes locked, a silent battle of two rock-hard wills. Tolek was infuriating, but I couldn't tell them the true reason I must go alone. If the Curse progressed, I couldn't have them near me.

"Tolek is right," Cypherion interrupted. "We're coming with you."

Reluctantly, I broke my eyes from Tol's and turned on Cyph. "I did *not* tell you all of this so that you would come with me. I told you so that you may create a distraction here. Hide it from my family." Keep the letters I'd written for each of them, because if I was likely to die in the process, I had to say goodbye.

"It doesn't matter why you shared it." Tol's voice had lost a bit of its heat. "We won't let you do this alone."

My broken heart stuttered at the sentiment.

"Well." I looked around us. "Rina, you will certainly need to stay and work the tavern."

Her face dimmed with resignation. "Ophelia, the tavern has been crumbling for two years. Closing it will make no difference."

That truth saddened me, but I saw it devastated her. It was not one I chose to push.

Refusals perched on my lips as I fought the urge to massage my wrist. Should the Curse claim me before I was able to complete the mission, I could have no one near me. The things I would be capable of…the destruction and bloodlust that would ensue.

I could not bear the thought of my friends being so near the threat. So near me.

But if the Curse claimed me, no one would be there to complete my task. Perhaps, if something were to happen to me, it would be best to have someone to carry on the mission. Or three someones. For whatever reason, Damien made it clear that this task existed solely for me, but he said nothing about what happened if I failed. Surely, it couldn't hurt to arrange a backup plan, even if his prophecy didn't transfer entirely.

"Fine," I conceded, the decision weighing heavily on my soul. Should anything happen to them, I was to blame.

Visions of the dangers that could befall them flashed through my mind, but in my heart, I swore that I would not allow my friends to meet such fates. I would protect them with every ounce of strength in my body. I was Ophelia Tavania Alabath, daughter of one of the most powerful Mystique bloodlines, future Second of our clan, and no one harmed those I loved without having to answer to me.

"We leave at dawn. We'll need horses, weapons, and food. Wear your training leathers. Rina, I have spares and can sneak extra weapons"—she flinched, not being properly trained, but remained silent—"but we will need another horse for you."

"My sister doesn't ride often anymore. She won't miss Calista for a few weeks," Tolek offered. Though his older sister had fought in the war, she, like many, had abandoned Mystique traditions two years ago. Training, riding, fighting—it was all tainted for them.

I nodded my thanks to him as the building creaked again. But this hollow sound was not the wind battering the walls. It was not the building, but the floorboards. In the stairwell.

"And I know where to get food," Jezebel announced from the doorway. *Of course,* she had been listening. I was remiss to expect otherwise.

"Jezebel, I swear to the fucking Angels, if you think you're coming with us—"

"If you think otherwise, you're a fool." She crossed her arms, the same stubbornness I used against my friends flowing from her. If Jezebel thought this journey would help me move on from my past pain, she would not concede. "We don't have time to argue. Dawn breaks in four hours."

CHAPTER FOURTEEN

FIVE MARES STOOD IN a line at the edge of Palerman, watching dawn break through the draping branches of the cypher trees that marked the western edge of the city. The air was still but for the muttering of the forest creatures. I felt their eyes and ears around us, monitoring the actions of the warriors in their presence and assessing any threat.

The land we would travel over was theirs as much as it was ours. We may guard the Mystique Mountain Range, the source of the magic in this world and all others, but those creatures pulsed with it, gifted to them by Gerrenth, the God of Nature, and Lynxenon, the God of Mythical Beings. They belonged to the power that ran in rivulets beneath the ground as much as we did. It was responsible for the bountiful growth in the plains, the temperate climate of our territory, and the steady hum in the air now. It controlled the balance of life and death, good and evil, strength and weakness.

We warriors were sworn to it. The earth and creatures worked in tandem with it.

Rolling green hills stretched out beyond the leaves, the grass shining with drops of rain from the previous night. You could smell it on the air; that scent of promise after a storm. Like anything could happen under the clear blue skies.

Sapphire shifted beneath me, her ears twitching impatiently. It had been so long since she had truly stretched her legs, using those powerful muscles we had honed over years of training. Since any of us had.

My horse read my tense energy and budding excitement, exhaling noisily. On my right, Jezebel's mare, Elektra, returned the huff, her coat and mane gleaming like a bolt of silver, carved from pure lightning.

"It's now or never," Tolek whispered from my left.

I looked to where he sat upon his golden mare, Astania. Her brown eyes were the exact shade of the warrior's atop her, as if they were cut from the same slip of soul. They both turned those deep eyes upon me now, awaiting my signal.

I listened to the forest, the plains, the buzzing of insects and flapping of wings. Birds of morning called to each other as the sun's pale rays flashed, igniting earth and grass and rock to call us forward. The pin my grandmother had gifted me for my birthday glinted on my chest where I'd forced it through the thick material of my leathers. I covered it with my hand briefly, tapping into the Soulguider heritage I contained, asking for guidance.

Then, I lifted my chin, a faint breeze gracing my cheeks, and inhaled the possibilities on the wind.

"It's time."

I nudged Sapphire with my heels, and she crossed the final boundary between our shelter of a city and what lay beyond.

The first hours of the trek dragged. The Palermanian sun—no, no longer Palermanian. We had left our home behind. This was the sun of the Wild Plains of the Mystique Territory of Gallantia. And it beat down on us, warm and bright, kissing away my doubt with each stride of the horse beneath me.

I could tell by the way that Sapphire pranced, her head high and tail swishing, that she appreciated the freedom of the open plains. Her muscles flexed and released, the most natural I'd ever felt her move. Every step became longer, more advantageous, seeking the next hill and the next valley.

She was swift, a starborn horse embracing the wild spirit of her heart.

And I sat astride her, following her unrestricted spirit, destiny burning in my veins.

Sapphire let out a high whinny, echoed by the four mares around us, and I called out with her. For the first time in two years, I felt my spirit shimmering within me, alive and wild and healing.

"I'll tie up the horses," Cyph offered when we stopped at dusk. He extended a hand for Sapphire's reins, the assortment of daggers strapped to his arms and torso glinting. I'd nearly laughed at how many he brought. But as I'd gathered what I needed for the journey, I'd slid the twin daggers he'd given me into my pack.

I kissed Sapphire's nose, running my hands through her deep blue mane. She nudged me as she turned, and a wave of understanding passed between us. Sapphire and I, we were one and the same, born to be outside of gates. Tasting the freedom on the air and following the call of the wind.

As she dipped her head to drink from the water Cyph provided, the sunset streaked out from behind wisps of clouds. The fading light turned the sky shades of pale pink and lavender, dancing across her hide, making her appear mythic and giving me a sense of calm.

The first day of our journey had passed easily. We had covered more ground than expected, barely resting until now. All of us had been at ease, free. The hours beside my friends—Tolek and Cypherion sparking debates with Jezebel, Santorina collecting interesting plants, and me savoring it all—had been bliss.

I could only hope for that to continue over the coming days. Though, as I sank into the shadows of the trees and watched tranquil dusk fall to dark night, I reminded myself that peace rarely lasted. And I had a tainted fate awaiting me.

Jezebel and Tolek were pulling food from our packs, setting out a small picnic of bread, cheese, and dried fruits. I leaned against the white wood of a cypher and breathed deeply. The ancient trees of our world, said to have sprouted up many millennia ago when magic first flowed through our land, buzzed against my back in acknowledgment of the power in my own blood. I let my eyes drift closed against the willowing branches to feel that mystical energy more deeply, allow it to support me.

With each step we took out of Palerman, my blood pumped faster, bursting with the world's energy. A small piece of me remained unsure about abandoning our home without warning, but each minute that passed affirmed my decision. The wind whistled in my ears and along my skin, telling me I belonged here.

This world—our world—called to me.

Only moments of peace lasted before Jezebel's and Tolek's voices interrupted my reverie, their sharp tongues lashing out at each other.

"Why, in the name of the Spirit-sent Angels, would you light a fire?" Jezebel questioned, her words harsh but a hint of a laugh hiding behind them.

"Well, I have no intention of freezing my damn balls off tonight. I rather like them." Rocks scraped together as he attempted to tease embers out of them, grimacing with each failed attempt. For a moment, I enjoyed the site of Tolek not being naturally gifted at something, exchanging a smirk with Cyph and Rina behind his back.

"Yes, why suffer a slight chill when you can attract a violent predator? That would be much preferred." Jezebel crossed her arms over her chest, the black leather of her training garb turning her body into a shadow in the setting sun.

Tol stopped his tinkering and turned a sharp expression on my sister, his brows rising as he shook his head. "Oh, by the ever-damned Angels," he muttered. "And just what threats are you expecting us to meet in this grove, Jez?" He was teasing her, a short breath of a chuckle passing through his lips.

But Jezebel's face turned to stone. "We don't know everything that lurks beyond those trees, Tolek Vincienzo. These lands are rife with magic. It would be naive to assume otherwise."

Her eyes were alight, the tawny harboring streaks of gold brighter than Angellight. From my perch against the tree, I shivered at the power in Jezzie's words, but Tolek did not flinch. He only locked eyes with her.

I bit my lip as I watched their battle of wills. Tolek and I goaded each other, but he and Jezebel had always been worse, tempers clashing like siblings ever since the day my three-year-old sister had grabbed Tolek's training sword. He, six at the time, had shoved her to the dirt, then immediately went wide-eyed at his action and bent to help her up. Jezzie, to her credit, had grinned and pushed him back. Even then, a deeper understanding passed between them. Maybe it was because they were both secondborn and therefore relieved of many of the pressures first children carried, but it was like they were pieces of a greater game in the universe, moving in tandem.

But I'd had enough of their arguing for one evening. We had days ahead of us on this journey, so I pushed off the tree and moved to interrupt. "Jez is right, Tol. We should be on alert and not draw unnecessary attention. We can use a mystlight lantern, but a fire will be too noticeable."

A frown cut across his face, but he dragged a hand through his hair and sighed. "Fine, I'll set out the sleeping mats, then." His black leathers hugged his lean muscles as he turned away.

Jez and I rolled our eyes at his male ego.

I discarded my weapons, folding my legs beneath me to join the circle of my friends around the lantern. But I kept Starfire and the spear close—just in case. Jezebel was right; much of Gallantia was a mystery. It was subject to the same magic we harnessed, but we knew not how the rivulets beneath the soil would be manipulated. At the source, the essence was a beautiful thing—raw and effervescent, promising and fickle—but it was wise to be wary of power.

I pulled my canteen from my bag and unscrewed the top, taking a deep swig of the burning liquid inside. It numbed the nerves that had been spreading through my body since we set up camp. The mares' low breathing helped me calm my own.

"Can I have a sip?" Cyph asked, setting aside the map he'd been holding to the light, rechecking our route. "I drained mine when we settled and would prefer not to search for a stream in the dark."

"This one's not water." I reached for my second canteen and passed it across the circle to him. The mystlight in the center cast a white-blue glow on his auburn hair as he nodded in thanks.

"Really?" Rina's voice dripped with accusation.

"What?" I asked, but her scowl told me everything I needed to know.

"You're going to drink out here?" Her sharp words dropped a silence over the group, and I felt the others tense.

I shrugged. "I only brought one canteen of it." *I'm dying anyway*, I added to myself as the spot on my wrist, hidden beneath my leathers, burned.

But Rina's narrowed eyes said it was not the amount that mattered. "Ophelia, you need your wits about you out here. You cannot spend every night drunk."

My eyes rolled before I could stop them. "I took a sip to relax myself. I will not be inebriated."

But I wrapped my hands tighter around the canteen. She didn't understand. I needed this one source of warmth and comfort to support me when my mind went to a dark place, but I would not—would *never*—allow it to risk the success of our mission.

Anger as hot and fierce as I imagined the center of the Spirit Volcano to be rose within me at the accusation in her dark glare.

How could she possibly believe I would ever jeopardize something so precious? I was the one who was given this task by Damien. I was the one who was going to complete the Undertaking. I was the *only one* who believed Malakai was still alive—who did not find that part of the mission pointless.

Rina's eyes slid to my grip, then back to where I'd pulled my lip between my teeth to keep it from trembling. After a moment, she sighed. "You're stronger than this. Please don't go down that road."

How dare she act as if this made me weak. I could admit it was a crutch, but I was anything but a fragile, shaky coward. To prove it, I uncurled my fingers from the canteen one by one, capped it, and tossed it to her.

"Fine, I'll let you mother me. You can decide when I have it. Water it down as you always do." I pushed myself to my feet and wiped my dirty hands on the thighs of my leathers to steady their trembling.

"I'll take first watch." I turned my back on their semicircle, but before I could take a step an arm wrapped around my waist. I was thrown over a strong shoulder, one hand gripping the back of my thighs to hold me in place.

"Vincienzo!" I roared, pounding on his muscled back. "Set me down."

Tol dropped me to the dirt a few yards from our friends, looking down on me with narrowed eyes. "Don't do that," he said.

"Do what?" I shoved myself to my feet. "Hit you? You're the one throwing me around."

"Don't run away." His voice was low, a mixture of command and pleading that shot through me, but I shook it off.

"I'm fine to take the watch, Vincienzo." I stepped away. "I'm not drunk."

He didn't break my stare but pressed the cold leather of Starfire's grip into my palm. I hadn't even seen him sweep her up.

"I understand that, *Alabath*," his lips curled around my name tauntingly, like he knew what game we were playing, though I did not. He stepped back, removing his own sword, the blade hissing as it slid from its sheath. Beside it hung his Vincienzo family dagger—the one he'd received on his sixteenth birthday, the ornate *V* catching the mystlight. "If you want to fight, we'll fight."

"I'm not in the mood."

His lips split into a grin. "That may just be my favorite phrase of yours."

"That's because you're constantly giving me a reason to utter it." The words were a growl through my clenched teeth.

Tolek shrugged, tossing his sword between his hands. "You're just afraid you'll lose against me."

"Fucking Angels, I'm afraid I'll put my sword through you because you're so infuriating." I clutched Starfire but did not lift her.

His lips quirked upward. "Ah, my dear Ophelia, you'd never be able to even if you wanted."

I nearly laughed at the absurdity of that statement. "I could. So quickly you'd never know what happened."

"Is that a threat?" His brows lowered, and he froze with eyes locked on mine. I heard our friends muttering but did not acknowledge them.

"I'm not doing this, Tolek." I sheathed my sword and tried to push past him, but his next words brushed against my cheek, a secret just for me.

"Afraid the alcohol affects your skill?"

My eyes snapped to his, mere inches away. "No," I snapped.

"Prove it."

I placed two hands firmly on his chest and shoved—hard. The anger that Santorina had stirred within me heightened until I was nearly shaking. Tolek lifted his sword, tilted his head to either side to crack his neck, and wiggled his brows. The smile lifting one corner of his lips told me that he knew he had me.

Without another word, I unsheathed my sword. My feet, legs, entire body shifted into a stance that felt more natural than any other—a defensive position, ready to guard from any blade or foe.

My eyes flickered over Tolek's body, awaiting his first strike, categorizing every twitch of his defined arm muscles and blink of his long lashes. He winked, distracting me enough that I didn't see his first blow coming. His sword skimmed the front of my leathers, not close enough to tear, but close enough to let me know that if he had wanted it to—that swipe would have ended me.

"Your reflexes seem slow," he said.

"That was a cheater's shot," I growled, but he was right. I should have dodged that.

"That's a loser's accusation." He reset his stance. "Come and get it, Alabath."

It took a few more strikes for me to regain my power, and in those close blows of Tolek's I began to understand Santorina's point. For years, I had only trained with my sister. I had learned her style so well that it was nearly impossible to surprise me, but fighting a different opponent highlighted my weaknesses. Where my stamina and reactions were not what they should be. I wasn't sure if it was due to the alcohol that my body and mind had, to some extent, become dependent on, or if it was due to the secret burrowing into my wrist, but regardless of the cause—I was weakened. The vulnerability turned to ash on my tongue.

Fury at my friends for seeing this, at myself for letting this happen, and at the Angels and Spirits that plunged me into this fate spread through my body. It encouraged my movements—made them more precise. I was not the fighter I should have been, but I posed a challenge for Tolek once again. With each strike, I resumed a bit of my old control.

The repeated clash of our weapons was loud in the darkened forest. I lost myself in the dance of chagrin, swords, and teasing smiles.

I was unsure who was winning, but each drop of sweat beading on my forehead siphoned away more of the anger that had boiled my blood mere minutes ago. Now, the heat pounded through my veins, tangling with assured spikes of adrenaline. Because this was what I was born to do, and I would no longer allow myself to be weak.

"You're merciless," Tol whispered when our swords met between us. "I think I like it."

A wicked smile spread across my face.

"There she is," Tolek muttered. His sword barely stopped my next swing.

But I recovered quicker than he did, knocking the weapon from his hand with the pommel of my own and twirling around him. I grabbed his wrist as I went, twisting his sword arm behind his back. Starfire came up to rest in front of his throat, lightly touching the skin there.

He chuckled. Our hearts pounded, but mine felt lighter than it had before the fight. A wind picked up, blowing my hair around us.

"Thank you," I whispered against his ear, making him shiver.

The Curse sent a shot of pain through my wrist that nearly knocked my sword from my hand.

"Anytime," he panted.

The horses whinnied wildly, stamping their feet.

"Cursed Spirits," Cypherion swore.

I stepped back from Tolek as a growl echoed through the trees.

Chapter Fifteen

I REACHED SAPPHIRE AS the predator released a roar that rolled along my bones, closer this time.

Jezebel threw me my pack and weapons as I pulled our horses' tethers loose and swung myself onto Sapphire's back. She didn't need my hurried instructions to take off down the wide path between the trees, away from the approaching beast. I'd never seen my horse scared until now.

Four sets of hooves followed, but they were quickly drowned out by the thundering steps of our attacker barreling through branches.

"What is it?" I called over my shoulder, my hair whipping my face.

"I don't know," Cypherion answered, picking up speed. His wide eyes caught the slivers of moonlight that poked through the branches, and there was true fear there.

Another roar pierced the night, and Sapphire sped up. It was cutting a path through the trees, parallel to the trail, gaining on us quickly. Too quickly.

Patches of moonlight reflected off a body that was scaled in places and fur-covered in others.

My stomach clenched.

A slitted yellow eye met mine as it turned toward us, charging through the trees. My fingers itched to grab my sword. Why were we fleeing when we could be fighting?

"Are those—" Tolek began, but his words were drowned out when the beast cut into our path.

It flared its gigantic set of wings. Covered in scales as dark as a moonless night and as sharp as knives, they blocked the entire path. With a hide of the deepest black and a mane of thin silver hair that glowed against the night, its body looked almost horse-like. But the armor of scales protecting its legs—legs that ended in claws, not hooves—and the spiked tail thrashing about behind it were of some other origin.

It towered over our mares on four legs, but it was breathtakingly large when it reared up on its hind legs. Wings flapping, it swiped out a claw. Sapphire pivoted, barely avoiding it, but a scream behind me chilled my blood.

Jezebel.

I yanked on Sapphire's reins to turn her and pulled my sword from its sheath. The creature was towering over my sister, her form so small on the leaf-strewn floor. Elektra danced on the outskirts of our circle, throwing her head back with a desperate whinny as she fought to rescue her rider.

With a bloody gash streaming from her shoulder, Jezebel raised a dagger and stabbed at the beast's leg, rolling away as it swung out. Its claws scraped her chest. When she pushed herself to a crouch, I saw the anger twisting her face.

The beast swung one wing across the space, knocking my sister to the ground again, and I screamed. It turned that slitted yellow eye back to Sapphire and me, and I swore it sparked with familiarity.

Without hesitation, we charged at each other. Warrior and horse against unknown beast. It was a clash of metal against scales as I fought to land a blow with Starfire. The way the creature moved—with cunning and fluidity—spoke of a power so old I didn't recognize it, but my bones and blood could feel it.

In my periphery, I could see Cypherion and Tolek trying to

strike the beast's defenseless sides, but the spikes in its tail swung lethal blows between them.

It snapped its jaws at me. I twisted, narrowly avoiding teeth as sharp as daggers. Its putrid breath skimmed across my face, hot and musty, like it had been sleeping for centuries. It was practically on top of us, raising a leg, claws shining in the moonlight.

I needed to get off of Sapphire. To send her running.

With a quick blow, I swiped Starfire between us, forcing the creature back a step. I jumped, landing in a crouch, and was raising my sword when the beast released an agonized howl. I chanced a look at its backside to see Jezebel had risen and brought her sword through the end of that spiked tail, severing the tip.

As I was about to take my chance, drive my sword into the beast that had tried to kill my sister with every ounce of weakened power I had in me, it flapped its wings. I staggered back from the wind it created.

Then, it took off through the trees with one last glance back at Jezebel. She narrowed her gaze at it, and it did the same, but there was no threat in the stare.

As it rounded the bend in the path back toward our initial camp, Jezebel collapsed.

"Jezzie!" I screamed, running to her side, but Santorina was already there, assessing her wounds and pulling water from her pack.

"She's okay," Rina assured me. "Look, the bleeding has already stopped. I think she just needs this." She removed a vial of salts from her bag, unstopped it, and waved it beneath my sister's nose.

My heart pounded in my ears until Jezebel's eyes slowly opened.

"Thank the fucking Angels," I breathed, crushing her to me, then pulling back to inspect her face. She blinked rapidly, scanning our surroundings.

"Let me clean your wound," Santorina muttered, and I let my sister go, not taking my eyes from her.

I was grateful for the instruction of Santorina's mother, who spent time studying in a Bodymelders encampment before her marriage, learning their medicinal practice and training with their healers. I thanked her Spirit for teaching her daughter how to care for wounds.

"I'm fine, I'm fine." Jezebel swatted us away.

"Don't be ridiculous—"

"I mean it." She flashed us the cut on her shoulder that was already healing thanks to her warrior blood and shoved herself to her feet. "Let's just get out of here before that thing returns. Or its pack shows up."

She marched away from us to where Elektra pounded her hooves in the dirt. I watched her go, unease creeping through my stomach at her unusual avoidance.

"What do you think it was?" Rina asked.

Cypherion shook his head, wiping sweat from his face. "I've never seen a thing like it."

"It felt ancient," I said, remembering its stare and the way it felt *familiar*. "Powerful."

"Well, whatever it is, let's leave before it returns. We'll never find out if we're dead." Tolek didn't take his eyes off the path when he spoke, but once Cyph and Rina turned away, he put a hand on my shoulder. "Are you sure you're okay?"

I looked him over, ensuring he was in one piece before I answered. "I'm fine. No more midnight swordfights, though."

He smirked as we turned toward our horses. "That's for the best. I'll find another way to win against you."

Once we were marching to a new camp, senses alert after the attack, I looked at my sister from the corner of my eye. Her tawny eyes were bright in the darkness, wariness and confusion still stuttering behind them. She was shaking, but something else swam to the surface of her gaze: a burning desire that I wasn't sure even she understood.

By the time the others settled down to sleep, dawn was quickly approaching. Too anxious to rest, I volunteered to keep watch. I had a feeling no one would find peace, though. I couldn't get the vision of the winged beast from my mind.

And its claws—as sharp and deadly as both its dagger-like teeth and the look in its eye. A shiver went down my spine as I imagined its gaze traipsing over me again. Whatever it had been, it was cruel and ancient.

I inhaled, flooding my lungs with much-needed crisp air, and wrapped my fingers around the pin my grandmother had given me. Its presence calmed me, guided me.

When my lungs felt full to the point of bursting, I slowly released the breath through my lips, a nearly silent *hiss* following the motion. Then, I repeated the pattern five more times, trying to release the image of that beast and my sister beneath it with each breath.

I reached a hand up, toying with the leaves on the hanging branches that draped to my chin. They were unique, the color of fresh apples. Vibrant and unmarred, as so much of the nature in our lands was. It was ironic that the people could suffer so severely, but magic kept the world pristine. I guess in people, the power only healed our external injuries. It left those on our hearts and souls to bruise.

Even then, there were some things that magic couldn't heal. I ran my thumb across my wrist, thinking of one.

The green-gray pattern continued to grow slowly. In the heart of the Curse, the spot where I could feel it burrowing deepest into my blood, the veins darkened to an onyx. That root crawled deeper within me, making itself at home beneath my skin.

As I sat there, looking intently at my wrist, I felt one of the Curse's extremities wrap itself around a vein, claiming me. My stomach rolled with nausea, and I braced my forehead against my knees.

You will not take me, yet. I repeated the affirmation to myself, thinking of Damien's prophecy. I had a job to do before I could die, and after tonight, that task felt so much harder.

Footsteps sounded behind me, muffled by the soft grass.

"Santorina," I muttered, straightening my spine and pulling the leather of my sleeve down, pretending the pain on my wrist wasn't excruciating.

Rina folded her legs beneath her in the grass next to me. "How did you know it was me?"

"Louder footsteps," I answered without looking at her. No warrior blood.

"Right" was all she said.

"Thanks for helping her," I whispered, looking over my shoulder to where Jezebel lay curled in the grass, Tolek and Cypherion on either side of her. We left our sleeping mats when we fled the beast, but they had given her the one blanket that made it out of the camp with us.

"She's going to be okay."

"I know." And I did—but I couldn't forget the fact that there was a moment when I thought she might not be. I didn't voice the guilt that ate at me every time that image flashed to my mind. It had only been one Spirit-forsaken day on this journey, and already I felt like I was unraveling. I groaned, burying my face in my hands.

"You cannot blame yourself."

"I can."

"No, Ophelia, you can't." She pulled my hands from my eyes, forcing me to meet her stare. "Whatever that thing was, it attacked Jezebel because that's in its nature. It could have been any of us."

My hands shook at the thought of any of them suffering. Spirits, this is why I didn't want anyone to come with me on this trek. If anything happened to one of them—

My breath lodged in my throat, and I couldn't answer Rina. Instead, I stared at the stars.

She folded her hand around my own. "I'm sorry for earlier." My eyes snapped up to hers. "With the rum," she clarified.

I exhaled. That argument felt like it had passed days ago; it seemed so small in comparison to what we'd just survived. "Truthfully, I'd forgotten about it." The weakness came roaring back to me, and I once again wondered how I ended up here. "I was not expecting those words, though."

She cracked a smile, white teeth bright against olive skin. "I mean them."

"Thank you," I whispered, returning her smile, the muscles in my cheeks loosening.

Tension lifted from her eyes. "Don't misunderstand my apology, though. I'm sorry for how I broached it, but I *am* worried about you."

"You need not be." The lie fled easily from my lips.

"But I am."

Our gazes locked, and we were evenly matched. Two storms of gritty determination and bold emotions, my twin force driving me to be my best.

"Rina," I exhaled, conceding slightly to her.

"Nothing can happen to you, Ophelia." She squeezed my hand. "I've lost too many. You're the closest family I have left." Santorina was a master at forcing me to face harsh truths, but for her to let down her own guard...for her to express this level of vulnerability meant something deeper than I could name. Guilt twisted through me, knowing I wouldn't be around much longer.

"You have them." I inclined my head toward our sleeping friends.

Rina smiled. "They're family, too. But it's different with you." Because I'd been there when she was told her parents had died. The moment she'd officially thought herself alone in the world. And I'd held her together.

"What are you afraid of?" I asked, gently squeezing her hand in return, and she knew I didn't mean the winged beast or the Undertaking.

"I am afraid of how many bottles I have emptied into your glass in recent months. I am afraid of the darkness I see lurking in your eyes until the first sip passes your lips each night. I am afraid of the fact that it is *each* night."

Her dark eyes shone with such honesty that I felt I owed her the same. I filled my lungs with air and released it slowly. "When I drink…it relieves the pain. It comforts me through blurry oblivion, but also with distraction."

Rina put her arm around me and hugged me to her. I surrendered into the embrace. "I know it makes you forget your grief," she whispered, her cheek against my head. "But there are other options for comfort and distraction. Allow us to help."

"That's not my strength."

"We all suffer weaknesses. You're fierce in most other aspects."

I rested my head on her shoulder, wrapping my arms around myself. My heart thudded slightly at her words. Maybe there were other methods to achieve the warmth I sought in the bottom of a bottle. Though I wanted nothing more than to douse tonight's events in the blinding liquor, I did not want to lean on that crutch any longer, weaken my body when I needed to fight.

"We dump the canteen in the morning," I said.

Rina nodded against my head.

We looked at the lightening sky, navy fading to pale violet as the stars slowly faded. All seven of the Angel constellations were still visible and the six gods with them. "Tell me about the constellations, again," Rina murmured.

With the dawn air cushioning my voice and our three friends sleeping soundly behind us, I whispered the legends of warrior clans and mythical beings to my incredibly human friend.

In the morning, we poured out the liquor.

I watched the warm amber that had become my lifeline seep into the dark soil beneath a cypher tree.

I turned my back on it.

Chapter Sixteen

"MALAKAI?" I WHISPERED. HOPE *budded inside me, like a flame threatening to fade into embers. He turned, an easy smile—that smile that made the stars seem dim—already on his face.*

"Ophelia." My name fell off his tongue as if he had been expecting me. It was full of pleasure and promises, but none of the utter disbelief that tumbled through my heart.

With long strides, he crossed the space between us, and as his boots swept over crumbling rock, I noticed where we were—or where we weren't. Every inch of our surroundings was dark, like a veil had been dropped, leaving one small ring of illumination around us. Shadowed outlines wavered in the distance, but of buildings or nature or people, I couldn't be sure.

Malakai stopped feet from me, and I wanted to close that gap between us desperately, but something prevented me.

"Where are we?" I asked.

Malakai shrugged. "Perhaps nowhere." His voice echoed with chilling power, the eerie undertone of his words and the spark in his eyes unsettling.

"How can we be nowhere?"

"Or maybe it's everywhere." He tilted his head, the dim light outlining the lines of his jaw and nose.

The undertone of his words was familiar, and I wracked my brain for the vague connection. It came to me slowly, hazily, as if from a distance: It is about everything that will be nothing if you do not act. *But how could Malakai know the Angel's words?*

"Malakai, what—" I stepped toward him but was thrown backward. A barrier had sprung up between us.

"It is all right, Phel." That smile that had once been my favorite moment of every day turned haunting. "It has to be this way."

"What has to? What's going on?" I beat my fists against the invisible wall. Each bruising hit rocked through my body, shaking my bones. It hurt deeper than that though—it hurt in my heart and soul. The Bind burned fiercely, and my heart sped with it.

"Malakai!" I screeched, but his name bounced off the barrier and swarmed around me, my own voice a taunting echo of what I could not have. We were in the same place, but we were not. My breathing turned into hysterical gasps as I planted my palms against the wall.

Malakai mimicked the movement, and I could almost feel his touch. Skin on skin, searing everywhere it would have connected. I imagined the warmth of his strong fingers lacing through mine. How his rough palm would feel pressed against my own, dragging down my body. His feather-soft kiss if he were to lift my hand to his lips. I wanted that—needed that. The fated connection we had built through years of childhood friendship that eventually budded into the innocence of young love. One so powerful that we'd tied our souls together for eternity.

Frantically, I searched his forest eyes for a sign of how he felt. His lips parted as little puffs of breath escaped in time with the gentle heaving of his chest, like he shared the desperation I felt.

But his wide eyes buzzed with an electric excitement. I realized it wasn't desperation from him—it was eagerness. *One I did not understand. He gave me a knowing smile that spoke of secrets, and it twisted my heart.*

"What do you want me to do?" The sound echoed around me.

His lips moved in what I assumed was encouragement, but I couldn't hear his words.

A tugging sensation wrapped around my waist. It pulled me backward—inch by painful inch as the Bind burned.

"NO!" I struggled against it, flinging my body forward. Carnal need and a refusal to believe drove me toward my North Star. A cursed instinct told me that if I did not fight, I would never again lose myself in his intoxicating presence.

Malakai's expression didn't falter, though. He watched me be pulled away with that same look of eager awe dashing through his eyes, an understanding smile puncturing his cheeks. He nodded as if to say it was okay, the bob of his head drawing his long hair into his eyes. I watched the swish of his dark bangs as if in slow motion, until the tugging against my gut was so forceful, I couldn't resist.

I shouted the only thing I could think to say, "I love you."

And I saw his lips form five words in response, Until the stars stop shining.

Then, I tumbled back, head over heels and into darkness with Malakai's green eyes burning an imprint in my mind.

I stumbled as the tugging sensation swooped through my gut. I couldn't see anything, but a series of sharp clicks met my ears, each one growing louder. A rattle joined them, more subtle than the clicks, but never ceasing. My teeth dug into my lip as I spun around, searching for the source, but only cold, dark air surrounded me.

The noises felt foreign, like they did not belong in this dream I was floating through.

I realized with a jolt—it was because they were real.

Cool night air kissed my sweat-damp skin and the stars shone down on me as I rocketed upward, back to the real world. And to the herd of small rodents tearing through our rations of food.

"Get away!" I growled, pushing myself to my feet, Starfire already in my grasp.

My shouts roused the others, and together we chased off the remaining creatures. When the last had fled into the brush, the five of us stood looking over our ruined sustenance.

"They ate it all." Jezebel dropped to her knees to sort through the crumbs left behind. "Every bit of dried fruit and meat. The bread and cheese, too."

"We'll find more," Cypherion comforted.

"We better—quickly," Jezebel snapped. Stepping between my sister and a meal was a quick way to find yourself with a blade at your neck. I touched Cyph's shoulder, shaking my head to tell him to step away.

"First opportunity we get," I swore. My head felt foggy, thoughts muddled as an ache spread throughout my skull. Two days. We'd only been out here for two days, and already our food was gone.

Jezebel extended a hand to gather up the remains, but I grabbed her wrist. "Careful, sister. The woodland creatures are typically friendly. If these were not, we don't know what contamination they may carry." I hated being distrustful of the animals whose land we roamed, but between the attack last night and now this, it was clear that something was off. "In fact, I think it would be wise to avoid them and their food sources as much as possible."

"You fear they may be contaminated?" Cypherion tilted his head as he observed the wreckage.

I nodded, kicking dirt over our ruined food pile. "The magic of the mountains provides for the animals of our land. They never take from travelers."

"But what will we eat?" Jezebel whimpered behind me.

"Perhaps they were hungry, Ophelia," Tolek challenged, rubbing a hand across his jaw and stifling a yawn. His eyes were still half-hazy with sleep, and his hair was pushed up on one side.

I swept my gaze across the trees, into the darkened spaces between the trunks. Remnants of my dream still floated through my mind, and I struggled to determine what was reality. Hallucinations were a symptom of the Curse—perhaps mine were only beginning. A shiver trickled down my spine.

Almost certain I could see slitted yellow eyes staring back at me, I gripped my sword tighter, but I blinked and they were gone. The forest felt like a menagerie of secrets and threats, not the promise of freedom I'd expected.

"The balance of power," I whispered.

"What of it?" Tolek asked.

Jezebel's stomach grumbled. "Oh, wonderful," she muttered to Santorina.

"For the sake of the Angels, Jezebel, will you be quiet for a moment." I clenched my eyes against the pain in my head, ignoring her muttered apology, and turned back to Cyph and Tol. "All natural-born creatures of the forests and plains should be peaceful. So why are they not?"

On Ambrisk, animals born of magic were loyal to the God of Mythical Beings, but it was a reciprocal relationship in which the god ensured their protection and health. In turn, the creatures were docile unless provoked. It had been such for the many millennia since some ancient being had shaped our world out of the effervescent dust of blooming stars and darkness.

"For rodents to scour our rations, something must be very wrong." Cypherion's voice dropped as if the words were hard to admit.

I twisted my lips to the side, brows scrunching together as I tried to decipher what could be the cause of this unnatural behavior. My dream—hallucination, whatever it may be—echoed in my mind, and I wondered how it all fit together.

"We should be approaching a stream soon," Cypherion panted from atop Erini.

"Can we discuss anything besides the lack of food and water?" Jezebel snapped from ahead. I glowered at her, but her eyes were on the horizon, in the direction of the mountains.

Crisp air filtered through my dry, cracking throat as Sapphire trudged along beneath me. My body ached from riding for so many hours in the day, legs and spine demanding reprieve, but we could not break until dusk. The reins slipped about in my sweaty, trembling hands, and I fought to steady myself.

In the two days that had passed since the incident with the rodents, food and water sources had become scarce. I was fearful of sharing the animals' food sources, not knowing where their taint was rooted, and we were reluctant to hunt. It was considered a bad omen to slay fellow mystical creatures. We had yet to come across any wild game that we were certain would be safe, but we were nearing the Solistine River each hour. We had kept to small portions of fruits, inspecting everything closely and praying to the Spirits that we would survive. Soon, though, both us and our horses would need stronger sources of nourishment.

My head pounded, as it had been consistently for days. The aches and trembling were likely also effects from dumping out my rum, but I tried not to consider that. I did not want to feel controlled by the desire to blur my reality, nor did I want to revisit Tolek's gloating expression from our sparring session.

"Have you decided on a name for your spear, Jezebel?" Cypherion asked calmly. Of all of us, he was the best at keeping his temper in check with the decreasing rations, though he was the largest and spent the most time working out when we stopped traveling. I smiled to him gratefully, and he cast me an understanding nod.

Jezebel pursed her lips, thoughtful. "I supposed it was insignificant, since I've been forbidden from completing the Undertaking."

"As have I," I reminded her.

My sister looked over her shoulder to me, her face unreadable. "Indeed, you have." Her eyes swept over the grassland surrounding us, blonde hair swaying as she turned back around. "But we all knew that would never stop you."

Her words hung on the air, wiping all thoughts from my mind. At the head of our group, Tolek stiffened, but he did not turn. A chuckle escaped Santorina's lips from Cypherion's other side, and he turned to her to exchange muttered words.

"You did?" I asked Jezebel in wonder, keeping my eyes on the clear blue sky above. The color calmed the tension building within me.

Jezebel shrugged, the spear on her back bobbing with the

motion. "You were born for it, Ophelia. We've all known, just as you have. *We* knew there was no keeping you from this, but it took an Angel to show that to *you.*"

I nudged Sapphire's sides to catch up to my sister, and the horse trotted through the tall grass and wildflowers with ease. "We are both Alabath daughters, sister. The blood of the warriors flows as strongly in your veins as it does in mine."

"Perhaps that is not the only destiny given to us. Maybe there's more." She kicked her heels into Elektra's sides to encourage the mare forward. Her parting words trailed after her on the breeze, "Besides, *I* was not called upon by Damien."

Elektra trotted away, shining as bright as the light in my sister's eyes as she contemplated her future.

"She certainly is a force," Santorina mused, sliding into Jezebel's abandoned post beside me. I smiled at her relaxed grip on the reins as she guided her borrowed mare, Calista. She grew more comfortable with each passing day.

"That she is." A force which had been tampered with when the winged beast attacked, but beyond her unusual silent stretches, I had yet to figure out how.

Cypherion caught up to us. The curved blade of the scythe strapped to his back was a shining silver arc against the cloudless sky. He was the only one of us who carried such a weapon, having found it in his mother's house five years ago. He had shown up to training with it one day, demanded he be taught to use it, and had never spoken of it since.

"Why did you ask about her spear?" I asked.

Cyph considered the question, wording his response as carefully as he did everything. I felt a bubble of anticipation rising within me. "There is something within Jezebel that others lack. I cannot name it, but I was curious what she has planned for her future."

"Jezzie wants to be a warrior. She has always trained like one."

With his sword strapped to his hip, scythe across his back, and a number of small blades sheathed across his chest and arms, Cyph made a formidable guard beside Rina and me. But the sharpest weapon in Cypherion's arsenal was his mind.

"Perhaps" was all he said before falling into his own contemplative silence.

I thought of the spear currently strapped to my own back, a physical symbol of Malakai. The cold metal pressed firmly between my shoulders, its warmth passing through my normally impenetrable training leathers, a presence demanding attention. The pulse it instilled in my veins quickened.

When we had dismounted last night and settled beneath a massive willow, I had removed the spear from my back and balanced it in my palms. Under my control, it slashed gracefully yet powerfully through the air, the blade so sharp it sliced cleanly through a fallen leaf.

Tolek had leaned against a tree, one leg stretched in front of him, the other propping a journal up as he watched, speechless. I shot him a devious smile, enjoying his observation as I worked.

He had raised his eyebrows, impressed. "It's as if it was made for you."

I had only winked and returned to my routine. My movements were already growing swifter as my quickened system worked to detox the last drops of alcohol. A dull ache had settled into my head, but I fought through it. My stamina, however, suffered. I had a sickening feeling that the web inside my right forearm was to blame.

Still, wielding Malakai's spear was freeing.

My heart lifted as I relived the feeling, all thoughts of thirst fleeing my mind.

"Come on, girl," I encouraged Sapphire, snapping the reins as Cypherion, Santorina, and I followed Tolek and Jezebel up the hillside.

The mares crested the top where rich green grasses reflected the sun into the valley of trees below, and we looked upon the descent. The halfway point of our journey marked by an invisible line in the grass at the base of the hill. I sighed in relief at the sight.

Thanks to our relentless riding, we had shaved a few days off of our journey so far. The Curse continued its slow progression through my veins. If we could keep pace, we'd reach the tundra—the bare expanse of land before the Spirit Volcano—sooner than originally planned, and the real fight would begin. I was equally excited for and wary of that promised point, aware that only a handful of days separated us from that moment.

My brow furrowed as a family of birds took off into the air from the opposite side of the hill. It was odd to see them flying so sporadically.

I kicked my feet against Sapphire's sides, urging her down the hill. But we froze when a battle cry sounded from the tree line.

Chapter Seventeen

MY HEART LURCHED INTO my throat at the gravelly screams of the men and women flying out of the ash-white cypher trees below. Their skin was pale, streaked with purple scars across their faces and exposed arms. Their moss-colored leathers had camouflaged them among the trees, but I cursed myself regardless for not sensing the threat. For not understanding the fleeing birds moments earlier.

The Engrossians were here.

My breathing hastened, deciding between fight or flight as their shouts grew louder. More menacing. Fleeing would be safest, but the blood in my veins heated and my hands twitched toward my weapons as I looked at those self-inflicted scars marring their skin. The sign of their loyalty to their clan—a sick tradition in my opinion, but one their power-hungry queen, Kakias, still enforced.

There were only half a dozen of them, all twice my size and intimidating, but only half a dozen. A rogue group. One of the many that denied the treaty that ended the war two years ago, turning their backs on their queen. As I heard the hatred in their cries and watched the light reflecting on their sharpened axes, I feared such revolution seeping into other tribes.

The air in my lungs turned to ash the longer I looked at them. Their clan was to blame for everything that had gone wrong in my life. These were the warriors who'd destroyed our homes and people. These men and women tried to tear Mystiques apart, and would have stopped at nothing to wipe us from the planet and assume our position as protectors of the mountains.

A need for vengeance fed the hum in my blood as I bellowed, "Fight!" and sent Sapphire flying down the hill toward the rogues and their waiting weapons.

Tolek, in the front of the group already, led the charge, Astania galloping full out. He unsheathed the long sword from his side, his muscles contracting as he swung it above his head, speeding toward the first enemy.

My blood pounded through my body in encouragement. My genes wanted a fight. I laid flat against Sapphire's neck, willing my energy into her legs to move faster, to catch up to Tolek and demand revenge for everything the Engrossians took from me.

The enemy in front raised a grisly-looking ax, a sickening smile displaying yellowing teeth as Tolek approached. He was still, the weapon poised to strike, eyes glinting like pools of death—dark and ominous, yet gleeful—as he anticipated my friend.

The motion of his ax launching from his hand was a flash in the wind. But Tolek was faster, swinging so far to the side on Astania that he had to wrap his long legs around her to stay on. He swiped out with his sword, slicing cleanly across the neck of the Engrossian.

The man fell to his knees, deep red blood bubbling through the wound in his throat and tainting the billowing grass. He hadn't even enough time for his eyes to widen in shock. The sound of his gargled chokes followed me as I passed.

Fucking Angels, Tolek Vincienzo was impressive.

Cypherion sped up beside me, heading directly for an Engrossian whose eyes were trained on Jezebel's back. My sister was facing down two enemies of her own, spear in-hand. Elektra shone beneath her, and together they were the image of legend, embodying a myth not yet written.

"Rina, stay back," Cypherion warned, ripping his scythe from his back.

Rina. She was untrained. Vulnerable.

But my friend sped up, steady on Calista's back, and snatched a knife from the strap around Cyph's arm.

"I will protect myself," she growled in return, directing her horse to the outskirts of the battle where the threat was minimal. Her stare held a heat I recognized—revenge. Rina had lost as much as we had. She may not be in the heart of the fight, but she would take down anyone who dared to touch her.

I smiled wickedly at my friend's strength and rocketed into the fray, pulling Starfire from my hip. "It's time for vengeance," I purred to the blade. She glowed in the face of battle. The sun warmed us both as we sank into a predatory mode.

My eyes locked with the largest of the Engrossians. His frame should have been intimidating, but I was thirsty for blood. His black eyes met my magenta, then took in the gold of my hair, and recognition dawned.

"Alabath," he hissed.

My eyes narrowed at the purple scars crisscrossing their way around his bald head, the pattern a unique map of his triumphs.

"You must be Victious." My gut coiled, and I knew I was correct without his nod of confirmation. Victious, once the leader of the Engrossian armies who fell from grace upon refusing the treaty and now led small bands of warriors in attacks against Mystiques.

Victious, who my father had nearly lost his life to during the war.

"I believe I have a debt to repay," I crooned, the sound almost seductive. Sapphire and Victious's deep gray warhorse circled each other, huffing. I timed my breaths to the mare beneath me to steady myself, turning us into one being.

Victious smiled hungrily, his scars standing out starkly against his skin. I wondered which were for the Palerman attacks.

"Your father will love to receive his daughter's head, I'm sure." He glanced to Jezebel as she ran her spear through the heart of an Engrossian, a victorious scream bursting from her lips. "Maybe I'll include hers, as well."

At the threat to my sister, my anger snapped and I charged.

It was uncalculated. Sloppy. Unlike my usual techniques.

And exactly the reaction Victious wanted to draw from me.

His ax met Starfire in a whirl of sparks. One. Two. Three times. I blocked each fatal strike of the Engrossian blade aiming for my neck, but even my honed skills were fading too quickly. Even more severe than during the fight against Tolek. For the first time since she was forged, Starfire was heavy in my hand. She did not feel like an extension of myself, but an iron rod, my wrist sagging beneath her weight.

My wrist…the affliction spreading through me, contaminating my blood and weakening me…

I continued to counter his blows, but his power was greater than mine. He kept me on defense, rendering me unable to attack.

"An Alabath who's not as good as rumors said?" He sounded hungry—for *my* blood.

But I was hungrier. Not only did I seek revenge, but that thing living inside me wanted fuel.

I snarled in response, then focused all of my energy on predicting his next move.

Cypherion, Santorina, and Jezebel fought the remaining three Engrossians, Rina doing all she could on the sideline, her knife bared. They dodged blow after blow, but it was so close. Too close.

"I'm going to kill them all," Victious mocked.

"I'll die before I let you touch them."

Fear for my friends kept me atop Sapphire, fighting to raise my sword arm though every muscle from my forearm to my shoulder to my obliques screamed in protest.

It was heavy, everything was heavy. Each strike echoed down my arm, bones grinding against each other, and I bit down on a scream.

"And die you will," my opponent purred.

I wasn't sure how much longer I would be able to hold off his blows. That sinking vulnerability returned as I realized I was going to lose the battle with Victious because of the Curse. It was a cruel fate, as I could tell I was the stronger fighter, but fate it was—and I could feel its cool hands reaching for me now.

My friends needed to run. They had to get out of here the second that blade met my neck. Victious would show no remorse, and they could be nowhere near my poisoned blood.

The sickening stench of Victious's sweat was overwhelming. His heavy panting and deranged growls drowned out all noise beyond our weapons clashing. I could tell he was closing in for the kill—gaining a position on me that I would be unable to fight my way out of.

My hand trembled as I met his blade, Starfire nearly falling from my grip.

His eyes darkened with victory, as a grotesque smile split the warrior's lips. The daughter of Alabath brought down by his mighty ax and sent to my father in pieces. I recoiled at the thought but willed my body to keep fighting until my friends were safe, so only one family may lose someone to this band of rogues.

Once Victious had me, he would be distracted long enough for my friends and sister to escape as he carved out my torturous death. If it was my last move, I would ensure they had that much. I would leave them with their lives. They would be safe, and I could die knowing that my last sacrifice was to ensure that.

And they would carry on my mission. I had yet to request it of them, thinking I'd have at least a few more days of life, but I knew they would do everything they could in my honor. Truthfully, what were a few less days when I'd known death lurked around me?

It was with those thoughts that I met Victious's crazed stare and was not afraid. Remembering the lives I was hopefully saving, I let the arm holding Starfire fall to my side, muscles screaming in relief. Victious's eyes glinted, the vengeance he sought against my father in his grasp.

I closed my eyes and exhaled for the last time.

"No!" A scream echoed, bouncing off the trees and hills around us.

My eyes shot open, my body going rigid when the ax didn't

meet my skin. I looked for the source of the shout, though I already knew in my bones who it was.

He had been watching. He guessed my intentions.

His scream caused Victious to hesitate for the slightest of moments, and it was all Tolek needed. I watched in horror as he pushed himself to his feet atop Astania's back and launched himself before me, in line with Victious's sharpened blade.

CHAPTER EIGHTEEN

I HAD NEVER KNOWN such fear as the moment Victious's ax swung through the air and lodged itself in Tolek's thigh.

Blood splattered across all three of us as he hit the ground, not moving. The coppery tang cut through the air. Sound stopped around me. Bodies moved, but senselessly.

I reached a shaking hand to my cheek where a drip of something was congealing, tickling my skin as it slid down. Not something—blood. *Tolek's blood.* There was too fucking much of it on my skin, hair, leathers.

No. Tolek had not done that. Victious had not done that. My vision turned as red as the blood flowing around Tolek.

I released a bloodcurdling scream that had even Victious's pale face slackening in fear. It was with little effort that I raised Starfire and brought her shining silver blade down across the Engrossian's thick neck. The grinding of metal through flesh, tissue, and bone that ricocheted up my arm was satisfying. His head tumbled through the air, an arc of blood painting the sky, and thudded into the grass. His body crumpled beneath Sapphire's feet, and I smiled.

Blood dripped from my blade as I panted, fury and fear battling within me. The sounds of my friends' battles ended, and I turned to see two more Engrossians fall, the third and final fleeing toward the tree line.

"*Absolutely not,*" I growled. I kicked my heels into Sapphire's side, and she shot off as if she, too, wanted revenge for our fallen friend.

We were gaining on the warrior, but he had a head start, and I knew that if he disappeared into the trees, it would be impossible to find him.

I reached behind my head and wrapped my fingers around the spear. The weapon warmed in my hand, begging to be used for this moment of vengeance. That familiar energy shot up my arm. Taking aim was significantly harder while Sapphire moved, so I pulled her reins to stop her. In one swift movement, I balanced the spear, aimed, pulled my arm back, and let the fated weapon fly toward my retreating target.

It shot straight through the back of his head with a *squelch* that I could hear across the clearing. I released a sigh at the sound. My breathing steadied as the enormity of what I had done hit me: struck a moving target from fifty yards with a spear. A feat by any warrior's standards—especially mine.

But that mystery would have to wait.

"*Tol,*" I breathed, remembering why I had chased the enemy down.

I retrieved Malakai's spear and raced back to where Tolek had collapsed. The gentle rise and fall of his chest lodged a sob in my throat. He was alive. Sprawled in the grass with his head in Cypherion's lap, pale and blood-soaked and shaking—but alive.

Santorina inspected his leg, giving Jezebel directions of what to pull from her backpack.

I threw myself down beside them, wrapping both of my hands around Tol's. Tears stung my eyes as I looked at the damp stain surrounding the ax still lodged in his thigh. Crimson pooled around the wound—splattered his face, leathers, and hair, tinted the grass red. Spirits, there was so much blood.

He cried out as Rina prodded the skin next to his wound.

"Sorry, sorry," she murmured. She sounded much calmer than I felt. "Hell, I can't tell what the damage is with the ax still in there. We're going to have to remove it quickly."

Tolek nodded without opening his eyes, but his grip tightened on my hand until his knuckles turned white and my bones ground together.

"Here." Cypherion removed the leather band around his arm, emptied the blades, and forced it between Tolek's teeth for him to bite on.

Santorina's face was hard, eyes narrowed in concentration as her slender fingers gripped the weapon. She met my gaze for a brief second, then tightened her grasp and pulled. The blood flowed fast, but Jezebel was there with a dressing, applying pressure.

"It didn't hit an artery." Rina sounded relieved.

"How do you know?" I asked.

She looked up. "Because he'd already be dead."

I swallowed, fear swooping through my stomach at the understanding that removing the weapon from his thigh could have been the end of Tolek.

The ax had sliced cleanly through his leathers. My stomach turned further at the consideration of what poison must have coated the Engrossian weapons in order to penetrate our reinforced garments. They were out to kill.

I was glad I'd ended them.

As if reading my mind, Rina said, "The magic worked into these training leathers may be the only thing that saved you, Tolek." Gently, excruciatingly, she cleaned the wound using vials and linen strips that I hadn't even been aware she had packed but could not have been happier for. Then, she stitched his skin back together using a Bodymelder thread that would fade into his skin as the wound healed.

I couldn't look away from the needle and thread that pierced Tolek's flesh, weaving in and out as if through mere cloth, each puncture thickening the sweat pouring down his face.

"This should have gone deep enough to either take your leg off or cause you to bleed out. But it didn't. You're lucky." Rina made the final stitch and tied off the thread with one skilled motion.

Tolek spit out the leather strip that his teeth had nearly gnawed through and grimaced. "I must be blessed," he panted. His face was too pale. Though the pain was evident, he looked to me, and his eyes softened.

As Jezebel and Santorina searched for materials that might help support the injury, I reached a hand to his hair. It was standing in disarray around his face, dark brown strands sticking up and out. I brushed my fingers across each sun-kissed highlight, his chocolate eyes melting in his blood-splattered face as he calmed with my touch.

"You're an idiot, Vincienzo." I shook my head. "Why did you do it?"

"Ophelia," he whispered, breathing through the pain. He fought to get the words out, his voice low and labored. "Why did *you* do it?"

Cyph glanced up from his friend's pained expression, but I avoided his eyes. A gash bled steadily from his forehead, staining his auburn waves. He didn't seem to notice.

I swallowed against the lump in my throat—the truth fighting to get out. "It was the only option." I couldn't let any of them die, but I could sacrifice myself.

"No." A modicum of energy returned to Tolek's voice as he repeated, "No, Ophelia. Never." His squeeze of my hand was merely a flutter, but it was reassuring and admonishing and concerned all at once.

I looked at the now-wrapped wound, wiping tears from my eyes.

"Tolek Vincienzo," I said, voice cracking, "never do *anything* like that again."

"No promises," he exhaled, wincing. My heart sank at the sight.

Spirits, this was my fault. All of it. Dragging my friends into this journey, into unpredictable danger. They did not deserve this pain. The attacks, the fear for their lives—they should not have seen any of it. These were risks that I should have faced alone.

Fear was a hot iron stabbing my innards as I remembered the weakness the Curse had plunged into my body. I almost lost

Tolek—my closest friend, my guiding moonlight in the dark night, and the knot that tethered me to reality—because of it. I wanted to rip the damned affliction from my wrist, claw it out one dark tendril at a time until it suffered as much as we had.

The Engrossians—this all went back to them. If I survived this journey, and was granted more time by the Curse, they'd be next on my list of targets.

A molten desire for revenge budded in my gut as I looked at Tolek's face, pale from loss of blood. If it hadn't been for his sacrifice, I would not have the chance to avenge those I loved so deeply. Though I hated the circumstances, perhaps there was something to be said for not moving through life on your own.

"We can't stay here," Jezebel said, wiping her hands on the grass and leaving it smeared with Tolek's blood. I assessed my sister. Her face was stern but steady. She was covered in dirt and blood—hers or Engrossians' I was not sure—but she seemed otherwise okay, save for minor scratches. Rina was similarly situated, with a split lip that swelled slightly.

"He can't ride." Cypherion sounded offended that Jezebel would even suggest it, and I knew he was going to spend the next few days guarding Tolek like a mother wolf.

"What if more rogues attack?" Jezebel asked, but even as she said it, her gaze flashed to Tolek's wound and uncertainty lit her eyes.

"I'll be okay," he insisted. His eyes were closed as he reclined against Cyph, hands locked above his head.

"Stop being a fool," Cyph warned.

Tolek cracked an eye open at the tone. "We need to move. Give me something to numb my Spirits-damned wound and replenish my blood. Santorina, I'm certain you have tonics for that?"

Rina was already mixing ingredients from vials in her pack. "I'm not certain how well they'll work given that I can't properly measure proportions." She sniffed a dark concoction, then dropped a white powder into it, swishing it until it dissolved. "Try this." She mixed a second one hastily, this liquid a deep crimson, and Tolek downed them both.

"Thank you," he said. Without waiting to see what effects the drugs would have, he dragged himself into a seated position. "Shall we?" he asked, looking at us all as if we were the reason we had stopped moving.

I chewed my lip as I considered the risks of each alternative. "We walk," I finally decided. Even that would risk Tolek's leg, but it had to be better than the jostling of a horse and the strain that would put on his thigh muscles.

Tolek's eyes flashed open. "That will be much too slow. Surely, I can get on—"

"You aren't mounting anything, Vincienzo." My voice was firm, but he laughed at the suggestion in my words. At least his humor hadn't been harmed. "I'll walk with you; the others will surround us on horseback. We send one scout ahead every few hours to check the way. Should there be a threat, we either divert to another path, or we throw you on a horse and pray to the Angels and Spirits for your health." Warriors healed more quickly than humans—I only hoped it would start to take effect soon.

His mouth was a tight line as he decided whether arguing with me was worth it, but whatever he saw in my eyes confirmed that it was not.

"Fine," he conceded. "Someone find my damned weapons and help me up."

Once Tolek was—painfully—on his feet, arm slung around my shoulders, spear strapped across his back, and sword secured in Astania's saddle, he said, "Oh, I believe I won our bet, CK."

"What bet?" Cypherion looked skeptical.

"I did indeed stand up on horseback mid-battle. I may not have fired an arrow, but I think jumping from the saddle counts for something." His grin warmed my chilled body as he squeezed me to his side.

Chapter Nineteen

Malakai

"Look at me," he seethed.

I did not. I *would* not. Because I knew what I would see in his gaze—an expectation of me to accept the truths as *he* saw them. And that was one of the few things that would break me. So, I kept my eyes on his dark boots, counting the scuff marks on the toes.

"You're difficult. I had not been told of your attitude." His voice was gravel against an open wound. Each word sliced deeper into me, tearing and grating.

I smirked against the pain because it was all I could do. Sweat-soaked bangs curled into my eyes, blocking the view of my captor, but he heard my amused exhale. I gripped the wooden arms of my chair and focused on the splinters cutting into my palms as I whispered, "I guess your lapdogs aren't so loyal."

There was a beat of silence, then his hand struck me so quickly I didn't even see him raise it. My head snapped backward, the impact rocking through my skull and down my spine. The force sent my chair tipping onto its back legs and my teeth sliced into my bottom lip as I bit back a growl. I swallowed the iron taste of blood and squeezed my eyes tight against the spinning world. He was wearing a fucking ring, and the large stone in it sliced my jaw, drawing a line of blood down my neck. From the thick gush, I knew it would scar, adding yet another mark to my body.

Fucking Spirits, why is he here? It had been over eight hundred days and he had never once visited. Not since the day he threw me in this cell.

His presence meant nothing good, and whatever purpose brought him here was likely an evil I couldn't avoid. With a deep breath, I looked up at him, and let the weight of the truth crash over me.

He sighed, and the sound carried years of pent-up aggression. "This could have been so easy, Malakai."

Hearing my name cross his lips caused bile to rise from my stomach, and I allowed my mind the pleasure of picturing myself vomiting on his smug face. In the stone cell, amid the rank odors of torture, the image was satisfying.

That rough voice continued, unperturbed. "If you had only followed suit, everything would have been okay. Now, we resort to *this* to protect the truth." I thought there might have been a note of regret in his voice, but then he added, "It is your fault."

His lies nearly drew a reaction from me, but I sucked in a breath and tightened my grip on the wood, counting as I exhaled my venom. *Eight...seven...six*—the thing that stung the most was that I didn't even think he thought his words were lies—*five...four*—they were his warped version of the truth—*three...two*—which meant I was insignificant—*one.*

Significant enough to keep, but maybe not enough to continue to torment.

"So, let me go," I growled. "Release me from these chains and return to your original plan."

"I cannot." His green eyes darkened, unrelenting. He was allowing himself to be controlled, and in two years, I had been unable to decipher why. Why resort to torturing me when I was already a prisoner? What was the end goal? I couldn't allow emotions to surface over that unanswered question, so I met his stare as he said, "If I release you, you will ruin everything." His voice wavered. The slice of hope left within me withered to a mere ember as I realized how much of a pawn he was in this. But in its place, a shadow of persistence rose.

"What is even left for me to ruin?" I closed my eyes, slipping toward defeat. The lies tasted like acid, but so long as he did not take away my one last shred of hope, I would never succumb. I would only act like I had.

"I am glad you finally accept it."

My fingers curled around the chair, and I counted the splinters slicing into my skin to force my temper down. "Why don't you kill me now? Or order my death, since you are too much of a coward to raise the weapon yourself." I may be forced to submit, but I would never make it an easy decision for him. He would feel each order of a blade or whip against my skin.

"You think that is what I want?"

My eyes flicked across the cell. "Is it such a surprise that I do?"

"You will understand it one day. Then, you will bow to me." He turned on his heel, gray overcoat a dark cloud swirling around him. As he reached the iron door, he turned. "Something is coming, Malakai. A promise-breaking threat I did not anticipate. But I am not sorry for what must be done."

He left, voice ringing in my ears as I gripped the planks beneath my arms with unrestrained force. Their splintering *crack* echoed around me.

Chapter Twenty

Ophelia

My heart hammered in my chest as I reconsidered the decision we were about to make. Reaching out absently, I dragged my hand down one of the many trees nestled at the top of the hill we perched on, feeling a splinter pierce my skin.

"I don't like this." I turned to my circle of friends, pulling the thin piece of wood from my palm as I searched each face like I must commit it to memory. After two attacks, thinking I might lose both my sister and my best friend, I was less inclined to take risks than usual. The fear that had gripped my stomach in those moments swooped through me again, and my hands shook.

"Ophelia, we don't have a choice," Rina responded. Her eyes were clear, as if she knew exactly what she was doing and believed in her decision. "There is nothing to fear."

I gnawed on my lip. "I should be the one to go," I repeated for the tenth time, but all four of them shook their heads.

From his spot on the ground—his leg too weak to hold him up for long—Tolek reiterated their argument, "You and Jezebel must stay here. You're much too recognizable as Alabaths." His soul-searching eyes stared into mine, and I had a feeling he had an ulterior motive for keeping me here, given that he was too weak to make the theft himself.

I sighed in resignation, looking down the hillside across the southern border of Turren and into the corner of the city where their market lay. The sun had barely risen, pale yellow light settling over the quiet streets, wooden stalls, and thatched roofs. Branches swayed in the gentle morning breeze. Soon, tradesmen would set up their wears for the crowds that would flood the streets. Customers would wind their way through the makeshift tents, buying fruits and meats and freshly baked bread.

It was a smaller city than Palerman, but large enough that they wouldn't miss the food we swiped from their market.

"Cyph, you should go as well," I instructed.

"I'm capable on my own," Santorina said, a bit of heat in her voice.

"I believe that, Rina, but two will be faster than one, and you'll be able to carry more together." We needed enough food for the second half of our journey, having gone days with nothing more than wild fruit, and blankets if they were able.

Rina nodded in understanding, and Cypherion took up his place beside her, leaving the majority of his weapons in our circle beneath the trees, including his scythe. He only kept a band of knives around his arm. "People will be less trusting of me if I'm cloaked in weapons," he explained when I raised my eyebrows in concern.

"All right," I agreed. "Go. Before I second-guess this plan."

They laughed at my nerves before heading down the hill. I watched until the long grasses swallowed them up, turning them into two bobbing shadows in the distance. They had two hours to make it into the market, another hour to wander around and fill their packs—illegally—and then a hike back up the hill. If they were not back by midday, I would go after them.

Jezebel's idea of finding an inn for a night was more and more attractive the farther Cyph and Rina went. My sister had pitched the promise of real mattresses and hot food, a night of solid slumber to refresh ourselves after the tumultuous journey thus far. But we all knew we could not afford to sacrifice the time. If we kept moving, we'd get to the tundra sooner.

I had been about to give in to Jez's persuasion when the pain in my wrist flared, the countdown on my life ticking toward zero. No, we had to keep moving.

Besides, my friends were right—I would be too noticeable in the town. The citizens of Turren were a mix of Mystique Warriors and the humans we harbored in our lands, like Rina's family. I had an inclination that fact alone was enough to make her want to explore the village below. She had but a few hours, though.

I huffed, dropping down in the tall grass and pulling a stretch of rope from my pack to distract me. My fingers traveled along the length of coarse material, tying it and untying it in intricate knots as my father taught me.

Normally, I would have turned to swords to expel this frustrated tension knotting itself behind my ribs, but I didn't feel up to the fight with how empty my stomach had grown and how weak my Cursed arm was. Not to mention the lack of sleep I'd had. The hallucinations kept plaguing my nightmares, waking me during the few hours each night that I'd drifted off on hard forest floors, forgetting the threats awaiting us for a moment.

The Curse was certainly not making my final days any easier. I worked the rope, hoping the repetitive motion of the configurations would spell me into a calm focus.

Tolek scooted across the ground to join me, watching my fingers as I tangled and untangled the same piece of rope.

"I'm surprised you agreed," he said.

I smacked his arm. "Shut up, Vincienzo." But it drew a laugh from me as he'd intended.

He wasn't wrong, though. Allowing Santorina and Cypherion to go without me went against every instinct in my body. But I was dying, and those instincts—that desperate need to protect everyone—would go with me. Letting them do this on their own was proving to myself that they'd be okay when I went. Still, I hated it.

"How's your leg feeling?" I asked him, without looking away from my new task—looping the rope around itself, recreating one of the stronger knots I knew.

"It's fine," he said. I narrowed my eyes. I did not believe an injury that deep was *fine.*

He laughed at my expression, the sound unknotting a bit of the tension within me. "I swear it, Ophelia. It hurts but it's not unbearable. I am fine."

My fingers continued to tie and untie as his words sank in. The image of him hitting the ground, Victious's blade embedded in his leg, flashed through my mind, and I squeezed my eyes shut against it. Fear coursed through me. I took a deep breath over the pain and let the rough material of the rope slide through my palms.

"You'll have a horrible scar," I whispered. The realization hurt me. "Good luck explaining that to your parents when we return."

Tolek's chuckle mixed with the breeze, but the sound was much more pleasant than his tone as he said, "They won't care."

"Of course, they will," I responded without looking up.

"No." He shook his head. "My family doesn't care what happens to me."

"Don't be ridiculous," I dismissed.

"It's true. The Vincienzos care about wealth and power more than anything. I'm not the heir." As firstborn, his sister would be his parents' heir. The one whose success weighed most heavily for their family's trajectory.

"That means nothing," I said, looking from him to where my sister organized our remaining supplies, much quieter than she usually was. Plenty of families had more than one child to carry on their name.

"To them it does. I'm only the reckless secondborn whose birth almost killed his mother." He swallowed, but no emotion seeped into his voice. "They see me as the one always stirring up trouble or hiding away in a book, never doing anything productive toward their *reputation.* Truly, they probably have not even noticed my absence. I'm sure it's more peaceful without me."

My hands froze. An undercurrent of pain slipped into his words at the end, and that twisted a knife into my heart. How had I known Tolek for my entire life and never known the way his family viewed him? I'd grown to depend on him so thoroughly these past two years as he helped me fight my darkness, yet I had no idea of his own ghosts.

The thought of his parents treating him in such a way heated my blood, but I knew him well enough to know he did not want pity. Instead, I tied another knot and asked, "What about your younger siblings? Do your parents treat them as they do you?"

"Those three?" He scoffed at the mention of the triplets born twelve years after us. I supposed it made sense why his parents had waited to have more children. "They are viewed as gifts after their blissfully easy births. No, it is only I given the honor of being the family disappointment, but I suppose someone has to set the bar low so others may surpass it."

I looked at him, taking in the slight downturn of his lips and the way he would not meet my eyes, and reached for his hand. "Please don't think of yourself that way. I don't care what your parents say—it's not true." Knowing they had planted this idea in his head, their names were quickly added to my list of those I sought revenge against.

"It's okay, Ophelia," Tolek whispered. "I'm used to being the least favored."

I was about to argue when Jezebel sat down next to me. Tolek dropped my hand, and I understood it as his signal that the conversation was over. I went back to my knots. "None of this is okay." One more swoop of the ends of rope around each other.

"No, nothing has been right for a long time. But it is, and it will be, okay," Tolek said.

"You know you don't always need to protect us," Jezebel added.

There it was—the guilt for their suffering, threatening to overwhelm me despite their words.

"This is my journey—my fault. If anything happens to any of you, I won't forgive myself." I tugged the ends of rope as tightly as they would go and held them up for Tolek to see: what appeared to be two separate loops, each feeding into the other, but it was really one string.

He brushed his fingers across it. "Looks great."

"It's called an infinity knot," I mumbled.

Jezebel pushed aside the tall grasses to lean back on her elbows. "We all made the choice to come with you." All I could see was her bleeding beneath the winged beast.

"She's right." Tolek scooted back to recline against a tree, and I could only look at his wounded leg. "I'm healing. Jezebel was hardly injured. Rina and Cyph will return with supplies, and we'll be on our way. As a group." With that, he pulled his journal from his bag and disappeared into its pages.

It sounded so simple coming from their lips, but I could not let go of the piece of me that wanted to jump in front of my friends at any hint of danger.

The hours dragged with the three of us sitting in our small circle under the cypher trees. At each shuffle within the grasses, I jumped to my feet, hoping to see Cypherion and Rina returning, but it was never them.

I continued to tie my knots, practicing for Spirits knew what, as Tolek and Jezebel argued over every Angel-sent topic they could think of. Currently they debated which bread was the softest, adding tallies of how much they suspected our friends would bring back.

"Maybe they'll find lemon cookies for you," Jezebel prodded, but I only nodded. Though I was not engaging in their conversation, their voices calmed my nerves. It was a hint of normalcy in this unusual journey.

From where she stood beneath the cyphers, Sapphire whinnied. I set my rope aside and moved to my horse. "What is it, girl?" I whispered, running a hand down her mane, carefully picking fallen leaves from where they'd gotten tangled.

They were crisp and brown in my hand, crinkling to pieces beneath my touch. I looked up, branches spotted with bare patches staring down at me. *Odd*, I thought, as I untangled the rest.

Sapphire's energy was anxious—it swarmed between us. "We'll be moving soon, don't worry," I muttered, brushing her until she settled. I was glad we had not decided to stay in Turren for the evening.

Finally, when the sun had passed its highest peak in the sky and started crawling back down, I couldn't take another second of waiting.

"Something's happened," I growled, swiping up Starfire from the ground. "I'm going in after them. Jez, stay and watch over Tol."

"Oh, hell Spirits," Tol grumbled from where he was handing small pieces of fruit up to Astania. I ignored his eye roll.

Jezebel ran to me, gripping my wrist over the spot where the Curse hid, pain shooting up my arm. I wrenched it from her grasp with a grimace, but she shouted, "Wait!" I followed her eyes down the hill to where two shadows moved among the grasses. The sun reflected off of Cypherion's auburn hair, and I slumped against Jezebel as a weight left my chest.

"Thank the Spirits," I mumbled.

"Are they back?" Tolek called, not even bothering to crawl toward us.

"They're back," Jezebel answered. Though she had acted unaffected by their extended absence, I heard a hint of relief in her voice.

I paced circles around Tolek, left hand rubbing the place where the Curse burrowed into my wrist, until Rina and Cyph reached us. They slumped to the ground, the weight of their journey pressing down on them. The tight set of their mouths and aversion of their eyes stopped my movements.

"What's happened?" I asked, looking between the two of them.

"Did you bring food?" Jezebel asked, digging into their packs and pulling out a piece of dried meat. She released a sigh as she bit into it.

"Something's wrong." I didn't say it as a question.

Cypherion distributed food to the group—sure enough, handing me an iced cookie that smelled of citrus—but I merely twirled it between my fingers, too nervous to eat.

Santorina threw Tolek a small jar of something yellow and fresh bandages. "Put that on your leg, and then I'll rewrap it for you." She stretched her arms over her head, rolling her shoulders. Her pack must be heavy. Good.

"You are an Angel, Santorina Cordelian," Tol gushed, doing as she instructed.

"We know that took longer than planned," Rina said, sitting down. "But we have good reason."

"Were you noticed?" Tolek asked, hands freezing as he unwrapped his soiled bandages.

Cypherion shook his head. "Nothing like that. We got supplies quickly and would have been back an hour ago, but we overheard something." He exchanged a glance with Santorina. She nodded for him to continue. "There's a tavern right by the entrance to the market, and a group of warriors were surrounding it, drinking ale, gossiping."

"And?" I pressed, knowing the early hour of their indulgence would not be cause to linger in a town where you had committed theft.

"We overheard them talking, and the things they were saying…" Rina's words cut off with a shiver.

"There's unrest," Cypherion explained. "People are suffering even worse outside of Palerman than we knew. Turren is one of the only towns where the market has been steady, and that's solely thanks to their position near the Solistine River. Most lost so many in the war that they can barely keep their families fed and clothed."

I sank to the ground, holding my head in my hands as he continued, "They're growing tired of it. There's talk of rebellion against the Revered."

"The Revered?" Tolek asked. He and I exchanged a nervous glance, the echoes of our encounter with Lucidius on my birthday coming to the forefront of my mind. He had not seemed concerned.

Cypherion nodded. "They think he should be doing more to help those hurting."

"We spread all of our goods throughout Palerman," Jezebel argued, but I knew from her slackened shoulders that she understood it wasn't enough.

"Palerman is not the only Mystique town," I deadpanned.

Unrest. Starvation. Rebellion. These were not things I felt equipped to face, nor were they things I had time to consider now. But my mind—my responsibility to my people—would not let me forget it.

"We will have to do more," I said. "We'll send food to other towns, too. We'll talk to Father when we return home and have him send word to the Revered. We will fix this." The promise etched itself into my brain alongside Damien's prophecy. Perhaps it was all connected, and this journey truly would guide me to save the Mystiques who suffered. If it did not, I'd see to it myself with every hour the Curse spared me.

They all nodded in agreement.

"There's more," Rina said, and my heart sank. How could there be more? "The oldest of the warriors—they had to be nearly five centuries old—they kept saying that they felt a shift coming. Like something was building in the atmosphere, waiting to combust."

A veil of unease fell across our group as her words sank in. "They did not say what?" Tolek asked, leaning forward.

Rina and Cyph shook their heads in unison, the former explaining, "No, but it was ominous. The way they spoke about it brought a trickle of something cold and terrifying slinking through the air. Like whatever it was, it was already here."

"They spoke of their ancestors, claiming tales from those who had felt it before. But it all sounded like fables to me." Cypherion did his best to sound reassuring, but his hands clenched at his sides.

I inhaled, holding the breath in my lungs for as long as possible before letting it hiss through my teeth. I was not sure what any of this new information meant for me, how it tied into the path I had carved out for myself. A slinking tendril of the affliction in my blood stretched out, curling itself around a vein with a tug. I had a sinking feeling that I'd find out.

Chapter Twenty-One

"If we survive this journey, Tol, you need to lose weight." I nearly buckled under his lean muscles as the hours I had been supporting him started to pinch my back. My Cursed arm shrieked in pain under Tolek's weight, but I bit back my groan. His injured leg dragged over roots and brush, and each grimace that crossed his lips pained me, but we had opted to stay close to the tree line since we would be moving slower.

"You could amputate my leg," he drawled, eyeing my sword. "That would take a lot of the weight off."

"Don't say that." I scowled up at him, but that pained shadow slithering across his face cracked my angry resolve.

His comments about his family came back to me, and I pulled his arm tighter around my shoulder as our friends' horses pranced around us. Cypherion led Astania, who demanded to stay close to Tolek's side, eyeing him with worried brown eyes. Sapphire nudged my shoulder, reminding me that she was with us. Her touch soothed a bit of that discomfort within me.

"I'm convinced that you love my muscles, Ophelia, and would in fact be very disappointed if they were gone." Tolek grunted as he lifted his leg over a knotted root. The amber specks in his chocolate eyes danced as he wiggled his eyebrows. "I've seen you watching in training before."

I reeled in my retort, reminding myself that if he was joking it meant he wasn't suffering too much. The wound was imprinted in my memory, shining muscle and bone flickering behind my eyelids with every blink. I could still feel the blood across my skin though I had scrubbed it away at first chance. It clung to my memory, the heavy, sticky sensation and stench of metallic death. Tolek's death. Tolek's blood. So much blood.

I ducked beneath the sweeping leaves of a willow and let them wipe the spiraling thoughts away.

"I don't know what you're referring to," I responded coolly, though I clearly remembered the way both Malakai's and Tolek's muscled backs and arms curved and flexed with each swing of their swords and slice of their spears. Cypherion, too, when he joined us. My cheeks heated at the memory of the days they chose to spar shirtless, the Palermanian sun causing a sheen of sweat to form across their golden skin, dripping down their backs.

Both of them were rather beautiful.

Tolek smirked, eyes on my blush. I had the impression he knew exactly where my mind had wandered, but then his foot dragged over a rock and his howl of curses cut through the air. I wrapped my arms around his waist, keeping him on his feet.

He turned pained eyes to mine, biting his lips to keep from crying out again. The horses stopped, Astania releasing a desperate whinny.

"Come on," I encouraged, all humor from our previous conversation vanishing. "We're halfway to the mountains. You'll heal faster the closer we get." The magic would work its way into his wound. It had to.

He nodded, his beautifully tanned face paling.

I met Cypherion's eyes, the blue wavering with worry. He offered me the reins, saying he would assist Tolek, but I nodded at him to continue. I needed to be close to Tol, to provide guidance through these bleak days. Steady him as he did for me.

"Talk to me about something else," Tolek coaxed.

I considered for a moment, watching sunlight stream through the high branches. "You still owe me a birthday present."

"That I do," he chortled, but didn't look at me. "Don't let me forget."

"That you think I could makes me feel as though you don't know me at all," I teased, pinching his side.

He squirmed, leaning into me as he stumbled over a rise in the ground. "Don't worry, Alabath, I know you better than you think." I nearly shivered at the realization that it was true—Tolek Vincienzo knew me better than anyone.

The laughter that slipped up my throat, genuine and bright, felt unfamiliar yet decadent. Too soon, though, it faded. Watching our friends meander before us, bruised and bone-tired, it was hard to forget the troubles we faced. And the fact that I may not be around to see us through them.

I was prepared to die, but Spirits, I would miss these people.

"What's wrong?" Tol asked, squeezing my arm.

I shook my head.

"You're worried about the animals and the uprisings," he guessed. He wasn't wrong, though I hadn't been thinking of it at this moment. But I latched onto the excuse.

"And the winged beast." There was no explanation for such unrest—spanning across clans and species and land. "The more I consider it all, the less confident I feel." Leaving Palerman had removed a veil from my eyes. I now saw the tapestry that formed Gallantia's strength, history, and beauty unraveling into delicate threads, so easily snipped.

"Why have our fields not replenished? Why are the people not being given food?" He voiced my own worries. Our territory should be in abundance thanks to the magic that powered the land, but it was clearly malfunctioning. And it had been kept a secret.

"Why are the forest creatures unhealthy?" I added.

"Should we seek out the Starsearchers?" Tolek grunted, ducking a branch.

I contemplated that as I pulled his arm farther around my shoulder. Consulting the minor clan could provide answers, but it could also expose a weakness. Not that we had any reason to mistrust the Starsearchers—or any minor clan—but after the war, I was uncertain of who we could put faith in.

"No. They may be able to read an answer celestially." I paused to wipe a drop of sweat from my forehead, though it was pointless. We'd been traveling for days with only streams to rinse off in. Our skin and leathers were covered in dirt, sweat, and blood. How I longed for a decadent bath with a variety of soaps, oils, and salts. "The Mindshapers may even be able to sort moods of those in the harmed territories and decipher where revolution is stemming from, but this is a Mystique problem first."

"You think we should..." Tolek trailed off, but I knew he understood.

"We have to tell the Revered. It is his responsibility to provide for his people." My heart clenched at the thought of Mystiques rebelling if this situation went unresolved for too long. I met Tolek's eyes and saw the same fear reflected there.

Tolek, to his credit, tried to keep moving even with the injury threatening loss of limb. In the days after his injury, though, we stopped more than usual and proceeded much slower, dragging out our progress. Still, only when I could feel Tol's body temperature climbing from exertion, or when the sheen of sweat crawling down his face and onto mine was so much thicker than the rest of ours, could I convince him to rest.

But every time, without fail, he pushed himself to his feet within minutes and insisted we keep moving. I didn't know if it was for my benefit or for his own restless heart, but there was an undeniable determination in his eyes.

So, I did not stop him. I allowed him the freedom he needed, and as we walked, his leg healed slowly. Proximity to the magic emitted from the mountains worked hard to knit his skin back together. Bring bone, muscles, and flesh back into their rightful places and siphon off the pain, just as it healed me. My head still ached dully—a steady consequence of my own actions that thrummed throughout our journey—but I could feel the healing power absorbing the withdrawal symptoms with each day we drew closer.

But it did nothing against the Curse.

"We're only a few days' journey from the tundra," I said to our group as we settled beside a bend in the Solistine River where the current was calm and the water deep. The melody eased some of the tension that had built in my shoulders. I rolled them back, massaging gently to work out the knots I was convinced would never leave. "We just follow the river north."

A flash of unease settled in the air between our group at the mention of *the tundra*—the expanse of dry land at the base of the Spirit Volcano. The first step in qualifying for the Undertaking, and the only one my friends would be allowed to accompany me on.

The steady flow of the river and animals scurrying through the trees were the only sounds as the realization of what waited sank into the group.

"It will be okay," I asserted, clutching one hand over my wrist as I said it. The Curse had been traveling up my arm as we journeyed, but slower than expected. I didn't allow myself to question its lack of progress, shutting down the hope that blossomed in my chest, but I was beginning to believe that I may be able to hide it from my friends until my mission was complete. Until the point where my life must be ended.

I had written a letter for that moment and tucked it into the bottom of my pack. It expressed everything in my heart—what had happened, how I felt about it, why I hid the truth, and why my life must end. I would leave it with them before it was too late. I hoped I would be able to explain everything myself, but should I not...I must take every precaution possible.

"Of course, it will be okay," Jezebel agreed, and I broke my reflection to nod my thanks for her support. I pretended not to notice that something had shifted about her when the beast attacked, but it was like she harbored a secret.

When my sister, Tolek, and Santorina reclined in the shade, Cypherion crouched beside the river. I watched his large hands gently apply oil over each of his blades, cleaning them as if they were precious treasures. Ironic given the blood I'd seen them draw.

Not wanting to interrupt his process, I pulled an apple from my bag and bit into it. My teeth sank past the crisp skin and an explosion of tart juice flooded my tongue. It was refreshing. The moment peaceful. He polished each dagger in silence.

When my apple was nothing but a core, I tossed it into the tall trees. A scurrying told me that an animal had snatched it up quickly, and I whipped my ahead around.

"You want to know what I think about them." Cyph jerked his head toward the trees as the sounds of the creature faded. I smiled softly at his quick intelligence, his strategic and insightful mind.

"They shouldn't be acting like this."

"They're as upset as the warriors." Cypherion slid each dagger home, one by one, taking care to ensure they were strapped properly in their sheaths before moving to the next. When he was done, I removed the twin daggers he'd gifted me for my birthday. Since the Engrossian attack, I'd taken to wearing them strapped to my thighs, always within reach.

Cyph helped me polish each. How he treated every weapon like it was its own entity and needed individual care was admirable. My inquiry hung over us all the while, and I appreciated his contemplation before answering.

"Have I ever told you of the fonder memories of my childhood?" he pondered, handing me a paste he used as polish.

The question surprised me, but I shook my head. We never pushed him to speak about his childhood before moving to Palerman, knowing only the few facts he had shared over the years.

"My mother wasn't always distant." He swallowed, not looking up. "There were early years when I remember her laughing. Caring for me. It's all blurry, but she was there. Not the vacant shell she became."

"What happened?" I swiped a bit of the paste over the blade, mimicking his movements.

"She never told me. I never asked, and she rarely speaks anymore. She simply *exists.*" He spoke matter-of-factly.

"It wasn't your fault, Cyph. Whatever happened, it was to her. But it's comforting that you have those memories." There was nothing else I could say, but sadness—cold and hollow—sprouted in my heart. I folded my hands in my lap to stop their nervous twitches.

"Maybe." He shrugged as if he didn't care but didn't give me a chance to argue. "But my point is that something *did* happen to her. Something sent her into a spiral so deep—broke her so thoroughly—she no longer cared for her only child. It's the same with the warriors. The same with the animals. Something is shifting, and it's driving them further toward that breaking point. What happens then, I don't know."

"Someone once told me that one has to break fully in order to heal." One hand drifted to the sleeve of my leathers where the Bind lay, then quickly back to my dagger.

His quiet laugh wiped away a bit of my sorrow, but his face turned firm as he said, "You needed to, Ophelia. Curses, you may still need to break—who am I to know? But I told you that because you lived beneath a veil, and it had to be lifted. I mean no offense by that claim."

Cypherion, always so pragmatic. A stark realist among us, who played by the rules and saw the world not only in a series of rights and wrongs, but also their implications and how each twisted the environment around it.

"There's no offense." And I meant it.

He handed my dagger back to me and laid a hand on my shoulder, squeezing gently. "*You* may need to break, but perhaps we can save the rest of them before that fate strikes." He looked to the trees, blue eyes narrowed as if inspecting each creature that roamed Gallantia, or perhaps the whole of Ambrisk.

I almost asked what he meant, unsure how it was in our power to do anything when we were not even certain what was occurring, but the shake of his head told me he was as lost as I. He brushed a wet hand through his auburn waves, attempting to tame them. I watched the locks fall stubbornly back where they wanted to be as I puzzled over the possibilities.

We sat in silence, heavy questions buzzing between us, until Santorina called out, "I'm going to see if I can find any ingredients for healing oils before we move again."

"Be careful!" I shouted back.

Rina waved me off as she disappeared into the dense cypher trees, black ponytail swinging down her back.

Jezebel rose to her feet, stretching her arms above her head and twisting her torso. Her spine cracked with the motion, a satisfied smile spreading across her lips. "Shall we go for a swim? You all reek." She wasn't wrong.

Her eyes brightened at a hint of something we hadn't experienced in a week. *Fun.* Jezebel had a confidence about her, an uninhibited ease with which she went through the world. It radiated from her as she peeled off her training leathers, baring her skin for all the world to see. All she wore was her golden necklace. There were few shames among adult warriors, and our bodies weren't one of them.

"Jezzie, at least pretend to be modest," I mocked.

"Why pretend?" She tsked as she strutted to a small cliff at the river's edge, stepped to the highest rock, and dove flawlessly, her tan skin a bright streak against the clear blue sky.

Tol and Cyph laughed at her brazenness, the latter standing to strip off his own leathers, though he left on his undershorts, and follow her into the stream. When they both surfaced, they swam to the other bank, Cypherion treading water against the river's lazy current. Jezebel pulled herself onto a rock, her torso hanging out of the water, and threw her head back so the sunlight hit her face. Unashamed and unabashed.

I smiled at my sister's freedom, the icy outer shell of my heart cracking with her happiness. I hoped she'd still be this radiant when I was gone.

"You may go join them," Tolek said, watching me with careful eyes as he scooted to the river's edge to splash water over his face and neck. "I don't mind sitting here alone."

The inside of my wrist flared in pain, as if I could forget about the secret burden I carried. I couldn't go join them. There would be no way to hide it if I stripped.

"I'm all right," I answered with a soft smile that Tol returned. I settled on the bank beside him and mimicked his motions, letting the cool water wash the dirt and sweat from my skin and take the more painful memories with it.

"Thank you," he muttered. "For everything."

I looked into his eyes then and saw his heart, that raw emotion that he hid but which I knew comprised his soul, swirling behind the amber flecks.

I watched as he stripped off the top half of his leathers, letting them hang open at his waist, and slowly brought handfuls of water to his shoulders, chest, and abdomen. It trickled along the cut lines of his muscles, slithering down his tanned skin and leaving it glittering in its wake. Drops drifted toward his waist, disappearing beneath the leather.

"I'll change your bandages," I offered, shoving away whatever coiled below my stomach.

Not waiting for him to respond, I unwrapped the soiled strips around his thigh. He reclined on his elbows, injured leg spread straight in front of him, a picture of pure bliss despite the injury.

Tol was silent, and I lifted my eyes to find him watching my hands intently as I spread a thin layer of Rina's healing ointment over the wound. It looked weeks old, not days, the Bodymelder string Rina had used fading into the scar, leaving faint black lines. The skin was hot beneath my touch, but for the time being, infection had been kept away.

Thank the Angels, I thought. My shoulders felt a bit lighter with the knowledge that Tolek was healing.

Jezebel's laugh drifted over to us, filling the space with her infectious energy.

"At least someone's relaxing," Tolek mused, watching my sister with a protective, brotherly gleam in his eye. The scruff on his chin had grown a bit longer over our journey, shadowing his chiseled jaw.

"I envy her sometimes," I admitted, without removing my gaze from where my fingers massaged his thigh.

His eyes shot to mine, his brow furrowing in—what looked like—anger. "Why would you?"

I watched Cyph dive low in the river and emerge to shake water from his long hair at my sister. She batted him away, swearing at him with a sly smile and revenge festering in her eyes.

"She's a unique combination." I smiled. "A forceful soul, but a kind one with the power to raise Spirits or barrel down her enemies. She knows what she wants in the world and takes it."

"She learned that from you."

That shell around my heart chipped further. With each fissure, I felt freer, like my spirit was opening up to those around me, flourishing in their presence. The cloud I had lived under for the past two years cleared slightly.

"She is a better person than I will ever be." *And that's okay*, I added. *She will have more time to live.*

Tolek fell into a contemplative silence as I closed the salve and started replacing the wrap. Jezebel's and Cypherion's faces had turned serious, their tones hushed.

"What do you think they're talking about?" I inquired.

"Perhaps Cyph is admitting an unrequited love for your sister." Tol averted his eyes, watching a butterfly float among the trees.

"Cyph knows better than that."

Tolek raised his dark eyebrows, and I could see his mind already churning with gossip. Spirits, he never could keep a secret. "Is there someone else? I imagine men fall at her feet." He raised a hand to his brow to mime the illusion.

I rolled my eyes, unable to help the laugh that escaped my lips.

"Truthfully, Tolek?"

"What?" He pushed himself upright.

"Have you ever seen Jezebel with a man?"

He thought for a moment before his lips parted. "Oh," he dragged out the noise. "How did I never know that?"

"Too consumed with your own affairs?" I mocked. Tolek certainly had his fair share of partners in Palerman, never committing to one, but enjoying plenty of men and women.

"Ah, yes, my many wondrous affairs," he drawled.

"But to answer your question—the boys in Palerman have pursued her for years. She has quite a bit of fun telling them off." I finished wrapping Tolek's wound and sat back. "And she's never met a woman she's wanted to keep around."

He was silent for a minute, watching the linen with which I had covered his wound. A breeze stirred around us, carrying the scent of spiced citrus mixed with the flowers and trees.

Tolek's voice was distant when he said, "She will find someone whom she loves. Someone who drives her existence, makes her fiercer and gentler at once. Who will match her spirit and truly see her heart. Who brightens life and makes it worth living."

"You sound as if you know the feeling." My mind fluttered to my North Star.

Tol's face twisted, but before he could respond, a scream cut through the air.

Chapter Twenty-Two

"Rina," I breathed.

I was on my feet, spear and sword in hand before her name had left my lips. I turned to Tolek, mind battling between dragging him to his feet and running.

"Go," he instructed.

"Thank you," I whispered, tearing through the trees in the direction of Santorina's scream. My heart pounded in time with my soundless footsteps.

White cypher trunks and thick green leaves flew past me, wild creatures jumping along beside me, following the source of my pursuit. I willed one of them—any of them that were untainted—to reach her before me. A friendly beast to tackle whatever predator had found Rina.

I hurdled over roots and ducked beneath low-hanging branches with innate swiftness. Senses perked, warrior blood heightening, following her human scent and another unfamiliar one in a straight shot from the river.

I burst into a clearing rimmed with bushes bearing wild berries. In the center stood Rina, a hulking figure behind her and a small silver blade pressed into the sensitive flesh of her throat.

Her pupils swelled, locking on me as she inhaled, a mix of relief and distress. Hands locked on her attacker's wrist, muscles straining to keep that dagger from pressing in deeper. Though she held a mask of bravery against this man, her lips trembled minutely. The woman who'd held a dagger against Engrossians days before was shadowed. She blinked furiously at me, afraid to make the slightest move, but I read that flurry: *Help*.

I mimicked her collected mask as I surveyed our opponent. A head taller than Rina, the enemy's shoulders and chest were broad enough to engulf her. Strong arms wrapped around her waist and neck. But it was his shirt that caught my attention—the style was formal, different than any in Gallantia with its shiny brass buttons, high collar, and thick fabric.

"You're not from here," I accused. Starfire was in front of me, sunlight reflecting off her pristine blade and into the face of our enemy, illuminating his sharp nose, wide eyes, and cut jaw.

His lips curled back, in a smile or a grimace I couldn't be sure. "You're correct," he muttered in a gruff voice. It wasn't malicious or harsh, but a tremor of unease ran through it.

"What do you want?" I kept my voice steady, though heated.

He tilted his head, the movement swaying his shoulder-length brown hair around his face, ears poking out. And Starfire nearly fell from my grasp. *Pointed* ears. I looked closer at his menacing half smile and saw the elongated canines.

Fae.

When he saw the shocked recognition on my face, he truly smiled, putting those gloriously sharp teeth on display.

"You're a faerie," I breathed.

My brain whirled, trying to remember every bit of history that had divided Ambrisk's three largest land masses between the three dominant magical groups: fae to the west, sorcia in the Northern Isles, and warriors to the east. We were given the responsibility of protecting the magic-fueled land of the Mystique Mountain Range for the good of all magical creatures, including the faeries of the western continent, Vercuella. The sorceresses, something different altogether, removed themselves from the conflicts of warrior and fae historically.

Faeries could not cross the sea into Gallantia, for they had a brutal history tainted crimson with bloodshed—particularly *human* bloodshed. My heartrate spiked as I remembered the reason a treaty was finally signed two thousand years ago, sealing this agreement. Ending the slaughter of innocent humans by the fae and allowing the escape of refugees to our continent.

Regardless of that, we all thrived off of the same magic—argued over ownership of it.

The faerie smiled, his teeth impossibly white, but his grip on Rina neither slackened nor tightened. "Correct again."

"You're not to be on our continent, nor to harm our people," I growled. "Release her."

I sensed movement through the brush behind me and prayed to the Spirits it was my friends coming to our aid. I needed to hold out until they arrived. While I could handle this brooding faerie on my own, the additional weapons and muscle couldn't hurt.

"You don't know what you're saying. She is no warrior." In a movement that was almost intimate, he inhaled the air around Santorina's temple. "She is something *else*; we have no deal with her kind."

"She is an ally of my people. She is with us."

My words hit him like a bolt of lightning. His muscles flinched as he understood that Rina was protected under our rule, and he was bound to the treaty.

Jezebel and Cypherion burst into the clearing, leathers barely buckled up, hair dripping wet, and identical looks of fury on their faces.

"Kind of you to show up," I greeted.

After one sweep of the scene, Jezebel spoke in a voice as soft and fierce as death's embrace. "Now, what is going on here?"

"It looks like someone wants trouble," Cyph said, eyes locked on that fae blade.

Jezebel chuckled. "I suggest you release her now, or my friend here will sink his scythe into your skull quicker than you can beg the Angels for mercy. Hurt her"—she raised a dagger and flipped it around her hand, a chilling smile parting her lips—"and I'll do it."

Cypherion raised his weapon with a threatening growl of agreement.

"I won't be begging to any Angels," the fae answered. Jezebel's hand tightened around her dagger.

"Stand down," I commanded my sister and Cypherion. They turned aghast faces to me. "He will release her now." I gave the faerie a look of pure ice, raising my chin and looking down my nose at him.

He bared his teeth, and I heard Jezebel's and Cypherion's identical intakes of breath. He gripped the knife tighter briefly but reluctantly shoved Rina forward, a pink line cutting across her throat.

"What are you doing here?" my sister asked without lowering her weapon. Santorina scuttled to my side, shooting a glare of pure vengeance at the faerie. Without breaking my stare, I removed a dagger from my thigh and tucked it into Rina's palm. Waves of relief rolled off of her as she curled her fingers around the handle.

"He was about to enlighten me," I hissed.

He held his knife at his side. "Threats to us and our magic are looming. I was sent here to discover what hold they have on your people."

Threats to the magic. The words landed like a hot weight in my stomach, another piece of Gallantia unraveling before me.

"What kind of threats?" Cypherion asked, his analytical brain likely already putting pieces together.

"You don't already know?" He relished in his advantage, his full lips tilting upward on one side.

"What is your name?" I fought to wrest back control of the conversation, my question cool though my blood boiled.

He thought for a moment, looking up at the interwoven branches before deciding whether to share his identity. "Lancaster," he finally answered. I did not know if it was true or not.

"Well, Lancaster, what can you tell us of this threat?" I asked calmly, sheathing Starfire in a show of alliance.

He dropped his dagger into his belt as well. "It will come for you—for all of us."

"What is it?" Goose bumps rose beneath my leathers.

"We are unsure." His tone was clipped, as if it hurt to say anything. "Our sources are tracking it, but we don't know much yet."

I nodded, tucking away each shift of his shoulders and buckle of his voice, clues to dissect later. "What you learn, we will want to know," I commanded, though I held no authority over the fae.

The forest was still, everything from the creatures to the trees watching. Waiting.

Lancaster nodded, one sharp bob of his chin as his hands clenched, reluctance pouring from every facet of his body and sharp-eyed stare. I suspected he was under orders to play nice with Mystique leaders.

"Now be gone, and do not harm any others in our land."

He looked to Rina. "I am sorry for the misunderstanding. We will meet again." He swept a deep bow before running from the clearing with the unmatched speed of the fae.

I leaned on Malakai's spear, allowing the weakness in my legs to creep up my body. Another thread being dangled before me, unraveling from the tapestry I had thought so perfect. It begged me to weave the mysteries back together, to clarify the muddled truth of a world much dirtier than I thought.

But the web became more tangled by the day. I was uncertain where each strand belonged.

"What did he mean?" Rina asked that night when we settled down to sleep. The sky was black, barely any stars peeking through the trees.

I laid my blanket next to hers, as close as possible, and curled on my side to face her, supporting my head with my arm. I was careful to avoid the central point of the Curse where the pain was the deepest, but I was growing used to the ache.

"I don't know." Something in my gut curled when I repeated

the faerie's warning to myself. *It will come for you—for all of us.* "But I have a feeling we'll know before long," I whispered into the night.

Rina remained on her back, the moon above us reflected in her wide eyes. She was purely human, yet she fought by our side on this journey, stepping into conflicts that were not her responsibility. For so long, she had shouldered so much more than she should have to.

"Rina?"

"Hm?" she hummed.

"If you weren't here, if the war hadn't happened and"—I took a breath—"your parents were alive…" She inhaled sharply. "What would you be doing with your life?" She was twenty-one with endless opportunities.

She turned her head to me and swallowed visibly. "I don't know."

"What did you want to do—before?"

I listened to the sounds of the forest, punctuated by the deep breathing of our friends while Rina considered her answer. I loved this time of night—when everything was still for a moment. Like the earth held its breath.

"Sometimes I thought I would become a healer. My mother loved it."

"That would be nice to honor her," I agreed, remembering her mother's gentle hands tending to wounds and how her daughter mimicked it.

"But when you all started the more rigorous training schedule, I wanted to do something physical, too." Her eyes searched the stars for an answer. "I started taking dance lessons. I think I'd like to do something with that."

Santorina had always been graceful, but I remembered that summer when the boys and I had been thirteen. We had been required to attend longer days of training and had hardly seen Santorina. It was the first time I'd truly felt the differences between our kinds.

Though I regretted never inquiring into her hobby before, I liked knowing that she had something she loved.

"That would be perfect for you," I said, rolling onto my back. "I'd like to see you dance sometime." I could picture her on one of those large stages in Palerman's arts district once repaired fully, spotlights gilding her. Leaping, twirling, every move controlled yet effortless, like she was floating. She'd be beautiful.

And if I did not live to see it, I'd guide her as a Spirit should, ensuring she found all the happiness her heart deserved.

After a beat of silence, Rina muttered, "I'm sorry about today."

I looked at the white light across her face and something warm flooded my chest. Similar to the feeling of a large sip of rum, yet different. More…peaceful, less blurry. I nuzzled into the sensation, letting it spread through my tired body.

"None of it was your fault. It was the damned fae male." The words were ash in my mouth as I watched the slight pink line on Rina's neck bob with each swallow.

She nodded slightly. "I need to train. I never want to be caught unaware again."

"Of course," I answered, guilt slicing through me at her fear. Why had I not insisted on this before? I had always strived to protect my friends, not considering that maybe they could protect themselves. "We can start tomorrow."

She reached beside her and handed me the dagger I'd lent her for the duration of the day. "This is yours."

"No." I shook my head. "You can keep it." It was one of the set Cyph had given me, but I had a feeling he would not mind us sharing them.

She nodded a second time, tucking the weapon to her chest. "The next time our paths cross with that faerie, he'll bleed."

I smiled at the steel glint in her eyes, the image and warmth in my body pulsing as I drifted to sleep. "That he will."

CHAPTER TWENTY-THREE

WHY HAD I HATED spears my entire life, when fighting with Malakai's in my hand felt so right?

Each time my arm slashed, I barely felt my conscious decision to make the maneuver. Like the weapon was an extension of myself. Even Jezebel could hardly keep up with me as we sparred, the sun beating down on us high in the sky.

"Don't look where you're going to strike before you do it," my sister coached, using the sleeve of her leathers to wipe sweat from her brow. "It's the only way I'm stopping your attacks right now. They're otherwise undetectable." Pride seeped into her words. Pride and a hint of relief as she caught glimpses of the side of me that she missed.

And I felt it, too, watching her in her element after such a perilous journey thus far.

"Right." I nodded, twirling the spear expertly between my fingers. How I could foreshadow a move I barely knew I was about to make was beyond me, but I did as she instructed. I tried to predict the power flowing through my muscles and control it.

Thankfully, the Curse seemed to be offering a reprieve for the moment.

We had risen before dawn and hiked the next stretch of rolling hills that morning, Tolek and I hobbling between the horses, his walking becoming steadier. When the sun rose high in the sky, we stopped to train in a small expanse of shaded grassland.

"Watch your stance," Jezebel ordered, tucking her hair behind her ears.

"Now you're finding nonexistent flaws," I fired back. I wiped the sweat from my forehead and shook out my tired limbs.

From his position lounging between the trees, Tolek barked a laugh and continued to write in his journal. Though his leg was healing—thank the Spirits—we insisted he sit out of our training session so he would have energy to continue on this afternoon. His eyes flitted between us and the spot behind me where Cypherion instructed Santorina on basic hand-to-hand combat, shouting instructions to both parties every few seconds. The dagger I'd given her glinted on her thigh.

"CK, good lad, show her the Alabath sisters' favorite move. The one that renders an opponent three times their size on his back before they've had time to blink."

"I believe that's their impressive charm," Cyph replied with a grin.

Jezebel and I rolled our eyes at them and prepared to duel once again. This time, she lunged first, but I moved to catch her blow with the hilt of Malakai's spear. She didn't follow through with the move—a feint, I realized.

I ducked her next slash to my left, losing my balance, and rolling across the grass before springing to my feet. I dropped the spear, unsheathing Starfire with the motion, and Jezebel laughed.

"Back to your sword?" she attempted to distract me.

"Why quit when it's a certain win?" I taunted.

She sighed, feigning boredom. "Always taking the easy way out."

I growled in response, Tol's laugh barely an echo as I honed in on my sister. I lunged. Unable to get her weapon raised in time, Jezebel lifted her wrist at the last moment. My blade landed against the metal guard she wore there, the clash echoing.

"You're lucky you still wear that," I reminded her, but the words were futile.

In the moments that it took me to speak, Jezebel had unsheathed a dagger from her thigh. In one motion, she brought it down upon me, a hairsbreadth closer than she intended.

The blade ripped through the sleeve of my training gear.

The fabric tore in slow motion.

Sunlight illuminated the discoloration of my skin as the material peeled back.

Each thread that was severed practically echoed in my ears, snapping the tentative hold I had on my secret one string at a time.

Jezebel dropped her weapon at the sight of the green-gray webbing printed on my skin, the black center nearly throbbing by the light of day. A wave of ice settled over me as my sister's horrified stare met mine.

Color leached from her heart-shaped face the moment Jezebel realized I bore the Curse.

Chapter Twenty-Four

"Keep fighting," I whispered, the world resuming its roar of motion and sound. I prayed Tolek had not noticed my sister freeze.

Jezebel only stared at me, her mouth popping open into a perfect circle of stunned silence, hands hanging loosely at her sides. I could not remember a time I saw her so shocked, tawny eyes so wide. Her chest rose and fell rapidly.

"Please, Jezzie," I urged. "Please, don't let them know." I adjusted my sweat-slicked grip on my weapons.

Jezebel's eyebrows rose, but I watched as she tried to work through the truth and slowly recovered her fallen weapons. Tremors wracked her hands, but she backed up a few paces, preparing to parry.

I looked over my shoulder. Tolek had risen to Rina's side and, using a fallen branch as a makeshift cane, was assisting with her stance. His eyes were locked on her feet as he stretched his cane forward to nudge them into the precise position.

I exhaled a sigh of relief.

"We're going to go rinse off," I called to their trio, grabbing Jezebel's wrist and pulling her after me into the cypher trees, low-hanging branches blocking us from view immediately.

I didn't stop walking until we were far enough away that their voices had drifted into silence. Only the noises of woodland creatures, a trickle of the stream, and Jezzie's ragged breathing surrounded us now.

Turning to my sister, I set my spear and Starfire on the ground softly, keeping my movements slow and controlled. Sunlight streamed through the branches, highlighting her horror-stricken face. I hated the expression painted across her features. It crawled beneath my skin and clawed at my gut.

She was terrified—of me.

I wanted nothing more than to embrace her, run a hand down her back to ease the many fears mounting in her mind. Chase away those shadows like our mother had when we were young and woke frightened in the night. But we were no longer children, and the fear was not sprouted from a figment of nightmare. It was real. The web on my arm was real.

Hiding was not an option.

"Jezebel, please," I begged softly, lowering my impaired wrist to my side. "It's okay, I won't let it get near you."

"What?" She jolted into motion, my words awakening her. Her eyebrows crinkled inward.

"The Curse..." I breathed, the words a tingle on my tongue. It was the first time I had spoken it aloud to anyone other than Damien. "I won't let it hurt you. It is my burden to shoulder."

She rolled her eyes, folding her arms across her chest. "Ophelia, if the Curse is in your blood, it is in mine, as well." She spoke as if I was being ridiculous. Her words were firm, but I didn't miss the subtle inspection of her own wrists.

Then I realized, the fear I had seen on her face was not fear of me. It was fear *for* me. Fear for what I was to face because of the Curse.

She raised her chin, only a flicker of that fear lingering in her eyes. "The hand has been dealt. We are Cursed. But if this is to be our plague, I will face it with you so that you won't greet darkness alone."

My stomach plummeted at her words. My sister—my strong, charismatic, fearless gift of a sister was prepared to look death in the face for me. It was a bit odd that she did not react more to the thought of her death, but I didn't question it. A warm air snaked around my shoulders, bolstering me.

I took two tentative steps toward her, assessing her comfort at having my scarred body so close. "Jezebel," I exhaled, relieved when she did not back away. I gripped her hand. "You were born fearless and have not let our corrupt world take that from you. I love that steel heart of yours." I shook my hair back from my face. "But you will not greet this with me."

Her fingers curved around mine. "What do you mean?"

"The Curse did not appear on Mother or Father. It has not soiled the blood of either branch of our ancestors, nor has it been reported on a single Mystique in the past two years. I am the lone case, and for reasons known only to the Spirits, it has chosen me."

Tears welled in my sister's eyes as she grasped the truth. "I will not lose you, Ophelia." She squeezed my hand tighter like she could hold me to the earth with pure will. "You will not walk this path alone."

Her words brought the stinging sensation to my eyes, too. "I don't have a choice."

"How long?" Jezebel asked, ignoring my affirmation.

"It appeared two days before my birthday."

Her eyes flashed to mine. "And you hid it?" When I nodded, she added, "Your speech." It wasn't a question, but an understanding of the toast I had given at my birthday.

I nodded again, squeezing her hand gently.

"You've been different. I thought—" She stumbled. "I hoped you were returning to your old self, but you were saying goodbye."

"Jezebel, I lost everything two years ago. The man I love, my future, our people." My voice rose with hysterics, words tangled between sobs and screams as thoughts I had not dared voice previously poured from my lips. "I have been wandering aimlessly, a shell of the person I was born to become. There was *nothing* in my life that could restore me. And when this affliction appeared on my skin…I was afraid, at first. But I was only afraid for Mother and

Father. For you. I was never afraid for myself. When I learned that I was the only one Cursed, I wept with relief. Relief because if this takes my life, I won't have to suffer anymore. I will no longer have to choose between fighting and surrendering."

I took a deep breath to steady my sobs. "I am tired, Jezzie. I am tired of trying to remedy things that may be beyond repair. If the Curse takes me, I won't have to try anymore. I can rest. This journey is my last battle, and I have every intention of seeing it completed, but when the Curse finally progresses, I will greet death with open arms."

Jezebel wrenched her hand from my grasp. "No!" she shouted in my face. "No, you're giving up."

"Is that so bad? I watched two of my closest friends nearly die—I watched you nearly die. I can't take any more pain."

"What happened to me was no mere accident, and I am *fine.* You don't get to use any of that as an excuse." She sighed. "You do not surrender, Ophelia. That isn't you."

I threw my arms out, gesturing to the air around me. "I don't have another option." And when I admitted those words, my own heart sank.

"We can fight it." She turned to the stream and paced along its edge, the slowly flowing water a mere shadow of her flustered movements.

"I am trying, but I don't know how. I can feel it burrowing into my veins, my blood. The pain..." I stopped at the look on her face. She didn't need to hear about the agony I'd been battling, even as it tore through me.

"It should have taken you by now." I could see her mind working feverishly, searching for an answer. A way out. "You should have died on your birthday, Ophelia, and yet no one has even noticed any symptoms. This is...I don't know what this is. But it feels different." Her eyes searched me from head to toe, silent desperation radiating from her.

Silent desperation and hope.

Hope that I couldn't bear to take from her, because doing so would be killing the spark of it that had formed within myself, as well. The spark that lit when I began this journey toward the Undertaking, and was fed each day by the spirits of my friends around me. One that wanted to turn into a roaring fire capable of forging my broken pieces back together.

No matter how accepting I was of the Curse, I needed that spark to face the end.

"You're right," I agreed. I watched the grass curling around my feet as I continued, "It is progressing slowly."

"And why did it resurface? Why now? Why you?" With her faith in me, her tan skin had assumed its usual glow.

I shook my head, blonde hair shimmering in the edges of my vision. "I don't know that either." Damien's words echoed through my mind—*Chosen Child.*

"Promise me something, Ophelia," Jezebel begged, hurrying to me and grabbing both of my hands between hers. "Promise me that you will fight it until your dying breath."

The silver blurring her eyes was impossible to refuse. They bared the feeble, fearful side of her so rarely seen.

"Okay," I whispered, squeezing her hands. "But we cannot tell the others. I need them to remain strong. I need their confidence to face what's coming."

With her nod, that singular spark of hope warmed my shattered heart.

Chapter Twenty-Five

THE LAST TWO DAYS of travel passed in a blur. Beneath an unseasonably hot spring sun, with little breeze to cool the sweat beading under our leathers, we marched toward the end of our journey.

The end of the trek, but the beginning of the battle.

I held up a hand, signaling Sapphire and my friends to stop along the spot where grasslands turned to barren desert. Black dirt and volcanic sand stretched before us, absorbing the heat from the sun and bouncing it into the air, ripples blurring the landscape. Tendrils of smoke, remnants from the top of the Spirit Volcano, drifted through the air, clouded our nostrils and stung our eyes.

In that vast expanse of desert, there was nowhere to hide. We were left completely at the mercy of the elements and whatever else lay in wait.

My stomach churned as I took in the tundra.

I looked to Jezebel on my left, and we exchanged a grim smile. The invisible cord of secrecy between us tightened with her nod of encouragement, reminding me that she would be at my side until the end. Beneath the linen covering I had fastened around my wrist, the Curse pulsed.

"Is everyone ready?" I asked, but the question was futile. Only stalling for time.

"We're ready," Santorina answered, her voice strong in the face of the unknown.

I looked to Tolek, atop his horse once again. My eyes landed on the dirty bandages wrapping his wound. "Are you sure? You can wait here."

His eyes hardened. "No, I cannot." He would not.

I understood.

I scanned the weapons strapped to my body. A dagger strapped to my thigh. Malakai's spear and Starfire. My own determination and desire to outrun the limit on my life. It was all I'd need.

"Let's go, then." I snapped Sapphire's reins and she stepped forward, one hoof sinking into the black sand. It took her a few strides to understand the earth beneath her. It was not the cool grasses she was used to prancing through. There were no wildflowers curving around her legs, brushing her coat and coaxing her forward in peaceful encouragement.

This ground was different. Energy radiated up through it, a presence of its own. Like the earth was somehow alive, and a sleeping giant had settled in its core, projecting its power up through the land. Shock waves passed through Sapphire, into me—the lifeblood of our entire world centralized within the mountain range we traveled toward.

The horses' steps were unsteady at first, but within a few strides they began marching across the sinister sand with ownership. I smiled at Sapphire despite the discomfort gnawing at my mind. She truly was a feat of the gods.

But this place was not. The barren land stretching out for miles between us and the Spirit Volcano did not reflect the sublime vision I had of our most sacred land. In the many times I'd visited Damenal as a girl, I'd never seen the tundra. A part of me was glad I hadn't. If I'd known of the way the air tingled against my skin or the slinking presence that pumped my blood faster through my veins, I may have been afraid.

I had no room for fear.

We had barely traveled fifty yards when the ground beneath us shook, that sleeping beast waking. Violent tremors rocked through Sapphire's body and into my own, my bones grinding against each other. I clenched every muscle in my body to stay seated atop my horse.

"Stay true," I called over the earth's roar. The two words the warriors spoke in a time of fear.

But the encouragement was lost among a swelling growl to the north. My heart pounded behind my ribs with the mounting sound. I swiveled atop Sapphire, unprepared for the horde of monstrous, wolf-like creatures breaking the horizon. Claws and teeth flashed in the tangle of sunlight and smoky haze. Yellow eyes honed in on their prey.

On us.

"By the ever-damned Angels," Tolek muttered.

Our mares took off like the wind, traveling south—away from the beasts—but I pulled on Sapphire's reins. We needed to go toward the Spirit Volcano.

But if we continued that way, we would intersect the beasts chasing us. Meet them head-on in a fatal clash of weapons and claws.

I swallowed my fear of that attack. We did not have a choice.

Sapphire yielded, understanding my direction, and her gallop quickened as she changed course toward the base of the volcano. Her movements were swift, the landscape beside us blurring into a mess of black ash as we flew over the sand. The horses' hooves kicked soot into the air. My vision blurred, eyes burning, but I blinked away the tears, laying my panic to rest with each flutter of my lashes.

I lay flat against Sapphire's neck and kicked my heels into her side, glancing toward the wolves. They moved with a preternatural speed and grace. Howls echoed from the pack as they surged forward in a flash of silver fur and onyx claws, traveling at a diagonal. Toward us, but also toward the base of the volcano.

Terror dug its nails into my stomach. If we didn't hurry, they would form a wall between us and the rocky surface. How had I not predicted this type of challenge on the tundra? I feared that the Undertaking would end before it even began.

No. I gritted my teeth. That couldn't happen. They could not be allowed to unify between us and the volcano. We could fight them one-on-one, pick them off as the pack traveled, but breaching a solid formation from this side would be so much harder.

"Faster," I breathed to Sapphire. "Come on, girl."

But the wolves were faster still. I flicked my gaze to them every other second. They gained ground.

These couldn't be normal wolves. Not with their unnatural size and speed. Much like the ink that etched my tattoo, the pack had to be enhanced. The aura of the unseen geysers of magic seeping from the earth worked its way into their systems, bulking their muscles and sharpening their senses. Building the strongest guardians for the first defense of the Mystique Mountains and the Spirit Volcano.

"They're imbued!" I called over my shoulder, ignoring the horror that gripped my stomach at the realization.

"How will we outrun the damn things, then?" Tolek yelled.

"Running from a fight, Vincienzo?" Jezebel coughed over the smoke.

Cypherion reached for his scythe. "I thought I'd never see the day."

"You still haven't," Tolek growled, speeding past me with his sword in hand.

Angels, they were ridiculous. But I smiled at my brigade of courage and chaos. I unsheathed Starfire from my hip, raising her above my head. Her blade became a beacon of light against the clouded sky and mountain-scape.

"We fight!" I bellowed. Four war cries echoed my own.

More than twenty wolves charged at us. I stood in the stirrups, my muscles screaming from the days of riding and hiking I had put my body through, but my heart sang louder.

In a mess of whinnies, howls, and screams, fur, flesh, and blood, we collided with the wolves. Sapphire reared up beneath me, and I tangled my hand in her blue mane, squeezing my thighs. My breath hitched when she used her front feet to knock aside a wolf as large as herself.

A devilish smile crossed my lips. *My warrior horse.*

I pulled Malakai's spear from my back, feeling the energy pass through my flesh. With a weapon in each hand, I greeted the first test of my Mystique Warrior future.

My heart pounded with each movement, but I latched on to the echoing beat as a point of focus, drowning out my terror. I raised the spear over my shoulder and brought it forward with all the force in my body. It sank into the closest wolf's side, not even deep enough to meet bone. When I pulled it out, a small but steady trickle of red seeped into the gray fur.

The animal crumpled to the sand, its growls ceasing within a cloud of black dirt.

I gaped at the wolf, unsure if it was truly slain.

One strike. And a nonfatal one at that. Its large chest continued to rise and fall as the blood slowed, but the animal showed no sign of moving. This creature was instilled with the magic of our mountains, but one puncture was all it took to defeat it.

My mind whirled, battle continuing around me. Magic always had motives. The wolves were no arbitrary guard. They were creatures of the mountains—powerful and mystical and protective—blessed by Lynxenon for a *purpose*, but not for unjustified destruction.

They were not here to eliminate potential warriors as they approached the Undertaking—at least, not all warriors. No, they were a threat that needed to be thwarted in order to advance. Draw blood and the candidate proved themselves worthy. Allow them to draw it first, and it may be the last thing you ever do.

"Do not aim to kill!" I called across the roar of battle. "They only need to be wounded." The Spirits' magic would heal them later.

"Drive them toward the volcano," Cypherion directed. I turned Sapphire at his words, aiming toward where he was chased by two wolves. I ripped my dagger from my thigh and launched it at one. It stuck in the beast's back leg, dragging it to the ground. I swiped it back up as Sapphire ran past the animal.

Our small band pushed back against the pack, the base of the Spirit Volcano looming ahead of us. But we were moving too slowly. Not gaining enough ground.

I slashed and stabbed any piece of gray fur that reached too near my body, losing count of the fallen wolves. But they *were* falling. Gray forms littered the ground, looking no more fearsome than oversized pups.

Catching my breath, I looked over the feud occurring on the tundra, seeking my next victim, but that brief pause left me exposed.

A set of shining obsidian claws grasped on to my left arm, sharpened points tearing into the skin and muscle. I cried out against the burning tear of my flesh. The only thing that kept Starfire in my hand was my years of training. *No one would take my sword.*

The beast's other paw reached up and sank into my side, tearing a second scream from my throat. The three-inch-long nails sliced through the firm muscle of my obliques. Dark spots clouded my vision. I tried to drag air into my lungs, nearly choking on smoke. My body begged me to give in to the pain.

"Ophelia!" My friends' screams sounded so far away, like they came from another place entirely. Here it was just me, the wolf, and the blinding slice of its claws.

The predator rose onto its hind legs, using my body to pull itself up. Each tug burned as it tore my skin further, the beast's weight ripping into me. In a swooping motion, it pulled me from the saddle, throwing me to the sand.

Somewhere, Sapphire whinnied.

Pain echoed through my body. A thunderstorm of agony that reached every inch of my bones so deeply, I was sure it would destroy me.

No, I swore as I looked into the yellow eyes of the wolf looming over me. Menacing drool dripped from its jaw, closer every second, until those shining obsidian teeth were all I could see. *No, I have come this far. I will not crumple.*

A strangled roar of determination and anguish broke from me as I rolled toward the beast, cradling my injuries. It snapped its jaw open, aiming for my neck. The flash of shining ebony teeth would haunt me for centuries to come.

I drove my uninjured elbow into the wolf's snout. The beast let out a stunned yelp, fading into an angry snarl. My fingers curled around Starfire's hilt. But then, hooves slammed into the wolf's side, forcing it back.

I breathed a ragged sigh of relief. With an unsteady motion, I dragged Starfire from the dirt and swung her over my body. She felt so heavy in my tired arms, but I swiped across the paw of the wolf—the only part I could reach. Blood splattered me.

As if one, the wolf and I both collapsed into the dirt.

For a moment, I breathed, watched the dust swirl above me, the roar of battle dull in my ears. Then, the air kissed the wounds to my arm and torso, stinging the damaged flesh. I wanted to scream, wanted to cry out against the searing pain.

Hooves pounded beside me, Sapphire's worried blue eyes gazing down at me. She lowered her head, nudging me to get up. She'd been the only one able to reach me as the wolf attacked. She'd saved me.

"Thank you," I whispered, dragging a hand down her nose.

But I didn't have time for anything else. Growls ripped through the air, weapons and grunts echoing. My friends were screaming out to me, begging me to rise. Before they became so distraught that the distraction got them killed, I pushed myself to my feet, leaning on Sapphire. Holy fucking Spirits, the pain was unbearable.

Wrapping my good arm around my torso and applying pressure to the slices in my side, I somehow swung myself into the saddle, squeezing my thighs as my only source of stability. The world spun. Pain took over my body. Bright red blood seeped from me onto Sapphire's white hide, and I cringed.

I chanced a look at my arm, the tangled mess of flesh and shining muscles nearly making me vomit. On my side, blood thickened beneath my palm, sticky and warm.

Please, whatever Angels and Spirits are watching, heal me quickly.

I forced my vision to focus on the battle that was still raging. We'd taken out nearly half of the wolves, but each that fell fueled their pack more.

Jezebel took out her last predator and broke away, galloping toward me, spear sheathed behind her back as she lay flat against Elektra.

"Stop!" I shouted over shaking breaths. It made my head spin, but I held up my hand as an explanation. The sunlight glinted off my crimson fingers, and our eyes met, a thousand unsaid words between us. Her face paled, devastation crumpling her delicate features: I was Cursed. She could not approach while my blood flowed.

Her lips formed a tight line, but she nodded, turning on an attacking wolf with renewed ferocity. Enacting her revenge for what they did to me.

"There are too many of them," Rina shouted, the use of her meager training against the beasts impressive.

Half of the wolves lay slumbering across the heated black sand, but there were still a dozen awake and hungry for our blood.

Their attack paused, and the world around me slowed. Horror tightened my chest as the pack worked with human-like determination, spreading out their ranks and forming a half circle around us. The silver hair on the backs of their necks raised, obsidian teeth snapping.

In the center of their formation, a wolf larger and darker than the rest nearly blended into the sand. It prowled on long, muscled legs, lifting its muzzle to the sky and howling. The others responded, flanking it protectively and echoing the sound.

My own pack's movement mirrored the wolves, coming to my side. They didn't bother to inquire after my injuries—they could see for themselves that I was not okay—but four pairs of eyes swept across my torn flesh and leathers. They knew that it would not stop me.

The yellow eyes of the central wolf narrowed at me, appraising an opponent, and I recognized the beast for what it was.

"That one." My voice was low and strained, but I pointed with my blade, injured arm throbbing as I extended it. "That's the leader. Take it out, and the rest follow."

"They'll never allow us near it," Jezebel cautioned, eyes locked on the creature.

Before anyone could respond, Cypherion broke from our formation and charged. Not for the leader, but for the right flank of their semicircle. To where three wolves waited for him, hunger in their eyes and growls echoing from their snapping jaws.

The movement was so sudden that all of the wolves looked his way, shifting to where he rode toward certain death at their paws.

"Cypherion, no!" The shriek left my lips before I realized what was happening. Every part of me screamed.

I snapped Sapphire's reins, and my friends launched into motion beside me. I willed my horse to fly over the earth. Move fast enough to catch him, to help him. Because there were too many wolves—even Cypherion Kastroff could not handle them alone.

But his eyes met mine, and I understood—he did not mean to defeat them. He rode toward those wolves knowing it was likely the last decision he ever made.

The leader, he told me with a flick of his gaze.

It is okay, his sharp nod said.

The determination in his bright blue eyes stilled my heart—not an ounce of fear lingered there.

He'd sacrifice himself for this. Provide a distraction to save us.

We all chased after him, but he barked, "Don't waste it," over his shoulder, and we froze.

No, Cypherion could not do this. He could not ride away from us. I would not stand another loss in my life.

But Cyph was fast atop Erini, and none of us would ever stop them in the race to those vicious claws. His sacrifice would be carried out, and *I could not stop it.* My hesitation would only risk the lives of the friends with us.

Giving into a moment of weakness, I squeezed my eyes shut, attempting to turn off my natural instinct to protect. Adrenaline pumped through me, my body understanding what must be done, though my mind refused to accept it. I shut down the reason in my brain, allowing my body to take control. I hated myself for it, but I could not squander Cyph's bravery.

I would not waste his sacrifice.

I pulled Sapphire back toward the volcano and turned my back on Cypherion, not watching what carnage came from his diversion. Tears streaked through the soot and blood coating my face, falling into the wind like it would carry them to him in a silent goodbye.

Sapphire and I charged the largest wolf, releasing every ounce of rage that flooded my veins at the thought of my friend giving himself to the pack. My inability to stop it.

My ruined arm pulsed with pain, my side matching it. My Cursed arm throbbed, the affliction a lightning bolt through my skin, but I ignored it all. It was nothing to the ache of Cypherion now tearing through my heart.

Sapphire took three long gallops and leaped into the air, soaring effortlessly over the massive form of the wolf leader. A tormented scream harsher than a riling storm left my throat as I swung to the side. My muscles…my wounds…every part of me echoed the roar as I fought with every ounce of strength I had left to stay on my horse, and brought Starfire down.

My blade connected, slicing true and strong across the alpha's shoulder before the steady presence of Sapphire disappeared.

The last thing I saw as I tumbled to the earth was the body of the giant wolf crashing to the ground. I sighed in relief as my head connected with the earth and darkness swooped in.

Chapter Twenty-Six

Malakai

BLACK FADED TO GRAY, spots of dim light puncturing the veil that had dropped over my vision. Why *the fuck* had they knocked me out again? To move me, obviously, but what about this move required my unconsciousness? What did they not want me to know? The questions swirled within my dizzy mind.

"Wakey wakey, Warrior Prince," the chilling voice of my usual guard cooed.

"Oh, shut *up*, will you?" The second voice sent a tremor up my spine, but I righted myself before they could see. *He* had returned. That explained the secrecy.

I fought to shake the remaining tethers of unconsciousness. I needed to be alert. Sliding my eyelids open slowly, I surveyed my surroundings. This was a new one: They had me chained deep within a cavernous room, wrists restrained above my head. Cracked rock walls surrounded me, reaching to the wide mouth of the cave. There was no door—they clearly did not expect me to get out of these chains—but the tunnel outside the cave's mouth branched in three directions and stretched on, an orange glow ebbing in the distance.

"Change of scenery today?" I projected my strained voice as best as I could, words slurring slightly. I felt oddly tired; the wound from the blow to my head was healing, but the dregs of drowsiness remained. More drugs, I reasoned. They were certainly becoming more liberal with their use of the substances lately.

My captor prowled closer, gray cloak dragging across the ground. The end and collar were in tatters as though picked apart by nervous fingers, and the thing smelled slightly like he hadn't taken it off in days. My skin tingled with each step he took toward me; even my body was aware that his recurring presence meant nothing good.

"You insolent *fool.*" He looked over with a searing stare. "You never will learn, will you?" His words landed heavily, like rocks dropping into my stomach one after another, but I kept my expression neutral.

"Appears I won't." I shrugged my shoulders as much as was possible with the position of my arms. The mouthy guard pulled my chains tighter. I released a pained groan but took the hint. Movement would be punished.

Even my captor flinched at the involuntary noise that escaped my throat.

"I've tried so hard to show you, Malakai." His eyes were dazed. Pupils wild. Unhinged. Nothing that I recognized lurked in there, like something inside of him had snapped. The leash he'd worn for the past two years tugged ferociously, pulling him deeper into the darkness that festered within him.

I knew that with each tug he fell further away from humanity, and that could mean nothing good for my future here.

I struggled against my chains, but they pulled tighter, twisting my arms. "Show me what?" I grunted. The scar his ring left across my jaw the last time we met twinged.

"The truth," he snapped. "To make you understand why it must be this way. Why *we* must be this way."

He was inches from my face now, and I searched his expression for any sign of remorse.

I was met with cold, uncaring steel.

"You've shown me nothing," I rasped.

"You have not been ready."

"You're vile and moronic." We threw the accusations at each other, both waiting to see whose insults would land first. When he did not react, I added, "It does *not* need to be this way." I would not beg, I would not plead, but I was not above persuasion.

He shook his head, hands coming to my face, dirty nails curving inward. With each one that dug into my cheeks, the rocks in my stomach piled higher. I tried to wrench my jaw from his icy grip, unable to bear the feeling of his fingers on me, but his nails gouged further. I was sure I'd have ten matching crescent marks on my cheeks.

"I am the truth, Malakai. I am power and destiny and unification." His voice rose to an airy, triumphant sound that ground an unsettled feeling deeper into my gut. In the years I'd known him, he'd changed. In those swirling, manic eyes, there was no hint of the man I thought I knew. Distantly, I wondered what had happened. How we'd both ended up here, chains around my wrists and darkness in his soul. But when he curled his fingers deeper against my cheeks, I shook off the questions.

"*Not like this*," I growled.

"There is *only* this," my captor snapped. He released my face and took a step back. As his eyes traveled over my body, catching on the many open wounds I had suffered at his word, I hated him more than ever.

He met my stare, eyes framed by dark brows and purple circles. "The reckoning is upon us. I fought so hard for it to not come to this, but the other players in our great game of fate are relentless. They were not easily deterred despite my greatest efforts." He shrugged, black hair skimming his shoulders, and lowered his voice. "*So be it.*"

He gathered himself, raising his chest in a show of power. The air around us stilled, and I felt the bomb he was going to drop just before it exploded. "She is here. And she will die."

It erupted, shrapnel shredding every inch of my skin, the heat of the metaphorical blast burning my eyes, blood, and heart.

"She..." My voice faltered, bile creeping up my throat. She...no. That was not possible. I lost all pretense of calm. "You can't!" My words tore through the air, my stomach contracting as heaves rolled through me. The rocks overflowed my gut now, filling my chest cavity. They would be my anchor, dragging me to my death.

I thrashed wildly against my chains, kicking until the cavern was filled with nothing but sounds of metal against rock and his haunting words echoing in my ears. My drugged muscles screamed in agony, straining against the cuffs that bit into my wrists and ankles.

My brain couldn't form words. The unconscious haze—whatever they had worked into my system—tried to take me again.

The one thought that had become my sanctuary turned to dust as his words sank into my bones. *She is here. And she will die.*

The promise that lit an ember of hope within me these past two years shredded.

The spark extinguished.

I was broken.

Chapter Twenty-Seven

Ophelia

Pressure. And pain.

The two alternated, cutting through the wave of oblivion until my entire body hurt.

The images came back to me. How I ended up sinking into this darkness. Teeth and claws, the wind on my face and Sapphire beneath me, the gleam on my blade as I slashed across fur.

Soothing hands caressed my face. They were gentle, beseeching. I wanted to lean into their touch and allow myself that moment of reprieve. But when a trickle of something warm ran down my temple I snapped to the present.

Someone was touching my face, where I was bleeding tainted blood.

No, no, no. No one could touch me.

My eyes opened. Tolek was leaning over me, worry creasing his battle-worn face. His cheeks were smeared with dirt, but he bore no obvious injuries. He looked into my eyes deeply, searching for a hint of life.

I was lying in the black sand of the tundra, trying to make sense of the mysterious way the sunlight streaked through the trails of smoke and organize my racing thoughts. My head was in Tol's lap, resting on his uninjured thigh as his hand gently stroked hair away from the wound on my temple.

"Hey," he said, his voice thick. "We've been waiting for you."

I scrambled away from him. The movement sent a wave of pain through my body, and the black earth around me spun. "Don't touch me," I wheezed over the soot in my throat. *Don't touch my blood.*

Rina halted where she had been dressing the wound in my side with strips of damp linen. My eyes went to her hands, and my stomach lurched. From finger to forearm, she shone crimson with my tainted blood. But she was human—she would be okay.

"Ophelia…" Relief vanished from Tolek's eyes, replaced by pain. "What's wrong?" He stretched a hesitant hand toward me, streaks of deep red across his palm and leathers. The world continued to tilt as I pushed myself to my hands and knees and emptied the contents of my stomach into the sand. Repeatedly.

I had worked so hard to conceal the Curse. To not only keep it from spreading, but to keep anyone from knowing. This was the result—my undeniably caring friend coming into contact with my blood with the intention of healing me. My already-broken heart was ripped in two, realizing what I'd condemned Tolek to. This was my failure.

Only when the bile had stopped stinging my throat did I raise my head and look around us to the empty landscape. The wolves' bodies had vanished.

"Where did they go?" I asked through a mouth that tasted sour. Tolek's cheeks drooped when I ignored him, but I could not face him yet.

"We don't know," Rina explained, still looking at me questioningly. "They went down as you did, and sank into the earth." She uncapped a canteen and extended it to me. I thanked her, using it to rinse my mouth out. Everything was still so muddled.

As I had suspected, the wolves were connected to the volcano. When I had slayed the alpha, it took out the rest. The leader—

My thoughts froze as the full sequence of events came back to me. I spat water onto the black sand and cleared my throat, afraid to ask the next question. "Cypherion?"

Tolek only inclined his head, still silent. I squeezed my eyes shut to fight the stinging rising to them. Spirits, Cyph—

"I'm here," a weakened, deep voice answered behind me.

I whirled toward it, ignoring the inclination to vomit again at the motion, and ran bloody hands through my tangled hair, gripping it at the scalp. Sobs lodged in my throat, relief turning my bones to jelly.

"Cyph." Despite my injuries, I staggered to him, falling to my knees beside his prostrate body, but keeping my distance to avoid shedding blood on him. My sister sat on his other side, legs curled beneath her.

"What happened?" I demanded.

Cypherion grimaced. "We needed a distraction."

I didn't want to chastise him for that now, but I swore to the Spirits if he ever did anything like that again, I'd murder him myself.

"How are you alive?" My side throbbed, and I wrapped an arm around my torso, but it seemed a good thing that I was moving.

"You were just fast enough, Ophelia."

I understood. He dove into the fray of the wolves knowing that it might mean his end, but also guessing that his sacrifice would fuel me with an unstoppable anger. He rode toward death thinking I may take out the alpha, and subsequently the pack, before his life was forfeit. But had he been wrong, he would have given himself regardless. To inspire my mission.

"You martyred yourself," I gasped. "Only the strongest of the Mystiques would have made that choice." I smiled through the gentle stream of tears trickling down my cheeks. His eyes lit with understanding of the words I wasn't saying.

He ducked his chin, but when his shoulders shifted, he groaned. My eyes scanned his body, taking in the unnatural stillness of him. Barely anything below his neck moved.

The world spun again. "You're hurt," I whispered.

But he's alive, I reminded myself.

"I am," he confirmed. Sweat stuck his auburn hair to his forehead, fresh drops forming despite the cooling air.

Silent tears fell from my eyes as I watched his eyelids flutter against the agony. He did this—risked his life—for me. One of my closest friends, who longed for a sense of where he belonged, sacrificed himself so that I could fulfill this twisted angelic prophecy. *Fuck the Angels*, I thought, not caring if they somehow heard me. *Fuck Damien and the rest of them for this mission and all it's brought upon us.* I needed these people alive, and this journey continuously threatened that.

Cypherion bit his lips before elaborating. "My back. Something snapped when I collided with the wolves."

There was so much pain layered beneath the thick tone of his voice. I swallowed my tears and the outburst that fought its way up my throat, knowing he needed me to be calm, to assume the presence he so frequently served for us.

"Can you feel your legs?" I asked gently, shifting slightly closer to look at the bottom half of his body. His feet did not move in their leather boots.

"Yes, I think I can move them, but the pain is too great to try." A muscle in his thigh twitched and he clamped his lips together, the veins in his neck straining. Jezebel used her sleeve to wipe the fresh beads of sweat from his face.

"We're waiting for the mountains to heal him," my sister explained, taking over the story to let him rest. Our eyes met, and I saw her silent plea of relief in the way her jaw wobbled. *I'm glad you woke up*, her eyes said. *And I'm sorry I couldn't stop him.* Her gaze flicked over my shoulder, to Tol's bloodied hands.

I shook my head.

"How long has it been?" I asked, glancing between her and Cyph, who had closed his eyes again and let his head fall back to the sand.

"Our guess is nearly six hours," Jezebel claimed.

I inhaled that fact. I had been out for *six hours*. Left defenseless for that long. Lost that much time getting to the volcano. But—"There's been no more attacks?"

Jezebel shook her head. "No, not a whisper of anything."

"I can feel it," Cyph clipped, eyes still shut. "The healing magic. Have for hours now."

"You can?" I leaned in.

Cyph nodded, his lips tightening. "Yes, it's tingling along my spine. It's like...ice and fire at once."

And when he said it, I felt it as well. Slowly, I peeled away the bandage Rina had applied. The edges of the wounds felt like they were rimmed in flame, but dancing inside—buried deep beneath the skin and inching upward—was what felt like a trickle of ice water.

The two sensations, heating and freezing, crawled toward each other in a deadly dance of burning and calming. Landing somewhere between pleasure and pain. Somewhere that I couldn't name. If it had been a physical place, I would have basked in it, but I had a feeling it also had the power to kill me. This magic, whatever it was, was fickle. Good and evil in one.

I screwed my eyes up against the sensation, giving myself over to the magic that had been building within me for hours. My friends around me fell silent, barely breathing as the visible signs of healing set in.

I squinted down at my arm, watching as the blood on my skin and torn leathers hardened. The flesh did not stitch itself back together entirely, but it inched closer before our eyes until the wounds looked days old.

The mangled skin of my left forearm now bore a new mark. Beneath the Bind, a series of pink scars took shape, ringing my flesh as a reminder of what we survived.

"Whoa..." Tolek breathed.

My eyes flashed up to his, and we smiled at each other. He reached down to run a hand along my hair, crimson fingers a beacon. I averted my gaze, sinking into the guilt that washed through me.

The sun had climbed high in the sky and was passing back down. We could not be caught on the tundra when it set, but one look at Cypherion had me clamping my lips between my teeth.

He gave so much; I could give this time for him.

But it was Cyph who said, "We need to keep moving." He had pushed himself to a seated position and reclined on his hands, though the curved arc of his spine and the buckling of his elbows did not look comfortable.

"Don't be ridiculous," Jezebel began. She and Tolek had spent the last hour arguing over who had slain the most wolves, while Rina cleaned our wounds one at a time and made us all eat something for strength. I had been careful to keep away from Jezebel and Cypherion until my blood had stopped flowing, nervously watching Tolek for any hints of pain. He'd come in contact with my blood hours ago, but I was not sure how long the affliction took to set in.

I twisted my hair between my hands—which were now clean thanks to the last of the water in my canteen—ignoring my desire to insist on moving.

"I'm being pragmatic, Jezzie," Cypherion responded, not unkindly. "We don't want to be on the tundra when the sun sets." We all glanced up to it. It had passed its highest point hours ago and begun its descent, dimming the clear blue of the sky as it went.

"Are you sure?" Tolek asked, eyes boring into his friend's with an intensity he rarely let others see. He stood with his hands locked behind his back, but his fingers fidgeted as anxiously as his eyes. I resonated with the pain flowing from him.

Cypherion nodded, though, and four sets of hands moved to help him to his feet.

After a minute of struggling, he was standing. Cyph was standing, with his arms around my sister's and Tolek's shoulders. He limped forward, his right leg dragging through the dirt as he winced. "It might take a bit longer to get back to normal. Maybe a visit to the Bodymelders." The minor clan whose power specialized in influence over healing, muscular repairs, and physical strength would certainly be able to restore Cypherion's balance if our mountains could not fully mend him.

"I bet you'd have a great time there," Tolek said. "Oh, shall we make a wager on it? What about—"

"No bets on this," I interrupted, then looked only at Cyph. "You'll heal."

I believed it fully because I had felt that magic heal near fatal wounds to my body. I knew what it was capable of. He *would* heal.

As I turned toward the volcano, grabbing Sapphire's reins to walk her, I heard Cyph murmur to Tolek, "What bet did you have in mind?" and I smiled to myself.

We walked slowly to cater to Cyph's limp and our exhaustion. Every inch of my body ached, begging for hours—days—of sleep that I couldn't indulge. I shut out any hint of weakness and channeled my energy into that of the mountains. *Draw from it, heal body and spirit, rise stronger.* That was my mantra in these final moments of calm.

When the sand turned to pebbles and the pebbles turned to rocks, we stopped. We had arrived at the base of the Spirit Volcano.

Though I felt as if I was leaving a piece of myself behind, I walked Sapphire to an area near the entrance to the volcano where it was clear that other warriors had tethered their horses before us. I left her loose though—I didn't want her tied up when I was gone.

Her eyes were endless pools of crystalline water when she stared at me. I tangled my fingers in her mane, bringing my lips to her nose. "Thank you for everything, girl."

Her exhale brought a stinging to the back of my eyes, and I couldn't help but hug her tightly, running my hands along her soft neck. Assuming I survived what waited for me in that volcano and the Curse did not take my life yet, I would be a new warrior the next time I saw her.

When I pulled back, she nudged my shoulder, as if to tell me to get on with it. To claim my destiny.

I met the others at the entrance to the pathway up the volcano when they were ready. We took in the towering mass of darkened rock before us. Ash and embers spewed from the mouth over a thousand feet above our heads, falling to the ground and sticking to our skin. Along the base of the volcano, the ash turned the ground a murky white color, like that of dirty snow. We stood at that line, holding our breath.

A tremor ran along my spine at the thought of what lay within those impenetrable granite walls. The Spirits that would decide my fate, awakened to deliver me to destiny or death. That eternal presence stalked me, drawing me to it. The essence waited beneath the lava for me to face it.

Alone.

When we reached the rim of the volcano, that would be the step of this journey when I said goodbye to my friends and dove headfirst into the unknown, be it to life or death. The ascent would be as far as they could go. The rest would be up to me, for it was my test to face. Their lives would not be risked in that forbidden sea of orange-and-red flame.

The thought of that goodbye stung more than I expected, tearing the breath from me. I looked at the group now, realizing how firmly I depended on each of them. For so long, I had ripped these relationships apart, but they clung to the tatters.

I ran, but they chased me.

When I isolated myself in a cave of my own making, my brigade fought through the darkness to reach me. With gentle smiles and calming hands, shoulders to cry on and moments of silence, but also with tough love and heartbreaking realities.

They were here. Beside me until the end.

Always waiting for me to come back to myself. And to them. They wrapped their spirits around my heart and held on, rocking me while I thrashed and soothing me until I was ready to return.

Provided that warmth of home for the day when I opened my eyes, so that I may not run in fear.

Home. Despite the outcome of this journey, I had found my way home to them. Since the moment the Curse planted itself in my blood, since the improbable appearance of an Angel in my bedroom, I had been clawing my way upward so that I may meet my fate with a resolved spirit.

As I stared up at the world of fire and ash swirling above me, I felt the four unbreakable presences at my side and closed my eyes in peace.

-PART THREE-

TISIPHONE

Chapter Twenty-Eight

Two Years Earlier

DAWN LIGHT WAS FILTERING through the curtains when my eyes cracked open, and my heart lurched into my throat. We had fantasized about this day all our lives, and now that it had finally arrived, something felt…wrong.

Undeniably wrong.

As if air had been sucked from the world and I was left lying there, trying to remember how to breathe. Like I was waiting for the black spots that would cloud my vision and lull me into a state of permanent darkness.

But nothing was wrong. Today was Augustus's eighteenth birthday. Today was the day he would embark on his journey to complete the Undertaking. I tracked specks of dust swirling through the morning sunlight, scowling because I would remain behind.

Shoving myself upright, I threw back the covers and kicked my feet over the edge of the bed. Bitter winter air snaked up my short nightgown and kissed my bare skin as mystlight flared to life in the hearth.

There was no reason to worry. Augustus would begin the trek to the Undertaking today, and in a fortnight, he would ascend to a full Mystique Warrior before returning to Palerman for a celebratory feast. In three months, I would follow.

Then, our lives could begin.

My heart fluttered at the thought of that future—eighteen years in the making—finally within reach.

I pulled the linens up on my bed, straightened the pillows, and tied back the drapes before selecting a pale blue dress from my armoire. Had our people not been devastated by the war, Isobeth, my attendee and friend, would have been in my room, tidying and helping me dress. She would have selected a spectacular gown for my farewell to Augustus and insisted on weaving gems into an intricate fashion in my hair. I would have let her.

Instead, I was on my own, and Isobeth was in the city tending to orphaned children as she had been since the war had ceased last month. *At least she survived*, I comforted myself as I slipped the dress over my body and struggled to tie the backing. Not everyone could say the same.

But today is a day to celebrate, I reminded myself, smoothing the soft material that hugged my skin closely, its velvet lining protecting me from the winter air. It cascaded over my frame, golden detailing shimmering in the light, giving me an angelic appearance.

I didn't quite care for this particular dress, but Augustus did, and today was about him. He always said that the color reminded him of the pale blue of the accents on Mystique Warriors' leathers. That it made my skin and hair glow. I preferred it for the former reason, but the memory of his fingers trailing across the neckline brought heat to my cheeks even on this cold morning.

The flush was quickly followed by a cold, sinking feeling in my gut that I couldn't place.

With nerves fluttering up and down my body, I skipped breakfast that morning, calling farewell to my family. I closed our heavy front door behind me and rested my back against it, breathing in the morning with a sigh. The air was crisp, the gray dawn wafting around me a sign of shifting weather. A breeze lifted the loose waves of hair around my face invitingly, teasing me with the promise of a fresh snow.

I watched the gray sky, awaiting those first flakes and all else the day would bring.

At midday, residents of Palerman paused their post-war restoration duties to gather in the town square and wish Augustus good luck on the Undertaking.

The morning had been pure bliss under a shadow of the encroaching farewell. We'd barely left each other's embrace, always a hand on the other at the very least. When Tolek and Cypherion chided our attachment, I let the words wash over us. They were right; he would not be gone for long, but something told me to hold on. To hold on and not let go.

I looked at the faces of warriors and refugees who bestowed best wishes on the shoulders of my partner. Old and young, symbols of our past and future, tan-skinned and bright-eyed. Despite their recent losses, all smiled at the promise of another warrior reaching his true purpose and fulfilling this destiny we all chased. Augustus was the embodiment of hope among our battered clan.

But when my gaze locked with his, I couldn't find the usual brightness there. The guard he had carried for the past few weeks sprang into place, and with it the foreboding I felt upon waking washed over me. A cold pit settled into my stomach when Augustus's smile did not reach his eyes, and it consumed me as we walked to the edge of Palerman where his mare, Ombratta, waited.

She released a pleased exhale as we approached, her black coat a streak of night against the snow that was starting to stick to the ground. Her mane shimmered around her, dislodging glittering flakes as she shook her head. His spear was propped beside her, the two ready to see him through the journey.

When we reached the point of our farewell, I tangled my arms around Augustus's neck, letting the heat of his body seep into my own and chase away the chilled unease.

Hold on and do not let go, that nameless voice in my head echoed. I didn't understand it.

His steady arms snaked beneath my cloak and tightened around my waist, crushing me to him as he ran his hands over the soft blue linen of my dress. Each stroke of his strong fingers was a silent message to me, imprinting his touch on my memory. His leathers were cold under my cheek, though I knew the reinforced material would keep him warm. His heart beat a steady pattern against my cheek, the knowledge of the Bind inked there warming my skin.

Just like that. We should have stayed *just like that* forever.

I slid up onto my toes, careful not to push away from him in the slightest, and pressed a gentle kiss to his neck. "Come back to me, Augustus," I whispered against his ear.

His breath hitched and a shadow formed behind his eyes as they drifted closed. The hands at my waist tightened. "My North Star," he muttered against my hair. "I love you, Ophelia."

"Until the stars stop shining," I forced out through an unsteady breath.

He brushed a gentle kiss to the top of my head, then each of my cheeks, and finally my lips. There was an urgency in the sweep of his tongue against mine. One that I returned, though I didn't quite understand it. All I knew was that despair in my gut and the tears stinging my eyes and his lips against mine, hungry and frantic.

Too quickly, he pushed away from me, taking slow steps backward toward his horse.

He walked away, and though I had every reason to believe he would return to me, my world shifted. I had felt the planet spinning beneath my feet with each beat of his heart, and when the tips of his fingers broke from mine, the world froze.

I became aimless, swimming through a dark sea without my North Star to guide me home.

Chapter Twenty-Nine

Present Day

THE VENTURE THROUGH THAT swirling mist of embers and ashes was treacherous. Smoke stung my eyes and clouded my nostrils, making the narrow switchbacks that protruded from the side of the Spirit Volcano even more precarious. I placed one foot directly in front of the other, toe to heel, not daring to look down. Not wanting to see where the soot floated past my feet and to the earth below. If I did, I was sure I wouldn't be able to see the ground through the haze.

Before hiking the cramped pathways curving through the rocky surface like a snake winding up the mountain, we had all looked to Cypherion. To where his hands draped around Jezebel's and Tolek's shoulders for support. He had looked directly at me, predicting the argument I was about to make. "I'm coming" was all he said, his jaw set and stare hard. He removed his arms from my sister and Tol and put his full weight on his own two feet.

His knee buckled slightly.

"Cypherion, this is a horribly dangerous idea. You cannot climb that." Hundreds of feet above, the volcano released a shower of sparks when I pointed at it.

"And when has a horribly dangerous idea ever stopped any of

us?" he countered, taking uneven yet determined steps toward the entrance to the switchbacks.

Uncertainty burned through me. "But this is different. One wrong shift and you'll fall to your death."

"I could say that about any of you," he argued, turning back to me and crossing his arms. His stare—so hard, so assertive, so unlike himself—seared me.

"We didn't nearly become paralyzed," Tolek snapped. Cyph glared at him, eyes flicking to the bandage holding Tol's leathers around his scarred leg, and Tolek quieted.

"Cyph, it is not a show of weakness to stay," my sister announced.

I latched on to her support. "If anything, it's a show of strength." To admit when he was hurt, to admit needing help.

"Ophelia, as you like to remind us, we have no input in your decisions." His words stung, but they rang true. How many times these past two years had I made that message *very* clear? "I have made my own decisions from a young age. I will not sit by, running my hands through the ashes down here while you all risk your lives."

I had no argument, so I chose the truth. "I just want to protect you."

His eyes softened. "I understand. And we, you. So, we must remain together." He staggered to me, placing a hand on my shoulder. "Let's ask our healer what her professional opinion is."

Rina, wringing her hands, scoffed. "Finally." She looked at me. "I believe if he's careful, he will be fine."

That had been that. We put Cypherion in the center of our line, behind Jezebel and in front of Tolek, whose leg had mercifully healed almost completely in the hours on the tundra. Rina brought up the rear, and I led our journey up the switchbacks.

Ashes drifted before me, each step treacherous as loose pebbles rolled beneath my boots, smoke fighting to get into my lungs. I was unable to shake Cypherion's words from my mind. *I have made my own decisions from a young age.* Though he shouldn't have been, he was correct, and the thought of such a lonely young boy angered me for an entirely different reason.

But he *was* capable of taking care of himself. I had to acknowledge that, bite back my arguments, and support him. It was not in my nature, but dammit I was trying.

I smiled to myself at the challenge, but my foot landed on an unstable stretch of rock. The world shifted beneath me as a two-foot-long gap in the switchback went tumbling to the ground.

I didn't even have time to register the danger before a small but steady hand gripped my elbow, shoving me against the wall. A sharp rock bit into my back as I caught my breath, the tender wound in my side flaring. Through my shredded leathers, a drop of blood slipped down my side.

"You're okay," Jezebel comforted, rubbing my arm. She looked to my freshly opened wound and winced. "Sorry about that, but do watch your step, sister."

I looked down the line of my friends, wide eyes peering back through the smoke. "I'm sorry. I…" My eyes landed on Cyph, where he stood with both hands digging into the rock, white knuckles the only sign of his strain. "I…got distracted. It won't happen again."

Jezebel nodded, tawny eyes bright in her soot-stained face.

"We're glad you didn't plummet to the earth, but this does pose a new problem." Tolek coughed. He nodded at the two-foot-long gap that now broke our pathway. Smaller rocks crumbled from its edge, bouncing down into the smoke. The echoes of their fall mingled with the crackles from above, forming a sinister cacophony. I flinched at each sharp note.

"It's not too large. We can make it." Jezebel wiped a hand across her eyes, red from the smoke.

She was right. On solid ground, it was merely a large step. But hundreds of feet in the air, breathing in hazy ash, along a narrow platform that was crumbling beneath our weight…it was more than worrisome. As we looked, another six-inch chunk of the rock broke off, widening the gap.

"Don't step too close to the edge. It's clearly not solid." I cleared my throat and looked to Cypherion and Tolek. "And you two," I instructed, pointing to each of their injuries in turn. "Be extra careful."

They didn't have any sarcastic responses.

With the smoke around us, it was difficult to see a mere yard beyond the gap, but a piece of me was grateful that in this step, it was only me versus this latest challenge. No distractions ahead, above, or below.

Tentatively, I stretched a foot across the gap. Jezebel braced me from behind. I prodded the ledge with the toe of my boot, ensuring it could hold my weight. When no stray rocks fell, I lunged. My core and the wounds across it clenched, every inch of my body focused on balancing my weight on the precarious surface. In a way, it was what I had been doing for years: teetering over the point of death.

My scars ripped further, blood dripping down my skin, but the stretch of rock was solid beneath my foot. I dragged myself across.

Both feet landed on the other side, my heart stuttering with relief. My fingers dug into the rock wall for support.

Scooting along, I made room for Jezebel, stretching a hand toward her. My breathing came in short, panicked inhales as her feet left the opposite side of the gap, a graceful, fearless leap across the distance. She stood about two inches shorter than me, and I prayed those two inches would not be her weakness.

They weren't.

Once my sister was safely beside me, our hands locked together to stifle our nervous energy. I nodded at Cypherion.

Awkwardly, he leaned his back against the wall for support, stretching one leg out to the side across the gap. In a moment that sent my heart plummeting to the earth, his supporting leg—the one healing much more slowly after his spinal injury—buckled.

Tol was there before I could gasp, pinning Cyph's shoulders back against the wall. He shook his head, honeyed highlights invisible under the coating of soot and ash. "None of that," he warned, gripping his shoulder tighter. "You're not allowed to fall."

Chocolate eyes met blue and Cypherion smiled at him in thanks. Then, Cyph threw his weight sideways and fell across the gap, his extended leg landing inches from Jezebel. With her steady hands gripping his arms, he used the functional muscles in that leg to pull himself across.

Tol followed smoothly on his freshly healed leg, and though I could barely see Rina through the haze, with her long, elegant steps she crossed easily—the most flawless of us all.

I released a relieved breath and looked up. Ash and soot fluttered onto my cheeks like snowflakes, but my heart lifted. The blazing mouth of the volcano was in sight through the swirling haze.

We had nearly made it.

Chapter Thirty

Malakai

Ophelia's face on the day I left had haunted me for over two years. Her dimmed eyes, usually so full of exhilaration and life, had searched mine for a hint of what plagued me. Her lips had pulled between her teeth, as she always did when she fought back words from that argumentative mind. Her drooping cheeks and stature, unbreakable grip around me, every inch of her body lurching to hold me back.

And that last request…*Come back to me…*

Like a part of her knew that I wouldn't return, but she stifled it to allow me the chance at my destiny.

I loved the fire that burned within her, but I was glad she held it back that day. Should she have voiced her concerns, I'm not sure how well my resolve would have held against her. It had already cracked each time I looked at her, lies leaving my lips. I hated deceiving her, and that day leading up to my birthday, on the Angel fountain, the truth was on the tip of my tongue.

But then I thought of what sharing that truth would do.

Not to the other parties involved, not even to myself, but to her. If she knew the whole story, she would have broken. A swell of guilt so powerful it could wreck an Angel would have engulfed her. Yes, she would have fought her way out of it, formidable as she was, but I know the path she would have taken then. It was not one I could accept.

So, I bit my tongue, tasting the shame of the lie as it spread through me, and learned to lock my heart behind iron bars. I said goodbye to the one person whose soul was wrapped around my own. We were one in so many ways, on a path together since the day we met.

Or so we thought.

All that time, another force had been at work, and it had other plans in mind for our paths. This—these chains, this cave, this torture—was mine. I could have told Ophelia the truth before I left, but the decision to tie myself to this path was mine to make. So, I had lied, and she had let me go.

It was another reason I loved Ophelia. She argued with the world, but when it came to me, she knew when not to push. The trust built between us since childhood ran deep, deeper than the blood in my veins and the Bind upon my chest. We each had a silent understanding of how the other's mind, heart, and soul worked.

Though I knew I made the right choice in hiding my secrets from her, a storm cloud of regret hovered over me. What did she think of me? I'd never know. We would never be reunited, but my final wish was that she knew the truth. I wished I had told her on my eighteenth birthday before I said goodbye forever so that we might travel our paths with clear understanding between us. I should have shared that final piece so that at the very least, she would know where I was. So that she would not be ashamed of my failures.

I only hoped that despite it all, she was happy.

Though I hated myself for it, I would do it again. Because what I did, I did for her. I would do anything for her.

She may never know it, but it was all for her.

Chapter Thirty-One

Ophelia

My legs ached by the time we arrived at the rim of the Spirit Volcano; my throat was raw. That final ten feet stretching above me felt like a mile, but we had come so far—I had come so far—for this moment. We traveled through the Mystique Territory, fought enemies, and brushed blades with death for this.

The moment I had trained for my entire life, the one on which I staked my dreams.

I had fantasized of this since my father first explained a Mystique Warrior's destiny and placed my first practice sword in my hand. Yet, I suddenly felt a trickle of fear snake through my body. Fear of what that plunge into the unknown held for me and what I could lose in the process.

I gripped my Cursed wrist as doubt spread through me. Completing the Undertaking was my destiny, and I was not scared that I would fail. I had always known I would succeed. But how would that trial change me? What warriors faced in the volcano was rumored to be horrific, aimed at exposing your weaknesses and guiding you through them. My father told tales of warriors who emerged scarred. Damaged. Incapable of overcoming those challenges.

Some did not return at all.

At the onset of this journey, I had thought I would face death in a matter of days. I didn't think I had anything to lose beyond my life itself, and I was at peace with that risk. Now—I looked at the four people at my back—my eyes had been opened, and I saw how truly wrong I was. How much I would be sacrificing in this dive into ash and flame.

But I didn't have room for fear of the inevitable.

The stars were barely visible among the smoke and ash, the lack of midnight light pressing on my shoulders like an omen. Much like the snow falling on Malakai's final day, this felt like a sign of change.

Jezebel stepped forward, uncurling my fingers from my Cursed wrist and wrapping them between her own. Over the rumble of the lava, she said, "I am proud of you, Ophelia. I know I have not always supported you, but you held true in your beliefs. Never forget how far you have come. Trust in your strength, sister, and we will see you on the other side." With one hand, she raised my Cursed wrist to her lips, kissing the linen wrap I had fastened around it.

I blinked away the tears rising to my eyes. "I love you, Jezzie. I would not be here without you." The unsaid goodbye hung heavy between us as she squeezed her hand around my wrist.

Jezebel smiled sheepishly as I removed my pack. I dug inside, my fingers brushing the pin from my grandmother that I'd hidden away, until I found the piece of soiled parchment on which I had written my final words to them all. Tucking it into her palm, I curled her fingers around it and dropped my pack at her feet. I would not be permitted to take it with me. Only the weapons strapped to my body were allowed.

Jezebel's hands shook as she clasped them both around the note, her eyes filling with tears of mixed denial and understanding.

I tugged her to me, dropping my voice to a whisper in her ear. "Carry on my mission, Jez, if I cannot myself. Find him."

She pulled back and for a moment I thought she'd insist it was impossible, but she nodded, tears streaking down her face now.

Squaring her shoulders under the weight of farewell, Jezebel stepped back beside our friends.

Cypherion approached next, wrapping his strong arms around me. "You're breaking barriers, Ophelia. Give the Spirits hell."

I laughed into his chest. "If I have even a small piece of your silent strength, I will be fine."

"Tell the Spirits that we'll all be there one day," he affirmed, stepping back with his hands braced on my shoulders. He ducked his head to look me in the eyes. "Once we're out of this mess, I'm going in."

"You will be next, Cyph. Mark my words." If anyone was strong enough to complete the Undertaking, it was Cypherion Kastroff.

He squeezed my shoulder and stepped aside for Santorina to say goodbye. Before she could speak, I opened my mouth. "Thank you, Rina. Thank you for never backing down when I needed to hear a harsh truth. For not placating my decisions, but fighting the wrong ones."

Her lips quivered as she pulled me to her, her black hair loose from her ponytail and falling around both of us. I allowed one silent tear to drip onto her borrowed leathers before pushing myself back.

"Good luck, Ophelia," she said. And in those three small words I felt everything she longed to say to me. Her need of me in her life and her distress at what I was about to endure. But she wouldn't voice any of it, forever the steadfast soul.

Then, it was only Tolek. He stood apart from our friends, hands clasped behind his back, dejected eyes burrowing into mine. With slow steps that prolonged the inevitable, he walked to me. I inspected his eyes, his pallor—no signs of symptoms, yet.

"There's nothing I can say to convince you to stay? Or to let me go with you?" He sighed, already reading my answer in my eyes.

"You know this is how it must be, Tol."

His arms curled around me, cradling my head against his chest. I wrapped my own arms around his waist and locked my hands behind him, reluctant to say goodbye. If something did happen to me in there and I truly never saw him again…I couldn't consider it. I swore that if I survived this, I'd find a cure for this Curse. I would not let it take him. My best friend through it all, something deeper between us. He was my guiding light in the darkness that had consumed my life, the tether tying me to reality, and I refused to be ripped from him.

Tol's chin rested on my head, and he whispered, "You carry a piece of my heart. Whatever happens in there, that will always be yours."

I nearly choked on the sob that tried to escape my throat, but I looked up at him. Those chocolate eyes were heavy with truths, and I was not sure I was ready to face them.

"And you, mine, Tolek."

His hand stroked longingly down my back as if imprinting the feel of me into his skin. I clenched my eyes, memorizing the caress of his fingertips through my leathers. When he released me, it took every effort to step away from him. He locked his hands behind his back again and watched me go.

The volcano shook behind me, calling to me. Reminding me that it was time. There could be no more delays.

I threw my shoulders back, shook my hair from my face, and raised my chin, forcing the tears to stop falling from my eyes. "Right." I took a breath. "When I go in the volcano, I don't know how long it will take me to get out. I probably won't have any concept of time. Do you guys remember the plan?"

Cyph spoke first, "We take the footpath to Damenal."

Jezebel continued, "To the temple where the flame pool waits."

"That's where warriors emerge after the Undertaking," Rina confirmed.

"That is where we will wait for you," Tol whispered, eyes still rimmed with tears.

I took a deep breath. "But stay out of sight," I reminded them. "Do not let anyone see you until I'm there. We don't want to raise suspicions of what we're doing."

They nodded in unison, and my heart shattered with each motion. But I had no more room for goodbyes in me, so I turned to the slope of rock behind me, took a breath, and climbed.

Here, unlike the ascension of the volcano, the ground was smooth from years of stray flames melting it. It made for a quick, steady final few feet of climbing before I reached the entrance. The rock around the mouth was so thin, I felt as though it would break beneath my weight. Ash rained down on me.

With each step I took along the ledge, the Curse inside my wrist throbbed. It felt alive, like a pulse of its own quickened. It knew. It knew something transformative was happening, and it burrowed deeper into my skin. This parasite that was killing me thrashed in fear of whatever waited for us below.

I took a deep breath.

Thick smoke clouded my lungs, but it didn't hurt. The ash here was sweet, as if once it left the volcano, the magic surrounding the mountain range changed it. The same magic that kept the smoke over the volcano and tundra, not allowing it to saturate the rest of the fresh mountain air. I let that power embrace me as I turned back to my friends, mere shadows in the smoky night.

I extended my arms at my sides, closed my eyes, and fell backward into my fate.

Chapter Thirty-Two

The fall was...grueling. Like setting my skin on fire and diving into the heart of a storm, unsure which way was up but feeling the hot agony swallow me. I waited for it to boil my blood, to melt my flesh until I was nothing but scraps of bone and the lingering drafts of a tainted curse.

Flames. There were so many flames. Blinding flashes of orange and red and yellow. Heat licked up my limbs. I thought I screamed, but any echo of my voice faded into the roar of the volcano. Embers singed holes in my leathers, leaving blisters on my flesh in their wake.

This heat was like living in the heart of a star.

In the distance below, a blue glow emanated. It was a speck from this height, barely visible through the tears streaking into the air around me. My eyes stung, the sweet-smelling smoke turning putrid again, but I would not close them. Despite the pain, I wanted to see every moment of this pivotal experience.

My heart tumbled through my chest, knowing that growing blue speck would be the hottest point of the volcano. The central stage of the fire that created this monstrous show.

The descent felt endless, the cavernous rock walls around me streaking past in flashes of gray and brown etched with veins of fire. Like the volcano was a living thing, the flame its blood. And that made me its foolish meal.

Though I had little concept of time, it seemed that minutes stretched. I thought of the height of the exterior and panicked. The structure was high, but the fall at this speed should not have taken so long. Had something gone wrong?

With a wave of doubt, I thought back to the night Damien appeared in my room. His words flashed through my mind in a rush, all blending together, nearly indiscernible from one another. *The task ahead will try thy spirit.* Not once did he explicitly claim the Undertaking as that task. Oh, for the love of the Angels, had I misinterpreted his Spirits-damned message? Had that ass of a First Warrior not thought to stop me from a grave mistake?

If after the brutal journey I put my friends through, I was not supposed to complete the Undertaking after all, I'd kill that Angel. The heat around me matched my anger at the thought that I had foolishly—willingly—given myself over to the Spirit Volcano. That I sacrificed myself to a ritual that had somehow malfunctioned.

I had a sickening feeling that this jump would be the end of me.

Oh, Spirits. This was what had happened to Malakai, wasn't it? The Undertaking was faulty, a fatal flaw claiming any warrior who attempted it. And I dove headfirst into that death like a reckless fool.

A plume of smoke rose up around me, and I choked on the soot. I coughed over the ash in my lungs, my chest seizing while the organs worked feverishly to dispel the poison. I continued to plummet through the air. This was it. This was the end. I'd curse Damien if I saw him in the afterlife.

The blue pool grew larger, its light radiating around me. I would land in it, and I would die at the heart of the flame. The irony of my death at the hands of the Undertaking—the future I was never afraid of—when I carried a deadly Curse in my blood was not lost on me. I'd made my peace with that fate days ago, but I hated that this was how it occurred. All I could do was tick off the list of goodbyes, sending each out into the universe with one final burst of love. My sister, my friends, my parents—

A flash of mist soared past me. Not the smoke I fell through, but a white cloud.

It circled around me again, and I tried to follow it, but it was too quick.

Then, solid braces caught my body, cradling my back and legs. My head snapped back at the contact, but it didn't hurt. None of it did, beyond the welts on my body. Whatever caught me had cushioned my impact.

I was tipped onto my feet, nearly toppling over at the vertigo from the sudden stop. I looked above me. The mouth of the volcano was so high up, the space I was in now as large as my family's estate in Palerman. My head spun as I took in the cavern, thick pillars of rock supporting the walls. To my right, the blue-white pool of flame flared, flowing in a quiet whirlpool, tendrils shooting high into the air. It was so much larger with my feet on the ground; it swallowed up a quarter of the cavern, molten white lava flowing into and out of the stone floor, dripping down the walls. Everything flickered—beckoning me—heightening my vertigo.

I fell to my knees and vomited up black smoke and ash.

When my body stopped heaving, I rose to my feet, wiping my mouth on my torn leathers. Before me stood three beings—no, they did not stand.

They floated.

Their feet hovered inches above the ground, and those feet—their entire bodies—were made of mist. Tinted white as if the color was being leached out of them, they were a stark contrast to the rock, fire, and smoke.

My jaw dropped, for as often as I had imagined this, I had never truly known what to expect when I came face-to-face with Spirits.

"Hello, Ophelia," the largest one greeted me, floating in the center of their formation. The edges of his misty-white form were rimmed with gold. "We have been waiting for you."

Chapter Thirty-Three

MOUTH AGAPE AND LIMBS trembling, I stared at the Spirits for a moment that stretched on, before falling to a knee, hand over my heart.

"Spirits of Mystique Warriors past, I come to thee for thy trial, honor, and permission so that I may pass through the Spirit Volcano and ascend as a Mystique Warrior." The words tumbled from my mouth in awe. As a teenager, I had recited the greeting for hours, until my tone and reverence were perfect, but none of that rehearsal mattered as it flowed from my lips. The essence of the Spirits before me pitched my speech beyond my control.

I didn't lift my eyes from the ground, watching the way the flame flowed through the volcano's thin veins beneath my feet. Sparkling trickles of reds bled into oranges, faded into yellows.

After a moment, one of the Spirits spoke, his voice deep and warm. "Rise, Ophelia Tavania Alabath."

I did as I was told, straightening my spine and shoulders. Despite the state of my appearance, I stood proudly. These injuries, the wrecked leathers, even the soot coating my flesh and hair, had delivered me to this moment.

The Spirit in the center, the golden-edged one, had a broad chest and shoulders even larger than Cypherion. His long hair fell below his collarbones, wild, as I assumed his demeanor was. "You come to us to grasp your destiny. We come to you to test your spirit." It was the same voice that had told me to rise. Though the words were ominous, he sounded somewhere between friendly and authoritative. "Each of us will present you with one riddle. One lyrical puzzle to determine your strength of mind. Then, we will decide your worth." Decide if I was to progress to the next level or rot in this flame-wrapped cavern for eternity.

I nodded, swallowing my intimidation, but I could not remain silent. "What are your names?" I needed to know these Spirits, to understand them. They had each been chosen for my Undertaking specifically, and deciphering why might lead to clues for these riddles.

The one on the right answered, his voice gruff to match his frown. "Inane girl. You do not question us."

"Peace," the golden-edged one said, turning to his companion. "She may ask us any questions she likes. We may answer however we please."

The harsh one scoffed, his slender body shimmering with the motion, but he folded to the one in the middle. "I'm Hectatios."

The Spirit on the left spoke next, her voice high and chilling. "I am Glawandin." Her oval face was flawless, with porcelain skin and delicate features. She smiled slightly at me, but only with her lips. When she shifted, the light caught her eyes. Instead of irises, they were solid orbs of milky white fog.

Blind. Glawandin could not see. I tucked the piece of information away.

"And I am Annellius." He brought a hand to his chest, dipping his chin. His wild hair cast shadows on the hard planes of his face. "Annellius Alabath."

"Alabath…" I breathed over the name.

"A distant ancestor, many generations prior."

His hair—flowing on a gust of warm wind—had a white tint to it, but beneath that film, I recognized the original golden shade. It was my father's and Jezebel's. It was mine. An Alabath Spirit.

"It is a pleasure to meet you." The tension eased from my shoulders as I spoke to my distant relative, settling into the Spirits' presence. "If I may ask, why does your frame glow gold while your companions do not?"

"Ah, unfortunately, that is not an answer I can provide." His magenta eyes—my eyes, I realized with a jolt—lit up.

"Your eyes…" I lifted a hand to my own.

"Another thing I cannot discuss."

Disappointment swept through me, cold and fast. But again, I tucked away that piece of information.

"Let's get this over with, Annellius," Hectatios growled, as if he had another appointment.

I looked at the Spirit, his silver hair flowing long down his back. With a cut jaw, full lips, and large eyes, one might have described him as beautiful—should he not have opened his mouth.

I braced my hands on my hips. "Why are you so rude? Is it not your *duty* to guide me?"

Hectatios's chest swelled at my words, hands clenched. I swore I saw Annellius smirk out of the corner of my eye, but I would not break my stare from Hectatios. "How dare you—"

"She's feisty," Glawandin trilled. "I'd like to keep her."

"She shares your fire, Hectatios," Annellius snickered. "By all means, begin."

Hectatios held out his hands and a veil lowered over the four of us, dimming the lights and heat of the flames. Annellius continued to watch me. At his side Glawandin stared at nothing, a pleasant smile brightening her face.

Hectatios spoke, his voice booming around us, the harsh tones amplified. "You began with hate in your heart. A cord of discord threatening to crush you. Now, you face us with a clearer mind because of this. What is it?"

I blinked at the Spirit. "What?"

"What is it?" Hectatios repeated each word distinctly.

"I have no forsaken clue what you're talking about," I retorted, heated frustration creeping into my voice.

"Ophelia," Annellius's voice was calming, his eyes understanding. "Think."

Think. What good would that do me? I looked between the Spirits, attempting to grasp whatever hidden meanings their words held. This part of the Undertaking was meant to determine your mental strength. This was neither physical nor emotional, but purely knowledge based. A trial for your mind, reaching into the depths of your brain to revive the cunning within yourself and hone that skill for any challenge a warrior may face.

The tundra and the ascent of the switchbacks—that was physical. The next portion I could only guess would be emotional. But this phase, this was when the Spirits tested your mental will, dedication, and ability.

I must *think.*

Anger bubbled up in my chest as I repeated Hectatios's words in my head. *Hate in my heart*...if anyone here had hate in their heart it was the silver-haired Spirit, not me. The way he watched me with smug eyes and a set jaw, his unrelenting rage poised to tackle me should I fail his test. Fury stirred within my gut, accusations working their way up my throat.

It was a fury I had not felt since...

I looked at the Spirit again. That expression on his face...I knew it well. The narrowed eyes, the angry exhales, the gritted teeth. It was one I had worn for two years.

And I understood Hectatios's purpose here. He reflected *me.* My darkest parts when I walked through the world letting the anger printed on my soul decide my every action. Rage at the universe for the fate that had befallen me. Distantly, I wondered what had happened to the silver-haired warrior to damage his heart as deeply as mine.

You face us with a clearer mind because of this. That was the answer I needed to find. There were endless possibilities, and I considered each as I paced the veined floor of the volcano. Patience, compassion, strength...they all were solutions to what I had faced. Each trait flourished in my heart, attempting to repair what was broken inside of me.

It seemed impossible that there was only one answer.

I stopped in my tracks and looked at Hectatios, deciding I needed to start somewhere. "Acceptance," I blurted out.

His eyes narrowed further if possible. "No."

"Patience, compassion, strength," I continued down the growing list in my head.

"No," he echoed. When I added three more guesses, he continued to deny me.

I threw my arms up. "But those are all pieces of me that got me here. How can none of them be correct?"

Now, a smile cut across Hectatios's beautiful face, and something shifted in his expression. That was approval dancing in his eyes. "Ah, you are looking inward. Perhaps, try the opposite."

The opposite, I thought, resuming my pacing. I ran my hands through my hair. I wished I had a rope to redirect the twitching energy within me and steady myself, but I had only my wit to rely on.

If the answer was not something *within* myself, then it must be something *without*. Something found in the world…or in others.

I realized there was not only one answer to the riddle. One grace, sure, but it was a result of many lives, something so vast that it took four to show it to me.

The answer came to me like a shooting star across the sky, illuminating everything in its wake and brightening all doubt. When I was a pit of rage, my heart warped and tainted, my friends and sister had pardoned my worst behaviors. They waited for me to return to myself, helped me get there through both patience and pushing. On the journey here alone, they showed endless fortitude and loyalty, and once I had dragged myself from the darkest of pits, they acquitted those worst pieces of me. Those shadows within my heart faded like dust in the wind.

I returned Hectatios's gloating smile. "Forgiveness. Not forgiveness of myself, but forgiveness from others. That is what cleared my mind and heart so that I may be here today. I would not be here without the forgiveness of my friends and sister."

The silver-haired Spirit nodded. The approval in his eyes glinted as he lifted his hands and the veil surrounding us dropped. The warmth of the volcano snaked around my shoulders, but I did not mind the heat this time. It bolstered me, riling my blood.

I turned to the two remaining Spirits, heart lifting in anticipation.

Glawandin's cheerful voice filled the space. "It is my turn." She swooped upward and spun in a circle, white flecks raining down upon me.

When they touched my body, my sight disappeared. "What's happening?" I screamed, turning in frantic circles. There was a roaring in my ears. "Bring it back! Bring my sight back!"

"Hush, child," Glawandin soothed. "Breathe. It will be all right."

It took me a few deep breaths to steady myself, but the roaring in my ears was eventually replaced by faint crackles of lava and exhales of smoke. I dug through the sounds for any indication of what was to come.

When Glawandin spoke beside me, I jumped. For a blind Spirit, she moved effortlessly through the air. "Thy sight is gone, oh, Chosen Child. But the difficulty shall be mild. To walk through life without the sense requires a skill just as dense. It is neither physical thing nor human being, but imperative instinct riling. You have not had it all the way, but it grows stronger in your bones each day."

Her voice faded into the darkness, the last sentences echoing around us and drifting up to the volcano's mouth.

Taking another deep breath, I channeled all of my remaining senses into solving her riddle. I listened to the movement around me—the crackles and snaps and whoosh of the flowing lava. The whisper of the Spirits stirring the air. Pungent ash filled my nostrils, fire heated my skin, and the ground remained solid beneath my feet as I gathered her hints.

Glawandin's words washed over me like a tidal wave.

Something neither physical nor human. An instinct that I had lacked but was growing within me. I turned my sightless gaze inward, exploring my own subconscious and heart. What had I struggled with?

Without my sight, my introspection felt omniscient, tunneling through my subconscious and seeing my actions and decisions as if from both the inside and the outside. It took me only minutes to discover that hidden instinct that had weakened so drastically in the past two years, a hole opening in my being. But the edges glowed a faint white light, stretching toward each other as I unintentionally nurtured this missing piece of myself, restoring it.

A piece I had recently acknowledged with Cypherion.

A devilish smile spread across my lips.

"It is trust. That is what I lack. I do not trust others. I assume responsibilities all on my own and do not ask for their help. I protect them all without believing they can do it on their own." Speaking the words brought a swell of warmth to my body, like a beast I had been denying was unleashed. Like warm honey flowed through my veins, comforting me and instilling a confidence I had lacked.

My vision returned with a flash, the space alarmingly bright after the darkness. Glawandin was gleeful, applauding me as she bobbed up and down in the air. "Wonderful, child! Truly wonderful. I warn you not to forget the words you have spoken."

I promised her I would not and turned to Annellius. The final puzzle standing between me and the next phase of the Undertaking. Success was so close I could taste it—victory sweet as sparkling wine amid the ash and soot.

Annellius met my gaze, and his frame glowed brighter. "This one is different. You will not be guessing something within yourself, but something within me."

I squared my shoulders at the challenge in his voice. "Understood." I was an Alabath just as he. I could look inside of myself and find a piece of him to guide me toward the answer.

Annellius raised one hand. The golden band at his wrist sparkled. "My veins danced with this hint of legend. It sparked within me since birth, a blessing and a curse. But I was greedy for the power. It overwhelmed me. It promised me the greatness of the First, but I did not understand its strength, rather tried to abuse it. Now, in my Spirit form, I carry the warning to future generations: beware the promises of greed."

When he finished, his face drooped as if weighted with remorse, so much pain resting beneath his mask. Annellius's riddle was not mere introspection. Whatever this warning was, he begged me to heed it.

What Annellius carried within him, whatever that power was, it was dangerous. A blessing and a curse. I looked at my wrist, but I knew that wasn't the answer. The Spirit was not Cursed in the manner I was.

What fate had befallen this ancestor of mine that was so threatening, he was now condemned to float in the Spirit Volcano and communicate the risk to future warriors? We had a power balance instilled across our continent—the Rapture made up of the leaders of every clan, responsible for ensuring a single person never grew too strong. Yet, here was an Alabath, telling me the very opposite had happened, and it had been his personal downfall.

Whatever this threat may be, I begged it to spare those I cared about.

My eyes washed over his body again, desperate for any hint of his suffering. The subtle golden light that echoed around his floating body pulsed when our twin eyes met. His strong form and perfect features appeared sculpted by an Angel himself.

An Angel...

Veins dance with this hint of legend...blessing and a curse...greatness of the First...

It was rare. So rare. It was unlikely, but not impossible. I swallowed loudly, watching as that golden light around Annellius Alabath shimmered. The gold source he would not disclose...it had to be the answer.

I opened my mouth to speak before I could rethink the guess. "You have Angelblood." It wasn't a question. I knew I was right as the words tumbled from my tongue.

A dim sadness entered Annellius's eyes. "I do," he confirmed.

"And you're an Alabath."

He nodded.

"So, our bloodline has it? Our entire family?" I gasped at the realization of what flowed through my veins.

But Annellius quickly punctured that awe with a shake of his head. "No. At my failure, the Angels removed their blood from our bloodline. Traces of it remain, but it is not pure. It makes us powerful, but it is not nourished as it once was." He hung his head. "I am sorry."

My shoulders slumped slightly, but I shook off the disappointment. I did not need Angelblood. I had gotten this far without it. If the substance tainted Annellius beyond repair, then it was a blessing that I did not have Angelblood.

"But I am right?" I pushed. "I have solved every puzzle. Forgiveness, trust, Angelblood." I pointed to each Spirit in turn. "I may pass?"

They nodded in unison. "Yes, you may," Annellius began. "But we have one more message." He swelled before me, appearing much larger than he had a moment ago.

I shriveled in his shadow, cold washing through me.

"Take caution, Ophelia. Should you survive the next phase of the Undertaking, your journey is not over. You have much more to face, and your future will not be pleasant. Your blood is strong enough to cause and end wars. But you do not need to face that blood-ridden future. You have another option. You may stay here, with the Spirits. You may remain, Blessed. Your soul…we sense something within it. We extend this offer to you."

My heart skipped a beat with every sentence he spoke, each more ominous than the last. I knew the Alabath line was strong, but to say I could cause and end wars seemed a drastic claim to me. I looked at the Curse on my wrist. Warfare and blood painted gruesome images across the vision of the future I did not think I would ever have.

"You…want me to stay?"

He nodded slowly.

For a brief moment, I pictured my life within the Spirit Volcano. The painful death that awaited me when the Curse grasped my life would no longer be a threat. I would remain in this sacred dwelling participating in the legends of our people, without any more agony to plague my life. Surrounded by the warmth of the fires twin to my own heat, assisting future warriors on their own Undertakings—

But there would not be any more Undertakings unless I proved I could survive this one.

Staying in the volcano and relinquishing my future would rip that chance from every Mystique. It may be the easier choice, to escape the pain the outside world caused me and the certain death that awaited me, but running from reality was not an option.

And I did not want it to be.

I may have an arduous end in the near future, but perhaps if I could have a few more moments of bliss before then and heal something for those who came after me, the suffering would be worth it.

I looked at each Spirit in turn. "Thank you. Truly, I am honored to have received the offer. But I have unfinished business in the outside world."

"As we thought," Annellius responded. Though he sounded unsurprised, a shadow of sadness crossed his face.

"May I ask one more question?" My heart pounded, needing them to say yes.

Annellius nodded.

"Can you tell me where Malakai is?"

I held my breath. My every hope hung on this one moment—on them being able to tell me where to find the man I loved. Annellius's pink eyes misted as he searched for an answer.

"We cannot."

My heart sank. I wanted to fall to my knees and beg, but I saw the resolve in his hard Alabath stare and knew there was no hope of convincing the Spirit to change his mind.

"Well, girl, get on your way," Hectatios said, not unkindly.

Glawandin glided over to the pool of blue fire and spread her arms wide, her melodic voice carrying throughout the volcano, "I believe you know where to go next." She pointed to the Spirit Fire.

I moved to her side on shaking legs and looked into the glowing depths below. One more step, and this would be over. One more phase to endure and I would ascend. A fall through this white-hot heart of the volcano was all that stood between me and the dream I clung to so desperately that it nearly shattered me. But this was the phase that broke the most warriors. The one that would try my emotions, raise things I did not want to face.

The fire swirled below me, shades of blue melding into a white pit of the unknown.

Before I could reconsider, I dove in.

CHAPTER THIRTY-FOUR

TWO YEARS EARLIER

MALAKAI

ASH SWIRLED AROUND ME as I stared into the pit of lava within the Spirit Volcano. The blend of yellows, oranges, and reds was eerily beautiful. Tantalizing.

I could do it, I thought, wrapping my hand over the wound in my shoulder that the wolf's claws left behind. I hadn't expected those beasts on the tundra. I don't know what I had thought waited for me, but a half dozen canine creatures lunging at me, jaws snapping, ready to rip life from me, was not it. Across my shoulder, one beast left behind long gashes to match its three sharp nails, but they had already partially healed on my trek up the side of the volcano, only slices of tender pink skin accenting my flesh now.

The switchbacks had been precarious, but I had almost wished they were longer. Wished I had more time before I reached this point. I was not ready to arrive at the top of the volcano, and all I thought about as I climbed those thin shelves was how I should have prolonged the journey. I should have laid beneath the stars of our territory for one more night. Should have soaked in the beauty of the world around me before it was too late.

But the lava was right there, churning below me, a living sea of fire. It would be so easy to break my promise and dive right in, face the Spirits, and emerge on the other side, ascended. It would take one step. Instinctually, my feet moved closer to the edge, the burn of the flame warming my skin and the sweet smoke filling my senses. My body longed to grasp the birthright that flowed through my blood.

Would the Spirits even accept me, though? With the secrets I held, I was not sure I would be deemed worthy. They could reject me, and then I faced eternity in their realm.

I supposed it didn't matter. Dead or alive, it was the same fate at this point. The heat of the flames was more enticing the longer I considered the option. I could…I kicked a rock over the edge of the void and watched it tumble through the air. I could do *that.* Free-fall through the smoke like that piece of gravel and let the flames do with me what they wished.

On instinct, my hand shot to the tattoo on my chest, exposed to the night air through the tear the wolf's claws left in my leathers.

No, I could not take that step.

There was too much at stake.

As if in answer to my mental turmoil, a figure rose beside me, dark and silent as the breath of a shadow.

"You could do it," he whispered, his voice one with the smoke. Sparks crackled out of the volcano and settled into the rock around us, inviting me in. I stared until the embers faded into the ground as if they had never existed.

"No. I cannot." I turned to face him, relieved that his face was hidden by the hood of his cloak. Maybe that made me a coward, but I was grateful I did not have to look into those eyes. "I have made my choice."

The lowered voice that came out of his shadowed hood was grim. "It is the right one. For all involved." His hand cupped my uninjured shoulder, and I cringed at the contact. I did not want this man touching me. He was the root of all that was wrong in my life, and now I was his.

A beacon of flame shot into the air, the precise golden shade of Ophelia's hair. "Let's go then," I muttered, heart breaking for the girl I loved. But I turned away from the golden light.

"Well, there is one more thing," the man said.

Before he could finish the thought, six armed figures emerged around the turn of the volcano, lining up amid the rubble at the base of the sloped ascent to the rim, waiting for me. Weapons glinted in the light of the flame; each man was strapped with at least three different blades. Their customary axes caused my stomach to turn. In their pale hands, the sharp tools were deadly. My own hands flexed, eager to reach for the spear across my back, though I wasn't worthy to wield it.

"What is this?" I growled at my captor, keeping my eyes on the six men below me and their deep green armor. I clenched my fists to keep my hands from shaking—in anger, in fear, I wasn't sure which.

Their line parted, and a dark, ethereal being emerged from behind them. She moved like a storm cloud, slow but sinister. Even with the smoke shadowing the moon, her skin glowed white aside from the two dark scars across her face. A cascade of black hair billowed around her, blending into the skintight, dark dress she wore.

A chill ran down my spine.

With her hands clasped in front of her, she appeared regal, but I knew the bloody history that coated those hands. The haunting smile that spread across her face told me she was aware of that fact.

I turned to the man beside me and repeated my question with vehemence. "*What is this*?" I gestured to the guards below and their maleficent queen.

"It is—" His voice stuttered ever so briefly, but one nod from that woman and his demeanor changed. He became rougher, more hideous. "This is a change of plans. Do not fight it, Malakai." A silent plea slipped into his voice on my name.

The laugh she released in response cut through the night like a shard of glass on delicate flesh. Unrepentant, jagged, and threatening.

A change of plans. Something heavy settled within my chest as her men charged up the smooth stretch of rock that separated us. Their threatening daggers and axes loomed closer. I contemplated falling backward into the volcano one more time but shut the idea out quickly.

Do not fight it, his instructions echoed in my head as hands gripped me, shoving me to my knees. If possible, I hated the man now more than I ever had before.

A boot collided with my stomach, and I hunched over, giving in to the shock that flooded my body as I understood the betrayal here. Something in my side cracked—a rib, perhaps. The pain shot through me, but they didn't stop. And I was not fighting back—I could not fight back for the sake of my heart—yet they beat me without remorse.

A fist connected with my jaw. Once. Twice. I lost count.

My teeth dug into my tongue. The copper tang of blood filled my mouth. I spit it out, the rocks at my knees turning crimson, and threw my head back to glare at my captor through an eye that was already swelling.

"Remove your hood. I want to see your face as you watch what you have done."

The men around me snickered, but I didn't care about them. They were nobody to me. It was not *their* lies that found me on my knees now.

My captor was still, his expression masked in shadow. Then, he turned and walked away to meet the woman waiting for him. He extended an arm, and the two began the journey down the switchbacks with unsettling ease. Every step he took cemented the betrayal now spreading through me as steadily as my blood seeped from my wounds.

As I was forced to my feet and pushed down the volcano, I thought back over every interaction leading up to this, questioning if I had been a fool to not expect this deceit. I supposed I had. For so many reasons, I wanted to storm at the man now descending the volcano—beat him as he had watched them beat me.

My blood heated. My chest tightened.

But one of the guards shoved my shoulder, and I remembered how precarious my position was. I swore I'd never show that man that side of me. The side that cried out at what was being done, begging for mercy. I locked my heart behind iron bars, tossing the key into the volcano with all my hopes of peace.

Biting my tongue, one thought echoed through my mind. I was not the coward here. *He* was.

Chapter Thirty-Five

Present Day

Ophelia

I THOUGHT I KNEW pain when I fell through the Spirit Volcano. I thought I knew pain when the wolf's claws sank into my body, tearing flesh and muscle. I thought I knew pain when Malakai left me standing on the edge of Palerman and did not return.

The dive into the Spirit Fire was all of those and more.

Every physical and emotional wound I ever suffered—every heartache and toil—was bundled up into one endless pit, thick and heavy, that I now plunged through. It hurt everywhere: body, mind, and spirit shredded apart until I existed only in useless scraps.

End it. End it now. End it quickly, I repeated the mantra in my mind. I did not care about anything; all I knew was endless agony and the tunnel of thick blue flames warping around me.

I couldn't find any breaks in the flame's power.

Then, something shifted. The blue flames flickered ice white for a moment, and in that flash, they soothed instead of tortured. I exhaled as the agony calmed into a peaceful melody, but it was as quick as a lightning strike.

The pain returned, burning stronger than before.

Bursts of white punctured the blue flames with an insatiable hunger. Within those white streaks lay strips of images that felt foreign yet familiar.

A girl and her horse.

A sword flashing through the air.

A piece of leather with stars printed on the material—

And I realized that they weren't arbitrary images. They were memories. My memories.

They battled the haze of agonizing blue flames to reach me. Image after image, they struggled to push into my mind, each one that landed easing the pain.

All pieces of myself. Threads in the tapestry of my life that made me a Mystique Warrior. A streak of short golden hair under a clear blue sky was imprinted against a hand trailing through a shining stream, leaving ripples in its wake, then faded into a pair of striking forest-green eyes.

I stretched a trembling hand out for them as I writhed in the flames, but they morphed before I made contact, becoming a curtain of jasmine and honeysuckle that parted to reveal the stark outline of the Mystique Mountains. A star brighter than the rest pulsed in the air above the highest peak, sending a sharp pain through my heart. Then, the stars rearranged themselves. They formed a constellation of a rope tangling into a knot I had tied many times before.

The images wove together. Threads merging to form my life, and I smiled at it, starting to recognize them for the whole.

But before I truly understood what they were forming, each delicate strand was severed, breaking them back into their individual memories. I felt the tear like a knife in my heart, like I was being shredded. They belonged together. All of those images, all of the memories that comprised my life—they formed one existence.

At the physical pain of them breaking, a scream wrenched itself up my throat. It felt as though a Spirit hand had punched through my chest cavity and ripped out my very heart.

In its wake, I was empty.

Make anew, a voice whispered inside my head. *We will restore.*

"Restore..." I muttered, my voice fading into the flames.

A cleansing. That's what the Spirit Fire was. My spirit...my soul...my being were all being cleansed, each memory ripped out of me. The fire was assessing what I consisted of, what my essence was built of, and deciding if it was the right composition. Ghostly hands crept through my body, searching my blood. Their presence ached.

The webbing on my wrist throbbed at its core, thrashing about in the dark epicenter of the pain. It burrowed deeper into me. I screamed out as I had longed to these past weeks each time I had to hide the affliction.

Then, that too felt like it was being drawn out of me. Just as the memories were. It was agony as that creature—that living Curse—was leached from my blood. It clung on, wrapping itself around my veins, and I didn't know who was going to win. Each individual strand of the web tore at me, like if it must leave, it wanted to extract my nerves from my body. The pain was so vast, I couldn't see the Curse losing.

With each memory expelled and examined, I felt closer to death. They were taking pieces of me, and I didn't know who or what I was without them. *End it. End it now. End it quickly.* I thought again as the green eyes reappeared in front of me.

Only this time, their meaning was lost to me.

End it.

Please.

End it.

I was at the end of my tolerance. There was no more room for hurt in my emotionally wrung-out body. I had suffered so much, felt burned up, and this was the final battle. The one that wouldn't only sever these memories from my consciousness, but sever my life from this earth. And I would be okay with that if it happened quickly.

But something flashed.

A memory clicked into place. A pair of comforting arms

wrapped around me under a moonlit night, tears falling freely from my eyes.

Another joined it. A darkened, wrinkled hand upon my shoulder and the knowing smile that accompanied it.

Blue eyes and tawny eyes, and a sleek, black ponytail.

The Spirit Fire was no longer pulling apart my memories, it was restoring them. The ones that formed my life as a woman of the Mystique Warriors. It gifted them back to me after their search of my heart and mind, finding the truth that lay within.

With each piece restored, I felt less like fabric with frayed edges. I was becoming whole. Each image made me stronger than before—stronger than I ever had been in my life. Because I needed those memories, the people in them, and the lessons learned, to be who I was meant to be.

I flexed my muscles, testing the theory, and with the slight motion, the blue fire around me pulsed. It no longer severed parts of my mind. I controlled it now.

As I watched, the flames healed my wounds, but I kept the scars on my side and forearm. White streaks against tan skin to serve as reminders.

I spun in circles, relishing the newfound strength. This was it. This was what I had waited for my entire life. The flames had healed my broken pieces, cleansed my tainted soul, and deemed me worthy of being a Mystique Warrior.

A bolt of flame wrapped around me and rushed me toward the surface. Tears threatened to fall.

In seconds I would emerge into the flame pool outside of the Mystique Temple. There would be questions to face, probably anger, but I did not care. Nothing could tarnish this moment.

The surface was closer now, a thin layer of blue flame keeping me from claiming that future. I closed my eyes, relishing in the fact that I'd done it. When everyone told me to give up, I'd fought against fate and won. With pride burning a hole in my heart and tears now coursing down my cheeks, I shot through the surface with a triumphant scream.

I'd expected a field of billowing grass set atop the mountains, surrounding the temple and the flame pool. Instead, I tumbled across cool, hard ground. The rocks cutting into my exposed flesh felt wrong.

When I opened my eyes, my heartbeat quickened. I slowly pushed myself to my feet, taking stock of the weapons strapped to my back and belt. I turned in a stunned circle, absorbing the rock walls, scent of ash, and orange glow in the distance.

I was not standing atop the Mystique Mountains with a clear, starry sky above and warriors surrounding me. There was no midnight breeze against my cheeks or soft grass and wildflowers around my knees.

I was still within the Spirit Volcano. Something had gone horribly wrong.

CHAPTER THIRTY-SIX

MY BOOTS PADDED ON the rock floor as I turned in a circle. Unease spread a cold pool behind my navel, creeping along my bones.

Ascended warriors were relinquished to the temple once completing the final phase of the Undertaking. The scene was one of legend: a warrior rising up from the flame pool atop the mountain like a phoenix rising from the ashes.

But I remained within the mountains, spit into a different cavern than the spot where I dove into the Spirit Fire. Smooth rock floors held me up, and cracked walls and ceilings towered over me. There were no veins of fire running through these surfaces. It was all gray stone and an aura of blue from the small puddle of flame that spit me into the cave.

As I watched, that circle receded into the floor, taking with it most of my light, leaving only the faded orange glow in the distance. I waited for my heightened sight to adjust to the nearly pitch-black air around me, panic ebbing further into my veins with each passing second.

I ran my hands over my torn leathers, feeling for any new discrepancies. My belt at my waist was still strung with Starfire, my dagger was sheathed at my thigh, and at my back, Malakai's spear was still a steady presence. A reassuring hand in this uncertain moment.

"How in the Angel-guarded hell did this happen?" I whispered into the cave, my voice bouncing off the walls and slithering around me. I wrapped my arms around myself at the sound and sank to a crouch on the balls of my feet.

The feeling of failure settled into my bones. I was trapped by the malfunction of our sacred ritual. The one thing I had always been certain I was destined for had betrayed me. Was fate all a great joke? Because it seemed to be making a comedy of my life. Loss and grief and guilt had been my constant companions; it only made sense that failure now mingled with them.

My fingers dug into my sides, gripping torn leather and flesh. I breathed through the tightness in my chest, through the crushing weight of disappointment, of inadequacy darkening my vision.

No, I thought, straightening my spine much more quickly than my reflexes were used to. It didn't matter how I ended up in this cave, but I did. Panicking wouldn't save me. This was not a failure; it was a redirection. I'd survived the Undertaking, was deemed worthy of the blood in my veins, and this was only a new challenge I must face.

I am Ophelia Alabath, and I am anything but inadequate.

The voice speaking in my head was mine, and yet it was different. It was sturdier, more assured than I had ever felt. This new echo was more than confident. It rang with infallible power and light, igniting the dregs of shadowed hope I clung to.

I stretched my limbs, and that was when I noticed the shift that my fear had previously hidden. It was subtle, not so much a reconstruction of self as it was an emphasis of everything that had already existed within me. The power in my blood—that birthright gifted to me by my ancestors—had been fed. I had honed my body for twenty years. I'd been denied the chance, but nurtured that power. When fate said no, I fought, and now the stirring strength inside of me was prepared to step into its legacy.

My muscles were firmer, control more eloquent. I unsheathed Starfire and sliced her through the air with deadly precision. Even in the dark, I knew the sweep of my blade could cut a hair on a man's chin.

I moved through the tunnel swiftly, twirling spear and sword around me in my usual training regimen. I had been skilled before, but now I moved as smoothly as a breath of deadly wind, ready to consume what stood in my path with silent vengeance.

The feel of my weapons—particularly the spear—was glorious. I had not known true weapon work until this moment. A grin bloomed across my cheeks, because I was an ascended Mystique Warrior, and the power within me was in endless wealth.

My sight grew stronger by the minute—better than ever in memory. My hearing, too—the dull roar echoing through the chamber felt like it came from within me. A silent beast breathing, and...something else. A sharper sound, like metal thrashing against rock. A shiver danced along my bones, ghostly fingers trailing down my spine, but my stomach swirled in anticipation.

I returned my weapons to their homes and braced my arm against the wall of cool rock, resting my forehead against it. "I did it," I mumbled to myself, tears threatening to overflow my eyes. This moment I had dreamed of and strived for...so many obstacles tried to keep me from it, yet I had survived.

I was alone, but I was whole. When the Goddess of Death finally greeted me, I would go as a warrior.

Death...I slowly raised my head to look at my wrist, having forgotten about the affliction lying in wait there.

The Spirit Fire had dissolved the linen wrapped around my arm, revealing the thin lines of gray-and-green webbing that still wound their way through my veins and branched up my forearm. The heart, where the pain had been the most excruciating, was still an orb of solid black against the inside of my wrist.

But I could not feel the Curse within me.

My arm no longer felt heavy—it felt restored. The pain, both the subtle residue of it and the agonizing throbs, were gone. Sucked from my veins along with the burden.

The Spirit Fire had wiped the Curse from my blood.

My body loosened, like a tension I hadn't realized I held suddenly lifted. The dark lines now resembled a tattoo—a symbol, a reminder, but not a threat.

I was healed. Tolek could be healed—that realization was like dunking my heart in gold and watching the relief shine through my pores. This knowledge could change everything should the affliction ever appear again. If the Undertaking had never been suspended, we may have known years ago.

Though the webbing on my skin lingered, I looked at it with an odd affection. I couldn't quite place it, but fondness spread through me at the sight. The Curse had changed my life in an unexpected way. I had been prepared to greet death, but found something worth fighting for. Had cowered so long in darkness, but was pushed to become who I was meant to be. The delicate webbing—uniquely beautiful now that it wasn't poisoning my blood—was a mark of the hope I'd held on to and would continue to nurture.

I stood tall in that dim cavern and looked ahead. Something had certainly gone wrong in the Undertaking to deliver me to this spot, but so many things had also gone right. I would find a way out of here.

My steps were featherlight as I moved to the edge of the cavern, my hair swinging forward when I peered around the corner. I was in an offshoot of an intricate set of tunnels—how long these had existed, I had no idea. There was not a person to be seen in this stretch of gray walls.

Hesitantly, I stepped around the corner. With so many paths, I chose one at the insistence of the twisting feeling in my gut. The shadows masked me between the orbs of mystlight gathered along the ceiling and moonlight seeping through cracks in the walls. We were near the outer wall, then, not in the heart as I'd supposed. Stars were muddled by the smoke, making the light a tarnished gray rather than the bright white I was used to, but it was bright enough to be certain.

My thoughts flickered to my friends and Jezebel as I crept

through the tunnels. Had they made it to the flame pool? Were they wondering why I had not yet appeared? Though I had no concept of time, it must be well into the night by now, creeping toward dawn.

I only hoped they were safe. I would crawl my way out of this maze if need be to find my way back to them.

I continued choosing routes that had that dull gray light filtering through spaces in the walls, afraid of losing the freedom of the sky. Was I traveling up or down? Was I walking in circles? I shoved the questions away, trusting my instincts would not steer me wrong.

My blood pulsed wildly through my body, a beast within me rearing to be unleashed. Something was coming—it could feel the threat. My back pressed to the wall, shoulder blades digging against the rock. With a hand hovering over the hilt of my sword, ready to strike, I crept toward the mouth of the newest tunnel and peered around the corner.

To my left, a deep orange glow flared in the distance. The heart of the volcano. To my right, more mystlight and a stretch of empty tunnel, reaching into the darkness. Pathways branched out from this one, deepening the maze. I did not know which side to give myself to.

The air shifted. A familiar but out-of-place scent wafted to me. That sound of metal against rock reached me again from the path to the right, growing louder now. Closer.

I looked between the darkness to my right and light to my left.

I turned right.

Chapter Thirty-Seven

Malakai

How long had I been in this cave? I'd lost count of the guard's shifts, but they switched every few hours, so it must have been at least a day. Without the window of my former cell and the moon to track across the sky, I was a victim to time.

My brain—still foggy from the drugs they gave me—pounded, my vision hazy. They must have continued to work it into my system even while I was out, because my neck muscles were barely strong enough to hold my head up. Soon, it would pass. Then, they'd likely dose me again—unless they were busy dealing with…someone else.

The wound in my side was bleeding, a fresh bead of crimson trickling down my body. It must have ripped open when I thrashed against my chains, but with my arms restrained above my head, there was nothing I could do to stop it. I tested my muscles, trying to swing my arms, but the chains clanged lazily against rock.

For the first time in my life, I was truly broken.

The horrific reality of what my captor was doing cut into my soul with each second that I remained in this cave, but still, I could not bring myself to fight. Each wound on my body seared, a reminder of what she may be suffering. I pictured the same marks being put upon her skin, and nearly vomited. When I closed my eyes, she was there, bloodied and bruised. And, fuck, if ever given the chance, I would ensure they all paid.

I tried to imagine any path in which she escaped. I prayed to the Spirits that I was not even sure I believed in, *If any of you are lurking nearby, please help her.* But it was futile. She was powerful, I'd never deny that, but she was one girl against an onslaught of soldiers and my captors themselves. I didn't see how she could win.

Would they let me see her when they were done? Let me say all those things I left unsaid?

Angels, why the fuck had she come here? She was supposed to be safe.

With a painful shudder, I wondered which moment would be the one in which she drew her last breath.

Footsteps echoed down the passage stretching before the mouth of my cave, quieter than usual. The bearer lighter—or stealthier.

A shadow-shrouded figure emerged from a hidden corridor halfway between where I hung and where that orange glow permeated the air. I braced myself, chains above my head clinking, and fought the slackening muscles in my neck. I may be chained, broken in every sense, but I would not show them how mangled my heart was.

I would look this guard in the face as they enacted their torture on me, and pray that they struck that final blow. Taunt them into it if need be. Anything to end this existence, because it no longer felt like a life.

Through my clouded vision, this guard looked smaller than the rest. Feminine. She did not seem familiar, though the shadows made it hard to tell. Clinging to the wall, she turned to look over her shoulder every few feet as if confused or disoriented.

This was the best they could do? I sighed.

My blood didn't quicken as she moved closer, and I realized I wasn't scared of what happened next. This guard didn't have the same bravado as the others. Even if she did, my body had grown so numb, I likely wouldn't feel anything. A twisted ghost of a smile split my lips—perhaps I could die peacefully.

She prowled through the shadows, seemingly unaware of my presence in the dim cave, but each step the guard took stirred a slumbering energy in my core.

A warm breeze drifted down the passage, a familiar scent floating on it, wrapping around me. It was a memory I had used daily to ignore the reek of my own blood—jasmine tangling with the crisp night air. My body welcomed it, a bouquet of everything that was good in the world, but I shook it off.

It is not real, I reminded myself. My mind was toying with me in this last desperate hour, conjuring fantasies of my deepest desires and fears. Falling victim to their tricks would only leave me more vulnerable.

Then, the scent shifted, and it became slightly wrong. Punctuated with a harsher undertone of ash and copper.

The fire in the distance pulsed—the orange glow lightening to vibrant gold for a fraction of a second, illuminating her—and my knees wobbled beneath me.

How—

Her face was in shadow, the light a halo, but that hair. The beautiful, soft golden hair that I had dreamed of nightly—I would recognize it anywhere, even under the thin layer of soot that coated it now.

The way it curtained her face—a shield to hide her deepest thoughts. How she always wore it tumbling down her back and lashing around her shoulders, whether training or riding or lounging among the wildflowers. It caught the light now just as in my memories.

Even from this distance I could feel the warmth of her body against mine, as if not a day had passed since I last held her. My hands tingled with the memory of soft skin that hid the depths of her soul from the world. The flicker of hope I had lost filled my veins in a roar of flame that rivaled the memory of her mouth against mine.

I opened my cracked lips, forced my voice through my dry throat, and exhaled, "Ophelia."

CHAPTER THIRTY-EIGHT

OPHELIA

MY SPINE STIFFENED AS that husky, strained voice reached my ears.

The ghost of a voice that had haunted my waking and sleeping hours, pulsed with every step I'd taken, and echoed every beat of my heart for over two years.

I hurried down the passageway, no longer taking care to stick to the shadows. All that mattered was finding the source of that voice. It couldn't be—it made no sense. Still, I ran.

My feet stumbled over one another in their haste, limbs shaking with every ragged breath. Ahead, I could make out the outline of a cave, no door or gate of any kind blocking it. That was where the whisper had drifted from, but my mind refused to believe what my ears heard. It was afraid to believe what my heart wanted. Afraid to let it break again.

Tension bracketed my muscles as I inched closer to that cave mouth, drawn to it. To whatever—whoever—lay beyond. What if this was a trap? A test of the Spirits. A trial to find out what I was willing to lose.

But did it really matter? Whether it was a facade or the real thing, I could not ignore it.

So, I stepped forward, and when I crossed into the dim cave, my soul lit up in flames, its missing piece in sight.

My jaw wobbled, eyes stinging. I was suspended in disbelief, body numb. My breathing quickened through the sobs working their way up my throat.

He hung—*hung*—from the ceiling, chains on his wrists pulled so tightly that his feet barely reached the ground, a matching set tethered to his ankles. The scent of blood mixed with sweat hit me, but his chest rose and fell slightly. Breathing. *Alive*, the thread of his soul tied to mine seemed to say as it tugged on the Bind.

"Malakai." My voice was a crackle of doubt against the warm air.

Those hooded forest-green eyes hadn't left my face.

"So formal." His lips parted into a whisper of a smile, and even through the dirt and blood, that gleam that met his eye was my undoing.

Something within my chest unlocked, tears spilling down my cheeks. I catapulted to him, colliding like two stars shooting through the sky. He groaned, but leaned into me, and I clung onto him. Thank the Spirits. He was here. Alive. Whole—but not undamaged.

Worn leather and honeysuckle was so much stronger than it had been in my memory, overpowering the blood and rust. Even here, despite his state, he still smelled like *mine*.

My hands locked behind his head, and I didn't miss the fact that I was half supporting his neck, but our lips crushed together before I could ask. I sighed into him; he tasted like home. My body lit up, heat coiling within me. The darkness I'd muddled through for years receded with every stroke of his tongue against mine.

Pressed together in a darkened cave, two years of longing unfolded into that moment, and I could have stayed like that forever. But the coppery tang accenting his cracked lips reminded me where we were.

I broke the kiss reluctantly, rested my forehead against his, stared into those heavy-lidded eyes that held a piece of my soul, and wept. Even through blurry tears and chains, he was the most beautiful sight, this moment sewing up pieces of my heart. Despite my vow, I truly thought I might not live to see him again, and that truth I'd avoided facing quaked through my body. If I had my way, I would never look away from Malakai again.

"How—" I couldn't finish the question, but how and who and why...I would get all the answers, and then I would slice the throat of every person who had a hand in him being here.

My fingers continued to support his head, his hair so much longer than I remembered. Like it hadn't been cut in years. It was thick and lush beneath my hands, but among that tangled mess lay a labyrinth of fresh scars and matted blood. A fresh one shone along his jaw. Each brush of my fingers over a raised bit of flesh sent a tangle of hatred through my body.

Who did this to him? Angels, I'd grind their bones to dust.

Malakai...my North Star...come back to me. How often had I repeated those words when *this* was what was being done to him? My pulse pounded—both *my* heartbeat and the one awakened by the spear.

It was that steady adrenaline that held my shocked frame upright as I pulled the dagger from my thigh and poked the tip into the first lock at his wrist. Barely knowing what I was doing, barely able to reach—dammit, did he have to be so tall? —I maneuvered the blade. *Please, please work*, I begged any Angel or Spirit that may be watching, but kept my expression neutral, sensing Malakai's half-closed eyes watching me for any hint of trouble.

The only sound in the cavern was the gentle tinkering of the blade within the lock, the distant roar of the volcano, and Malakai's labored breathing. The rasp in his throat had me rotating the knife faster, forcing my hands to remain steady.

Malakai dropped his head to my shoulder and inhaled. "Why are you here?" he choked out, voice only a whisper against my skin, but I thought he sounded angry.

So many questions from us both, but I couldn't waste time with answers. Not when whoever locked him here could return any minute. Not when that light in his eyes was growing more distant by the second and his head felt heavy against me. I flicked my gaze down his body and realized how slack it was. He'd lost some of his muscle, likely not having been allowed to work out, but the mountains kept him relatively strong. It was the drooping stature of his frame that concerned me more. Something beyond the chains kept him sedated.

"Listen, Malakai," I whispered hurriedly, lowering one hand to lift his face and turn it toward me. He leaned into my touch with a sigh. "I need to get you out of here. I need to get these chains off."

My free hand fluttered over his body, taking stock. So many scars. There were *so many scars* on his skin. His back, arms, and chest were all littered with them. My stomach turned over at the fresh-looking one on his right pectoral—directly opposite the Bind. Four points in a vertical line and two more to the right, forming a square with the top half of the line.

The Engrossian constellation—the Ax. Someone had carved that forsaken symbol into his flesh. I saw red when I looked at it.

My fingers slid through a sticky trail of fresh blood on his ribs. A puckered pink wound appeared to have reopened, exposing a deep slice into the muscle. "Fucking Angels," I cursed.

Malakai released a breath of a laugh at my curse. "Spirits, I've missed you, Ophelia."

The words tore at my heart, and I wanted nothing more than to hold him. Hold this broken man before me and never let go as I never should have let him go on his eighteenth birthday. But I needed to get us out of here first.

And murder whoever had dared to touch him. Looking to the Ax, I knew who my enemies were. Though that didn't explain why he was *here* of all places.

I turned his face to me, gently brushing his cheekbone with my thumb and pressing one quick kiss to his lips. A reminder that I really was here. "Just give me one second. I'm getting you out of here." The promise in my eyes was urgent even as his lids drooped.

"The drugs—they'll move out of my system soon." He sounded as though he was trying to reassure me.

Later. I forced myself to take a steadying breath at the mention of drugs. *I will get revenge later.* I placed my hand beside the Bind and kissed the tattoo, reminding him of what truly mattered; then, I returned my focus to the lock.

After what felt like an eternity, there was a click, and the first cuff opened. Malakai's arm fell to my shoulder. I freed his other wrist and gently lowered him to the ground.

"Just one more minute, Malakai," I encouraged us both, desperation and determination tangling in my voice.

He watched me work on the shackles around his ankles, only breaking the silence to whisper, "My spear?"

The weapon flared hot against my back, energy spreading through my spine. "I've been keeping her warm for you." I looked up to him as the first ankle cuff sprang free.

His eyes softened, but something troubled lingered in them. "You hate spears."

"I like this one." I blushed at the memory of how right it felt to hold this spear, heat creeping through my body, but that agitation didn't leave his eyes.

The second ankle shackle opened, falling to the floor with a clatter. I sighed in glorious relief and shot to my feet. "Do you know how to get out of here?"

Malakai shook his head, long black bangs falling into his face. "They've always kept me blindfolded or drugged when they moved me."

Drugged. The word echoed through my mind, solidifying the vengeance in my gut into a burning hot need for revenge.

In the time it took me to free him, Malakai had regained a bit of his strength and color, and he leaned against the wall as he struggled to push himself to his feet. I slid my arms around his torso to help him up, but he tensed beneath me.

"What is it?" I asked.

A voice behind me drawled, "Leaving so soon?"

My head whirled, hands still supporting Malakai, and the figure in the gray cloak nearly knocked the breath from my lungs.

"Lucidius?"

Chapter Thirty-Nine

Lucidius Blastwood rounded the edge of the cave, his gait oddly predatory. His gray cloak nearly blended into the stone walls around us, making him appear as a living piece of the volcano. His eyes went first to his son, standing weakly with arms around my shoulders. Beneath my hands, the muscles in Malakai's scarred back tensed.

The Revered's gaze swept across his son's unchained wrists and ankles, then to the dagger returned to my thigh, absorbing the scene. I watched him process what I had been coming to terms with since my eyes landed on Malakai—the gruesome truth of what had happened two years ago when his son disappeared. I waited for the disbelief, the grief, the anguish to splash across his features.

"Lucidius?" I repeated, breaking his stupor. Malakai's fingers curled against my shoulder.

Lucidius lived in the Revered's Palace in Damenal, the city atop the peaks. He rarely returned home to Palerman. Was he realizing as I had that all this time, his son had been so close? Was he toiling through the guilt of a father not sensing the pain of his son? Did he blame himself for not stopping it sooner?

"Lucidius," I said louder, an edge of pleading seeping into my voice. "We need to get out of here. Malakai...he's weakened. We have to get him out. Can you show us the way?"

He must know how to get out of the Spirit Volcano. He was

the Revered, and this land was under his jurisdiction. He had found us here, within these cavernous walls and flame.

The unmarked shift in his being that I noticed at my birthday struck me again, an unidentifiable emotion trickling down my spine. How had he found us?

"No, Ophelia," Malakai rasped. He cleared his throat. "He cannot help us. Or rather, he will not."

I looked from father to son, struggling to grasp the hatred in Malakai's eyes. So bright. Burning. A flush rose to his cheeks as he glared at his father.

No, I refused, biting my lip to keep from shouting the words throughout the cave. *It can't be.* The trickle down my spine spread along my bones, and I finally recognized it for what it had been—a warning.

But even as the denial roared through my brain, my heart knew it to be true. I stared at Malakai, my mouth agape, but he kept those smoldering eyes on his father, the venom in them returning a semblance of life to his face.

"He brought me here." Underneath the malice in his words, I heard the breaking of Malakai's heart that followed that confession. Like it was a truth he had been refusing.

The volcano could have erupted around us, and I would not have heard it. No sound or thought reached my mind other than the echo of those words. *He brought me here.*

My hands stumbled over the long scars crossing the length of Malakai's back. From lashings. His father…*his own father* had done this to him.

"But—" I looked at the Ax carved into Malakai's chest, grasping on to the first thing I could. "The Engrossians."

"Working with him," Malakai clipped.

The man standing before us, the Revered Mystique Warrior, protector and leader of our people, upholder of justice, was responsible for the disappearance and torture of his only son and heir. The love of my life and my partner. Not only that, but he betrayed our own people, those who relied on him, by conspiring with our greatest enemy.

Red tinted my vision as it narrowed in on Lucidius's grimace. All I saw across his sharp features was my blinding desire for revenge. How could anyone enact such treatment against his own son? There was no justifiable answer, but I knew that it meant something within Lucidius had been warped. Changed into this despicable, disgusting being that stood before me.

"Why?" I growled at the man. "You kidnapped and tortured your son. You must have a very good reason, *Revered.*" I spat the title at him, satisfied to see him flinch at my ire.

A shadow of emotion flitted across his face. Was it remorse? I didn't care. No amount of penance could absolve him of the acts he committed.

I'd kill him. No matter what he said next, what explanation he offered, Lucidius Blastwood would die at the end of my blade.

"I did not intend for this to be the outcome." The Revered stood feet from us now. My sword was at my hip. In two strides I could end this, get my revenge and silence him for good. My hand flinched toward the hilt, but I froze when Malakai leaned into me, his body warm and steadying, communicating his thoughts with a gentle nudge. *Not yet.*

We needed answers. He needed answers. And the longer Lucidius spoke, the more strength Malakai could gain back.

"I may have believed that once, Father. But you did not stop it either."

I tightened my arms around Malakai's torso, sending him reassurance. *I'm here for you,* I channeled the sentiment into that merged piece of our souls in the Bind. Whatever he needed to say, whatever happened next, I was here.

"I only wanted to protect you. I had no control over *this.*" Lucidius waved a hand at the chains hanging from the ceiling, and his gaze hardened, an unreadable mask slipping over whatever emotions he truly felt.

"What are you talking about?" I snapped. "We are in your domain, certainly you are responsible."

The Revered's eyes darkened, the circles beneath them deepening as he angled his chin down at me. The condescension in his gaze was infuriating. "Ophelia." An angry growl rumbled in Malakai's chest when his father said my name, but Lucidius remained unbothered. "Do you truly believe I would torture my son?"

I was silent, unsure what to believe of the man before me anymore. The one who had been appointed Revered as the most powerful Mystique alive, but had brought shame to the title and himself. He wasn't who I thought he was—that much was clear—and that meant I couldn't know what lengths he would go to.

The question still hung in front of me: *Why did he do this?*

As if he read that unspoken inquiry, Lucidius said in his chilling voice, "Over two years ago, I made a deal with Kakias."

"Queen Kakias," I breathed, my hands stilling against Malakai.

Lucidius nodded. "She demanded Malakai in exchange for the end of the war."

"So, you handed over your heir? Just like that?"

"It was not an easy decision." His features were unreadable. "I saw how our people suffered, and I made a sacrifice that has eaten away at me every day since."

"You're lying!" Malakai barked, energy slowly returning to his drained muscles where they draped around me.

Lucidius looked between me and his son, eyes dejected. "We would have been entirely extinguished by the Engrossians thanks to the sorcia they partnered with. Alone they couldn't have beaten us, but with her..." He swallowed. "The Mystiques would have become extinct. The Engrossians would have ruled over the mountains. I couldn't have that. I thought Malakai would be presumed dead and live out his days in solitude. There's a cabin in the northernmost region of the range. I did not expect torture and—"

"Do you truly think that is the truth?" Malakai scoffed, and Lucidius flinched. "Or do you forget that I knew *everything* before coming into this Spirit-forsaken volcano? It was not tortured out of my memory as you may have hoped. I held on to it all for when this day might come." Malakai turned his gaze to me, voice softening a touch. "What he said is not the whole story, Ophelia."

I looked at him for only a brief second, afraid to take my eyes off of Lucidius, but I saw such pain festering behind his green irises that it could only be from one thing—betrayal. "What is the truth?"

Malakai deflated. "He's painting his actions as a sacrifice on his part, but every decision he made was selfish. He does not care about me."

Lucidius's jaw tightened. "That is where you're wrong, son."

"Am I?" Malakai gestured to the chains at his feet.

The Revered nodded, but his expression did not falter. "I never wanted this."

"But you caused it. Your actions for more than a century brought this about—your nefarious plans and dreams." Malakai pulled me closer to him. Whether it was to protect me from the truth or to lean on me for strength, I was not sure.

Silence surrounded us.

I did not care what Lucidius said. What truth he thought was correct. He had known that his son was being beaten for two years. *Two years* of scars and lashes and...carvings. I held no sympathy for the man, regardless of the tale he spun.

I raised my chin to the Revered, wrapping my fingers around Malakai's hip and squeezing to communicate that I understood. "But you still have not explained why, Lucidius. What do the Engrossians gain in eliminating Malakai from rule? We would have chosen a new ruler after you. With the end of the war, we were rebuilding. You cannot expect me to believe Kakias waged an entire war simply to get Malakai out of the way." Even for the queen of darkness, that was a steep cost.

In a blink, something in Lucidius's face shifted, and I knew I had found the exact question he had hoped to steer me away from. His veil of feigned remorse dropped completely. His brows lowered, and the shadows under his eyes deepened until his expression turned into a cold, cruel image of nightmares.

The gray of his cloak suddenly did not make him a piece of the volcano, but a commander of the sinister actions contained within. Understanding coated my bones with cold dread.

"The war wasn't a surprise, was it?" I guessed.

He laughed, the sound passing through me like a cold spirit. "I'd hoped you may believe my facade. We could have used you, but you have always been too smart for your own good, Ophelia. And apparently my son's brain has not been as addled as I intended." His casual shrug had my blood roaring in my ears.

"Very well, I shall tell you the full tale." A sneer twisted his lips. "Then, I shall dispose of you both."

My grip around Malakai tightened. Lucidius was a skilled fighter. If it came to that, could I survive the battle with him and escape with his son? Malakai's heartbeat quickened beside my head, waking a fierce determination within me. As long as the stars shone, I would not let that heart stop beating.

Lucidius's voice was harsher when he spoke again, as if the confession unleashed the truly sinister being hidden within him. "You are correct that I knew about the war before it began, but this plan has been in the works for decades. Much longer than either of you have been alive. It begins with my mother." His scowl deepened. "As a young warrior, barely a century old, she grew restless. She had not traveled since her summer exchanges as an adolescent and was eager to see the world, but she never made it past the Engrossians."

My brows cinched together, and Lucidius saw my confusion.

"No, she did not die there. But she did have a brief dalliance with a highly ranked Engrossian soldier. Nothing more than one night, but thus—I was born."

"You're...you're half Engrossian?" If that was true, he did not have the right to the Revered title of his Mystique father's bloodline.

Lips curling into a grin, Lucidius prowled around us as he spoke. "I am. But my mother hid it from everyone, especially the man I thought was my father. She went home and convinced him that the child was his. I was born with her tanned skin and dark hair, so there was not much question. Though, my eyes always favored those of my true father." He gestured to his face, and I swore I saw a bead of pride in those eyes—the ones Malakai had inherited.

"My mother died when I was only sixteen, but not before sharing her secret with me. And unaware of the truth, the Mystique man raised me as his own."

My mind raced to rewrite the history I thought I knew while also figuring out how this led to where we were today.

Lucidius continued, "I tried to force that other part of me away. The Engrossians were our rivals, after all. I grew up detesting them and their thirst for our power." His voice slithered over those last words, nothing but admiration in his tone. Based on the slight tremors rocking his body, I knew that Malakai heard it, too, and was as disgusted as I was.

"But I couldn't deny it." Lucidius remained lost in his tale, unfazed by our reactions. "I wanted to know the other half of my heritage. I wanted to see if I could fill this void within me that had formed when my mother told me the truth. So, a few years after her death, I started taking annual trips to the Engrossian Territory under the pretense of diplomacy. My Mystique father never would have let me go otherwise, for I had outgrown the age of summer exchanges, but I learned their history, their culture, and their strife, directly from my biological father. And that was when I met Kakias."

Lucidius's eyes turned a hungry green, so deep it was almost black. Barely darker than his son's, but in them I saw an emotion I recognized.

"It was more than just a treaty," I breathed. The end of the war, the diplomacy he masqueraded behind in signing that agreement, it was all a farce. The relationship between Queen Kakias of the Engrossian Warriors and Lucidius Blastwood, Revered of the Mystiques, was—could it be called love? Something rooted in such vile goals, manifesting into such atrocious actions, was surely a different kind of burning passion.

"I believe you two understand. A connection that deep cannot be explained, nor can it be severed." His eyes flitted between us, narrowing at the Bind on Malakai's chest. "She was everything to me, but only for that month of every year. For the rest of the year, I was to remain in the Mystique Territory, learning to rule from my false father's hand."

"If you were truly loyal to the Engrossians, how did you ascend to a full warrior?" The Undertaking surely should have killed him.

His answering smile was spiteful, as if he had been waiting for me to ask. "The pools of magic in the Engrossian valleys are rife with dark secrets."

Bile coated my throat. He had fooled our most sacred ritual. Made a mockery of it. Though I did not want to believe it, with each piece he revealed, his story became more irrefutable.

"The years went on, and it was clear that my father intended for me to marry another woman of a great Mystique bloodline."

At the sneer on Lucidius's face, Malakai and I both released low growls. *Akalain.*

He scoffed at our reaction. "She was beautiful, yes, and a talented warrior. She would make a good match for a future Revered, promised strong offspring, but my heart was elsewhere. When I told Kakias, she offered to kill the other woman—no questions asked—but we both knew that was a temporary solution to our larger problem."

His face softened a bit as he spoke of the queen, but my stomach rolled. Akalain was a true warrior, not this monstrous woman whose legacy was coated in unnecessary bloodshed.

"Kakias's mind is a wonderful thing. So ambitious. We found our solution. I would marry whomever my false father appointed, become the Revered Mystique Warrior after him, and Kakias would be the queen of her people. After decades of strife between Mystiques and Engrossians, my wife would die, and I"—he took on a tone of mock sadness—"the poor widower"—his voice turned cold again—"would propose the idea to unite the two most powerful clans, bringing honor to our Engrossian bloodlines that had been shunned for generations." He panted as his plan formed fully before my eyes, his chest rising and falling with unhinged aggression.

They'd been planning this for *decades*. Every clash between our clans in that time—it was all calculated. They'd created strife only to give them cause for a union when the time was right. It was cruel, calculated, a plan fitting of the queen I'd heard rumors of.

But somehow it had gone wrong. My mind sped ahead of the story, grim understanding spreading through me, making my limbs heavy with sadness for the man I loved. "But you messed up. The marriage was consummated, and you had a son with Akalain. A son and heir to the Mystique Warriors."

He nodded, his eyes shifting to Malakai. "I'd successfully avoided an heir for so many decades, until twenty years ago." He paused, and I could not read whatever emotion flitted across his face. It almost looked like uncertainty, but he masked it. "You were never intended to exist. *You* were the foil to our plan."

Anger flared hot and deep within me. It was an effort to remain where I stood.

Lucidius turned his eyes back to me, as if his son truly did not matter. "Kakias and I had a son the same year Malakai was born. A warrior who is three parts Engrossian and one part Mystique."

That final, key piece of information slid into place in my mind, and I gasped. The bastard-born heir to the Engrossian throne was...Lucidius's son.

Malakai's half-brother.

We had seen him before. Fucking Spirits, it had only been in passing during exchanges, and rarely for long enough to speak, but I dragged his face to mind now. The untamed black curls, the strong jaw and shoulders...if it wasn't for his mother's sneering grin and icy skin, he could have been a twin to the one I loved.

I scrambled to put my thoughts in order, shove away all emotional reactions to unpack later. As unbelievable as this was for me to discover, I knew it was harder for Malakai to hear. He had been so still as his father spoke. The only sign of life was his pounding heartbeat, but I squeezed him tighter and reminded myself why I needed to focus.

I no longer doubted Lucidius's threat to kill us.

"You staged a war—slaughtered thousands of innocents—in order to get this child into the Revered's position." I thought of the unrest now brewing within our territory. "Do you even care for the dozens of Mystique cities that are now going hungry, living in devastation thanks to your greedy grasp for power?" And for what? He already had power; he just could not share it with the woman he desired. Desperation born of love could truly turn you rotten.

"Don't you see? They need to suffer before they can be liberated by their future king. My true son will save those that survive." *His true son.* As if the one that stood with us, sharing his blood, meant nothing.

"So, you thought that by faking Malakai's death you would be able to usurp his title, place this other child into Mystique rule and unite the two clans? After the war it would look like a show of good faith to restore peace. You would send the people that make up half of your bloodline into such turmoil, take their honor away, to what end?"

He'd planned it all. The dismantling of trade deals between cities and clans. The lack of funds for quicker reconstruction. It all went back to Lucidius. I wondered if he was somehow involved in the disruption of the forest creatures and appearance of the beast that had attacked us, in the fae strife. He'd likely known of the talks of rebellion. That's what he'd wanted—to drive Mystiques to such desperation and then send in his new heir to save them.

The instinct to fight tore through my bones. While the man in front of me may be powerful, I was fueled by injustice, and that passion upheld a promise of revenge.

"The Engrossians showed me honor that the Mystiques never did. The Mystiques taught me to be a ruler, the Engrossians taught me to be a conqueror. They taught me what it takes to be a man who leads his people to glory."

I laughed, one breath of disbelief. "You are not a man. What you have done to your son…That is shameful; that is not something a man does."

"Everyone must sacrifice something, Ophelia. That is a truth you must learn if you wish to play this twisted game. I chose what I was willing to sacrifice, and before this is over, you will have to, too." Lucidius shrugged.

I did not want to play *this twisted game*. I did not want to play any games unless they ended with Starfire piercing Lucidius's heart and Malakai's spear impaling the queen's.

"You have deceived Malakai and betrayed him!" I screamed. "You have betrayed the Mystiques, and *you* will die for it, Lucidius."

He grinned, giving his son a knowing look, and a spark of unsettling glee lit his expression. "Betrayal? Oh, she does not know, does she?"

"What don't I know?" I looked to Malakai, but he cast his glance away. "What don't I know, Malakai?" I repeated in a whisper meant only for his ears.

But it was Lucidius who replied, "I did not deceive Malakai at all. Perhaps I did not know about the torture, but Malakai and I struck a deal. He knew about his half-brother and my allegiances. I told him before the end of the war. He was aware of my plan, signed the treaty himself, and he knew that when he left for the Undertaking it was to be a sham. Malakai left that day understanding that he would never return to Palerman." He took a step toward me and lowered his gaze. "That he would never return to you."

As it had the day Malakai walked away, my world tilted. His guarded behavior before the Undertaking, my mounting suspicion, and the reluctance I felt in letting him go…it had all been right.

Lucidius knew where to strike to hurt me the most. My grief, my rage…none of it had been a secret among our people, surely not those close to my family. He knew for two years what Malakai's disappearance had done to me. And he knew now what this revelation of Malakai's choice to leave would do, the wedge it had the power to form between his son and me.

I pushed away from Malakai slightly, still careful to support his weight, but far enough to breathe my own air. "Is it true?"

His nod didn't just tilt the world on its axis. It flipped it upside down. Never would I have believed that, given a choice, Malakai would have hidden these deeply spoiled truths and walked away from me. I could not have done so from him. We did not hide harsh realities from each other; we never had secrets. Or so I thought.

My North Star...his voice wove in and out of my mind. But he had not come back to me.

"Why?" I fought tears as this fresh sting of betrayal settled in my heart, shattering every sealed-over crack I'd worked so hard to heal.

"Ophelia." His voice cracked. "I didn't have a choice. I was saving lives, ending the war. And beyond that, he—they—threatened *you.* If I didn't agree to silently disappear, they would have killed you." Each word was punctured with the threat of tears.

"But you—" I fought to form sentences. "You chose to leave. You didn't tell me." My life may have hung in the balance, but it meant nothing to me without him.

He tried to bring a hand to my face, but I dodged it. "What choice did I have? If anything had happened to you, I couldn't have lived with myself."

I only shook my head, his choice unfathomable. I had spent two years searching for him. had risked everything to get here—the journey across Gallantia, the tundra, the near losses of our friends.

And he had lied.

"Oh, don't get angry with the boy." I had forgotten Lucidius's presence entirely. "It was his sacrifice that kept you alive. If he had told you, we would have taken you both." He leaned against the wall, crossing his arms. "You were a far greater prize than Malakai, anyway."

"What do you mean?" I asked, voice shaking.

Malakai's knees buckled. I gripped him tighter to support him, but he felt foreign against me—like the lie had changed him.

"Surely, you've put it together by now, haven't you? Or was I mistaken when I said you were smart?" Lucidius took slow steps toward me, watching me work through his words. There was nothing but pure malice in his gaze.

I was a prize. They wanted me either dead or remaining oblivious in Palerman, but not informed in any sense. *Why?* What pawn was I in their game? Was it that they wanted me safe in Palerman until the day I could be of use? That was likely the day they'd have killed me, regardless of any deal Malakai signed. I was willing to bet that they would not honor their word once it served them otherwise. They got Malakai out of the way and had me distracted and grieving, a lamb waiting to be led to the slaughter.

My mind swirled with pieces of everything I had learned, but the answer to his question felt like it hovered right in front of me.

"Malakai is not a full Mystique Warrior," Lucidius continued, laying out pieces of the puzzle, trying to tease me into solving it. Still, with his son hurting beside me, Lucidius treated this as a game.

"Neither am I," I admitted. "My maternal grandmother, she's not Mystique."

"And that small segment of your blood, combined with Alabath blood, is what makes your existence so delicious, Ophelia." He was close now, his face only a foot from mine. I could see the shadows swirling behind his eyes, tainting his soul. It was much too close for comfort, but I was frozen.

He looked at a point above my shoulder. "Haven't you wondered why that spear works so well for you?" The golden tip reflected in his dark eyes, gems sparkling.

"How did you—" The energy of the spear flared deep within me. "Did you send it to me?" The thought of him so close in the clearing that night when I was sick made me shiver.

"No." Lucidius shook his head. My relieved exhale was short-lived, because he continued, "That was not me, but after everything I've told you, you can't truly believe that we weren't watching you. We knew when you decided to complete the Undertaking. We knew about the little guest in your room the night of your birthday, and the affliction to your blood. Though, that seems to be cleared up. Unfortunate for me, as it would have made my job so much cleaner."

Damien. The Curse. Lucidius knew about it all.

"Who do you think sent the rogue Engrossians after you?" He smiled with malice. "When you threw the spear through that warrior's skull, everything I suspected was confirmed."

My heartbeat pounded faster with each word. At this proximity, I could smell his sweat and greed, but I would not be the one to back down.

"For reasons much more convoluted than I care to discuss right now, the spear belongs to you. Not Malakai. You are meant to be the Revered of the Mystique Warriors, Ophelia—proved the most powerful warrior of your generation. Not Malakai. The Alabath blood, descendants of the Angels, runs through your veins."

"It was removed from our bloodline. Annellius confirmed it." I couldn't get myself to speak the word *Angelblood* aloud, and I did not know if Lucidius would know who Annellius was, but it was the only thing I could think to say. The only explanation that everything he said was false, and the mysteries he was spinning were merely a labyrinth of lies.

"Was it now?" Lucidius turned away, but I saw a hand slide within his cloak. "Regardless, your life is a promise I have staked my loyalties on." He paused. "So, you see why you have to die."

I sensed the attack right before he turned.

I shoved Malakai to the ground, diving in the opposite direction. Lucidius's dagger grazed my temple as it flew past me.

Blood sprayed across my face as I rolled, obscuring one eye.

I jumped to my feet, unsheathing Starfire from my hip, and turned to face the Revered. One of the most renowned fighters alive. His movements were swift. Deadly. He did not care if I walked out of this cave. To him, my life was dispensable. *A prize*, he had said.

It was a blessing, then, that I felt the same about his.

I fought bitterly, but Lucidius was much more practiced. He

met each swipe of my sword easily, like I was a child with a stick. I cursed him for suspending formal Mystique training for the past two years, but the blame only fueled my anger further.

He swung his sword, a massive weapon with a silver hilt inlaid with black stones—not the blue gems typical of Mystique weapons. This was Engrossian. Curious that he did not carry an ax.

The lethal point skimmed the front of my leathers, nearly gutting me. Malakai screamed in distress, but I was quick. I spun around Lucidius, raising my sword at his back.

He turned and met my blow with unprecedented speed, the force throwing me backward.

Lucidius stalked toward me. In a flash of silver, a blade sailed past his ear, grazing the skin. Malakai had recovered Lucidius's dagger and chucked it at his father in a rage. He could barely stand, but he fought for me. Always protecting me.

I met his steel expression, and the nod he gave me said everything. He believed in me to end this. He gave me permission to, no matter how painful it would be to see his father die before him.

"You've always been a nuisance," Lucidius growled at his son, ignoring the blood flowing from his ear.

I lunged while he was distracted, but the Revered countered my move. We became a flash of silver blades, my golden hair, and his swirling cloak as we danced around the cavern. Both of our strategies were merciless, each aiming for the demise of the other.

He swiped his sword to my right. I lunged to avoid it, but he was ready. A blade, small and quick, sliced against my upper arm. In the moment I took to react to the pain, Lucidius raised a booted foot to my chest and shoved.

The crunch of my skull and spine colliding with the wall echoed in my ears. I collapsed to the floor.

Two roars punctuated the air as my vision faded: Lucidius, victorious—and Malakai, a tormented strangle I hoped to never hear again.

Chapter Forty

Dim mystlight filtered down as my vision focused. I braced my palm against the floor, clenching my eyes over a wave of nausea.

Metal, not rock, chilled the side of my body, and my fingers brushed something flaky. Dried blood. However long I had been unconscious—for the second time in as many days—had been long enough for the blood dripping from the wounds on my arm and head to solidify beneath me. I scraped it with my nails while my brain caught up to my senses, waiting for the world to stop spinning.

Lucidius. Malakai. The Engrossians. Was it all true? The deluge of information the Revered—no. He did not deserve that title.

The deluge of information *that man* had poured into me overwhelmed me as I pushed myself to a seated position. I touched the spot on my arm where Lucidius's dagger had sliced. The wound had already healed over, tender pink skin replacing the blood.

Bars surrounded me on three sides with rock at my back. Metal barriers and solid granite. *Caged.* Like an animal, Lucidius had thrown me into this metal box, wounded and unconscious. Every inch of my body throbbed when I struggled to my feet. Though I was healing, my muscles were exhausted. The cracking of my body against that wall reverberated through my skull, but nothing critical must have broken because I was able to stand.

My vision flickered before me at the sudden movement, and a

wave of dizziness buckled my knees. The bars caught my fall. Cold metal—so out of place in the volcano—bit into my flesh as I wrapped my hand around one.

"You should sit down." Malakai's voice was gentle as he spoke, and the familiar sound flooded me with relief, before my memories caught up with me, burning a hole in my chest and filling my throat with a rotten taste of betrayal.

I turned to my right. A cage identical to mine was built into the rock wall. Malakai watched me from inside of it. He appeared much more alert than he had been in the cavern, but wary. Not from the drug—which had passed through his system by now—or from any newly sustained injuries, but from the look of fury on my face when my eyes met his.

"Ophelia..." he began, his voice utterly broken.

"How long have I been out?" I interrupted.

His face fell at my dismissal. "It's hard to tell without windows. Maybe half a day."

"Half a day?" I turned away from him, inspecting the bars of my cage for weaknesses.

"Could be more or less."

"Helpful," I muttered in a tone I had never used against Malakai before. The rage that had pooled within me since he left mounted again, feeling familiar and foreign all at once. I thought I had escaped the shadow of fury that followed me, but it was like an old friend lying in wait. Malakai's lies had opened that door again. This fresh wave of anger was for him.

But I wasn't ready to face it, yet. I needed to survive Lucidius first, though a part of me wondered which was more likely to kill me: Malakai's betrayal or his father.

"Where are my weapons?" I asked, still not looking at him.

"Lucidius took them when you fell. Unstrapped the ones from your belt and thighs and the...spear." He stumbled over the word.

"The spear. It's mine?" Mine, not his as I was led to believe my entire life. It had felt like an extension of myself from the first moment I held it, felt that pulse pass between us. I attributed that to Malakai's lost presence, but I should have known. That feeling went deeper, the weapon calling to my blood. Awakening something within me.

"Yes." My heart cracked further, a hole widening within it.

"Okay."

"Ophelia, let me—"

"No, Malakai." I finally looked over my shoulder to find his gaze burning into me. "I'm not ready to hear any excuses from you. I don't want them."

Silence.

"How do we get out of here?" I asked, turning away again, unable to face the conflicted pleading and ire that mingled in his expression.

"The bars are sealed magically. Only fire melts them. I've seen them used. If we get out of the cage, I'm not sure where to go. But we can find our way out, together." His voice was stronger than before, as though finding a way out of this would fix something between us.

Together. I had longed for *together* for so long. But now that it was here, just an arm's stretch away, I was not sure if I could feel it.

I walked to the side of my cage that faced Malakai's and knelt down, the metal sending chills through the knees of my leathers. Malakai scrambled to me, gripping the bars on either side of his face, awaiting my next words.

I took a ragged breath over the hole in my chest. I wasn't sure if there was a future in our *together*, but that didn't wipe away the past or the present.

"And you're…are you okay?" My voice cracked over the words. They sounded ridiculous, because I knew there was no world in which he was okay at all. But, Spirits, please let him survive. Despite everything—no matter what came next for us—I needed him.

He sighed, shoulders drooping as his hands slid down the bars. "I don't know," he admitted. I waited for him to continue. "Physically, I'm fine right now. The magic here heals all of my injuries and pushes drugs through my system quickly. Mentally…emotionally…I don't know."

My heart cracked with each word. I looked into the green eyes I had missed so desperately, but lies and deceit clouded my view of them. I thought back to the utter perfection our lives had been before he left, and it felt tainted. Like we had existed in our own realm. The spotless glass that held our relationship shattered, and I was left standing among the shards. Perhaps it had always been an illusion—that bliss nothing more than a figment of young love.

I pushed away from the bars and settled against the rock, letting the solid presence of something natural steady me. Questions continued to fall stoically from my lips. About Lucidius's past. About what he planned for us. About who else may be here. And I told him about the Curse, about Damien's quest, and about the journey to the mountains.

But we never spoke about us. Never spoke about the betrayal Lucidius revealed, and never spoke about what would come next, should we survive.

Anger lifted Malakai's voice every so often, but he stifled it—answering my questions quickly and obediently like a lashed creature. It twisted my gut, because he *had* been lashed, and here I was, salting the wound instead of nurturing it.

But I was also hurt, and there was a long road before healing. Despair sank into my bones as I wondered if we would ever heal. Could things ever be the same, or were we destined to be torn apart? I ran a thumb over the tattoo on my arm, feeling his dampened spirit twisting along that thread in my body.

As I looked at the bars towering above us, one realization came to me. I at least wanted a chance to decide if healing was possible. A fierce determination sparked within me. Because healing would not matter if we died here.

Chapter Forty-One

I COULDN'T BE SURE how long we sat in silence after my questions trailed off. It may have been minutes or hours, the only sounds Malakai's and my uneven breathing, each listening intently for any move from the other, but neither wanting to break the still truce we had fallen into. No matter what came next, we were in this together for now. We had to be if we wanted a chance to survive. But the truth hovered between us—rotten and putrid.

Everything I had learned in the preceding hours swarmed through my mind on repeat. Each time I got to his deceit, it was like a fresh slice to my heart. But he had wounds, too. Physical and mental.

We were both hurting. I had to remember that.

Finally, boots echoed down the hall, and a masked guard opened the iron door to our prison.

"Hello, Warrior Prince." My eyes flashed to Malakai at the name, and he tensed. He knew these men, and from the subtle shift in his posture, I guessed he knew what their presence meant.

Malakai pushed himself to his feet roughly, muscles flexed to fight, but his voice was lethally calm. "You can have me. Leave her."

"Malakai—" I started.

He turned to me, his eyes pleading. He got here by protecting everyone else, including me. I didn't put the chains around his wrists or wield the weapons against him, but the physical, emotional, and mental scars he bore were the result of the undying love he held for me. What he had done to protect me and what he would continue to do.

But he was making another decision about my life without consulting me, and that was what tainted our relationship two years ago. The war, the Curse, the Undertaking, and our life together had all been affected by his lies, and I'd had no say.

No more. Despite my anger, I would not let Malakai sacrifice anything else for me. I would not let him continue to choose my fate. We had bound ourselves together by the tattoos on our flesh, partners and equals for eternity, but he had turned his back on that. Now, I would make my own choices.

Because Lucidius had revealed that I was born to be the greatest warrior of our generation. With newly-ascended strength thrumming in my blood, I would fight for myself and for Malakai.

I raised my chin and turned back to the men, assuming the same composure I had seen on Malakai. "Don't listen to him."

I heard Malakai's protests but shut them out.

The guard in front shook his head. "Touching, really, but stupid." A smile was barely visible beneath his obsidian metal mask. "It doesn't matter anyway. She wants to tend to you both herself."

Tend to us. Kill us.

He stepped aside and no less than a dozen masked guards filed into our prison, half approaching each cage. They gave me the same size guard as their *Warrior Prince*. So, they knew about my heritage. They knew that I was as lethal a threat as Malakai—perhaps more so. The thought brought a satisfied smile to my face.

The closest guard, a broad-chested figure with a tangle of purple scars down his exposed arms, spoke in a rough voice. "Stick your hands through the bars, girl." When his mask shifted, I could see something in those black eyes. Regret? Apology?

I latched on to it and slid behind my own mask. I shut out the fear, the heartache, and became the vicious creature that lurked beneath my bones, revenge-driven and cunning. Lucidius had said this was a twisted game. If it meant survival, I'd learn to play.

I took a step back from the bars, shaking my head. "No, I don't think I'll make it that easy for you, *sir*."

The kind-eyed guard balked.

I merely shrugged, my smile widening sweetly. "Did you really think I would?" I lowered my voice, as if sharing a secret. "You know who I am, don't you? I assume you do, otherwise you would have stationed more of your guards around *him*." I flicked my hand in Malakai's direction and walked to the front of my cage, leaning against the bars with ease and tossing my bloodstained hair over my shoulder. "I am a daughter of Alabath. I am the most powerful warrior of my generation." I leaned in conspiratorially. "So, truly, what did you expect?"

They were silent. Two guards in the back of the room shifted slightly as if they were going to step forward, but a third halted them. The picture of calm, I picked flecks of dried blood and dirt from my nails as I waited, masking the storm brewing within my blood.

"Griffus! What are you waiting for?" an Engrossian from beside Malakai's cage shouted at my tender-hearted guard.

"Griffus, is it?" I looked up at him through my lashes. Tension radiated from Malakai across the room.

The same guard from Malakai's side of the cavern called to me now, "Let him chain you. Or your lover will suffer the consequences." I straightened my spine, my pretense of control slipping as he uncoiled something sinister at his hip.

A whip.

I will not let Malakai sacrifice anything else for me.

"Ophelia, don't listen to them," Malakai pleaded. "They'll torture me regardless; you can't give in." His voice called to that nest of guilt in my heart.

There was a commotion on his side of the cave, and he was thrown back from the bars. His scarred back crashed into the rock wall behind him. The guard in front burned through the bars and all six of them entered his cage, forcing him against the wall and aiming various blades at his flesh.

It was a challenge to fit both of my wrists through the narrow bars, but I did it quickly, with steady hands. They would not see me shake. The rope was rough as they wound it around my scarred skin.

They burned my bars with volcanic fire, and Malakai and I were pushed into the center of the room, bumping against each other. Blindfolds cinched across our eyes, but even the feel of his muscled skin against mine was comforting. I wanted to sink into that feeling. For a brief moment, I allowed myself to fall back into our clearing and the endless nights we spent there. The cool breezes guarded me in a cocoon of jasmine, honeysuckle, and him.

But it was a false safety that belonged to people entirely different than the two standing in this cave. Someone prodded me in the spine. I shook my head and started forward.

The guards marched us through the maze of volcanic hallways, and I tried to memorize the dizzying path of my steps. The silence of the mountains was threatening, looming up and around us with ghostly whispers of warm volcanic winds. Even beneath the blindfold, the essence seemed to swallow us whole, like it knew what fate we were walking toward and the Spirits in this sacred place wanted to save us.

They couldn't though. We were alone.

Flashes of tarnished moonlight passed through the fabric across my eyes. *We must be near the outer edge*, I noted.

I pictured the way the light would land on Malakai's hair and skin, the scars attracting the white glow and pulsing before my eyes. Each flash embedded a silent promise in my mind. I would not die until one Engrossian guard fell for each scar on Malakai's skin. Then, Kakias herself would suffer. A slow and painful death, toying with her the way she had our lives.

I pictured the night sky again, and one star in particular, shining brighter than those around it. Demanding to be seen. I held the North Star in my mind with every step forward. Even now, amid this chaos, it remained a reminder of my own hope.

Pulsing. Beckoning. Reminding me to fight. If I could get

Malakai out, it would all be worth it. He may have hurt me—we may be broken—but he deserved to live after what had been done to him.

A devious smile curled my lips, rich with promise. Maybe this was the path to execution, but it would not be our own.

Chapter Forty-Two

THE AIR SHIFTED AS we stopped walking, volcanic warmth wrapping around my battered body. A hazy orange glow pierced the blindfold across my eyes, but that wasn't what caused my pulse to quicken. Even without sight, I could sense the authority in the room. Her power and the reverence of the warriors surrounding her was palpable, crawling up my skin, exploring me in a way that felt violating.

Sightless, I listened. Heels clicked against rock, every step louder than the last, the only other sound a crackle of fire. My breath quickened with each echo, but I steadied it. I held control.

The steps paused before me, mere inches away based on the way that unavoidable power engulfed me. It turned alluring, though I wished it were not. Invisible fingers tickled my skin, awakening my senses and enticing them to bow to her. My stomach rolled, but I straightened my spine, muscles straining against it. Against her. How she was capable of this, I did not know.

The blindfold fell from my face, and I stared into the cold, calculating eyes of Queen Kakias. She quirked a brow at my reluctance, reaching up to cup my cheeks with pristine hands, slender fingers ending in pointed nails. Her skin was soft against my own. These were not the hardened, calloused hands of a warrior who spent their life bearing weapons. No, these were the hands of a dictator who relied on the soldiers around her to do that. Kakias was only the mind that guided their abominable actions.

I took in her white skin, like an iced-over lake, not a crack visible but for the faded purple scars stretching from the center of her forehead diagonally across the left side of her face and disappearing under her sharp jawline. They eerily didn't twist her expression at all, looking more like paint than puckered skin.

The deep black of her hair was a stark contrast against the rest of her face, except those eyes. They felt endless, like I would fall into the dark irises forever and never return to myself. Regardless, I held her gaze defiantly, refusing to show any uncertainty, as I wound my pinkie into the knots at my wrist and fought to keep my spine from bowing to her power.

"Hello, child," she cooed, as if I were a baby. A chilling smile broke across her cheeks, pointed white teeth stark against red lips.

For a flash, I pictured those teeth dripping with blood, as her hands should be for all the pain she brought upon my life. For all the pain she brought upon this *continent.* Lucidius may be responsible, but I'd be a fool to forget the artful contrivance of this woman. While many barreled forward with strategies and swords, historical circumstance taught some to nurture a skill even more powerful—manipulation. Kakias had undoubtedly pulled the strings of fate to her advantage throughout the centuries of her life until I stood before her today. Hands tied, soul battered, but broken heart still beating. A twisted, vengeful desire gripped me.

I tilted my head, her own taunting smile mirrored on my face. "Hello, wicked queen."

Ire pinched her face, but it was gone in a flash. The queen released a haunting laugh, echoing off the rock walls around us.

When she took a step back to circle me and Malakai, I maintained my indifference. I did not allow my gaze to follow her, instead scanning for anything that might aid our escape. Malakai was to my right, brows lowered, gaze assessing. The twelve guards formed a semicircle at our back.

In the shadows, a cloaked form lurked. Lucidius. His presence riled my blood, but I forced myself to maintain my cool demeanor.

The cave was the largest I had seen so far. Even larger than that in which I met the Spirits, with towering ceilings and pointed tapers of rock hanging down from them. A set of large steps was built into the wall on one side, as if a crowd could gather in the space, and to my other side a bubbling cauldron sat above a fire. A rack beside it held—

I gasped, my resolve slipping for a moment.

My dagger, the spear, and Starfire winked at me in the flickering firelight across the room.

"Oh, you've seen my little welcome present?" Kakias intoned. My eyes were glued to my weapons. "Or perhaps a goodbye present is more appropriate?" Her dark dress dragged along the floor, the train a serpent in her wake.

The fire, the cauldron, the forge.

Her *present* was drastically clear. My precious weapons, the defenses that saw me through the journey here, the trusted presences at my side, were to be melted down and forged into something new. Engrossian battle-axes most likely. To deface any warrior's weapon was a disgraceful act among all seven clans, but this...this level of destruction. It wiped the warrior from existence, erased any honor they bestowed upon their people, and blurred any memories of their triumphs.

This was vile.

My eyes locked on Starfire, the blade that had trained me into the warrior I was today, then the spear, the weapon I had only begun to explore, and the rage I had so carefully contained was unleashed.

"You're a disgrace to all warriors, present and past," I seethed.

A cold hand snaked around the back of my neck. She whispered in my ear, her breath a hot sting against my cheek. "I would expect nothing less from you, Ophelia. You're rumored to be a ferocious little thing."

If that was what was expected of me, then I would oblige. I'd unleash every bit of fury that had festered within my bones for two years. Allow the power I'd honed to feed on it. I'd play her game of tactics and manipulation, striking low and without remorse.

"And you are rumored to be a cowardly ruler who has others torture innocent men to achieve your deranged goals." I jerked my chin at Malakai.

She circled back to face me. I caught the flash of hatred in her eyes when they flicked to Malakai, and I realized that his torture had been for no reason beyond her own revenge. The pain she felt over Lucidius having a child with another woman.

"I prefer ambitious, visionary, loyal to my cause," Kakias said, resuming her control.

"*Loyalty* does not justify the thousands of innocent lives you took in your sham of a war," I spat. How twisted her views were, how contrived her motivations. "Your ambition is tainted with death, Kakias."

"It is called *sacrifice*, dear," she sighed. "You'd be smart to become acquainted with the skill, to learn to conquer the ache it leaves behind."

I found it hard to believe that she knew anything of sacrifice. She operated on greed, ensuring others felt that jarring pain, the black hole it rooted in their soul. Kakias did not sacrifice—others did as a result of her plans.

"Why is that?" I growled. Fury and revenge became molten within me, and I'd unleash them if she thought to make a *sacrifice* of someone I cared about. My newly adapted strength begged to lock my hands around her slender neck.

"Because you will be the greatest sacrifice of them all."

My breath caught in my throat. For a moment, I forgot to fight the power driving my spine into a bow. I stumbled but recovered before she could win that battle. That wicked queen would not get my reverence, she'd not get my life—I'd ensure it.

Kakias stepped closer, until we were toe to toe. "It's a shame. We could have made a great team." She shook her head, actual pity in her voice.

Malakai practically growled, but Kakias paid him no heed. The hatred was clear in the tight set of his mouth and shoulders. He looked quickly to my wrist—where one finger tangled with the knots—and blinked in understanding.

"And explain to me, Kakias, why would we *ever* be a team?" I forced myself to resume an essence of that false sweetness.

She dropped her gaze for a moment, and I stilled my fingers, my heart rate speeding.

She was not looking at my hands, though. In her own she held something thin and silver, a blade as delicate as an icicle. She twirled it between her fingers. Black gems lined the handle, sending a myriad of colors around us where the firelight touched them. The reflections were searing poison against my skin. Lifting the dagger to balance it carefully between her hands, she regarded it like a treasure on display for its victim.

"Well, surely after that one is disposed of"—her eyes landed on Malakai briefly before turning back to me—"you will need a new lover. I have someone in mind."

My blood chilled, fingers gripping the rope. "Your son?"

That malicious smile returned. She grasped my chin between cold fingers and jerked it upward. With her other hand she brushed the hair from my forehead, prying it from the patch of dried blood. The hilt of her dagger pressed into my cheek. "He likes pretty things. I think he'd be pleased to have you as his own."

There was a shuffle behind us, a guard stumbling, and Kakias averted her attention for a moment. I looped my finger into the rope and tugged.

Then, she tightened her grip on my jaw and shoved my chin up farther. "But, alas, you would be too much trouble. I can see it in your eyes—the way they swirl with that unbridled power." She considered. "I think it's something we share, Ophelia."

"We share *nothing*," I spat, wrenching my chin from her grasp.

Her sharp-toothed smile was hungry. "The innocence of the naive is truly remarkable." Thoughtful eyes raked over my body, but she tutted, "It does not matter. My son wields enough power without you, so it will be cleaner if I simply take what I need now. Besides." She gripped my left forearm. "This would have to go."

The cool tip of her dagger traced the Bind where my leathers were torn at the elbow. Each second of the slow drag fueled my anger.

When she reached the tip of the star, she dug the dagger in gently, a bead of crimson blood forming around it, sliding downward over my scars. That dark power around my bones loosened as she watched it, hunger burning at the sight, distracting her.

Her eyes met mine, a cruel joy festering there, and I knew what she meant to do. It would not be enough for her to kill me; she had to break me first. Little did she know I had already been broken so severely by the man standing beside me that her attempts would be futile.

She tilted the dagger as if she would drag it down my arm. The ropes fell from my wrists. Her eyes widened, and I smiled sweetly.

"Oops," I whispered, before raising a fist and bringing it firmly against her jaw. The echoing crunch was satisfying, but I could hardly appreciate it before the room around us erupted.

The guards pulled axes. I ducked one and swiped two daggers from the owner's waist. I turned to Malakai, slicing through the binds at his wrists without looking and shoving a weapon into his hands.

"Show no mercy," he muttered just loud enough for me to hear.

"It's not in my nature to," I purred as my dagger sank into the side of a guard. Together, Malakai and I faced the host of Engrossian guards.

I couldn't help but grin as my blade repeatedly met flesh. I was not killing them, but I was inching toward the fireplace. Toward the weapons beside it. If I could get my hands on Starfire or the spear—

Cool fingers wrapped around my throat, crushing my windpipe and throwing me to the ground. The air blew from my body, and my head smacked into the rock. Black dots clouded my vision.

"Enough!" Kakias shouted.

Her bloodied warriors froze as her claws gripped my hair and dragged me to my feet to face her. The silver slit of her dagger pressed against my neck as she walked me backward. I couldn't fight, couldn't struggle as it sank deeper.

One motion, and that would be it. My blood would spill, my life would be ended. Malakai would die next, and the Mystique Warriors would forever be at the hands of this hell-sent queen with the soulless eyes and bloodied hands.

My legs hit a table beside the forge, and she forced me onto it. Splintered wood cut into the skin where my leathers were torn. I felt trapped. I did not understand the power she wielded to hold me here.

"The box," she called without taking her eyes from the place her knife met my neck.

A guard brought whatever she demanded, placing it on the ground beside the table where I couldn't see it.

I raised my chin, daring her to make that final slice.

"All of this precious blood wasted in a worthless girl," she whispered.

My chest tightened, but I refused to let Kakias see even a flicker of vulnerability. Malakai was on the ground, struggling against the guards.

The queen smiled as the first bead of blood trickled down my neck, a thin line of heat tickling my flesh, signaling that it was time to die. Metal caressed my skin like a welcome kiss, as if the Goddess of Death knew I had evaded her recently and had come to claim me now.

The blade pressed deeper. It was sharp—one slice and my life would be over. My eyes locked on Malakai, face drained of color and eyes wide, and I sent my goodbye to him with one slow blink, sending him riling against his captors.

Then, I met Kakias's cold stare, watched her lips split into a victorious grin. The blood thickened on my neck. Slowly. She was going to do this so Angel-dammed slowly. Make me feel every second of life leaving my body.

There was no preparing for it, nothing I could tell myself to make it hurt less. I was trying to grasp that grim reality when a flash of green armor threw aside the queen, knocking both her body and dagger away from me.

He tore his mask from his face, but it wasn't pale skin that shone in the firelight as he looked down at me.

It was tanned skin.

Brown hair with honeyed highlights and chocolate eyes fueled by vengeance.

Chapter Forty-Three

"VINCIENZO?" I GASPED, CONFUSION shooting through me. Fighting erupted around us again.

"Hey, Alabath," he breathed, fear and relief deepening his eyes. He glanced over his shoulder at the stirring queen, and his frame tensed. Turning back to me, he pulled me from the table. "I'm glad you're alive." He placed a kiss on my cheek, whispered, "I've got to go," and dove toward Kakias's body.

Stunned, I watched my best friend roll across the ground with his hands around the neck of the Engrossian queen.

Before I could move, one of the guards forced my hands behind my back. I thrashed, kicking the air wildly, but their grip was too solid. Panic formed a vise around my stomach as they forced me out of the fray of battle.

They shoved me toward the wall. I spun, poised to attack, but a gold chain with a crescent emblem and purple gem dangled around the guard's neck.

"Jezebel?"

She removed her mask and winked at me. I had never been more grateful to see her mischievous eyes. "Hello, sister. We're just in time, it seems."

"What—how did you get here?" I gaped at her, taking in the deep greens of her full Engrossian armor and weapons. I looked over her shoulder, and should not have been surprised to see

Cypherion fighting beside Malakai. Ax slicing through enemies, his scythe nowhere in sight.

Where he joined Malakai and Tolek, the three moved like a thread connected them. If one faltered, another struck, shifting as one along that instinctual rope. It was the beauty of their years of training tied up within their bond as brothers, and I wished that our lives weren't on the line so that I could marvel at it.

"When you didn't emerge from the Undertaking, we figured something had gone wrong. We returned to the Spirit Volcano and went in after you," my sister reclaimed my attention, a proud glow emanating from her. "We completed the Undertaking ourselves and have been prowling these tunnels in search of you." I understood then that the radiance around her was more than pride, it was the blood within her veins awakening.

At the sharp clash of weapons, Jezebel added, "I'd love to tell the tale, but we really can't let them have all the fun."

Malakai and Cypherion faced all nine of the Engrossian Warriors while Tolek circled their queen. I pushed Jezebel aside to run to them, but she grabbed my wrist. "You'll need these." My sister sheathed my dagger at my thigh and pressed Starfire's cool hilt into my hand. She warmed in my palm as if in greeting. Silently, I told the blade that I missed her, too.

"Thank you," I breathed, grabbing the spear from its place on the rack and launching myself at the Engrossian guards.

"Malakai!" I screamed as I ran. I threw his spear—my spear—and he swiped it nimbly from the air. In one motion, he ran a guard through, shoving the man's body to the ground and turning to take out another behind him.

With Starfire in my hand, I took up my place beside Malakai, guarding each other's backs as we were meant to do. Three Engrossians faced me, axes and daggers raised between them. The first lunged, and when his ax made it past my defense and sliced a small cut across my collarbone, I grimaced at my misstep. Malakai groaned as if he felt the pain himself, but he kept his focus on his attackers, leaving me to handle my own.

I smirked at the Engrossians before raising Starfire and slicing a delicate pattern between the three and myself, pushing each back and knocking two to the ground. My sword's weight was impeccable in my hand—the balance even more precise after the Undertaking. I swiped down across the back of the third Engrossian as he turned to flee, leaving his spinal column exposed to the warm air.

As he fell, one of his companions kicked out from where he lay. His booted foot met my ankle with a crunch, and I stumbled, screaming in pain.

Malakai's steady arm gripped my waist, supporting me. I brushed my fingers across the back of his hand in a quick acknowledgment that I was all right.

Ignoring the throbbing pain in my ankle, I charged at the fallen Engrossian. His eyes only had a second to widen. I brought my sword down and sliced his head from his neck, relishing the vibration of metal through bone. A vicious smile graced my lips.

When I looked up, seven guards had fallen to the blades of three fully ascended Mystique Warriors and Malakai. Two guards remained, retreating to where their queen fought Tolek with only a dagger.

We crept after them, circling our prey. I limped due to my wounded ankle but continued.

"Tolek Vincienzo, I am grateful to see you, but I swear on the fucking Angels, you better kill her now," Malakai said to his friend as he approached, cautious eyes trained on Kakias.

"Ah, my dear friend, I have missed you," Tolek responded in his most carefree voice. "Must she die? She could be so fun to torment."

Kakias's eyes darkened. "Those are words you'll regret, child." She sent her dagger flying toward Tol's heart.

He leaned so far backward I thought his shoulders would meet the ground. But he righted himself.

"That was your mistake, Your Highness." Tolek's voice took on a threatening hum rarely heard from him.

He launched himself at the unarmed queen, weapon poised to swipe diagonally across the front of her body, but one of her guards was faster. He impaled himself on Tolek's blade before his queen, sending his body smashing into Tol's. The two tumbled to the ground, and in the mayhem, the final guard grasped his queen's arm and ran.

We raced after them, Malakai stopping to help Tolek up, but when we reached the mouth of the cave, Lucidius stood in our path. He had cleverly avoided the battle thus far—a coward in every sense of the word.

I heard my sister and Cypherion quietly questioning his presence, but I couldn't take my eyes from the vile man before me. This all started with him, and now it would end with him. I knew from our last encounter that Lucidius and I were evenly matched fighters when it came to our swords. This would have to be a different kind of fight if I wished to defeat him.

Starfire clattered against rock as I tossed her aside, the noise sounding like a protest. "It is just you and I, Lucidius," I snarled.

He smirked, lowering his sword. "From the day you came into this world, Ophelia, you have been the bane of my existence."

I clenched my hands, refusing to be distracted. "You took so much from me, and now, I will get my retribution."

I flew at him, catching him in surprise and knocking him to the ground. Lucidius had brute strength—but I had swiftness.

We rolled through the cave, punching and scraping and kicking, but my friends knew not to interfere. This was *my* kill. My injured ankle barked in protest when he brought his foot to it, kicking the spot before the healing magic could set in.

I retaliated with a sharp knee to his gut. He released the hand he had on my wrist, and I shoved him to the ground. I wrapped my hands around his neck, feeling his life squeeze from his body. He landed a punch squarely against my cheek, whipping my head to the side, but my grip held.

Spitting out blood, I looked back to his purpling face and whispered, "You are a shameful man, Lucidius Blastwood." I tightened my grip. "Responsible for bringing so much pain into the world. It is time you experience some of it yourself."

I could feel life slipping from him slowly, sliding between my fingers. But he gripped my shoulders and threw me into the ground so hard that my vision clouded.

He was atop me in a breath, knees pinning my arms as he sat across my chest, sneering down at me.

Everything that had delivered me to this point flashed before my eyes. The first time I grasped that spear in my hands. The green-gray webbing that worked itself up my arm and the black heart at its center. The golden glow of Damien hovering in my room. The winged beast atop my sister. The ax that buried itself in Tolek's leg when he jumped in front of me. The fae knife digging into Santorina's throat. The yellow eyes of the wolf leader that I stared into while Cypherion sacrificed himself for our cause. The revelation of Malakai's secrets.

But with these images came brighter memories. The delicate, fleeting sparks of joy. The last dawn over Palerman, and the feeling of the wind in my face while riding Sapphire. Tol's smile as he shouted instructions to me and my sister during training. Cyph and Jez laughing in the stream. The moon reflected on Rina's hair as I guided her through the constellations. The hope in Malakai's eyes when they first met mine in the cave.

And for those reasons—those sparkling stars bursting through a clouded sky—I fought.

Lucidius's weight on my torso was slowly cutting off my breath. One of his legs pinned mine, but he was sloppy, leaving the other free. I lifted my injured foot behind him and drove it into his spine, hearing bones crack. The agony from my wounded ankle sent a shooting pain up my leg and a tortured cry escaped my throat, but he toppled off of me.

I pushed myself to my feet, ready to finally end this, but someone was there first. Santorina's long dark hair swirled around her as she dragged Lucidius up by a white-knuckled hold.

I stalked toward him, dragging my dagger from my thigh, a predator moving in for the kill.

Lucidius locked eyes with his son and whispered, "There's so much you don't know."

My eyes flicked to Malakai. Arms hanging loosely at his side, face twitching as if about to crumple, he looked conflicted. But it was his defeated sigh that sealed my decision.

Without another thought, I sliced the blade across Lucidius's neck. The sound of tearing flesh was both satisfying and heartbreaking as I realized what it meant for Malakai.

Santorina dropped Lucidius's body between us, facedown in a growing pool of blood. Her eyes raised to mine, black hair a flowing shadow around her as we caught our breath. Blood dripping from the blade to the floor was the only sound in the cavern.

Chapter Forty-Four

We dragged the bodies of Lucidius and the Engrossian guards into the hall to give ourselves a semblance of peace, but their blood left a red trail as a reminder through the cavern.

I set the former Revered's body apart from the others and stood over him for a moment. Skin pale from blood loss, darkened eyes staring into the unknown, he looked more Engrossian than ever. Still, I crossed his arms over his chest and lowered his eyelids before turning my back on him forever.

When I returned, Malakai remained kneeling beside the puddle of his father's blood, the curve of his spine and drop of his head forming the image of a broken soul. Firelight danced across the crimson in a breath of life, but his tear-lined eyes were unseeing. Despite it all, he mourned his father. Or maybe, he mourned the man he once thought his father was and the life that had been ripped away from him.

"Thank you," he muttered, raising his eyes first to Rina and then to me. "I could not have done that myself."

Rina relaxed, as if she had been awaiting a blow of anger and those words set her guilt free. She nodded, and something about her seemed different, but I could not place it.

My hands shook at my sides as the realization of what I had done—who I had *killed*—sank into my bones. Not only because Lucidius had been the Revered, but because he was Malakai's father. No matter his despicable actions, that fact would always remain true. Looking at Malakai now that the heat of battle had calmed, seeing how broken he truly was, I worried how my decision would affect him.

Neither of us spoke for a long moment. We exchanged gazes hardened by circumstance. Then, he looked back to the puddle.

"What happened?" Tolek's whisper was a knife through the tension and shock radiating from us all. He dropped to his knees beside Malakai and slung an arm around his shoulders. Cypherion sat on Malakai's other side.

Malakai shook his head, eyes clenched, the pain of it all still too raw to share.

So, I did it for him. My friends and sister were silent as I exposed the truth of Lucidius and Kakias's plans. Where Malakai had been for the past two years when they believed him dead, his father's secret family, and everything that had happened since I said goodbye to them atop the volcano. Through the story, everyone unconsciously drifted closer to Malakai, as if to shield him.

I even divulged my secret—the Curse I'd hidden from them and how it was lifted. There were a number of outbursts at that.

"This entire time, you were going to die." Rina gaped. The pieces clicked to place in her mind. My insistence throughout the journey, my decisions that were somehow rasher and more reckless than usual.

"I should have told you, but I needed you all to remain normal." Be strong when I could not. Anything else would have been admitting I might not survive to see my mission completed. My eyes stung, speaking to all of them but mostly to Tolek. "I should have told you when you touched my blood. But I hoped I'd survive—to fix it."

"You should have told me even before that," he said, but there was no anger in his voice. "You should not have felt the need to fix it alone."

The effects must not have had time to take root in his veins before he completed the Undertaking. I thanked the Angels for that.

"I don't understand how, though," Cyph said. I only shook my head, having no answer.

The only piece I left out of my explanation was the mention of the Angelblood in the Alabath line. That was my secret to be picked apart and deciphered down the road.

Malakai did not move as I spoke. He simply stared at his father's blood as it hardened into the rock floor. Tolek and Cypherion remained at his side. I watched the spot where Tol's arm draped across Malakai's back, hand gripping his shoulder, and two pieces of my still-broken heart ached at the sight of them together.

"But how are you all here?" I asked when I finally tore my eyes away.

"It seems you weren't the only one destined for the Undertaking," Jezebel answered.

"Lucidius forbade the ritual," Cypherion elaborated, the fire dancing in his blue eyes like a beacon against the crystal sea, "not for the well-being of Mystiques, but to our detriment." His gaze met mine, shoulders squared and jaw tight. "It was a guaranteed way to ensure the Engrossians rose above us."

I nodded as the deceit deepened. Lucidius had betrayed so many people.

"How did you get here, Rina?" I asked. "You can't have completed the Undertaking."

She shook her head. "When they went into the volcano…I couldn't wait up there, feeling useless. I thought there might be another way in, so I started down the switchbacks, and at the spot where we nearly fell, I noticed an inconsistency in the rocks. The side is false, and it opens into a slim tunnel. I think that's why the pathway was so weak. I crawled through it and trusted my instincts. Prayed to your Angels and Spirits that I would survive and let their gentle hands guide me—or whatever it is you guys say." Her tone was dismissive, but when her eyes met mine I saw pride in those dark irises.

Malakai's voice was cracked and haunting when he said, "That's how they came in. The Engrossians. They couldn't go through the top of the volcano, so they built that secret passage. We need to seal it." His words were listless, his eyes distant, but he was speaking, which lifted my battered heart slightly.

Rina responded quietly, "Yes, I assumed so. There were a number of discarded weapons in the entrance." She gestured to a dagger sheathed on her own hip.

I embraced my bold and fierce friend, squeezing her tightly to me. She who had no responsibility to our people, yet risked everything on this journey. She who was not privy to our secret rituals, yet entered the volcano fearlessly.

Perhaps that needed to change.

"What do we do now?" Jezebel looked to me, along with Tol, Cyph, and Rina.

Swallowing my hesitation, I pushed my shoulders back and assumed every bit of authority that rightfully ran through my veins. "We'll need to summon the rest of the Mystiquc Council." I assumed Lucidius sent them away. He likely had not invited the Chancellors of the minor clans to Damenal either, in order to avoid exposing his plan. "A meeting will need to be held to discuss everything that unfolded tonight. Let's send messages to each clan leader and host a Rapture—"

"We can forget about Kakias," Jezebel interrupted at my mention of the official meeting.

"That wretched bitch," Rina whispered.

"I cannot believe I didn't kill her." Tolek shook his head.

"No, Tol," I said. "What you did was more than enough. Malakai and I wouldn't be alive if it wasn't for you."

He gave me one of his soft smiles, but averted his eyes quickly as Malakai squeezed his shoulder in gratitude.

"If it wasn't for all of you." I looked among the four people who had given so much for this mission. Without them, I would not have survived even the first few days of the journey. Hectatios's and Glawandin's messages from the Undertaking came back to me, and I smiled at the forgiveness and trust that forged these relationships, tying us together for every challenge ahead. "Thank you." The words would never be enough, but I had a feeling I would be repeating them often—particularly now that they knew how much I'd hidden from them, yet they had not turned on me.

I continued, "We'll include the Engrossians in the Rapture. Kakias likely won't attend, but it needs to appear as her choice to the minor clans." My friends murmured their understanding. "We'll need to notify our own families of our safety and tell them we'll be staying in Damenal for the foreseeable future." Looking to my sister, I added, "Everyone who worked with Lucidius will need to be questioned in order to confirm that the corruption stopped with him."

Her lips pulled into a line, but she nodded. I prayed to Damien that our father was innocent. But it was a problem for a later date.

My voice was quiet on the last instruction. "And we must dispose of the bodies." We had to burn the Engrossians outside of the volcano, or their spirits would remain here for eternity. I would leave the decision of Lucidius's fate to Malakai.

"We can take care of the Engrossians," Cypherion said, pulling Tolek to his feet, and they nodded in agreement when Rina said she'd assist them. Jezebel offered to hike to Damenal and secure the correspondence we needed.

That left Malakai and myself.

He lifted his eyes from the patch of crimson steadily sinking into the floor and met mine. The hollowness that lingered behind that stare crushed the piece of my soul tethered to his, and the threads within me stretched at the pain.

It was everything from the past two years—the torture, the secrets, the death of his father—swallowing him whole. And in that moment, it threatened to break me, as well.

But I couldn't let it.

There was so much that we had avoided since reuniting. Everything that drove a wedge between us, making me feel more distant from him than ever. Before anything else, we had to discuss this betrayal that was now festering in our bond, rotting more by the second.

We locked eyes, unsaid words passing between us. I nearly sank to my knees under his broken stare, but I held my ground, looked into the dim forest green of his eyes that I had missed so thoroughly, and nodded once before turning to leave the cavern.

Chapter Forty-Five

I WALKED DOWN THE tunnels without direction, taking countless turns until I came to a set of rooms dug into the walls of a corridor, forming a sort of abandoned barracks. We had to be deep within the mountains now. But the rooms had doors, which meant privacy.

I chose an empty one, devoid of most comforts save for battered furniture, and marched across the threshold, eyes locked on a pair of shutters set into the wall. I only turned when I heard Malakai close the door.

Looking at him nearly shattered my resolve, everything from the past weeks rushing in at once—roaring in my ears and clouding my vision. Before I even fully had him back, I felt as if I had lost him again.

He knew. *He knew.*

For over two years, I wandered aimlessly, a lost soul amid a sea of abandonment, holding out hope that he would come back to me. Yet Malakai had walked away from me that day knowing he would not return. Knowing that my world would shift, my heart would shatter, and he still made that choice to leave me in the dark.

Because that was what it was—a choice. One that took away my own autonomy and set rage curdling in my gut.

My parting words to him echoed in my mind.

Come back to me.

Come back to me.

Come back to me.

And yet, he did not.

His jaw tensed when my face shifted into a razor-sharp glare. The dim mystlight in the corners of the room illuminated the remnants of blood, dirt, and scars covering his skin.

"Ophelia," he started, voice so low that if I hadn't been watching his lips move, I wouldn't have known he had spoken.

"No," I interrupted, stepping farther away in the small space. The back of my legs met a writing desk, and I let it support me, my hand coming to my throat to hold back the sobs that had built up since I first laid eyes on him. I'd forced them down, but now that I faced the truth—faced him—the hot sting in my eyes was overwhelming. "How *could* you—" I whispered.

My question was cut off when I met his haunted stare, but he understood. *How could you lie?* How could he break the one thing I was so sure of—break us—by lying to me?

"I couldn't tell you. You wouldn't have let me go if you knew." He appeared somewhere between desperation and anger. If he had one minute or one century left to live, he would spend it trying to make me understand.

And he was right. Had I known that he was walking away for good, I *never* would have let him go. My fate be damned, he mattered more than my life.

But still— "You. Left." My whisper sliced through the air, sharp with accusation.

"I never wanted to." Frustration broke his voice, the low timbre like a storm waiting to unleash its first clap of thunder.

"You walked away and did not return." My shout strained my throat, and I threw my arms out. "You *knew* you would not return."

"Lying was my only choice." He clenched his hands repeatedly before turning and slamming his palms against the wall. "Fuck," he muttered.

The muscles in his back rippled beneath their scars as he took a second to breathe. When he turned back to me, he leaned forward, hands open before him as if searching for an answer. "What was I supposed to do? It was the only way to keep you safe."

"My safety is *my* choice, Malakai. We could have found a way together."

"They wouldn't have allowed it. They wanted me, Ophelia." He placed a hand on his chest, both bracing himself and emphasizing the harsh reality. "They wanted *me* in exchange for Mystique power. To consolidate it and corrupt it. And Kakias wanted to torture me as her own Spirits-damned toy to get revenge on my father for even having me, and he was—I don't know what happened to him, but he was different. He let her do that to me. But no one besides them knew that you were the rightful heir to the position, so I thought if I left, it would hide my father's shameful plan and keep you safe. They promised you would not be harmed if I gave myself up." His voice rose with each truth.

"As if you should have believed them!" I raged. "They would have used me anyway." Paired me as the Engrossian prince's submissive partner or killed me outright—somehow they would have used me.

"I didn't know that!" The storm within him finally broke, and he shouted, "I did what I had to do, and I would do it again."

His panting breaths filled the tense space between us.

"I will not have my future controlled, Malakai. Not only did you keep your family's secrets, but you hid my blood right from me, as well." Did he not see how twisted his decisions were?

"I'm sorry for not consulting you, but what choice did I have?"

I inhaled, fighting through my anger for a moment to see the pain in his eyes. Malakai was not the root of this problem. "Lucidius brought shame upon himself." Malakai recoiled at his father's name, a knife to my gut. But Lucidius should feel that remorse, not Malakai.

"Listen to me," I tried to speak calmly, waiting for his eyes to meet mine before I continued. "*He* is the only one that should have been ashamed of his actions." Ashamed for offering up his own son in search of power he masqueraded as love. Ashamed for turning his back on the Mystiques who trusted him.

Malakai took a deep breath, letting my words settle. "I know you think I took your choice from you, but my father played the only game I would let him win. He knew that if he threatened you, then he would have me under his thumb."

I couldn't take this. Spirits, I couldn't take any of these truths. I sank further into the desk behind me, fingers curling around the edge until the wood bit into my flesh.

"Fuck them," I spat. "Fuck the Spirits and the Angels and all of them. We would have found a way. Together. As we always should have been."

He shook his head. "The only reason I could leave was because I knew it was keeping you safe. If you had given yourself over, and they had tortured you as they did me…" He swallowed heavily over the end of the sentence, shuddering. "I would have lived centuries in this Spirit-forsaken hole, faced any means of torture, if it meant you would live out your days happily."

I scoffed, hot tears cutting a path through the dirt and blood on my cheeks. "Happy? Do you know how I spent these past two years, Malakai?"

He shook his head again, hair brushing his shoulders, eyes not leaving mine.

I ran shaking hands through my hair, forcing myself to keep speaking, to make him understand my anger so maybe I could keep it from turning into a toxic leech between us. "I spent them searching, desperately hoping to find a way to restore our lives. Clinging to the piece of my soul that insisted you weren't dead, only to find out that you knew what you were facing when you left me, and you hid it from me. When you did that, you broke something in me." I wanted to tear the room apart, throw something only to watch it break as irreparably as his decisions had shattered what had mattered most to me.

"Did this mean nothing?" I shoved my left arm forward, brandishing the Bind and the fresh set of white scars wrapped around my forearm. "To me, this meant that we were partners—

that we faced life *together*. Yet you knew these secrets and chose to face them without me. You may as well have burned this from my body."

He recoiled at the scars both on my body and within it. The exact pain he wished to avoid by leaving me. If possible, the shadows in his face darkened. The avoidance of his eyes tightened my chest with the realization of an even worse truth.

"Did you know when we received the Bind?"

His whole body tensed. "I didn't know. Not everything—"

"You said this was so that we could always come back to each other!" I screamed, voice cracking, fingers locking around the Bind until my nails dug into my flesh. "It was all *lies*."

"I didn't know everything, Ophelia!" Now he was shouting, too—a wild tangle of desperation, anger, and hurt seeping from every part of him. "I was figuring it out, if you will let me explain myself."

I had no interest in excuses, but I remained silent.

"I hadn't trusted my father since the war began. The last time I had seen him—after the Curse first appeared—his lack of concern…It made me want to push him from the top of the mountains myself, the Spirit-forsaken bastard." He ran a hand through his matted curls, fingers getting caught on the way back.

The shock of everything I hadn't known about these pivotal moments of my life froze me.

Malakai cleared his throat. "Before the treaty was signed, he returned to Palerman for one night to see me. To threaten me, actually. At that point, I had my suspicions about his loyalties, but even I hadn't imagined the full extent of his history. Or his plans." He sighed, his eyes falling closed. "I had seen the bloodshed, Ophelia. Had seen the orphaned children and families in mourning. Me signing the treaty—agreeing to hand myself over—it would stop all of that. You can't expect me to have not agreed. What is my life when it could save so many others?"

To me, it was everything.

But he was right. If I had had the power to save so many, I

would have sacrificed myself. This was bigger than my pain, bigger than us. This was about the unfair deaths of thousands of warriors in an avoidable war. Shame at my own selfishness swept over me, but it did not wash away the taint of his betrayals.

"You should have told me from the moment you first suspected your father."

"A part of me wanted to deny it all. He was my father—" His voice broke over the word. "Part of me didn't want it to be true."

Lucidius had made it clear to us both that Malakai was unwanted, nothing but a foil to his deceitful plans. Malakai, who had grown up honoring that man and hoping to one day follow in his footsteps. It was a miracle by the Angels that he still stood before me, showing even an ounce of fight against this twisted fate.

But the tattoo on my arm stung.

"You haven't answered my question." My grip on my arm tightened.

He took a shuddering breath. "When we received the Bind, I had already signed the treaty."

The little air that had found its way into my lungs was squeezed out again. *So that we may always come back to each other.* All meaningless letters strung together in words of false sentiment.

"When I told my father I wanted the tattoo, I thought he'd kill me on the spot. He forced my hand into the treaty that night. I was so afraid of him, I barely knew the extent of what I was signing, only that I was handing myself over in exchange for the end of the war. But I did know that if I didn't sign, the war and Curse would have continued to destroy Mystiques. And if I spoke a word of it, they'd have killed you as well." Sadness crept into his obstinacy. "I thought this was the only way."

The only way for thousands more lives to be saved. The only way for me to live.

His shoulders drooped under the weight of everything that he had suffered. Every heart-shattering truth that unveiled itself. That was the true gift of Kakias's wrath. It was not enough for him to be handed over to the Engrossians at the hands of his father and face years of physical and mental torture designed to ruin him. A selfish part of the queen had wanted to hurt the child Lucidius had with another, and Lucidius had been weak and twisted enough not to fight her on that decision. Maybe once Kakias had broken Malakai, she'd have finally killed him, but first she had to crush his spirit. And mine in turn.

They took this most precious thing between us and destroyed it. We couldn't rebuild it from the fragments—not with the lies that lay among the rubble. We could possibly forge something new from the heat of our pain, but it would never be the same. The glass had shattered around our innocence, our eyes opened, and healing those emotional scars would be complicated.

Maybe some things were meant to stay young and beautiful.

I swallowed that truth that I wasn't ready to accept.

His father—*his own father*—was responsible for the broken man before me. I looked again at the scars that littered his once flawless body, forever reminders. Thoughts of war, Curses, death, and despair shadowed my mind—and one chance to stop it all. I recognized his bravery in those wounds. My anger didn't subside, but my resolve finally cracked.

"Augustus," I whispered, the name breaking the shield I had put up between us.

The utterance of that name from my lips was all he needed to stride across the room, arms sweeping around me. I didn't try to wipe away the tears that flowed over my bloodstained cheeks. I let them cut a path through the dirt, sting the cuts, until they mixed with Malakai's, dropping one by one onto his chest.

His forehead came to rest against mine, hands cupping my cheeks. He gently brushed his thumbs over my cheekbones, tracing the bruise his father had left in our fight and wiping away my tears.

"Ophelia…I would never have chosen to leave you had I found a way to end this otherwise. You are my heart." I was his heart, yet he had broken me. "The thought of you alive and whole was the only means by which I survived." His words were soft, imploring me to understand the promise that echoed through each syllable. I didn't miss the lack of regret, but I pushed it aside, needing this moment more than I needed to argue.

"I was not whole," I corrected him. "You took a piece of me with you when you left. If you only knew who I became without you..." My voice trailed off as I brought my hand to rest against the Bind on his chest.

He ran his thumb across the matching tattoo on my forearm. "My North Star..."

I shivered in his grasp, taking a steadying breath. "I'm so angry with you." He stiffened against me. "I need you to understand that I will be, for a while. And I don't know how we fix this." I tilted my face up to his, our lips brushing against each other as I said, "But I will always find you," and closed the space between our mouths.

Though I was still furious with him, the betrayal of his deceit lingering in my bones, I arched into the familiar warmth of this embrace.

"Fucking Angels, Ophelia, I missed you," he whispered against my ear, his lips glossing over my jawbone. "No more damn secrets." I tasted the sweetness of his promise as he brought his mouth back to mine.

His tears slid down my skin, leaving a trail following his kisses. Down my neck, across the tear in my leathers that the Engrossian blade sliced across my collarbone. Over the fresh, pink layer of skin that was already knitting itself back together.

"No more damn secrets," I gasped, his kisses blurring my senses. Fucking Angels, his lips were a drug, and I was addicted. Despite the anger coiled in my gut, I wanted him. Needed him. Desire awoke within me, mixing with that fury to form a dangerous, vicious combination.

He paused the exploration of his lips and pulled back to look into my eyes. The green spark I loved was brightening—not fully returned, but swimming closer to the surface, trying to push past the pain smothering it. "Thank you for never giving up. For finding me."

That white-hot tangle of need and anger exploded within me.

I couldn't wait any longer, twisting my fingers in his hair as I pulled his lips down to mine, rougher this time.

This is real, he is real, I reminded myself as he lifted me, my legs wrapping around his waist. Malakai was back. Those were his hands beneath my thighs, his muscles that my fingers stroked, and his groans filling my mouth. He was scarred and broken—Spirits, I was scarred and broken—but he was here. We were here together.

The room was sparse, but there was a volcanic fire in the hearth and a rug spread before it. Our mouths refused to break apart as he walked us toward it and lowered to his knees smoothly. The hard length of him pressed into me, only encouraging me. I clung to him as if he was breath and I was drowning. He kissed me as if I was water and he was dying of thirst. Each a source of life for the other.

My hands drifted down his back, his breath hitching when I traced the long scars decorating his skin. I shuddered at the images passing through my mind.

"I'll kill them," I muttered from where I sat across his lap, legs tightening behind his back, crushing him to me. "Every last one of them will suffer for each mark on your skin."

His hands tightened around my waist as I spoke, pulling my chest flush against his. "I love when you threaten people for me, but can your grand revenge wait until later?" he asked, fingers slowly removing what was left of my leathers, deftly unhooking the buckles between us, and lips tracing a path from my collarbone to my shoulder.

I rolled my hips against him in answer, relishing in the groan he released. "Later," I promised, kissing him deeper and biting his bottom lip.

In one swift motion, Malakai had me on my back. He followed the wrecked material of my leathers as it bared my skin with lips and hands and teeth. Kissing and feeling and biting every inch of me, like he also could not believe this was real. Could not believe I was real.

Each spot his lips met was an electric storm. Each gentle drag of his fingers across my skin sent a ricochet of sparks through my body, my blood alive with his intoxicating presence. He trailed kisses down my stomach, along the inside of my thigh, stopping just at the apex. Malakai muttered things about how much he missed me that I barely heard, his breath against me the most wicked tease.

I cracked my eyes open and found him watching me. Wanting to see me come undone beneath his touch after we had been starved of this connection for so long.

"Please," I breathed, hinging on desperate.

He hooked one of my legs over his shoulder, lowering his mouth to me. And when his tongue dragged slowly up my center, circling my most sensitive spot, my back arched off the floor, head falling back. It was better than I had remembered.

I tangled one hand in his hair, guiding him, though he held my hips in place. As he destroyed me with his tongue, he slid two fingers inside me, moving sinfully slow. I could relish in the heat of his skin against mine, in the stroke of his tongue and fingers pushing me to the edge, in the hand holding my hips, forever…but I wanted more. I needed all of him.

"Malakai," I sighed. He hastily returned his lips to mine at the sound of my voice, as if he needed to consume that, too.

He sat back, kicking off his shorts and freeing himself. I took in his scarred body, a map of what he'd suffered. In the flickering light of the flames, he was beautiful. Once, I'd known that body better than my own; as I took him in my hand, dragging slowly from base to tip, I swore I would again.

Our hearts beat erratically as he lowered himself on top of me, pushing into me slowly after so much time apart. I gasped, but he captured it with a kiss, pulling his hips back and easing forward again. Each stroke was a question, and I answered in turn, digging my ankles into his back so I could feel more of him.

This, I thought, as he buried himself within me and dragged a moan from my lips, *This is right.* I didn't want to think about the rest of it, about what came next. Just this moment, and our own personal dance of passion.

He rested his forehead against mine, stilling for a moment. I looked at him through lowered lashes, reaching up to trace the planes of his face. When my fingers trailed over the fresh scar on his jaw, his eyes drooped closed, and I could see him slipping into that dark place.

Not now, I thought. I twisted our bodies so that he was underneath me, lowering down on him slowly until he reached so much deeper—giving us both so much more of a distraction.

He raised his eyebrows in surprise, but when I circled my hips my name slipped from his lips like a curse, and he hurried to meet each motion. I braced my hands on his shoulders, nails leaving crescent marks on his skin until he hissed. A part of me—the part unable to forget about how we got here—thought it was fair.

He must have seen it in my eyes because he sat up and pulled me flush against him, his bare chest brushing my breasts and making me arch into him.

"If you're angry, then take it out on me," he commanded, coiling a hand in my hair and pulling my head back to look at him. "But I'll love you until the stars stop shining." He kissed me harder then.

I didn't say anything, just tightened my grip on his shoulders, ripping my mouth away to kiss his neck, biting the skin less gently than I once would have. He moved quicker, hands tightening on my hips as he thrust harder, getting us to what we both needed—a release for all of the unfathomable emotions welling up within us.

Anger and desire and betrayal and love coiled within me as I slammed my mouth back against his, making up for the years we lost. Sweat dripped down our bodies as we got closer. He lowered his hand between us, his thumb circling exactly where I needed him. Tingling heat coursed through my body at his touch, molten and ready to destroy me.

I placed my palm on his chest, feeling the thudding of his heart beneath the Bind, and my shattered world felt slightly less broken as my climax ripped through me. We went over the edge together, the passion between us burning away the darkness.

Chapter Forty-Six

I SLEPT WITHIN MALAKAI'S arms for the first time in two years, and when I woke beside him, I was unsure what to make of the storm of feelings within my chest. A bit of that black hole that had festered between us had eased. The pain was not gone—forgiveness had not been given—but I was grateful to be with him in that moment, with his scent wrapped around me, his breath against my neck, and his heart beating a steady pattern against my back. I could not deny the fact that something had changed, but I chose not to face it yet.

A subtle golden glow crept around the shutters. Had it truly been two days since my friends and I had been preparing to cross the tundra? Everything that had happened since then flashed through my mind like a mirage of dream and nightmare.

I watched the light brighten and listened to Malakai's steady breathing, hoping he slept peacefully. But the shade of the sun outside our room was wrong—too bright to be the dull haze of morning. Its golden essence ebbed and pulsed, alive and calling to me.

Slowly, I disentangled myself from Malakai's grasp and ensured he stayed asleep on the rug while I pulled on my wrecked leathers. My body ached from both the battle and the sex—which I supposed had simply been another kind of battle.

His head turned toward the fire and the light warmed the deep shadows across his face. I placed a whisper of a kiss on his forehead before crossing to the shuttered doors. They were made of metal and should have been cool beneath my skin, but when I reached for them, warmth spread through my palm. Intuition told me what waited outside. I stole a breath, bracing myself before opening the door and stepping onto the rocky ledge jutting out from the mountain, forming a balcony of sorts.

"Hello, Ophelia." The Angel's golden glow spilled into the room as I pulled the door shut after me. He gave me a knowing smile. "Sleep well?"

I rolled my eyes. "Hello, Damien. I suppose I'm not surprised to see you." I kept my voice low to avoid it drifting inside and waking Malakai. As much as he needed the sleep, there was also a piece of me that did not want him to see Damien. I had told him about the Curse and the prophecy that sent me on the journey to the Undertaking, but him meeting the Angel felt personal.

The First Warrior chuckled where he hovered. "Congratulations are in order." His voice still carried that familiar booming echo, but outside, amid the magic of the Spirit Volcano and the Mystique Mountains, it blended into the dawn, filling the air around us with his essence. Like he owned the very mountain range before us.

As it had on the night of my birthday, his presence sent a trickle of cold unease down my spine. I crossed my arms in front of my chest, appraising this legendary being. "Yes, thanks to little help from you, I may add."

"You know I may not interfere, Chosen Child." His golden curls drifted in the wind. I met his purple eyes, shades away from my own.

"Why do you call me 'Chosen Child'?" I repeated the question I asked all those days ago. I was a different person then, but I still chased the same answers. "I am not a child, nor have I been chosen."

He smirked. He seemed much more relaxed here than the last time I saw him, comfortable, able to joke, even. "Compared to me, you are a child. And yes, you have been."

"What do you mean?" I demanded, narrowing my eyes.

Damien turned to watch the sun rising over the snowcapped mountains. Pale yellow light painted everything in its path with a promising radiance that dulled in comparison to the Angel beside me.

"Time will tell." His voice was a low caress over the landscape and myself. Though I ached to protest, his words carried a finality that I knew couldn't be pushed. A warning pulsed inside of me, insisting that he spoke true. Only time would unravel the enigma before me.

"What's happening with the forest creatures? And the fae?"

Again, Damien said, "Time will tell." This time it felt final.

I inhaled the heaviness of that and let it settle into my shoulders, trying to accept the unknown that it cemented into my future. Lifting my chin, the cool morning breeze washed away any weariness threading through me. We watched the dawn in silence for a few peaceful moments before I could no longer stand the tide of questions churning through my head.

"Annellius," I began, and I felt Damien's curious eyes shift to me, though I kept my stare on the horizon. "He said the Alabath line is descended from Angels."

"Did he?" Damien asked, bemused. I turned to him, frustrated at his feigned ignorance, but his face was amused. Teasing me. "It is true," he added when he saw my expression.

"So, my family had Angelblood in our line?" I had to be sure. I had to hear it from the lips of the Angel himself.

"You do."

That word nearly stopped my heart. *Do.* "Annellius said it was removed because of his greed."

"It was." Damien nodded, his curls falling into those purple eyes.

I groaned, flinging an arm out. "Why must you be so cryptic? It was removed yet I have it? None of your messages make any sense."

"You will understand in time," he promised, and I didn't know why, but I believed him. Something within his omniscient gaze told me to.

I searched desperately for a question he could answer. Anything to solve this lingering web that wove itself through my life. "The Curse is gone." It was not a question.

"Is it?"

I conceded to playing his game. "I felt it lift from me when I was in the Spirit Fire. The mark has stayed, but the Curse is gone." I extended my arm for proof.

His gaze narrowed, and he tilted his head to the side, looking like a curious child. "Can you be sure it ever lived within you?"

"I felt it." I rubbed my thumb across the web, remembering the pain of the Curse rooting itself within me, thriving on my blood. That excruciating ache as it reached further into my veins and drank from me would haunt me until the Spirits claimed my life.

"Maybe you felt what you were meant to feel." Maybe he was not as much a curious child as he was devil's advocate. His gaze followed a wisp of cloud as it drifted across the mountain peaks. I watched his eyes track it, waiting for a response, but that moment of playfulness faded from him.

"What in the damned Spirits does that mean?" I finally asked.

"Do not swear at me, Ophelia. You may be frustrated, but I am still an Angel," he scolded.

"I could have said worse," I muttered.

A knowing smiled twisted the edges of his lips, and it unsettled my stomach. "That affliction on your wrist was a pretense. Planted by the powers that be and lifted when they deemed it fit. You were never at risk of suffering from *that* Curse."

"*That* Curse?" I repeated.

He watched my thumb continue to scratch at my new dark scar. "That ghost of an affliction may be gone, but your curse runs deeper, Ophelia."

The words chilled my blood, though I didn't understand his meaning. "I was never going to die?" Tolek had not felt the Curse because it had not existed.

"Everyone dies, Ophelia. It is what we are meant to do before the Spirits call your soul into darkness that matters. If you have truly lived, when you join the stars, the dying will not seem as scary."

Before I could ask what *I* was meant to do, Damien vanished.

"Stop doing that!" I growled as the sun fully crested the mountains. It bathed the range beneath it in a breathtaking light, rising and falling with the slope of each magic-imbued peak. The sight should have relaxed the tension budding within me. The vision of a newly dawning day should have been a comfort after the horrors I'd faced, but my heart remained cold with the memory of Damien's words.

All I could think of was the haunting echo of Angels and curses, darkness and stars.

Chapter Forty-Seven

Malakai

I WOKE ALONE IN the room in which I had taken Ophelia. The memory of being buried inside her still burned into my skin, everywhere, but she wasn't there. For a moment, I feared I had dreamed it all. That I was still a captive within my father's prison, and torture lay just outside the door. But my fears eased when I rolled to my stomach, because the rug still smelled of her. That unforgettable swirl of jasmine tinted with citrus brought me back to my senses.

I retrieved my shorts—the only article of clothing I had. Bloodstained and battle-worn, they remained a vivid reminder of the past days' activities. As were my sore muscles and stiff neck from sleeping on the floor with only Ophelia's pile of golden hair for a pillow.

I should have been happy, waking to a freedom I thought I'd handed over permanently, but the aching reminder of my past haunted me. I stared into the dying flames, lit by the volcano itself, and recited the truths as I knew them.

"My father is dead," I whispered.

"My father who had me tortured is dead."

My father who had me tortured in order to bring glory to my enemy, his second family, was dead at the hands of the woman I loved.

I couldn't bring myself to say that one aloud, didn't want to face it.

I closed my eyes, taking a breath to steady the emotions ricocheting throughout my body—a tangle of anger and grief and shameful relief that I knew I'd have to face—but all I could see behind my lids was that silver blade slicing along my father's throat. The blood following its trail and spilling down his chest to the floor below. His face when he fell into that crimson puddle.

His wide eyes, apologetic as he spoke his last words. *There is so much you do not know.* Fucking Angels, what cryptic message had he tried to communicate to me?

My hands clenched at my sides as I tried to steady my breathing. It was all too much—so many emotions bottled up within me. For years they'd sat there, rattling the cage I'd locked them in. I'd refused to feel, refused to hurt. They'd tasted that sweet freedom in the last few days, once I'd finally thought myself broken. But now, I tried to lock them up again. If I didn't, I'd drown in the force of grief and betrayal, the memories of what he'd allowed to be done to me.

There was a small part of me—and I was ashamed to admit this—that was relieved that he was gone. That this was all over.

That Ophelia had found me.

Ophelia…

I crossed to the iron doors of the balcony and eased them open. There she stood, the sun forming a pale halo around her head when she turned to me. Her face—which had been pinched in consternation—relaxed, the lines easing.

The smile that lifted her expression was an arrow to my heart, trying to forge a bead of happiness that I didn't deserve. Bringing that smile to her face was something I would willingly die for, any day of my life. The knowledge that she lost it for so long because of my choice to leave haunted me.

Guilt rattled the cage, but I tucked every rotten emotion into my heart and imagined iron bars sealing across the damn thing.

I stepped onto the ledge and wrapped my arms around Ophelia. The tension was clear between us, but when I rested my cheek against her head, the light of this moment dulled the pain of the dark nights I spent in that cell. Each rise of my chest against her back was a silent patch to the wounds buried deep within my soul. It would take many stitches to heal them, but having her here was a start. I pressed a kiss to her temple, letting my eyes drift shut, and thanked the Spirits.

Yes, I could force away my emotions for the time being. I'd face everything later.

Ophelia wrapped her arms over my own, still wearing her torn training leathers. I supposed she would be needing official Mystique Warrior leathers now. When I said as much to her, she smiled and reminded me she had crafted her design over a decade ago in anticipation.

She's finally receiving what she deserves, I thought, with only a dull shadow of jealousy. When she had described the pain she felt the last two years, it broke me more than any of the torture I suffered, but I locked that in the cage, as well.

I had thought that after I left she would be safe, but I had been wrong. She was not safe from herself.

I had hoped the others could make her happy. Tolek and Cypherion, Jezebel and Rina. But still she suffered. Never again would she hurt because of me. I pressed her to me as I made that silent promise and felt the beating of our hearts alternating between us.

"There is another thing that's rightfully yours now," I whispered into her hair as we watched a pair of birds soar over the mountains.

"You?" she asked dully.

"Until the stars stop shining," I muttered, squeezing my arms around her. "But that's not what I had in mind. The spear."

She craned her neck to look me in the eyes. "Your spear," she whispered, but it wasn't a challenge. Simply a reminder of what had changed.

"*Your* spear," I responded, assuring her with my gaze that there was no hostility behind my words.

It was rightfully hers. It had been all our lives. Her eyes searched my own before turning back around, and I hoped she saw everything I wanted to convey. That the spear, the position of the Revered, it was all hers. Even if it had truly been mine, I didn't want it. I couldn't after the truth of my father's deceit.

"Do you have a name for it?" I asked, expecting her to say she needed time to wield the weapon before finding one that fit it.

She surprised me when she spoke immediately, in a far-off voice. "Angelborn."

I stood atop the Mystique Mountains, gazing out the tall windows of an empty room in the Revered's Palace overlooking the white marble temple below. The place where my father lay. Despite the evil he brought into the world, his body would be embalmed in the palace's temple by the Master of Rites before being tossed into the volcano. It would be up to the Spirits to decide where he would go from there.

Thankfully, beyond saying goodbye with my mother once she arrived, I didn't have to do anything.

From up here, the temple looked so small. Its steep staircase leading to a square structure surrounded by pillars could have been a plaything of children rather than a house of worship for the Angels. The columns appeared so feeble, capable of being broken by a breeze. Even the Revered's Palace felt lackluster. With its sweeping walkways and endless lifeless rooms, all pale stone and white marble, it was a cold maze of hazy memories.

The one place that hadn't felt void of life was the vaults beneath the palace. Built into the mountains, they'd held the Revered's wealth for centuries. Ophelia and I had visited them, searching for an idea of what type of staffing she could appoint in the palace. With news of my father's betrayal spreading, understanding of his corrupt rule dawning, more Mystiques were returning to Damenal, and Ophelia wanted to employ those she could.

Descending the stone staircases into the bowels of the mountains had felt ominous, like eyes lurked in the shadows, but the vaults themselves teemed with wealth. Gold littered every inch, shining in the mystlight.

The realization that my father had hid this in order to weaken Mystiques that could have been saved made me furious. I wanted to storm out of the palace, out of the city, and never return. Instead, I added the emotion to my cage.

Near-silent footsteps echoed on the marble, pulling me from the memory. Two sets of them. I forced a smile, but as their presence settled around me a sliver of tension lifted from my shoulders. I had forgotten how much I relied on their steady comfort prior to the treaty.

"It's odd, isn't it?" I said without looking at Tolek and Cypherion as they stood on either side of me and beheld the world beyond.

The world that now stood at our feet to guard.

"What's odd?" Cypherion asked. He knew. I knew he knew, but he needed me to say it.

And I needed to say it. "My father is gone, and this all falls to us now, but I don't feel unsettled about it."

With the death of my father came the assumption of a new Revered, and it would be Ophelia. I had no doubt that the Rapture and the Mystique Council would be uncertain about a twenty-year-old taking up the position, but there was no debate to it. The Spirits had named her the rightful heir.

It unfolded before my eyes, the life that would be built in these halls that my father had called his own—families and fights and festivities—and it felt okay. Better than that, it felt right. Like I could breathe freely for the first time in years, even though a shadow hung over me. One I would need to face soon, but not today.

"Yes," Cyph responded, his voice a calming hand to the guilt I felt over my father's death. "It is odd that it is all falling into our humble laps, but you're right. It feels like something in the universe is being fulfilled."

Tolek grasped my shoulder. "The fates and stars have always written a great destiny for you, my dear Malakai." He paused. "For both of you."

Both of us. Me and Ophelia.

I took a step back from the window and turned to my closest friends, grateful that they had been much more understanding of my deceit than Ophelia had. When I had explained, I saw the hurt in their eyes, felt the chasm between us, but I also felt the agreement. They would have done the same to protect those they loved.

"I owe you both the greatest debt. Ophelia told me how you protected her, both in Palerman and on the journey here. How you kept her from sinking into that dark place within herself." The one I allowed to form by leaving. "That is an act I can never repay, but my life is yours." I pressed my hand to my heart over the new linen shirt I wore, the material I used to don daily now strange against my scarred skin.

Cyph mimicked the gesture. "You don't need to thank us, Mali," he used my mother's childhood nickname for me. "We love her as a sister."

Tol removed a hand from behind his back and held it to his heart, as well. "Cyph is right. No thanks necessary, Mali. We love her." There was an edge to his words, a stifled emotion I couldn't place, and I did not wish to when I saw the way his shoulders tensed.

I lowered my hand and they did so, too. "I missed you, boys."

They swept me into a crushing hug, and in it I felt all the sentiments we couldn't bring ourselves to speak aloud. All the longing we wallowed in during those years apart, for losing their friendship was another sacrifice I made when I left.

"Let's go see how poor your spearwork has become," Tolek teased.

"He likely won't last ten minutes," Cyph added.

Tolek's face lit up. "Shall we bet on it?"

I shook my head, smirking. "You're on, but I think I'll try a different weapon."

CHAPTER FORTY-EIGHT

OPHELIA

JEZEBEL HAD ASSUMED THE chambers at the far end of the opposite corridor from me and Malakai, a wide stairway separating the hallways. "I do not wish to share a corridor with the two reunited lovers each night, thank you, sister," she had said when I requested she move closer.

Malakai had smirked at her implication, and I felt the glow of his male ego from across the room. I had ducked my head, choosing not to voice the fact that we were arguing over his lies much more than we were in bed together—though the latter had become my favorite distraction. Not to mention the fact that the suites were so large, she'd never hear anything through the multiple rooms we each had.

It was a bit odd how we had all settled so smoothly into the Revered's dwelling over the days following the Undertaking. The glamorous palace was lacking most staff due to the Revered's actions, so for the time being, the six of us had it mostly to ourselves, warriors searching for work trickling in slowly.

For two weeks, we rose every morning, trained in the large arena on the palace grounds, and spent the afternoons wandering Damenal. We explored the city atop the peaks, seeing which shops had survived the war and which had closed, purchasing whatever we could from gracious owners. Each haggard face was another promise that I would restore what we'd lost.

In the evening, we'd settle around the long table in the dining room, draining bottles of wine over rich food. At first, Jezebel had prepared our meals. We'd offered to help, and often kept her company while she cooked, but it normally resulted in her yelling at Tolek for touching something he was not supposed to. For their sake, we'd hired kitchen staff quickly.

And after dinner, when the world was quiet and holding its breath, I'd stand on my balcony and look out over the city that was coming back to life. At the world that buried secrets tangled in threads of lies. At the mountains that remembered the heartbreak I was still enduring, and just breathed.

It was peaceful, but it would not last. This was the calm before the storm that I was beginning to fear would break over my head and drown me. The Chancellors of the minor clans would arrive for the Rapture within the week, and we'd begin restoring what Lucidius ruined.

I assumed no one would arrive from the Engrossians. That was another battle we would have to face in the coming weeks. For now, I let the solitude of the Mystique Mountains soak into my skin, rejuvenating my spirit.

I stood on a platform in Jezebel's dressing room as the seamstress we had summoned fluttered about me, measuring and pinning and cutting. She wasn't just any seamstress. She was Divina Delantin, and she was the esteemed worker of Mystique leathers in Damenal.

On the floor at my feet were the renderings Jezebel and I had recreated of our desired leathers. I remembered the nights we spent as young girls, sketching these awe-inspiring garments by candlelight when we were supposed to be sleeping, and the moment felt surreal.

Divina circled me, pinning scraps of material into place as I swiveled in the light streaming through Jezebel's tall windows. Everything in the Mystique Mountains, including the sunlight itself, brought a new realm of beauty to the world. The seamstress's expert hands folded a stretch of fabric around my hips, achieving the precise vision I had dreamed as a girl. My skin tingled in anticipation of three days' time when she would return with my finished product.

I was picturing the feel of the leather against my skin so vividly that I missed Jezebel's rambling. "Ophelia? Are you in there?" she asked as she unfolded from her position on the lavender chaise—her favorite in her chambers, even though it was in the dressing room—and approached me. Her eyes met mine in the mirror.

I turned as Divina instructed and looked down at my sister. "Sorry, what was that?"

She rolled her eyes. "Daydreaming again?" But her lips quirked up in a smile, and I knew she was relieved with the shift in my mood over the past few days. Even more relieved when she had learned that the Curse we had feared was taking my life was in fact a farce, brought about by the Angels. She had burned the note I gave her before the Undertaking—dropped it into the mouth of the Spirit Volcano when I told her what Damien had admitted. We'd watched it turn to ash while questions lingered between us.

Jezebel toyed with her necklace's pendant where it fell to her chest. "I said Father will be here in a few days."

My stomach sank. "He will." And he would be sequestered with the other Mystique Council members until they could be questioned about aligning with Lucidius. We fell into a contemplative silence, neither voicing the possibility of what that would mean.

"How did you feel after it? The Undertaking?" Jezebel asked, reaching up to fiddle with the ends of my hair.

I considered, unsure where she was heading. "I felt…whole. Like a piece of me had been fulfilled. And I felt powerful."

She pursed her lips but was silent.

"How did you feel?" I asked, turning back to face the mirror and running a hand through the fringed fabric along my thighs.

She bit her lip for a moment before speaking, and tension radiated from her. "I was underwhelmed," she admitted. Jezebel's tawny eyes met my magenta, our faces so similar, but our insides so different. "I thought I would feel as you did, but I did not." She paused, and I allowed her the time to gather her thoughts. The only sound in the room was Divina's stitching. "Something within me shifted, and I believe that was the moment you are describing. Like a spring that had coiled in my gut all my life finally sprung free, but it was not fulfilling as you said. Like perhaps this piece of me that I gained was not the piece I sought."

"You are a full warrior now, Jezzie." I placed a hand on her shoulder, and she turned her face up to mine. For a moment, she looked so young—so uncertain. A girl with questions on her heart and dreams in her mind. "You have fulfilled that piece of yourself. Now, we can find the other pieces you feel are missing."

She smiled softly and leaned her cheek against my hand, soft hair falling across my arm. "I think they may be far off, yet."

"How far may that be?" My heart jumped, afraid of what she would say next.

Our eyes locked. "I am unsure, sister, but perhaps very far indeed."

"Are you ready?" Malakai's head peered around the door of our dressing chamber, his freshly trimmed black hair falling around his face. It still curled in messy tendrils, but the few inches we sheared off after our ordeal seemed to take some of the memories with them. Jezebel had enjoyed cutting it so much that she'd insisted on Cyph letting her do his, as well. Tolek had threatened to draw his dagger if she came anywhere near his precious hair.

Malakai's eyes lit up when they landed on me—almost like they used to. The subtle shift inflated my heart. "Ophelia..." he whispered with awe in his voice, coming to stand beside me in front of the mirror. The tension between us took a reprieve.

He ran a hand across my collarbone, over the leather strap around my shoulder, and down my arm, taking in the beauty

Divina had crafted. A chill followed in the wake of his fingers, my skin reacting to his touch like lightning shooting through my veins. His path lingered on the tattoo on my arm, then the scars below, drawing delicate circles over the permanent marks with his thumb as if he could brush them away.

His gaze traced the warm brown leather framing my chest in a heart-shaped neckline, parting low between my breasts, with a panel extending down over the greater part of my rib cage. My stomach was bare to expose the three long, white scars that wrapped themselves around my waist. A proud reminder of what I suffered for our people.

The skirt began below the scars, a thick leather belt holding Starfire. "Stars?" Malakai asked, tracing the design imprinted in the belt. Four tiny ones building to a final larger one with four main points and smaller beams between them. My own personal constellation.

"The North Star." I smiled up at him as his fingers brushed over the biggest star, nestled beside Starfire. "A last addition I asked Divina to include."

His bewildered smile nearly took my breath away as he eyed the skirt beneath the belt, strips of leather forming a fan around my thighs. As I moved, they spun out around me, lifting slightly. Perfect for the range of motion I would need.

The whole outfit was designed with purpose—to show off the sacrifices that proved my worth and also allow the freedom I required. Divina had suggested adding golden wristbands, but I denied them, wanting all of my scars on display. When Rina saw the leathers, she'd asked if I should require more coverage, to protect myself.

"I do not plan on needing protection," I'd responded simply. Besides, should a true battle loom, I could don full leather garb and gilded armor.

I finished lacing up the knee-high boots Divina made to complete the outfit, and strapped Angelborn across my back before turning in a circle for Malakai, my hair flowing out behind me. I couldn't help the smile that spread across my face as I watched my dream take shape.

Malakai's hands settled on my shoulders, fastening the sky-blue cloak without breaking his gaze from my eyes, our mouths so close I could feel his breath against my lips. Unable to help myself, I reached up and brushed the unruly hair from his forehead, appreciating the unfathomable softness of it under my fingers.

He is here, I reminded myself for the hundredth time. *We survived.*

I caught his gaze with my own, a flicker of pain flowing through his green eyes, and my stomach dropped. Tension coated the air between us, a stark reminder of what he had suffered—what *we* had suffered, I had to keep reminding myself—and the broken pieces resting inside of us. Shards of glass poised to issue fatal punctures with one misstep.

I shrugged out of his grasp, needing a breath of my own air. In the same moment, Malakai banished that echo of hurt from his eyes. We did what we'd become so adept at: ignoring our pain.

The anger between us had not vanished, but it gave way to this moment. Instead, we watched the fabric trailing behind me catch the light, shimmering like the crystal surface of the sea, and emphasizing the blue threading within my leathers. The color of our people. A sign of hope for us both.

"It's perfect," he whispered, planting a kiss to my forehead.

He stepped back, and I frowned at his linen shirt and plain pants. He bore no leathers because he had not officially completed the Undertaking, but I chose not to raise the conversation.

As we approached the Rapture chamber doors, Malakai bent to whisper in my ear, "I have to say…while you look every bit the powerful Revered Mystique in those new leathers, I'm more excited to see how they come off later." His breath was a soft caress down my neck.

I winked at him in response. The shiver his words caused faded as we came to a halt in front of Tolek, dressed finely in his own sleeveless leathers with his hair combed back yet slightly ruffled, like he couldn't leave it perfect.

"Jezebel and Cypherion have gathered the masses within," he told us. Those chocolate eyes swept up and down my body, taking in the freshly crafted leathers and lingering on every inch of the exposed skin around them. Not in a leering manner, but in astonishment. Quickly, though, the look vanished from his face. "Shall I tell them you're ready?"

Malakai watched the shift in his friend's expression, and the narrowing of his eyes nearly unsteadied me, but I did not have time to address it now.

"Yes," I responded, and Tolek disappeared through the double doors.

I ran my hand over my leathers once more, ensuring that everything was in place. This was my first impression as acting Revered. This moment—what happened behind those doors—would decide my fate and the fate of my people. If my rule was supported, or if we would fight for allies.

Malakai sensed my hesitation and lifted my fingers from where they scratched at the dark scar the Curse had left me. I hadn't even realized I was doing it. He brought my hand to his lips, kissing it gently. "You are the most powerful warrior of our generation, Ophelia. But more than that, you are fierce, kind, and loyal. Your heart burns with the hope of the Mystique Warriors. They will see that and they will honor it."

I swallowed my fear, shook my hair behind my shoulders, and lifted my chin. Though talk of curses and glory echoed through my mind like a haunting vow, I remained determined. Malakai's words were true, and I felt the strength within me to prove that.

"Let the trials begin," I muttered.

With Angelborn across my back, Starfire at my hip, and Malakai's grip firm within my own, a wealth of unanswered promises burned through my veins. I pushed open the double doors of the Rapture chamber to claim my fate.

EPILOGUE

DAMIEN

"THE GIRL HAS STARTED on the path," I muttered the words into the cold air as eight sets of eyes, including my own, traced her movements through the ancient piece of Angelglass. A crack running down the center cut a jagged line directly between her and the boy as they stood with hands locked, whispering to each other.

"Now that she is fully ascended, the progress should be quicker." My words rang with a hopeful promise of chances long lost.

We watched through the glass as she entered the council chamber, missing shards adding dark spots to the scene. The marble doors sealed firmly behind her. As the last sliver of light disappeared, the air within our room felt heavier. We could not interfere in the affairs of the warriors, only guide. My attempts recently had been too blatant, the punishment I received for them still ringing through my blood. The taste of the poison on my tongue.

"Good," he responded as he turned his back on the glass. "I am tired of waiting, Damien." He prowled the circular stone room like a captive beast, and I supposed in a way he was.

Everything we planned, though, was not only for him. I looked around at the others who lined the walls, and thought that the cause ran deeper—millennia in the making, awaiting this moment. And it all rode on the slim shoulders of the golden-haired girl. The Chosen Child.

"We will soon reclaim what was taken from us," I promised. "That and more."

Around the room, six voices echoed my sentiment. Though they clung to the shadows, their dull light pierced the darkness. Many were afraid to approach our master as I did, but I knew he could not achieve his plan without us. Without me, in particular.

He needed the girl, and I was his key to her.

"You have done well, Damien." Pride swelled within my gold-tinted body, easing the remnants of recent failure. The ancient beast within him woke with each word, its head rising and muscles tensing, no longer dormant as it had been rendered for so long. "She has been delivered to this pivotal moment, but we have seen this achievement before."

"And fell from this point, as well." Bant's whisper was a growl from the shadows, but our master tensed at the reminder of the history. I did not dare to look at the Angel behind me.

A ghost of white light trailed after our master as he unfroze and continued his prowl around the circular room. A flash of that light lashed out, striking Bant. The Angel yelped.

Then our master whispered, his voice tired from the effort, "Yes, Bant. Thank you for the reminder; though, I advise that you in particular keep your mouth shut."

It was an order. Neither Bant nor anyone else dared speak again, the air growing heavier still. I imagined that had we needed to breathe, it would have been impossible to draw breath.

"This will restore everything that was once lost to us," our master finally muttered. His back was still to the room but those white tendrils pulsed and twisted around him in a dance of edgy glee. "It rests within her, but she will never willingly relinquish it to us. She must be led blindly, for she cannot learn what lives inside of her yet."

He turned toward us, the power trapped within him sending that unique, bright essence swirling around his figure, lifting the strands of his long silver hair so that it flowed behind him as if caught on a gentle wind.

His milky eyes narrowed against golden skin, dark brows lowered, and he decreed, "It will be either our salvation or our undoing—the Curse of Ophelia."

ACKNOWLEDGEMENTS

This book was born out of many pent-up emotions that I didn't know lived in me. It started with the idea of a heart-broken girl angry at fate. It became so much more. But it wouldn't have been possible on my own.

The biggest thank you goes to my parents. When I told you I wanted to quit my job and move to London to pursue my MA in Creative Writing, I had a whole speech prepared. The fact that you supported it from the get go–so much so that that speech was pointless–speaks volumes. I've always been a writer, but I never knew if I had what it took to be a published author. You guys did, and you always made me feel proud of that.

Thank you to my brother for your support. It might take you months to finish a book I write, but you still do it. And to my aunt, uncle, cousins, and Grandma, for the encouragement. To Poppy, Grammy, and Gopah, I hope you're proud, and I wish you were here to see me achieve my dreams. I know you always believed in me more than I did.

To my gorls, Monica and Jillian–our friendship means so much to me. Something that spans decades is pretty special. To Chey, for talking me off too many ledges to count, never questioning the weird things my brain produces, and always understanding my typos. You're the best mate a girl could ask for. To Liz, for championing this story from the very first day and founding Tolek Vincienzo's fan club. Thank you, Carmen, for always checking in on me and reminding me that I don't have to do everything alone. To Taylor for being a solid critique partner, and Monica for alpha reading everything.

To Noods, for listening to endless complaints and rotting. To MJ, for the Jersey Shore binge during which I started writing this book.

To the Heir Fan Club, for every laugh. To Mick and Madi and Mina for every read-through, text, and piece of advice. To every single beta reader whose hands this story passed through. And to Katie for answering every self-publishing question I had. You made this scary process so much less intimidating.

To Julie for taking my author photo that one day we went to the London Zoo (and not making me feel weird for it) and for being my piece of California in the UK. To my friends in London who I miss so much—I wish we were celebrating this release at the lanes. Thank you for making London home.

Thank you to my editors: Kelley, for cleaning this story up until it shined, and Megan, for every final check and word of encouragement. To my cover designer, Fran, for an absolutely jaw-dropping design that will brighten shelves. To Lorna for designing this final version, and to Abigail for allowing readers to enter Ambrisk via that stunning map. To Rebecca for the assistance on the pronunciation guide, and every artist who has brought my characters to life.

An incomparable thank you to every freaking person I've met through bookstagram and booktok! Seriously, you have all pushed me further than I can explain. Ophelia was a baby of the online book community, a product of all the love we share for our favorite stories. From the first ideation, you showed me endless support. This book wouldn't be published without you.

Honestly—to myself, for not giving up when this felt impossible. To Ophelia's chaos brigade for rooting themselves so deeply in my mind and heart that I didn't have a choice but to tell their story.

And, finally, if you've made it this far—to you, reader. Thank you, from the bottom of mine and Ophelia's cursed little hearts, for giving us both a chance to find a home with you.

Until the stars stop shining,

Nicole

About the Author

Nicole Platania was born and raised in Los Angeles and completed her B.A. in Communications at the University of California, Santa Barbara. After two years of working in social media marketing, she traded Santa Barbara beaches for the rainy magic of London, where she completed her Masters in Creative Writing at Birkbeck, University of London. Nicole harbors a love for broken and twisty characters, stories that feel like puzzles, and all things romance. She can always be found with a cup of coffee or glass of wine in hand, ready to discuss everything from celebrity gossip to your latest book theories.

Connect with her on Instagram, TikTok, Facebook, and Twitter as @bynicoleplatania or at **www.nicoleplatania.com**.

Did you enjoy *The Curse of Ophelia*? Add the second book in the *The Curse of Ophelia* series on Goodreads now!

Printed in Great Britain
by Amazon